THE
NORTHEAST
KINGDOM

PETER COLLINSON

JOVE BOOKS, NEW YORK

THE NORTHEAST KINGDOM

A Jove Book / published by arrangement with
Multimedia Threat, Inc.

PRINTING HISTORY
Jove edition / August 2002

Copyright © 2002 by Multimedia Threat, Inc.
Cover art by Complete Artworks Ltd
Book design by Julie Rogers

Visit our website at
www.penguinputnam.com

ISBN: 0-515-13361-2

A JOVE BOOK®
Jove Books are published by The Berkley Publishing Group,
a division of Penguin Putnam Inc.,
375 Hudson Street, New York, New York 10014.
JOVE and the "J" design
are trademarks belonging to Penguin Putnam Inc.

PRINTED IN THE UNITED STATES OF AMERICA

10 9 8 7 6 5 4 3 2 1

BEFORE THE FIRST DAY

THERE ARE TWO TYPES OF POLICE TRAFFIC STOPS: "HIGH RISK" and "unknown risk." "High risk" are stops of vehicles fitting the description of a stolen automobile or of one suspected of being used in the commission of a crime. Every other stop represents an "unknown risk" because a police officer never knows, as he or she approaches a vehicle, what might be going through the operator's mind at that moment on that particular day. The element of surprise, and therefore the advantage, is always on the side of the driver. The "low risk" traffic stop does not exist, unless the officer finds that he has pulled over his own mother.

The big man wedged behind the steering wheel of the white Ford cargo van was not Deputy Sheriff Brian Kearney's mother. Brian's mother was a fading violet named Annette who, at six o'clock on a dusky August evening in Huddleston, Montana, was already settled in on her back porch not three miles away, a second small bottle of Michelob Light soaking a water ring in the imitation redwood patio furniture Brian's father had been assembling for her on the night he died. Brian's mother's second husband, Perry, a semiretired bank manager and the reigning Border County Tenpin Champion, always took care, Brian had noticed, never to set his own drink, nor the little cigarillos he left smoking in plastic Bank of Huddleston ashtrays, on any of the porch furniture, the assembly of which Brian had completed himself that long night between his father's wake and funeral. That bit of family respect was what had sold Brian on his stepdad, that and the fact that his mother was happy again and no longer alone. At this hour Perry would be sitting right next to her looking up at the mountains and the sun dipping behind, content to share her small beers from the beat-up Igloo cooler between them and tapping his foot in time with the rockabilly music playing through the screen door. Brian lived just a couple of streets away from them, the same mountain shadows falling over the ranch house he shared with Leslie and their twin daughters. Leslie had mac and cheese on for the girls, who were both fussy eaters, and last night's leftover Shake 'n Bake heating in the microwave for Brian who, when he pulled over the Ford van with Arizona tags, had been on his way home.

Brian was alert as he left his Bronco and approached the suspect vehicle. Huddleston was a small farm town, but being just south of the Canadian border, it saw its fair share of trouble. Some drug couriers got lazy, thinking they were home free after passing the border checkpoint, and let their attention to lawful driving slide. That part of Montana, the furrowed brow of its northwestern face, was also separatist country, a small but militant portion of the population saw the police as invasive agents of an unfriendly government. Six years before, on a stunted mountain named Paradise Ridge, just down the road from where Brian now stood, a white separatist facing eviction from his cabin home had held the FBI at bay for more than a week in a standoff that had culminated in a near-riot in which a federal agent died preserving order. Since then Paradise Ridge had become a monument for antifederalists and reactionaries of all stripes, a wailing wall for militant radicals, and the adopted Pearl Harbor of a local fanatic order of separatists known as The Truth. The Truth had fallen on hard times since their church-bombing, race-warring sociopath founder, Jasper Grue, had been sentenced to life plus life plus forty years in a federal penitentiary; but the movement was still alive in the area, and always a law enforcement concern.

The van was long and windowless in back. As Brian walked past the rear bumper, he saw the driver watching him in the side mirror. Brian twirled his finger in the air to get the man's window down, then put his thumb and forefinger together as though turning a key.

The driver's side window went down obediently and the engine shut off. The driver placed both hands on the wheel where Brian could see them, and Brian moved to the window with more confidence. The driver appeared to be alone.

The first thing Brian noticed about the man up close was his scar, thick and bubble-gum pink, drawn across the base of his neck just above his sternum. A shirt with a collar, such as the flannel one crumpled on the passenger seat, would have covered it.

Beyond the scar, there wasn't much to see. A beefy white male wearing a Marlboro baseball cap and a faded yellow T-shirt, cheap sunglasses hanging on a bright orange cord, sparkless brown eyes. Peanuts and coffee, those were the smells.

Brian didn't make a practice of hassling out-of-state motorists, so he told the driver straight out that he had been stopped for speeding. The man had his license and registration ready, as well as a shipping invoice for the cargo he was carrying: a load of ladies' dresses.

Brian took the paperwork back to his Bronco. The van was registered to a company in Tempe and the driver's name was Durwood Roby. The tag and the license both came back clean. That nagged at Brian. There wasn't much call for profiling offenders in Border County, but the man's necklace of scar tissue had raised Brian's antenna. He took a second look at the registration, noting the model date. The vehicle year was listed as 1995, though it seemed to him clearly a newer '98 or '99. Brian and Leslie had been over at the Ford dealership in Little Elk the month before, as the girls were out of car seats now and the repair bills on the station wagon were testing their budget, and Brian had admired the sleek lines on the millenium models, more curved and aerodynamic like this one. It was another pebble of the suspicious side of the balance scale. Brian radioed for police backup—the sheriff was on a two-week angler's holiday in Idaho—and returned to the van.

Roby was waiting patiently, drumming his thumbs on the steering wheel, the skin around his cuticles picked raw. Brian stood with his holster away from the door. "Mind my asking where you're coming from?"

Roby smiled, an unfriendly man trying to be friendly. His teeth were like little pills. "Alaska."

Brian saw Canadian coins in the open ashtray. He saw some dresses behind the driver's seat. "Do you know what model year this van is?" he asked.

Roby shrugged. "Got me. It's a company car. I just drive it. I'm a workingman."

Brian nodded, stalling, still deciding. Backup was minutes away, but waiting meant being even later for dinner and enduring Leslie's scolding. This was not the first time Brian had pulled someone over on his way home. He glanced up and down the road. It was hedged by woods to the turns at each distant end, quiet and untraveled at dusk.

Brian backed away from the door. "Mind stepping out of the vehicle for me, sir?"

Roby's first expression betrayed that he did in fact mind. "No problem," he said, opening the door and stepping out. Brian was awed by the man's size and his right hand moved casually to the pepper spray canister on his belt.

Roby strolled toward the rear of the long van. He seemed used to being hassled, a big, ugly-looking guy with a scar, and the thought of such discrimination shamed Brian but did not deter him. Beneath the tight cuff of Roby's T-shirt were two letters seared into his triceps, raising a scar.

"Quite a tattoo," Brian said.

The man looked down at his arm and proudly fingered the brand.

"*BR*," read Brian. "I have your first name as Durwood. Ever serve any prison time, Mr. Roby?"

Roby was still admiring his arm, smiling like a flat-nosed dog pressed up against a wire fence. "Naw. I did this myself."

A police car rolled down the road earlier than Brian had expected. His hand eased away from his belt and his confidence again lifted. "Okay if I take a look inside your vehicle, Mr. Roby?"

A trick question, a standard law enforcement trap. Answering "No" naturally invited further scrutiny beyond the threshold inquiry. The process of trying to establish legal grounds for a probable cause search could stretch on for as long as Brian wanted it to, even if Roby was ultimately found clean. Answering "Yes" was a waiver of the individual's Fourth Amendment rights and a consent to a police search.

Roby weighed those options as he stared at Brian, his dogged agreeableness faltering. "It's just dresses," he said. "I'm on a schedule here. They checked me across the border."

"Then you won't mind if I take a quick look?"

Roby stared at him, deliberating, and at that moment Brian knew there was something hidden inside the van.

"Sure," Roby said, with a flick of his wrist. "Knock yourself out."

The cruiser stopped in front of the van and Merce Patterson climbed out, a short-limbed, mustached man, chewing his Nicorette gum. Brian nodded him over to Roby and then went around the front of the van to the passenger's side door.

Brian checked under both front seats and inside the well beneath the radio. He used the butt end of his four-battery Maglite to pick through the fast-food litter on the floor.

"Do you have a passport, Mr. Roby?" Brian called out to him. There was no answer. "Can't get across the border without a passport."

Nothing from Roby. Either he was thinking or no longer cooperating. Brian could see Merce Patterson through the open driver's side window, his mustache riding the movement of his jaw, but Roby was obscured by the wall of the van. The look on Patterson's face told Brian to move it along.

He pulled the keys from the ignition and went around to the rear doors, opening them and facing a rack of dresses sheathed in cleaner's plastic. He removed one of the hangers and looked the dress over: a matronly blue cotton pullover with snaps up the top half, a loose bib front, and a matching rope belt. The rest were all variations on that same basic style, some with buttons instead of snaps, some floral patterned or striped, some with collars, some without. Brian removed some hangers in order to reach through, finding a second garment rack. Beyond that lay more piles of plastic-coated dresses, which he poked and probed with his flashlight, finding nothing. He stepped back from the fender, shoving the dresses back inside. Around the open door he could see the back of Roby's head and neck, and Merce Patterson standing wary of him.

Brian opened the side door and stepped onto the running board. There were dresses everywhere, folded on the floor, stacked lengthwise and bundled with bungee cords, lying loose. He waded in, feeling around, and eventually uncovered a stack of long, white cardboard boxes near the back left wheel well. He quickly opened the top box: more dresses. Discouraged, he pulled back and surveyed the interior of the van. The scar on Roby's neck drove him back to the long boxes.

Moving the top one off the others required an enormous amount of effort in relation to the task, half emptying the box, sliding dead dresses around, and then balancing the box on his hip as he opened the one below: still more dresses. He gave them a defeated stab with his flashlight butt and struck something hard.

A muffled *clink*, like a small sack of nails dropped on

the floor. He listened a moment for Roby—it was silent outside—then, with the first long box still balanced against his holster, swept away the top layer of dresses.

He had dented one of dozens of small, red boxes of rifle cartridges packed in neat rows. Brian pulled out one of the tapered, copper-jacketed rounds, then shoved the rest of the dresses off the far end of the box.

He had uncovered a sizable brick of U.S. currency sealed in plastic wrap.

The first box fell to the floor as he backed out of the van, the shimmering plastic-wrapped dresses swirling at his feet, slinking off the running board to the ground. Brian fumbled his flashlight back into the loop on his belt and unsnapped his side arm, moving around the rear doors. He saw Merce Patterson and pointed to Roby's back, nodding fast, all the while trying to keep calm. Merce Patterson's face paled with concern and his hand went immediately to his own gun.

"Mr. Roby," Brian said. His voice came out dry. "I need you to turn around and face the van, sir."

Roby only turned a little, his eyes tracking Brian as Brian circled in front of him. Merce Patterson was still getting out his gun.

"Turn around and face the van, sir, please, right now."

Roby looked at the two of them there, at ninety degree angles to himself. Merce Patterson had drawn on him but Brian still had not.

"You don't want to do this," Brian said—not at all certain exactly what Roby was doing. "You really don't want to do this, Mr. Roby."

Brian remained ready with his hand on the butt of his side arm, and just when it seemed he was going to have to make a move, Roby sneered and turned to face the van.

"Flat up against it, sir," Brian said.

Roby did as Brian commanded, lacing his fingers behind his head and spreading his legs. Brian advanced on Roby's back, not bothering to pat him down, pulling out his handcuffs and going directly for Roby's wrists. But

Roby's hands would not meet behind his broad back, and with his free arm strong between Roby's shoulders, Brian motioned to Merce Patterson. Merce linked his cuffs with Brian's and finished the job.

Brian rushed through Roby's Miranda warning. Roby looked at him contemptuously now, mean and dead-eyed, refusing to speak. He refused even to acknowledge having been informed of his rights.

Two more cruisers arrived in the time it took Brian and Merce to unload the van. Thirteen semiautomatic AR-15 assault rifles lay on the side of the road, with the cash and ammunition stacked to one side along with, curiously, a child's chemistry set. The bottom box had been removed whole. It contained four objects: a long, tube-shaped barrel, a wire connected to a small box, a hand trigger, and something like a sighting mechanism. The casting and texture of the metal parts all had the feel of military issue, although large sections along the barrel were filed down.

Roby, asked to identify the unassembled device, stood mum.

The last item was a Chock Full o' Nuts coffee can. Merce peeled back the lid and pulled out a small plastic sandwich Baggie full of white powder. He gave Brian the knowing cop look, and Brian nodded back, though a fistful of cocaine did nothing to explain the assault rifles, the money, the unidentified device, or Roby's forged identification. Merce handed Brian the bag—actually two bags, one Glad-style bag sealed inside an airtight Ziploc—and Brian worked the package with his fingers. It had a sticky, oily texture, more like laundry detergent than cocaine.

"You don't want to open that," Roby said flatly.

The big man wore a teasing smile, a grin even uglier than his jagged scar. Brian, an affable, reasonable young man, felt a flash of anger heat the nape of his neck. But Roby would not elaborate. The tow truck arrived and Brian dropped the bag back into the coffee can, impounding it and the cash and transporting it all back to the stationhouse the sheriff's department shared with the local Huddleston police.

Roby was uncuffed and fingerprinted without incident. The company listed on the van's registration returned "No Known Address" in Tempe, and Brian decided to wait at the station for Roby's prints to come back through the computer. He left him to be processed into a holding tank and ducked into the sheriff's office to call Les, apologizing, telling her he'd explain later. She wasn't happy. Then he called the emergency number the sheriff had left, getting neither an answer nor a machine. Brian would have to sort through this mess alone.

He rejoined Merce Patterson in the conference room, and they laid out the evidence on a dusty meeting table. Merce broke the seal on the cash and counted a bundled stack. There was maybe $50,000 total, all circulated bills. Brian shook his head. He took the loose packet of currency and fanned it under his nose.

"Too much to trust to the evidence locker," he decided. "We'll double count it, you and me, start a chain-of-custody form, then padlock everything in the sheriff's office overnight."

"Right," said Merce, taking a whiff of the cash himself.

Brian picked up one of the AR-15 rifles, drawing a bead on a pretend target, then set it down and worked on assembling the four-piece puzzle. It came together more easily than the porch furniture that had killed his dad. Brian arranged the open, box-shaped sighting mechanism at the busy end of the barrel, and after a moment of weighing the contraption in his hands, hoisted it up onto his shoulder.

It was one of those surface-to-air missile launchers movie terrorists use to blow up helicopters.

"Jesus," said Merce.

That solved, Brian set the launcher carefully back down on the table and turned his attention to the double-bag of white powder.

"Drugs," said Merce. "Or anthrax."

"Right," scoffed Brian.

Still, neither of them moved to touch it.

"A narcotics rap is nothing compared to running rifles and missile launchers," said Brian, recalling the man's taunting grin. "Reverse psychology? Maybe he wants me to open it?"

"Didn't seem like a psychology major, that guy. I think he was just playing with us."

Brian pulled the bag of powder toward him. He lifted the airtight pack carefully out of the loose bag, soft and squishy, almost like a bag of dough.

"Thirteen small arms," he said, "thousands of rounds of ammunition, a missile launcher."

"And a little bag of white powder inside a Chock Full o' Nuts can."

Brian massaged the bag, feeling its weight. "And the driver, likely a convicted felon looking at the rest of his life in prison, surrenders without a fight?"

He thought of Roby grinning at him again. The condescension, the ex-con looking down on the deputy sheriff. This was a big collar for Brian. He passed the bag of powder lightly from one hand to the other. He did not want the guy's respect, but did not deserve his insolence either.

Brian pulled apart the top folds of the bag, breaking the seal.

GILCHRIST WAS A SMALL TOWN NESTLED IN A VALLEY IN THE broad upland hills of the small-town state of Vermont, in the heart of the region known as the Northeast Kingdom. Geographically defined by the counties of Essex, Orleans, and Caledonia, the Northeast Kingdom forms the bulge of the top-heavy Green Mountain State as it leans, casually, onto New Hampshire and the rest of New England. The Kingdom is modest, conservative, remote. The Kingdom is old country. Glacial lakes and boreal forests, cut from the same rugged stock of timberland that roughs Canada's wilderness. Farmland that yields its owners a modest living, and dirt-floor general stores run by generations of the same family. It is open, available, and, in parts, still wild and free. Driving through the Kingdom is like taking a trip back through time. This is the place old men talk about when they talk about America.

A man in a somber black suit eased a polished Fleetwood Limousine along country roads grayed with winter, his normal evening commute. He steered the gleaming automobile with slender hands and long, unadorned fingers, navigating corners and hills with the care and concentration of a battleship captain forging a winding strait. Gilchrist Common, as the Fleetwood left it, was postcard Vermont, a white clapboard school, town hall, and steepled church all set around a wide, tree-bordered common featuring a prim, white bandstand. The names of the streets outside the common were like signposts to the town's past. Railroad Street. Mill Road. Abenaki Way. Then the roadside stops of commerce, such as Corey's Satellites, Reynolds's Gun and Archery, and the Pit-A-

Pattern store where catalog orders for JCPenney were placed. Then the land really opened up.

The Fleetwood followed the power lines strung along old telegraph poles, two-lane roads linking homes and working farms with expanses of land in between. In early January, the land was generally shin-deep with snow, drifting and settling like time-sand against the crooked stone walls marking century-old property lines. The air was clean and cutting and arctic cold. He passed a mobile home up on cinder blocks in front of a struggling farm. Yellow light spilled out of a kitchen window as children in hand-me-down snowsuits made desperate fun in the fading light, tramping around a yard cluttered with cars in various stages of salvage. A handful of men stood around a pickup in a driveway of frozen mud, neighbors and hunting buddies jawing. One of them waved to the Fleetwood as it cruised past, and Tom Duggan, town undertaker and church sexton, pulled his hand from the smooth steering wheel and waved back.

It was dusk when he arrived. The driveway had been cleared by the Department of Public Works as a favor to him, and he nosed the long Fleetwood under the carport. He could just make out high, curling cirrus clouds, usually welcome as a harbinger of fair weather, though these had been streaking and multiplying all day, the wind increasing from the north, tree branches creaking behind the house. Forecasting weather was a lost skill, another task trusted to radar and computer. The Weather Channel was calling for six to eight inches, but Tom Duggan judged it would be more than that, perhaps much more. If the wind summoned the right momentum, he thought they had all the ingredients for a low-grade blizzard.

He let himself into the house and hung his black undertaker's coat neatly on the peg in the closet and moved through the kitchen and the dining room to the parlor. The timers had come on, the tasseled floor lamp in the corner spraying sandy light over the tired furniture, the house dim and warm. The radio was playing—it was always playing— tonight, a sports talk show from New York. The broadcast did not matter, only the voices, the companionship.

She lay in the recliner they had picked out at the Wal-Mart in Burlington, her slippered feet up, eyes closed, hands at rest in her lap. She stirred as he approached, opened her eyes, and smiled. "Tommy."

"Evening, Mother," he said.

She smiled again, drowsily, radiantly.

"It's Friday night," he said. "And you know what that means."

She gave it some thought before answering. "Franks and beans."

"As always."

She reached for his hand and held it a moment. "Shall I get up then?" she asked, and worked the control of her automatic chair to do just that.

Tom Duggan cooked in the kitchen while his mother sat in the breakfast nook watching the Channel Six news. Like the radio, the TV helped fill the absence left by his father, deceased six years now. Tom Duggan's mother was eighty-six and in good health, careful about fire and stairs and determined to live alone. She was a mortician's widow, and therefore disabused of the usual superstitions and phobias of death. But recently Tom Duggan had sensed an uncertainty in his mother, a fear of the dark, a creeping loneliness not assuaged by television or radio. He dropped by every weeknight for supper, remaining until she fell asleep, usually around eight-thirty.

In the outside world, an aging bachelor such as Tom Duggan would have been the subject of some gossip, but in Gilchrist, home to many Quaker families, the lifestyle of the "Yankee Amish" was widely understood. While not a peculiar man, Tom Duggan was by now quite set in his ways, a man of routine and purpose; and at his age it was easier to go on living as a bachelor, beholden to no one but himself and his church and his town.

He called to her from the stove. "Snow might get in the way tomorrow. Sure you feel up to it?"

The delays before her responses were growing longer, as though she were communicating with him across greater and greater distances. "I don't think I'd miss it for the world."

He felt a proud tingle behind his eyes, the warmth of nascent tears. "No, Mother, I don't think you would."

Tom Duggan was being honored that next day for having saved Gilchrist from extinction. The town had originally been founded in 1788 by Colonel Coleman Gilchrist, one of Ethan Allen's Green Mountain Boys, a band of civilian revolutionaries who fought to preserve the independence of the New Hampshire Grants, as Vermont was then known. The Boys joined the American effort during the Revolutionary War, winning a key battle alongside Benedict Arnold at Fort Ticonderoga. Colonel Gilchrist survived a lead ball through his lung in Quebec, and after Arnold's treasonous plan to surrender West Point to the British was uncovered, the colonel was engaged by Thomas Jefferson himself in an effort to recapture the traitor. Failing in that enterprise, Colonel Gilchrist retired his commission and settled in the area with his wife, Marguerite Estelle Duggan.

Now in its third century of existence, Gilchrist had seen prosperity come and go. The railroad boom of the late nineteenth century had lasted no more than two decades into the twentieth. The millworks had failed to survive a third generation. Mining briefly revived the town in the 1950s and '60s—but it was an asbestos mine, and the good times were not to last.

Forgotten among the boom years of the 1980s was the economic downturn of small-town America. Money that flowed vitally through arterial city streets recirculated there without reaching the extremities, and by the end of the decade many rural communities had turned necrotic and began to die. Geography also had a hand in Gilchrist's recession. The high, cloud-snaring mountain peaks to the west, north, and east isolated the town, and the nearest state highway was nothing more than a two-lane road with the number 17 posted next to it, fifteen minutes on the other side of brake-wearing Planter's Rise. So there was little hope of Gilchrist refitting itself to appeal to the recreational dollar, as had the thriving ski resorts to the south, or luring a light manufacturing plant, as had Essex Junction with IBM. In truth, many Gilchrist residents would rather have watched the town fade quietly into history than endure the lifestyle changes commercial solutions would have engendered. And so into the last decade of the twentieth century, Gilchrist continued to wither on the vine.

The town's financial woes came to a head in late 1991. There were only three public streetlights in Gilchrist, all of them posted around the historic town common. Tax revenues for that fiscal year were such that, not only was the town unable to pay the electric bill to keep the streetlights shining, but it lacked even the funds to afford the service charge required to shut them off. Gilchrist was broke and in trouble. The migration of younger families to more centrally located towns, coupled with the depressed local economy, rendered Gilchrist "tax-base poor." State aid dwindled, and in the final accounting the three-member board of selectmen came up $49,344.84 short of anticipated revenues, which for a town of Gilchrist's size meant bankruptcy and certain ruin. Long-delayed maintenance on public buildings had become a safety concern. The church cemetery was nearing capacity. The town truck needed a new slide-in sander, the cost of which the Department of Public Works—a seventy-year-old diabetic named Dickie Veal—officially tagged at "pricey." And $763.14 raised at bake sales and barbecues was not enough even to fund the *volunteer* fire department. But the most severe blow came in the form of a town referendum in early March of 1992 when cash-strapped residents decided they could not afford to contribute any additional local aid, forcing a vote to deny tax-limit overrides for Gilchrist's two most expensive mu-

nicipal institutions, the police department and the board
of selectmen. A mostly quiet crowd followed Police Chief
Roy Darrow down Main Street that evening after the
meeting and watched him padlock the tiny clapboard stationhouse. The four-member force was officially dis-
banded and the Vermont state police were alerted. The
next day, with a few strokes of the ceremonial town quill,
Gilchrist's government was downsized to exactly two employees: a jack-of-all-trades administrative clerk, and an
emergency town administrator nominated from among the
three selectmen.

That town administrator was Tom Duggan. A selectman for twelve years, he had devoted much of his life to
the town and was known for his levelheadedness and a
shrug-and-roll-up-his-sleeves attitude. The business of
saving the town required the patient temperament of a
man accustomed to heating soil before digging graves below the frost line.

Tom Duggan took to his duty piously. He spent all his
off-days researching the matter, driving west to the uni-
versity in Burlington, usually in the Fleetwood but occasionally in the hearse. He would bring books and notes
back to Mae's Pantry, nursing a wedge of lemon pie by
the front window, and voices would hush out of respect
and newspapers would stop rustling as he pored over figures, a two-inch-long pencil in his cramped hand.

At a special town meeting convened on the common
on a cool evening that June, Tom Duggan faced the gathered townspeople from the crumbling front steps of the
town hall. He was exhausted from checking and recheck-
ing his math late into the night. Word had spread throughout town that he had a miracle bailout proposal that would
be Gilchrist's salvation.

It was a kind of industrial plant, he announced. So
specialized an industry that highly trained technicians
would relocate with it, thereby eliminating the obstacle of
attracting new workers. The plant was virtually guaranteed never to go out of business, as there was an unyield-

ing demand for the service it would provide. In fact, it was recession-proof, a unique business invulnerable to changing economic concerns, public fashion, even competition. And as it provided a service, rather than a manufactured product, there would be no negative environmental impact whatsoever.

At that point people were shouting questions. What was this revolutionary new industry?

A federal correctional facility, he told them. A United States penitentiary.

He quickly laid down some background in the face of their stares. The business of American justice was a growth industry doing one hundred billion dollars–plus annually. One out of every four males in modern America had an arrest record. This fact so clouded the minds of those gathered, whose own doors were never locked and whose own children never disappeared, that he had to repeat it twice. More prisons had been constructed in rural areas during the previous fifteen years than in the past two centuries. Communities that had sued the government in the 1980s to keep prisons out of their backyards were bidding for such projects now, requiring reliable sources of tax income in order to survive. Prisons were to millennial small-town America what military bases had been during the Cold War. The domestic "War on Crime" had created a public works project of immense financial proportions. The urban crime wave had become a rural bonanza.

Through inquiries to the Federal Bureau of Prisons, the agency responsible for maintaining federal correctional facilities nationwide, Tom Duggan learned the BOP was exploring sites for two new penitentiaries in the northeast. Based on similar projects across the country, he pegged the construction cost at roughly $120 to $130 million, payable by the federal government, bringing Gilchrist some $275,000 in annual taxes right off the top, with various generous "hidden" financial benefits to follow. What gave Gilchrist the edge on competing communities, he argued, was the wealth of town-owned land lying fallow to the north and northeast, arguably Gilchrist's sole marketable asset. His recommendation was that one hundred acres be offered to the federal government free of charge. Existing access roads and local utilities would have to be modernized to accommodate a state-of-the-art prison facility before a bid would even be considered, necessitating an approximately one million dollar bond issue—an enormous financial gamble for the town. And Gilchrist would be competing against other aggressive and similarly desperate small towns in neighboring New England states. But Tom Duggan viewed the prison as a last ditch effort.

"Our inaction here," he proclaimed, "will mean our ultimate demise."

He contended that the prison would in no way interfere with Gilchrist's integrity or daily life. The town would go on as it always had, uncompromised, with the only measurable change being the influx of prison employees and their families, the quantity of which could be set by the town. Indeed, housing subdivisions would have to be planned and constructed, requiring the sale of hundreds of acres of privately owned farmland at prices easily ten times the current recessionary rate. This last fact was not lost on the oldest families in town, who owned the most land and wielded the most influence.

And so the motion carried. The bond was issued, roads were built, pipe and wire were laid, and in the end the long shot paid off. Gilchrist won its prize prison. Tom Duggan himself ceremonially heated and broke ground on the 312-bed facility in the northern outlands, before a cookout on the town common to celebrate the return of solvency to Gilchrist.

And now, tomorrow, a bust of his likeness was to be installed inside the town hall foyer, alongside the rest of the town's founding fathers and Revolutionary War heroes, including Colonel Gilchrist himself.

Tom Duggan rolled the swelling franks around the pan

with a wooden spatula, still concerned about the coming snow. Clara Nibe had passed on two days before, so with her wake soon after the ceremony, he had arranged for Dickie Veal to drive his mother home. He would check the propane tank outside before leaving. She had plenty of food. It was the isolation of the house that bothered him.

He sliced the franks and served them with the beans and a splotch of ketchup, fixing place mats on the table as he told her about the wake arrangements, making conversation.

"Wasn't Clara Nibe whosit's sister-in-law?"

"Yes," Tom Duggan said. Family pride prevented his mother from uttering Marshall Polk's name.

"Think he'll come down out of the hills for that one?"

"I doubt he even knows about it."

Marshall Polk had been the town postmaster for forty-four years, cranky yet beloved, as much a Gilchrist institution as the town hall. But he had been one of the two sitting selectman removed from office when Tom was anointed town administrator; and he never forgave the town for its slight, nor was he ever the same afterward. When Tom proposed his prison bailout plan, Polk formed a small but vocal opposition group. He retired from the postal service and turned vehemently antigovernment, protesting at town meetings in his lumberjack coat and fur-lined boots, railing against the dark specter of federal intrusion on Gilchrist land. Toward the end, even his small cadre of supporters abandoned him, but Polk persisted as the lone voice of dissent, growing more and more radical, eventually calling for the destruction of the town either by his own hand or by God's. He fled before seeing the turnaround of the town's fortunes. On the first day ground was broken at the prison site, Polk announced his secession from Gilchrist and declared war on the town, withdrawing into the northeast mountains.

People claimed to see him fishing now and then, or

rummaging through the abandoned buildings out by the
asbestos mine. Some sympathetic outland residents left
food for him that routinely disappeared. But never had a
single shot been fired in this one man's revolution. And
he had departed the town before what would have been
partial vindication for him, Tom Duggan's one glaring
error of judgment.

Among the five official security-level classifications of
the Bureau of Prisons—high-security, medium-security,
low-security, minimum-security, and administrative, listed
in that order—Tom Duggan had reasoned that "administrative" dealt with the lowest-risk inmates, and neglected
to investigate the matter any further. He later learned,
along with the rest of the town, that in fact an "administrative" facility is a specialized institution charged with
the containment of extremely dangerous, violent, or
escape-prone inmates.

The Administrative Maximum Unit Penitentiary at
Gilchrist became the United States's twenty-first century
Alcatraz, a high-technology Devil's Island of no parole,
no release, no escape. It was, in the words of one pundit
on TV, "the latest advancement in the Bureau of Prisons's
legacy of maintaining 'Control Unit' penitentiaries, the
government's instrument of revenge upon the country's
most infamous or dissident criminals."

But this incredible gaffe was overlooked by the townspeople as soon as the enormous financial benefits began
to roll in. The guards' neighborhood, a seventy-house sub-
division in the old village of Gilchrist Falls, went up like
a boomtown, a planned community of three-bedroom
colonials, thirty-by-fifteen-foot asphalt driveways, and
freshly sod front yards. The police force was rehired full-
time and repairs were made to the crumbling granite steps
of the town hall. The three streetlights were updated and
two new ones were added, bringing Gilchrist Common's
total to five. The town truck got four new all-weather tires
as well as its slide-in sander, and the iron fence around

the cemetery next to the church was widened and improved. The 312 felons were quietly added to the population rolls, allowing for even more tax income due to census-based state support. With the growing budget surplus, the school and fire department buildings were revamped and the old police station was replaced by a modern brick facility. Five years after the penitentiary received its first inmate, tax rates had plummeted to a thirty-five-year low. A high, white flagpole, the second-tallest structure in town after the church steeple, was erected next to the bandstand on the common. Town revenues grew and grew, allowing for a second snow-clearing truck for public roads, a two-man DPW staff and a generous retirement plan for Dickie Veal, a modernized water and septic system, and, by special vote, the construction of a municipal golf course and country club at the foot of the eastern hills.

But, for the most part, the town went on as before, only more prosperously. The prison in the northern outlands turned out to be an excellent, if exceedingly private, neighbor.

"How are the beans?"

"Delicious," Mother said.

"That's the brown sugar."

It was a conversation they had shared many times before, but Tom Duggan found comfort in the repetition. His mother's house was a sanctuary, unassailable by time. He often thought of the fine mahogany he kept in storage over at Fred Burnglass's mill, the other half of the order that he had placed for his father. And he had saved yards of the best ivory satin fabric over time. Knowing that she would be well attended at the end pleased Tom Duggan as much as it did his mother. It gratified him to know that she was a woman at peace.

A waxy paper bag from Mae's Pantry lay atop the table, full of the usual Friday night treats: a plain cruller for her tea and a Bavarian crème donut for him. Tom Duggan smiled during a quiet moment, watching his mother's dry, hardening eyes focused on the television as the lively theme music from *Wheel of Fortune* played.

THE FIRST DAY

THE STORY OF REBECCA LODEN'S DIVORCE REACHED A WIDER AU-
dience than her recently published novel, the bestselling
thriller *Last Words*, ever would. The upheaval had begun,
in true literati fashion, with a cheeky blind item on "Page
Six:"

> Bodice-ripper from the pub biz. It's no mystery that
> the business side of this rising industry pair is get-
> ting breathless and bare-chested with the bestselling
> author of another genre. Note to heaving bosoms:
> Close the office shades. This city has eyes.

Rebecca phoned Jeb that day to see if he had the inside
scoop on the offenders' identities. That was how unprepared she was for her husband's infidelity. If she had been
holding the telephone more closely, she might have heard
the office blinds being drawn.

The Other Woman was a celebrity romance writer, a
miniseries-spawning, household name, so the imbroglio
quickly went national, splashed onto magazine covers and
decried in chat rooms and alluded to in the presidential
campaign in a stump speech on modern morality. In two
weeks Rebecca Loden went from being a mid-list thriller
author to the poster wife for spurned spouses everywhere.
The just-released *Last Words*, bursting with pre-pub ac-
clamation and already touted as Rebecca's breakout book,
went back to press eight times, riding the sudden surge
of public awareness all the way to number four on the
New York Times Bestseller List, her very first charting.
The scandal pushed the book into early buyers' hands; but

it was the story itself, that of a rookie female FBI agent tracking a sociopathic militia leader across the American west, that clicked with readers. Now one year later and three weeks into its softcover release, the paperback was number one on the *USA Today* top fifty, while the romance author, whose affair with Jeb did not outlive the scandal, had failed to chart with her subsequent offering. It seemed that romance readers would tolerate adultery neither from their cherished characters, nor from their favorite authors.

But victories of morality and commerce had meant little to Rebecca. The breakup of her marriage was a car wreck, an absolute broadside, she hadn't seen it coming. She endured the usual crises of mind, body, and soul. The blame was all Jeb's, and yet still she searched for reasons. That someone once so compassionate and smart could fail her so badly. He had pledged to change, to restore love, trust, intimacy. In fact he begged her to stay, to go with him to counseling and give him another chance. She agonized and he apologized and she prolonged the suffering by going back and trying to make it work. But Jeb wasn't interested in repair, he was interested in syndromes, compulsions, addictions, he wanted to convince himself that he was blameless, that having a poor character was not a flaw but a disease. They had been more than a couple, they had been a team, a single ambition, she the author and he her literary agent, but somewhere along the way she had lost him to himself. Somehow he had changed without regard to Rebecca. The sweet, tender, dedicated man she had loved perished in that car wreck—that was how she mourned her marriage. The Jeb she had admired was dead.

And yet the new Jeb was still in her life. He had been profoundly responsible for the business side of her success, argued her lawyers and accountants, giving him a potential legal claim on future earnings. Why forfeit an extra fifteen percent to another literary agent on top of whatever earnings settlement he might attach? The emotional toll of retaining his services—Jeb was a top agent—seemed too great, until anger caught up with her and Rebecca decided that Jeb should have to sing for his supper and not cost her a penny more than he was worth. So the alter-Jeb remained her agent, a doppelgänger negotiating the deals for her current work-in-progress, the much-anticipated follow-up to *Last Words*.

After the divorce was settled and they embarked on separate lives, every block in Manhattan, a city they had discovered together and made their own, became a monument to betrayal and defeat for Rebecca. Central Park was now a wasteland of softball games and summer picnics. The entire Upper East Side, where they had lived for the last year of their marriage, was off-limits to her now, as though cordoned off by yellow crime-scene tape. The street noise distracted her, and she was unable to write more than a sentence or two without losing her way. The rest of their property had been divided equally, but she found she could not share custody of the city with him. Friends expressed concern about the radical nature of her move, from the Upper West Side to rural Vermont. "Depression" is a word even close friends don't use lightly. But she wasn't fleeing New York City so much as she was returning to the only safe place she knew, the only world she could trust now, the world of her writing.

It was writing that had first brought her to Vermont. She had stalled near the end of the first draft of *Last Words*, whose nemesis she had modeled on Jasper Grue, the leader of the vicious band of backwoods survivalists known as The Truth, who had bankrolled their segregationist militia with a spree of kidnap-murders in the mid-1990s. A scrap of research about his current residence, the Administrative Maximum Unit Prison at Gilchrist, prompted a long drive north into Vermont in an attempt to break the mental logjam. She never got any closer to him than the penitentiary parking lot, but that was all she had needed. She retreated to a nearby country inn and

completed the novel that night in a torrent of creative
energy.

She now lived a half hour north of St. Johnsbury in a
two-story post-and-beam house of exposed wood and high
ceilings and magnificent views of the unnamed mountain
that was her only neighbor. She wrote at a converted carpenter's desk in a sunroom off the kitchen, late into each
day until the sun cycled behind the cap of the mountain.
At night, her world revolved around the broad-mouthed
fireplace. This was a period of hibernation, of recovery.
Her novel had occupied her full-time, its completion her
sole focus.

She felt confident returning north to ADX Gilchrist.
Driving her big red Mountaineer, feeling the rhythm of
the road under the tires, gave her a sense of independence,
something else she had reclaimed from Manhattan. There
the city set the pace, traffic lights, train times, escalators.
In Vermont, she traveled at her own speed. She slowed
now, taking in the regenerative beauty of the Northeast
Kingdom. As she crossed the town limits of Gilchrist, the
noon sun glinted off crystalline lakes in an ice-laden valley, the snow shining like sugar on the roofs of the cozy
lakefront homes. She passed a Christmas tree farm, an
acre of neatly spaced rows of blue spruces of graduating
heights, and started to feel good again. Nothing very bad
could ever happen here.

ADX Gilchrist looked less like the most secure prison
in the country than it did a vocational high school fortified
against a terrorist attack. The penitentiary was set behind
high fences inside a wide clearing of high birch trees cut
back from the perimeter in a perfect, sacred square. Rebecca pulled into the main lot and stepped out into a thin,
crunchy layer of packed white dust, pulling on her parka
and zipping it against the cold. She left her handbag in
the car, carrying neither a notebook nor a tape recorder.
Both were contraband on the inside.

She stepped past muddy snow plowed into tight piles
and across a damp gravel road to the entrance, putting

herself in the place of an arriving inmate. She passed under a squat guard tower and there was no one about. The entire prison compound looked like a border checkpoint at the crossroads of nowhere.

The outer fence was twenty feet tall, topped by taut strands of barbed wire angled inward. Inside the fence were bales of gleaming, spiraled concertina wire, stacked three wide and five high. They looked springy if you ignored the two-inch razor blades. Still, the visceral effect of the fence and the wire surprised her. She proceeded to a grille of thicker steel than the fence, with no visible lock or handle, barring her from a steel mesh tunnel inside. There were no buttons to push, no telephone receiver to pick up.

"Your name, ma'am?"

She found the source of the voice in the observation deck over her right shoulder. The guard stood impassive in a white shirt, black tie, and wide amber-lensed sunglasses of the type usually available through a special TV offer. A rifle leaned against the sliding glass window.

He found her on his list—it could only have been one name long—and with a slow rolling rumble the steel grille opened to admit her. She walked the twenty paces to the second grille, feigning poise as the first grille rolled shut, effectively trapping her inside the enormous sally-port cage. She heard a low ambient humming she realized was the electrified fence. When the second grille did not immediately open, something interesting happened. Rebecca began to panic. The electric fence, the tower, the glimmering wire, all roused a basic fear, one of humanity denied, of freedom revoked. She trembled, and yet even in the grip of this unreasonable distress, the writer in Rebecca thought, *Remember this. Use this.* When the grille clicked and rolled open finally, she squeezed through to the other side and did not look back.

The boxy, austere building ahead did not intimidate her as she imagined a super maximum security prison would. The façade was white limestone and square windows, cold and uninviting but not fearsome, with no outward symbols of deterrence. Certain embassies in New York City inspired more dread.

Warden Barton James met her at the administration building's door. He was tall, no older than sixty, stooped at the shoulders like a career butler, although his hand, when she took it, was warm. Baldness articulated the shape of his skull, tipped forward deferentially on his long neck, and at times his sentences began with a mild stutter. Capillaries of red and blue showed maplike beneath the thin flesh of his face, giving him a sense of frailty that interested Rebecca. Oddly, she noticed his fingernails were trimmed to various lengths, as though he observed some obsessive grooming routine that allowed time for only two fingers each morning.

She had him pegged as a bachelor, a man with nothing but order waiting for him at home, so when he mentioned that Mrs. James was a loyal fan of hers, Rebecca was, in a writerly way, intrigued by her error. *Keep surprising me*, she thought. Another man and a woman met them inside, Special Agents Gimms and Coté, two FBI agents assigned full-time to the federal penitentiary, and both admirers of *Last Words*. They shook hands and exchanged pleasantries, then Rebecca continued with Warden James to another imposing grille, this one a grid of two-inchsquare steel bars rising from the floor.

"We don't get many visitors," he said, excusing the agents' attention.

"But the inmates must," said Rebecca, uncertain she had used the right term. Convicts? Prisoners? Criminals?

"They're allowed one per month, but we find ourselves in a rather remote location here, and these men aren't that well-loved. We've actually cleared very few outsiders since Gilchrist went online five and a half years ago. Which, frankly, is just how we like it."

"I appreciate you bending the rules for me."

"No, not me," he said, pleasantly. "I just do what I'm told." He led her under the raised grille to another guard wearing a white shirt, black pants, and black tie, standing at an inner checkpoint. Rebecca clipped a laminated ID card to the smooth wool of her sweater. "You'll have to bear with us now, there are certain things, regulations, we must insist upon. A pat search, to begin with. You received the appropriate clothing list?"

"I did."

The only restriction that had affected her, aside from the prohibited colors black, blue, and orange, was the one banning brassieres containing wire supports. She wore a sports bra beneath her boyish sweater, a prudent, if somewhat defensive, choice of apparel.

She followed a secretary named Donna into a secure room and surrendered her car keys, coat, and belt, and stood for her very first frisking. Donna's technique was efficient and businesslike—she had the busy, no-nonsense demeanor of a well-caffeinated young mother—and Rebecca smiled and never squirmed. After more scrutiny from a metal detector wand, Donna asked her to raise her sweater up to her shoulders. "Body alarm," Donna said, attaching an adhesive patch to Rebecca's chest, just above her heart, connected by wire to a red, pager-sized device, which clipped to the waistband of Rebecca's khaki trousers.

"We call them 'triple deuces,' " said the warden, back outside at the lobby checkpoint. "That was the prison system's old method of sounding an emergency alert, dialing two-two-two on any facility phone. Pressing that black button on the transmitter sends an electronic signal directly to the Command Center, which controls everything inside the prison. The device also tracks your location anywhere within the perimeter at all times. Every officer here at Gilchrist wears a body alarm, and every one of them will answer a triple deuce running. The pulse rate monitor is a backup device: A read over one hundred and sixty will trigger the alarm if, for instance, a gun to your head is preventing you from signaling. If the electrode wire disconnects, same thing. But don't let that scare you. We haven't had a triple deuce here in . . ."

"Twenty-seven weeks," answered the lobby watchman, one eye on his closed-circuit monitor.

"Twenty-seven weeks. Thank you, William." The warden passed her a clipboard. "And of course, that was a false alarm."

She signed the liability waiver, as well as an autograph for Donna, who was markedly more personable now that her official duties were complete. "I can't wait for your next book."

Rebecca asked her full name and, inscribing the autograph, asked her what it was like to work at ADX Gilchrist, leaving the part about "being a woman" unsaid.

"Super," Donna said, brightly. "Pay's good. Job security, real safe."

"I notice you don't wear a weapon."

"No one does inside, except the extraction teams. There's really no need. We have rifles at our desks in the event of an emergency. We're retrained each year."

"Really," said Rebecca.

"I like the M-14," said Donna, eager to impress.

Other than shooting skeet over the rail of a cruise ship on her honeymoon, Rebecca had never held a firearm in her life. A retired police captain from the Bronx edited her fictional gunplay for accuracy. Here was a young mother six inches shorter than she who could handle an M-14.

"My kind of reader," Rebecca said.

She continued with Warden James down a long corridor of granite terrazzo polished to a high sheen. "Up Front," as the warden referred to the administrative area, had the antiseptic charm of a hospital morgue at night. Their footfalls echoed. Warden James offered her a tour and was surprised and a little disappointed when she declined.

"I hope you didn't go to any trouble on my behalf," she apologized. "But I'm really just here to see Trait."

He gestured graciously with his hand. "My office, then."

The interior was routine upper-management, which disappointed her. The office of the warden of ADX Gilchrist could have been that of the president of a small-town savings and loan. Her eye was drawn to the commendations on the wall and a crystal vase full of butterscotch candies on his desk. He picked up his telephone and said without dialing, "Please make Mr. Trait available."

Rebecca sat in a firmly padded vinyl chair, mindful of the body alarm wire squirming against her belly. The warden hung up and faced her, standing against the sill of a barred window, fences and cushions of razor wire visible behind him.

"Is it fair to ask what you're working on?" he said. "Or is that off-limits?"

"Perfectly fair," she answered, "although I don't have a one-line synopsis worked out. I can tell you what it is not. It's not a prison book. Very little of it will actually take place inside a prison. There might be a scene like what we're doing here, with a character entering a high-max penitentiary for the first time. I must say, these triple . . ."

"Deuces. Triple deuces."

"The body alarms are a great detail."

"I could get you some technical specifications." He was moving toward his phone.

"Oh, no, thank you. The fence outside, it's electrified?"

"Five thousand volts." He settled back against the sill with an incongruous smile. "We lose a few birds every spring and summer." A moppy spider plant browned at the fringes spoke to the aridity of his office. "I gather you're doing something on Luther Trait."

"Something, yes. There are similarities."

The odd smile again. "I'm wondering what you think you'll get from him. From meeting him face-to-face, I mean. None of my business really, but we do take our

jobs seriously here. I'd like to think there's real interest
here on your part, in prisoners, in crime—not just in ex-
ploitation. I'd like to think you are something of a student
of the criminal mind and not just another writer stirring
the pot. I'm hoping that your coming here isn't just a
publicity stunt."

She nodded, feeling tested. The truth probably fell
somewhere in the middle. She was certainly conscious of
the publicity value of this rare meeting with Luther Trait.
And she was aware of the market pressure to follow *Last
Words* with an even bigger book, thereby reinforcing her
bestseller status and putting her on track to getting her
scratchboard portrait on a Barnes & Noble tote bag. She
knew from experience that quality was rarely enough to
get a novel into buyers' hands, that there had to be a hook,
something to reach beyond everyday readers and tap at
the shoulder of the public at large. Something topical,
something urgent, what they call in the trade "that Big
Book feeling." Something to push it to the front of the
bookstalls. The Holy Grail of publishing was the Contro-
versial Bestseller.

At the same time, she was writing about crime, and
not a multigeneration romance or a mother-daughter
weeper or a memoir. Criminals and their methods and
mind-sets. Where was the appeal? This was something she
thought about more and more often. What was it about
violent crime that attracted her interest at all?

"I just want to get things right," she said.

The warden smiled a moment, distant with thought.
"Well, I'm not sure what you'll be able to do with Trait,"
he decided. "Not much entertainment value there. But—
I suppose I might've said the same about Jasper Grue."

She smiled wanly, sensitive to people confusing her
fictional antagonist with his real-life model, or assessing
the relative entertainment value of her work. But more
than that, the warden's remarks reminded her that she was
now indeed inside the same building as Grue. Sharing
space with such a creature, breathing the same square acre

of air. She wondered suddenly if she had given this visit sufficient thought. She asked the warden who else was incarcerated there.

"We have them all. Anyone you can think of, and some you probably can't. Not merely the most violent, although we do house them. But some of these men have a certain drive, something innate, an indomitable criminal will. It takes work to keep your sanity while confined twenty-three-and-a-half hours each day in a windowless, double-doored, six-by-eight pod, denied all human interaction. We've seen some breakdowns. You remember Feretti, the New York mafia don?"

"Sure."

"Hallucinations. Self-mutilation. We finally had to ship him out. His family's lawyers were going to sue, but that would have meant their don's condition leaking to the New York papers. He's no tough guy anymore. Off the record?"

She was not a journalist, never had been. "Sure."

"For the worst of the worst, a life sentence means freedom. Take away their fear of death, all hope of eventual release, and what do you have? You have empowered a criminal, over whom you no longer wield any influence. We are not a vengeful society, but order must be kept, a certain decorum. Our goal is to restrict a prisoner's freedom, not establish it. The system *requires* something more, some penultimate level of punishment short of death in order to keep these career criminals in check. That is the primary function ADX Gilchrist serves in the federal prison system. This is hell on Earth. A necessary dungeon. No fraternizing allowed. No contact visits. No central mess hall or congregate recreation yard. No weight training. A regime of absolute silence. No sleeping between six A.M. and ten P.M. No work opportunities, and no pacifying movies or television. And for many, twenty-four-hour video surveillance. We move inmates through the facility electronically, opening and closing all gates and doors by remote control, thereby eliminating most

contact with guards. We have not had a single violent
incident since we went online. What you see here is the
future of high-tech penology. In a sense, we are no longer
jailing these irredeemables. We are merely watching them
until the day God Himself commutes their sentence here
on Earth. This place is more like a nursing home than a
prison."

"A nursing home."

"You can use that." He straightened, as though to in-
dicate he was back on the record. "We care for the most
dangerous, the most escape-prone, the most famous and
infamous, the most threatening and most threatened criminals in the federal prison system. Terrorists. Serial killers.
Members of the Medellin and Cali drug cartels. Mariel
Cubans. The Libyans who tried to blow up the New York
Stock Exchange. The heads of every major national prison
gang, which we call 'disruptive groups.' The Aryan
Brotherhood, the Black Guerrillas, the Mexican Mafia—
these men didn't get to the top by a vote. Witness Security
cases, and prisoners who have to be separated from one
another. All the big CIA spies. And your man, Grue. Take
the worst of the rotten apples from every Level-Six institution system-wide, seal them inside Gilchrist to rot together, and thereby improve the quality of the harvest
overall."

He was pushing it a little with that harvest metaphor,
which sometimes happened, people getting grandiloquent
in a writer's presence.

"A real rogue's gallery," he finished. "A treasure trove
of bad guys. Enough to keep you going for an entire shelf
of books, I'd imagine."

His telephone buzzed. Trait was ready. Warden James
opened his office door and led her out, ever considerate,
intent on playing Virgil to her Dante.

"Now, Luther Trait," he said. "He's got the thickest
jacket in central file. Everything about him is recorded—
movement, meal consumption, books read, everything.
Trait is a 'blue-book' inmate, a resident of Echo Unit,

'The Director's Unit' as it's known, thirteen underground pods that are the most isolated in the facility. Yes—even in this place, there has to be some higher level of punishment for these men to fear, because that is all they respect. Echo Unit is the hardest time in the federal prison system. That's where Feretti was when he cracked. The most notorious cases, spies, terrorists, dissidents. It's both political and symbolic. Trait has 'walkalone' status outside Echo, meaning that if he travels anywhere inside the prison or out—the rare occasions when he is subpoenaed to testify in an accomplice's criminal trial—he travels in four-point restraints in the company of our number-one extraction team. We can put on a pretty good show if we want to. The cameras in his pod go dark one hour each week, per court order; other than that, he's always under the glass. But let me say this."

They stopped before another rising grille. Rebecca watched the steel curling into the ceiling.

"I'm not impressed much by criminals. The images the media creates—supercriminals, evil geniuses . . . I'm a career corrections officer who rose up through the ranks. I've worked with all kinds of felons, all my life, and I'm here to tell you that every single one of them, almost to a person, is in essence a pathetic excuse for a human being, a narcissistic, low-intelligence opportunist, and a failure. Weak-minded predators, all. So when I say that Trait is an exception, understand that I am not given to hyperbole or mislaid awe. This institution, built to break such men as Luther Trait, hasn't even touched him yet. On the contrary, he seems to be thriving. The regimen, the military routine, the ascetic existence: I believe this place has been good for him. He is a better man here than he ever was in any other lockup, and certainly better than he was on the outside."

A dying fly flopped on the floor and the warden stooped to pick it up before continuing ahead.

"The Brotherhood of Rebellion gang he headed up at Marion was unique among disruptive groups. It was more than just a criminal racket hiding behind tribal colors: It was a culture, a religion. He had members of different races and backgrounds all willing to fight and die for him. And they ran Marion from the inside, which was no playschool itself. The BR was the biggest threat to the security of the American prison system we'd ever seen, and Trait was both its czar and messiah."

They arrived at the Command Center, an imposing, circular guard station like a phantom tollbooth. Double doors opened inward to find eight guards working the room like air traffic controllers, monitoring dozens of viewing screens and issuing instructions into headset microphones. Assault rifles, handguns, and boxes of ammunition were stored inside glass cabinets at the compass points of the room. One man walked away from his post to tell the warden that Trait was on his way, pointing to a computer screen showing a black man in drab gray clothing and chains walking down a hallway surrounded by a phalanx of helmeted men. On another monitor nearby, Rebecca noticed the words *Visitor: LODEN, R.* superimposed above the time, date, and her current location, *C. Center.* Between the lines of text, a small red graphic animated her rising pulse rate.

The warden explained that the penitentiary was designed so that the entire facility, the gates, doors, cameras, lights, thermostats, and alarms, could be operated from within the Command Center, the fortified brain of ADX Gilchrist. It was to be the last post evacuated in the event of an emergency.

They stepped through a small sallyport trap into a new hallway, short and bright and sealed off on either end with steel grilles, blocking stairs she would not want to descend. The walls were different there, a sad, gray concrete that left the corridor still and cool. She was suffering through the dreamlike dread of knowing she was in a place she should not be.

The first door on the right opened into a small room where a corrections officer stood waiting against a side

wall. There was a closed door near him that perhaps led
to a bathroom, and a Formica-topped table with two blue
chairs. Nothing else but the walls.

Warden James said, "Trait's pod in Echo Unit is underground, closed off from the outside hallway by grilles
and an electronic door that seals off noise. For security
reasons, no one from the outside is allowed into Echo."

"No complaint from me."

"This is the disciplinary hearing room. Our kangaroo
court—right, Carlos?"

Carlos grinned behind square-rimmed, top-tinted eyeglasses. "Yes, sir."

"Carlos came over with me from Florence. He'll wait
with you here. Normally we would do this in our visiting
area with each of you on opposite sides of a Plexiglas
wall, but Trait has never been allowed that far up front,
and I'm of the opinion that certain inmates should remain
generally ignorant of prison·geography. So special arrangements have been made. You'll be face-to-face here.
No extraordinary restraints. Trait will be wearing a stun
belt, activated remotely at the extraction team's discretion,
delivering an immobilizing electrical charge. If by chance
Trait does misbehave, your interview will be terminated
and he will be removed. The encounter will be recorded,
of course." He indicated two cameras in the corners of
the ceiling. "I don't suppose I have to instruct you not to
initiate any physical contact with him. Oh, by the way—
we could not, by law, compel him to attend this interview.
The choice was his. Were you aware that he has turned
down every other media request for an interview, until
today?"

"No," she said. "No, I was not."

"This is going all the way back to his tour in Marion.
Can you think of any reason why he would desire to meet
with you in particular?"

She was spooked now. "No—certainly not."

The warden shrugged, smiling obliquely, and walked

to the door. "I hope you get whatever it is you're looking for."

"You're leaving?" she said.

"It's best that I wait back at the Command Center. My presence here would only be a distraction."

Carlos showed her to a chair at the table and then returned to the wall without a word. Rebecca tried to get comfortable, overthinking her posture and conscious of the body alarm electrode pasted over her heart. Her nerves were on display inside the Command Center. It was not the rate of her heartbeat that troubled her, but rather its force, its bass depth, the heaviness of which seemed to dislodge something in her chest that rose to obstruct her throat, a lump of intimidation she tried to swallow back. Why had Luther Trait agreed to this visit?

She heard chains approaching and clasped her hands underneath the table.

The door opened and the room was scanned by two men in riot gear: helmets, flak vests, jackboots, lineman's gloves, black truncheons. They entered and Trait followed in his chains, backed up by two more men in riot gear and a fifth, the team leader, wearing yellow latex gloves.

Trait wore prison scrubs, thick blue cotton washed to gray. Both his leg irons and handcuffs were shackled to a belly chain that draped around his stun belt like the tassels of a ceremonial dress. He did not shuffle but instead used the entire length of ankle chain to stride from the door to the table. His eyes were fixed on her, and images from his criminal trial came flooding back to her mind: slow-motion video of him walking in and out of court, staring defiantly at the cameras, smiling when his verdict was read. Rebecca tried to meet his stare across the table, certain her body alarm was going to go off screaming. ADX Gilchrist was an athenaeum of killers, and these librarians had just brought to her table their rarest book.

The team leader held the plastic back of the chair as Trait sat. A pair of guards remained at the door while the other two moved peripherally away from him, almost to the walls. The lead man remained between Trait and the door, muttering softly into his headset. His hand was poised over an instrument on his holster belt that must have been the stun-belt trigger.

Luther Trait looked no older since his trial, only slimmer and more compact. His forearms, neck, and face had all lost muscle, his brown skin appearing to have faded in tone. Still, he bore none of the criminal ugliness one usually sees in a murderer, but rather a sense of nobility and pride. Only his eyes hinted at his malevolence. Light brown, nearly yellow, the irises blemished and cracked like gems miscut by a jeweler, they were eyes that had split public opinion: To some, they were evidence of a mystic intelligence attributed to Trait; to others, they were an outward manifestation of his evil soul. Still others found symbolism in their shattered appearance, with regard to the abuse he had suffered as a child. To Rebecca, they stood out like negative images in an otherwise developed photograph. It seemed to her that eyes so singular in appearance must also view the world singularly.

He was studying her too. "I don't know you," he said. "The phone is off the hook. They record every conversation."

It seemed an odd prelude to their discussion, a warning. "Okay," she said.

"They said you are a writer, a novelist. Are you going to write about me?"

"I am writing about someone like you."

"There is no one like me."

"I am writing about someone who is in a position similar to yours."

"A black man in prison."

"A leader. A prince among criminals."

"A man of revolution. A criminal to your society but an innocent in the eyes of the true man, the eternal man: the warrior."

Trait's unusual eyes bore none of the recalcitrance of a sociopath, but instead his gaze drew her more intimately into the encounter. He was like a thick wire humming with electricity. He emanated power. She felt his radiation working on her. His voice was deep and commanding, and she gave in to it because she was safe. There were guards and cameras.

"At Marion," he said, "the warden would parade visitors by my cell. Nobody wanted to leave the zoo without seeing the lion. The king of the jungle is safe in his cage and all is well."

"That's not why I'm here," she said.

"This so-called dungeon: It is my temple. It was built to worship the warrior Luther Trait. For six thousand years the civilized man, the weak man, the modern intellectual, has constructed laws in order to protect himself. He has branded the warrior a criminal in order to confine the dominant male who would otherwise be his master. You see before you a strong man in an age where strength is feared. How do you punish the unpunishable? I am a riddle they cannot solve. That is why they watch me constantly: to study me, to learn from me. All of mankind's worthiest impulses, shut up in this museum buried in the frozen earth. Everything you see here—this table, these guards, these bars, and walls—it's all about one thing."

"What's that?"

"You. It's all about you. Imprisonment is population control. The dominant male is the mate attractor. You, the female, are the great prize."

"A prize?" she said. He was just pushing her buttons, seeking her out. "Is that what I am?"

"Take away these chains, these jails, and laws. Turn every man loose in the world to fend for himself. Where would you be then? Who would you run with for shelter, for protection, for survival? A smart man? A cultured man? You would align yourself with a criminal." He leaned closer, dragging a few links of steel over the edge of the table. "You would run with a warrior. You would run with me."

"Oh," she said, sputtering now, offended. "Please."

"You have something for me," he said.

He was leaning close to her. He wore a musk of confidence.

He was waiting.

"I don't understand," she said.

He said again, "You have something for me."

She wanted to dismiss this as horny bravado, but could not ignore the pale sulfur of his eyes. In them were scrutiny and insistence, and she was struck cold. She sat still, forgetting her quickened pulse rate transmitting through the body alarm. For the moment there was no one else in the room and no warden watching them on camera. There was no one else in the penitentiary.

It was as though he knew something she did not. All she could think was that there had been some gross miscommunication regarding the circumstances of her visit.

"Maybe there was some mistake, I—"

"There was no mistake."

His stare was different now, more probing than provocative, more evaluative than involving. He finally sat back, and there was perhaps a hint of relief in his eyes. None of this meant anything to Rebecca. But like a plug pulled from a wall, the connection between them—at once so forceful and immediate—was broken.

Rebecca was mystified. "What is it that I could possibly have for you?"

Trait stood abruptly. His chair scraped violently against the floor and his surprising agility froze Rebecca.

"I'm done here," he said.

He doubled over before he could finish speaking. He dropped to the floor as though struck on the back of the head. He lay on his side, grunting and twitching, chains rattling as he contorted.

The two nearest guards moved in immediately. A *Clear* order was issued, and they reached for his armpits, jerking him to his feet. The group leader opened the door, muttering into his headset.

Trait had not made a move for her, as far as Rebecca could tell. Still, she wasn't sorry they had dropped him, only that the interview was over.

Trait's livid brown eyes found her. His face was proud. He bore the abuse nobly, shaking off the electric charge that had humbled him and assuming his former poise. The guards released him and his hands trembled as he stood to full height.

"Next time we meet," he said, through gritted teeth, "it will be on my terms."

The guards fell in around Trait as he turned and strode unassisted to the door, the chains slithering like serpents at his feet.

TRAIT CAME OFF THE STAIRS INTO THE BLEAK SILENCE OF THE underground corridor and walked the range of granite and steel, his handlers keeping stride with him like the five points of his star. His thoughts were divided. As usual, he was measuring the distance of the hallway in paces, counting off the steel doors, watching the hacks and how they signaled to the cameras to rack up the steel grilles. He didn't get out of E-Unit more than three or four times a year and made the most of every opportunity. He listened attentively to the click of the automatic door locks. He studied the camera positions and observed the sight lines down each range. He noted the way the hacks communicated by hand gestures in observance of E-Unit's regimen of silence, and thought of the various ways that this could benefit him.

They walked him to the examining room inside the E-Unit entrance trap. The doctor was waiting but nothing happened right away—no strip search, no examination—and Trait realized who they were waiting for.

In the other half of his mind, Luther Trait was not in the penitentiary at all. He was a Nubian king strolling along the banks of the River Nile with his wartime advisors under the beating African sun. He was the leader of a complicated system of tribes that reigned over a powerful seventh-century empire stretching from modern-day Egypt into modern-day Ethiopia, descendants of the early Nubian kingdoms who battled with Egyptians for power in the vast Lower Nile region, long before the campaigns of Alexander and the age of Christ.

This was not a dream. His thoughts represented a spir-

itual journey to the source of his strength and will, a pil-
grimage to his inner homeland. The bars and walls around
him had reality in space but no reality in time, and freedom from the senses of his immediate environment unlocked the universal. Anywhere he wished to go, he freely
went. In an instant he reassembled the kitchen of his early
youth. He was kneeling on a chair at the gouged wooden
table by the window. He picked up a Dixie cup, felt the
texture of the ribbed place mat underneath his forearm,
smelled the food stains hardened in the grooves. He shred-
ded a paper napkin into thin strips. He reached across the
table and tasted a pinch of sugar from the chipped bowl
as he looked out the steamed window, its grime etched
into his brain like a Rorschach blot. He walked to the
closet in his mother's bedroom, the one he had spent so
many hours of so many days locked inside. The padlock
was nothing to him now. He opened the door for the little
boy sitting on the musty shoeboxes beneath the hanging
old coats, squinting into the sudden light.

His journeys were not fantasies or delusions, nor empty
masturbatory voyages.

The foster homes of his youth: They were as real to
him as the examining room he was in now. He returned
often, prowling the shadows of his past, assembling the
houses before him room-by-room like a god—every stick
of furniture and the people who owned them. The little
boy eating cereal at the breakfast table knew what he had
to do to get back to his mother. It was all prearranged.
Leave the back door unlocked or free the latch on the
bulkhead before the happy family leaves the house for the
day. She was careful only to take little things that
wouldn't be missed, and he smelled her in the rooms,
Winstons and spearmint. Then she would reclaim him and
he would be back home for a few weeks of her and the
closet until the time came for her to give him up again.
He did whatever he had to do in order to return home
again. Then there was the last house, the big one on the
hill in New Jersey. The polished marble foyer and game

room, pinball and soda, and his own bedroom and his own TV. Their daughter was three years older than he and she let him play with anything he wanted. He liked it there. He let himself stay too long. When the homesickness came, before a day-trip to the Central Park Zoo, he cranked open the downstairs bathroom window just a few inches, so that it might not even be noticed. He left it up to fate. That evening he smelled his mother in his bedroom, the smoke and the gum, and at once was ashamed. The next morning, the father noticed his paintings missing. The silver was gone from the dining room and the coins from the cabinets of glass. Desk drawers had been pried open and important papers taken, bank accounts drawn on. The police came and talked to Luther but he fooled them with his answers. And he had been with the family all weekend. He couldn't wait to return home, and the ensuing days were agony. Finally he called the number from a pay phone after school. His mother's telephone was disconnected. After that, he was rarely sad anymore, only angry.

Sensory deprivation was for Luther Trait the ultimate freedom. Like the boy in the closet, he transcended consciousness, able to project himself to any place and time in every manner of being except the realm of the physical—the very realm he was working on right now.

The door opened and Warden James stepped inside. He had paled during his tour at Gilchrist, same as his prisoners. Trait had not seen him in perhaps two years.

"Initiate a search log," the warden said.

The doctor had a clipboard prepared, snapping on examination gloves as he faced Trait. The egg salad on his breath was stomach turning. "Does the prisoner request an X ray in lieu of a digital search?"

Trait nodded.

The warden shook his head. "No more than two nonmedical abdominal X rays per year."

The doctor was bored with this routine. "Sign the waiver," he said, holding the clipboard up to Trait.

Trait was looking at the warden. Not with malice, just
studying him, tracing the veins beneath the thin veneer of
the man's pallid face and wondering if the face of a prison
was the face of its jailer.

"Prisoner refuses to sign," declared the warden, taking
the clipboard and pen from the doctor and authorizing the
search.

The doctor started with Trait's ears, curling them inward and running his fingers behind and inside, his sickly
egg breath pushing into Trait's face. He tipped Trait's
head back to fully expose his nostrils, then probed them
with a short nasal speculum. He held Trait's jaw and slid
a plastic bit between his teeth to prevent him from biting,
then used a wooden blade to lift Trait's tongue for inspection. The doctor's latex thumbs entered his mouth and
fished out the insides of his cheeks. This was the intrusion
Trait enjoyed most, a white man checking the quality of
his teeth. He felt aligned with his slave brothers, slaves
who built the South, who built the pyramids, who built
everything. All this time the warden watched him patiently.

The riot sticks in the hacks' hands were truncheons,
yard-long black sticks tipped with steel ball bearings. "Rib
spreaders," they were called, separating the ribs without
breaking them or leaving any bruises or marks. There was
a symbolism in those sticks, only partly phallic, of the
agents of the state reaching through the bars of the rib
cage of a free man to get at his soul. Trait slept with wet
toilet paper stuffed in his ears, to keep out their hammering on the bars every hour on the hour, ostensibly checking for sawed pieces but really just banging on a man's
mind, whacking away at his sanity: *Bang! Bang! Bang!*
He had to fight to survive, every step of the way.

The hacks tore apart the back of Trait's prison shirts,
seamed in Velcro for just that purpose, sliding it down
over his manacled hands to expose his back and chest.
His shoes were removed and his feet inspected, the soles
and the spaces between each brown toe. The stun belt was

removed and one hack grasped his cotton pants at the elasticized waist and pulled them to his ankles, and the doctor lifted his dick for inspection, then his sack. Trait remembered the first time he had stood for this, in a county lockup outside Milwaukee. He had proudly urinated in the examining guard's face. But he was young then and his anger had lacked focus.

"Bend over the table."

The Nubian kingdom fell in the fourteenth century as claims on the Nile by outside countries were defended and won. Aside from a few artifacts and ruins, none of the Nubian culture survives today except the language. Even the name was taken away. The lesson of history, as Trait understood it, was that every great empire believes itself the anointed, the eternal, the last. And every great empire eventually falls.

"What could she have had?" said Warden James.

The warden's face was near his own, his voice was soft and intimate in his ear. In five years, he had never once addressed Trait directly.

"What did you think she could possibly have had for you?"

Like flashes of true insight to a cloistered monk, communication was a rare and beautiful thing to a man in total isolation. In a life as rigidly controlled as Luther Trait's, there was no room for coincidence—and so the woman's visit, scheduled one day before the beginning of the beginning, had demanded his courtesy. The message he had expected from her, in fact the only message she could have carried for him at that late hour, was one of abortion, of the failure of their great plan. His relief at her ignorance eclipsed his displeasure at the distraction her visit had posed, at that very late hour when demands upon his concentration were at their highest. No—she had been sent to him for some other reason, one that he had not as yet divined.

Trait looked at the warden's venous face, his dewy eyes, so impassive and near. He pitied the man left holding the keys in a kingdom of open doors. The doctor continued his manual prodding, an exercise in humiliation, a thorough search for something when they knew that nothing was there. As the cold steel table chilled his chest, against his bare back Luther Trait felt the burning desert sun, and in his ears he heard drums of war, and water lapping patiently at the sandy banks of the ancient and holiest Nile.

HOW WARM AND REASSURING WAS THE RAMBLING GILCHRIST COUNtry Inn: the warm blond oak of its floors, the ornamental wreaths and pewter sconces hanging on the walls, the framed homilies ("God made us Sisters, Life made us Friends"), the brass registers breathing warm air through the floors. The formal prose of the inn brochure, printed in violet ink on heavy ivory stock, delighted Rebecca.

> *The Inn is a recently renovated Victorian farmhouse, constructed by descendants of the original Gilchrist family. Located on seven secluded acres just outside the historic town common, Gilchrist's only lodging establishment is a unique four-season retreat. Its ten bedrooms offer guests a relaxing and comfortable lodging experience, most rooms featuring well-appointed private baths and thermostats for your personal comfort. Bedrooms are spacious and individually decorated with heirloom antiques, a queen-size canopy bed, and handmade patchwork quilts. Afternoon tea served weekends.*

The bell on the reception desk—an actual handbell, set next to a spice-scented candle of caramel-colored wax in a squat canning jar—brought the proprietor and innkeeper, Fern Iredale, out of the kitchen. Fern was about sixty, solidly built, strong and broad but not tall, with short salt-and-pepper hair and a relentlessly upbeat manner. She appeared wearing a yellow apron tied over a work shirt, khakis, and moccasins. Rebecca remembered her first visit, and how five minutes chatting with Fern at

check-in had completely deionized her urban cynicism. It
turned out Fern was a fan of "strong women" thrillers.
She had made Rebecca promise that if she ever came near
Gilchrist again, she would spend another night or two at
the inn and Fern would organize a reading in town. And
Fern was so warm and dear that Rebecca could not let her
down. There were worse things she could do for herself
than enjoy a weekend of Fern's mothering.

A carton of paperbacks sat behind the desk, ready for
the next evening's event. Fern checked her in, then
proudly led Rebecca around to the back of the house via
the enclosed farmer's porch. A painted sign above the
communal bookshelves read, "Take a book. Leave a
book." On a small stand on the highest shelf was an autographed, plastic-sleeved hardcover copy of *Last Words*,
with a handwritten sign below it reading, ". . . Except This
One."

Dinner was an adventure. Vermont cheddar-cheese
soup, homemade oatmeal-maple bread, cob-smoked maple ham, potato pie, and maple-butternut squash, with not
a green vegetable in sight. Apple cider was the beverage,
apple betty the dessert. Guests sat family style at one long
table in a room of latticed windows looking out on the
night and the trickling snow. Rebecca noted that the sage-
green floral wallpaper matched the fabric of the seat cushions, the tablecloths, and the linen.

Fern hovered over dinner, a body in perpetual motion,
returning again and again from the kitchen with platters
of food. Later, dishes of Ben & Jerry's Phish Food would
follow them into the parlor, as well as Granny Smith apple
wedges dusted with nutmeg and cinnamon. Also "sugar-
on-snow" was a local treat—maple syrup boiled and
poured over a bowl of freshly fallen snow. And coffee,
tea, and homemade oatmeal-maple cookies.

The other guests were generally pleasant. Normally
Rebecca resisted groups. Anytime strangers are brought
together in a closed social system—a doctor's waiting
room, an airplane, a checkout line—a sort of existential

jury is formed. Judgments are passed from stranger to stranger, if only silently, and any action taken by one within the group becomes collusive. If at a large dinner one person is inexcusably rude to the waiter, then by association the entire table is held responsible for his bad manners. Naturally, Rebecca's mind carried this to extreme "lifeboat" scenarios. Who in the group would be the first to crack? Who would betray the others for his or her own gain? Who would hoard the drinking water? Who would emerge as the leader? Especially since her divorce, Rebecca had a hard time surrendering to anything that was beyond her complete control.

Fern, a platter of ham on her arm, posed an icebreaker—"What was the best meal you've ever eaten?"—and Rebecca enjoyed what the responses told her about the others.

First there was Terry, a bonds analyst from Fort Hill, New Jersey, who was in Gilchrist to research the prison-bond offering as a model for other towns pursuing similar projects. He wore a blazer to dinner, his buttery hair still damp from a shower. He was boorish about his job, eager to impress, but at least he kept the conversation going. His favorite meal was a luncheon he had attended in London, where he had been seated two tables away from the CEO of Sun Microsoft Systems.

Mr. Hodgkins was a gentleman in his late-fifties, polite and well-groomed without being particularly handsome. He had the air of a man of travel, a seen-it-all self-possession that made him difficult for Rebecca to read. His hair was graying and fading off the top and sides of his head, his eyebrows were wiry, his eyes cool blue. There was a whiff of money and manner, which Terry in particular deferred to, sensing a soul mate, but Hodgkins would give nothing away. Evidently, he had been at the inn for a few days already; perhaps he was looking for retirement property in the region. He declined both wine and dessert and retired to his room immediately after dinner. His favorite meal, he said with a fond smile, was a lamb dish at Maxim's in Paris, "With a lady friend—but that was twenty years ago."

Mia, a social worker, was from the Montreal area, traveling on vacation with her young husband, Robert. They both seemed younger than their twenty-four years. This was their first night in the United States and, in contrast to Hodgkins, the couple possessed an abundance of youth but clearly little cash, reminding Rebecca of her hungry years with Jeb. Robert was slender and goofy with a honking laugh, while Mia, when not enthusiastically defending the poor, was shy and quiet, the fabric of her black turtleneck stretched from her pulling the front fold up over her pale lips. They were a couple one looks at and wonders how they ever got together, and yet is greatly relieved they did. Mia's favorite meal was a picnic the two of them had once shared in the middle of a soccer field on one of their first dates, cold chicken and pasta under the stars. After some deliberation Robert agreed, although he also liked Mia's beef stew. The couple withdrew to a cushioned deacon's bench after dinner to play Yahtzee, a game Rebecca hadn't even known still existed.

Dr. Rosen was a tall, thin, sandy-haired podiatrist from Boston. He looked natty in a blue cardigan sweater, corduroy trousers, and tan loafers, sitting in an easy chair after dinner with a copy of *Yankee* magazine open on his knee; his attention was split between the game of Yahtzee to his left and a *Jeopardy!* match to his right. Dr. Rosen smiled with self-satisfaction when he knew the *Jeopardy!* answer, and switched his attention to the dicing game when he did not. He was content to monitor the matches rather than play, and to his credit meddled in neither. He could not think of a favorite meal but pledged to come up with one before the end of the evening. He wore a wedding band, although it was clear—to Rebecca at least—that the woman he was traveling with—a short, young, thick-waisted salon blond named Darla—was not his wife. Her favorite meal was "a cruise to the Bahamas—the entire cruise was just one big meal!" A small gem linked to a delicate gold strand around her wrist was a constant source of distraction. It took very little deducing to figure out that Darla and Dr. Rosen were in the early stages of a May-December extramarital affair.

Bert and Rita Noonan, a married couple near Dr. Rosen's age, were visiting northern Vermont for a weekend of antiquing and cross-country skiing. They were florists from Connecticut, having left control of their small chain of stores in the capable hands of their eldest daughter. Bert and Rita were very much a team—so much so that they were nearly one person, Bert-and-Rita, two heads thinking as one. In the parlor, each opened a different newspaper and read articles to the other over decaf tea. Their favorite meal was a salmon dish served at Canyon Ranch, a spa in the Berkshires they visited twice a year. They were eerily fit and friendly, these semiretirees in casual slacks and half-glasses, like forty-year-olds suffering from a mysterious aging disease.

Coe, a teenager who worked for Fern, was tending to the wood fire in the parlor, running the carpet sweeper over Terry's cookie crumbs, and collecting empty bowls, dishes, and plates. "Done with that, Miss Loden?" He wore a woolen court-jester hat of the snowboard generation, even indoors, and was very much the postmodern dude. No one asked him what his favorite meal was. From the look of him, Rebecca would have guessed frozen pizza.

Later that evening, sitting in a quilt-backed rocking chair with a china cup of blackberry tea on the chessboard table at her elbow, blissfully content, Rebecca noticed Coe returning from an outdoor task with a markedly jauntier pace. Smiling to himself and meeting no one's eye, he carried a few scraps of kindling to the fireplace, breezing past her, the flaps of his untucked flannel shirt emanating the unmistakable fragrance of marijuana. The boy kneeled at the wide stone hearth, his tattered jeans frayed at the hems, the dirty white strings dripping with snow, and attended to the crackling pine wood with rapt concentration. Rebecca watched him wistfully, envying his carefree youth.

She was not the only one. On the other side of the fireplace, in a wide club chair near the player piano and the French doors leading out to the porch, a guest named Mr. Kells sat with the *New York Times* dipped just a few inches below his eyes. In them, fleeting yet unmistakable, was the same wistful expression that had clouded her own eyes, the same glimmer of the fuddled memories and exquisite indolence the tender aroma of pot aroused. At precisely the moment she became aware of him, Mr. Kells looked up and became aware of her—prompting her to glance away, embarrassed and protesting her innocence with a return to her copy of *Vermont Life* and a feature story about chain-saw art.

Mr. Kells was a football coach at a small northeastern college, in Gilchrist overnight to scout a quarterback recruit. At least, that was the occupation her writer's mind assigned him. Big hands held the newspaper, football hands—brown-skinned, ringless, and hairless. He was in his mid-forties, thick-chested, his weight well-distributed over his tall frame but just beginning to round out in the middle, the stone build of his youth starting to soften. The plate of oatmeal-maple cookies that found its way to the piano bench near him was empty now, but for the crumbs. A few tiny woolen pills remained stuck to his white polo shirt, from a sweater he had pulled off after dinner. But his belt matched his shoes, and in general, Mr. Kells bore an agreeable, everyman look, a rugged, one-of-the-guys familiarity that belied his actual behavior.

He was the only guest aside from Mr. Hodgkins not to succumb to the geniality of that pleasant, fire-lit evening. He had kept to himself at dinner, seated next to Mr. Hodgkins, eating methodically. They were the only two not to ask any questions about Rebecca's interview with Luther Trait. Since dinner, he had spent the evening ensconced behind the *New York Times*—not hiding, necessarily, but separated from the rest, an outsider. Perhaps it had something to do with his traveling through all-white Vermont. But would a college football coach lavish the better part of an evening on the *Times*? Rebecca could not get a good read on him. When pushed for his favorite meal, he pointed to his plate as he chewed. "This is it," he said, "right here."

Rebecca found herself missing the *Times* for the first time since leaving New York. She kept up with it online, but news was so ephemeral in cyberspace. Printed on paper, it seemed intractable, authoritative, final.

She roused herself out of the rocking chair. In the sitting room near the kitchen there was an overstuffed sofa with navy blue throw pillows sunk like napping children in the curves of its plush, welcoming arms. The sofa was Fern, the pillows her guests.

"In here, dear."

Fern was inside the saloon doors, past a sign that read *Employees Only.*

"Oh, never mind the sign," she said. "That's just to keep out the riffraff."

Rebecca pushed through into the warm kitchen. "You get a lot of riffraff here?"

The room was square, arranged around a large, central butcher-block island. The sink and countertops had been wiped down, the trash paper bagged, recyclables separated and ready to go. Fern fed muffin pans to a large stove built into an exposed brick wall, then pulled the string on her apron, lifting the neck loop over her neat, peppery hair, and padded in moccasin shoes over to the faucet to refill the kettle. Fern struck Rebecca as an old-guard lesbian, a distinguished veteran of the gender-identity wars, her commission honorably resigned. If she was alone, it was certainly by choice, and yet she wasn't alone. She had her guests and, as Rebecca set her cup on the counter, Ruby the cat came rubbing against her leg.

"Hi, there," said Rebecca, kneeling to pat Ruby's slinky black coat. "I remember you."

"Ruby, come here," Fern *tsk-tsk*ed, pouring a dish of

milk and setting it on the floor. Ruby's belly pouch swayed as she sauntered over to the dish on silent, white-mittened paws. Fern stroked her tail as the cat lapped.

Rebecca asked, "Is she an indoor or outdoor cat?"

"She's no mouser. She's too lazy. *You're lazy*." Fern worked the cat's soft head, scruffing the blaze of white between her forehead and her nose. "She's too skittish, the old girl. I don't know what she'd do with herself if she ever got outside. She's too sheltered. *You're too sheltered*." Ruby had stopped drinking altogether, back arched, eyes narrowed to a squint as she luxuriated under Fern's small hand.

"Thanks again for arranging things."

"Don't be silly," said Fern. She was up and washing her hands in the sink. "I'm thanking *you*. When's the next one coming?"

"Soon, I hope," said Rebecca, as Fern pulled a bag of oranges from the pantry and spilled them onto the butcher's island. She halved them with a long knife pulled from a magnetic strip on the wall. "I don't suppose there's anywhere I could get a New York newspaper at this hour?"

"No. I know that Mr. Hodgkins has been driving up to Newport for his. He usually leaves it around here somewhere."

"Mr. Kells has it," she said. The dishwasher began to breathe steam and Rebecca slid down the counter away from it. "Has Mr. Hodgkins been here awhile?"

"Four days. A nice, quiet guest. Private bath, uses a lot of towels. He must have some friends near town. He's always driving off."

The kettle whistled and Rebecca filled her cup. "What about Mr. Kells?"

Fern paused to think, her knife blade poised over a Sunkist as though determining its fate. "His second night. He skipped dinner yesterday. I don't know him that well. Funny thing, though."

"What?"

"No skis. Neither of them. No winter sports gear what-soever. This time of year, that's usually what I see. Not people traveling alone and without skis."

"I'm traveling alone," Rebecca said. "And I don't have skis."

"Ah," said Fern, winking and pulling a juicer out of the island cabinet. "Everyone is a suspect."

Rebecca returned to the parlor with her tea. Dr. Rosen and Darla had slipped away, and Robert and Mia were chatting in French over a game of Mastermind. Bert-and-Rita had moved on to back issues of *Consumer Reports* they had brought along with them. Terry was watching *SportsCenter* with the volume turned down. Coe was still tending to the fire.

The *Times* was folded on the piano stool next to the plate of crumbs and Kells was gone. Rebecca picked up the wrinkled newspaper and glanced at the headlines, then dropped it back onto the stool. She was less interested in its content than she had thought.

She opened the French doors onto the glassed-in porch. The chill was refreshing after the heat of the parlor fire-place and the warmth of the kitchen stove. She couldn't find a light switch, so she followed the dim passageway toward the darker rear of the house, letting her eyes adjust. She set her teacup down on a wicker plant stand and crossed her arms to the cold, looking out at the snow shaking out of the unseen sky and tumbling onto the grounds. A glowing white carpet stretched to the bare trees at the foot of the mountains and the silence was absolute. She wondered at the strangeness of the day, a study in contrast: ADX Gilchrist and Luther Trait standing in sharp relief against the agreeableness of the inn. She thought of killers and innkeepers and bestselling sequels and wondered what direction her life and her career were taking.

"Excuse me."

The voice was low and perfunctory—but still Rebecca

jumped as Kells walked out of the shadows at the dark end of the porch, stepping past her.

"Didn't want to startle you," he said.

"Right," she said, nervously touching her throat with her hand. "Thanks."

He was already on his way back to the parlor door. She stood there a moment, angry with herself for being spooked, then she turned her attention back to Kells. There was an air of tensile strength in the way he carried himself. What had he been doing on the porch?

She returned to the parlor door, but he was gone again, as was the plate of crumbs. Rebecca ignored the growing cold and continued stealthily along the outer porch almost to the front entrance of the inn, stopping at the twin French doors. She saw Kells there, just inside the saloon doors, handing Fern the small plate and saying goodnight. Rebecca edged back from the wall to avoid being seen, and peeked out again as he moved past the reception desk to start up the carpeted stairs to the guest rooms, a hard-cover book in his hand.

She made her way back to the porch door. She found her cup of tea on the plant stand and then, curious, she rounded that last corner, following the porch to the end. Another pair of doors led to an outside stairway going up, and they were locked. Before the doors was Fern's communal library, the built-in bookshelves packed with chipped paperback spines of varying widths and lengths: chubby romances, thin humor books, self-published Vermontalia, and the familiar stripes of last year's thrillers. But what surprised her was the top shelf where earlier that day she had viewed Fern's autographed copy of *Last Words* above the sign admonishing borrowers, ". . . Except This One."

The wire display stand was empty.

THE SECOND DAY

REBECCA AWOKE LATE THE NEXT MORNING TO THICK SNOWFLAKES drifting like downy feathers outside her room's calico curtains. She showered until the hot water ran out, dressed, and arrived downstairs just as Mia and Robert were leaving. Bundled in mittens and mufflers, Mia gave Robert a playful punch in the back as they pushed through the doors.

Bert-and-Rita were the only ones left in the dining room. Rita was done up in a violet snowsuit, and Bert was sporting a ridiculous pair of gaiters wound to his knees. She disparaged them because she envied them. Here was a good, working marriage, two healthy people growing old together. Rebecca said "Good morning," then fixed herself a to-go cup of coffee at the serving table, leaving them swapping sections from the local newspaper.

She took a drive around the town. The falling snow kept everything fresh and white without yet impeding movement, so that the Mountaineer rolled along confidently. Snow was the great equalizer, nature's cream base. Even the most beautiful town in the world profited from a little touching up. It whitened out the rough edges, filled in the cracks where things were wanting, and brought to life the colors that survived its steady march—the sorrel of a tree trunk, the stark black dome of a short silo, the bright brick of a heated chimney.

Outside the town center, life was more rugged and lonely. Collapsing barns. A solitary tree wilting in a field of snow. A makeshift house constructed around a mobile home. A tractor driven by a watchcapped man of flannel and wool. Horses rooting through snowfall for food, near squatting cows, lazily watching her drive past.

She made a circuit of Gilchrist and was back at the common by noon. The Gilchrist General Store, first stop on the right as you come from the inn, was a wood-planked floor of three narrow aisles, a mix of old and new, glass bottles of Moxie and plastic half-liters of Sprite. The post office was there, a scale and a stamp machine and a government seal behind the register. In back was a selection of fishing and hunting gear, and next to the deli counter was a bulletin board of Polaroid pictures of camouflaged men, photos taken at all times of the year, hunters holding up a string of fish or kneeling in the back of an open pickup twisting the head of a dead deer toward the camera. The old man behind the meat case wore a stained smock, drying his hands on a brown paper towel.

She ordered a sandwich and stepped outside. A crowd was gathering on the snowy common, townspeople milling around the gazebo. The historic white buildings spaced around the blanketed common looked like a movie set, *The Nineteenth Century New England Village* backlot. Dates were printed above the doors, as though a flatlander might question their authenticity: Gilchrist Town Hall, 1854; Gilchrist Masonic Hall, 1841. Rebecca's cynical eye sought out the anachronisms, things that would have to be framed out of the camera's view. The snowmobiles lining the curb. The North Face jackets. A placard in the window above the general store advertising Tai Kwan Do.

Yet something about Gilchrist touched her, triggering a sense memory which, despite its authenticity, warmed her heart. It was the simple innocence of a small-town past shared by most Americans, despite their true pasts—memories assigned in seventh grade, with the first three chapters of *The Adventures of Huckleberry Finn*. This was Rockwell's America. Rebecca wandered over to the common with her wrapped sandwich.

The bell rang in the church steeple, calling the gathering to attention. It was a ceremony of some sort, the dedication of a bust about to be unveiled. The honoree named Tom Duggan, stood on the bandstand wearing a hangman's coat. Rebecca remained on the edge of the crowd, biting into her sandwich discreetly and listening to a top-hatted man speaking without a microphone. He was the town historian, joined onstage by the uniformed chiefs of the police and fire departments and the selectmen and other elected officials, reciting from index cards something about the history of the penitentiary and Tom Duggan's role in bringing it to Gilchrist. But Rebecca was more interested in the conversations around her.

One old salt in a dingy pea coat decried the turnout. "Saturday afternoon, for chrissakes."

"Town's changing," sang his buddy, with the cadence of an oft-spoken refrain.

"Seen all them outer-state license plates these past coupla days?"

"How's that?"

"Strangers riding around. At night."

They all resembled each other in some vague way: hearty, red-cheeked, dour. Lots of beards. Kept the chin warm. Rebecca turned her attention to a middle-aged woman talking to a hard-faced neighbor.

"You heard about Lemsie?"

"Drinking again?"

"Tractor stolen last night, right out of his barn. Chief Roy don't have no clue."

"Like Dickie Veal's snowplow two nights ago." The man *sheesh*ed. "Crime follows money, don't it."

"Like shit follows dessert."

The snow was coming down harder, thick flakes rushing to the earth, the groundfall thickening and muffling sound. The bust was unveiled to applause and a few whistles—it was granite and chip-cheeked, just like Mr. Tom Duggan—and then the man of the hour began to speak, slowly and shyly. "Louder, Tom!" came the cries, and he smiled with embarrassment and opened his mouth to start over.

Instead of speech, there was a series of short horn

blasts, as from an old civil-defense alarm. All heads
turned toward the source, a narrow stone tower just visible
behind the roof of the library.The sequence repeated, and
the common hung in stunned silence for a few moments
before people started to talk.

"Fire alarm."

"That's not the fire alarm. This one's different."

"Police emergency?"

"Not police either."

"Got to be the prison."

This last rumor spread quickly through the crowd. Rebecca saw Tom Duggan on the gazebo, one hand still
resting on the crown of his granite head, which appeared
stately and confident while the man himself looked bewildered.

The police and fire chief hustled down the slippery
bandstand steps and strode quickly across the common.
This excited no one at first, the people just milled about,
confused and drifting into tighter groups as the siren blasts
continued. At one point Tom Duggan tried resuming his
speech, but gave up, his voice lost in the din. Then people
began to disperse. They walked off in different directions
with faraway eyes. Their expressions unsettled Rebecca.
It was like they had all suddenly remembered last night's
shared-nightmare. She returned to her Mountaineer and
eased it through the thinning crowd back to the inn.

Fern was with Kells in the parlor. She wore a loose
sweat suit, he a parka and wet boots. He was standing in
a small puddle of melting snow.

On the television, a local news anchor had cut in with
a bulletin regarding a disturbance at the prison at Gilchrist.

"Oh, my," said Fern, her small hand going to her
mouth.

"What have they said?" asked Rebecca, but Kells
shushed her.

The anchor said that a small group of inmates had reportedly seized control of the prison Command Center.

"The Command Center," said Rebecca.

Kells turned. "What's that?"

"The brain of the prison. They control everything from there."

Kells returned to the television for more news, but they were cutting back to a talk show.

Noises at the front door, others returning. Fern looked up with a start. "I better get some tea on," she said, making for the kitchen.

Rebecca was excited. She followed Fern as far as the sitting room, as though expecting a messenger, but it was only Darla returning, shaking snow off an orchid mohair scarf. "What is that god-awful *noise*?"

Rebecca led her back into the parlor. Only a few chunks of melting snow remained where Kells had stood before the TV. There was a chill in the room because the outside door had been left ajar. Rebecca reached the porch door just in time to see a white Jeep Cherokee pulling out of the driveway.

He had shushed her rudely at the television, and she was wondering about him now. Remembering her sleuthing the previous night, she followed the enclosed porch around to the bookshelves before returning inside. She saw that *Last Words* was back on display.

The alarm went silent an hour later, by which time all of the guests except Hodgkins and Kells had returned to the inn. They all stayed close to the television in the parlor and pressed Rebecca for details about the prison. She described the security regimen and praised the professionalism of the Gilchrist guards, belittling the chances of a few disgruntled inmates against crash gates, electric fences, and underground sensors.

At dinnertime, Fern's forced enthusiasm belied her anxiety while the guests chattered excitedly, the way people get when they find themselves near news. Twice Darla quieted everyone, claiming to hear helicopters overhead. Kells did not return for dinner, and neither did Hodgkins.

The mood after dinner was much different that night.

They migrated back to the television, with Terry com-
mandeering the remote and switching between channels
at the most inappropriate times. The snow was coming
down more heavily with each hour, hampering the press
coverage, but in a way the lack of video only made the
story more alluring. The twenty-four-hour-news networks
kept replaying the same choppy footage over and over
again, that of badly wounded guards arriving at an area
hospital in an ambulance fitted with a snowplow blade.
Otherwise, the reports focused primarily on the all-star
roster of criminal personalities involved.

"Craziness," Terry declared. "I'm out of here first thing
in the morning."

Rebecca said, "I think it's kind of exciting."

The network newscasts came on at six-thirty, leading
with the riot. Due to the guard casualties, the warden and
his administrative personnel had reportedly been forced to
evacuate the prison. They were awaiting more support,
which, like everything in Gilchrist, was slow in coming.
Snow had closed the nearest airport in Coventry.

Terry cut to the Weather Channel, which showed a
forecast of more of the same: heavy snowfall, strong
winds. Despite the traveler's advisory, cars rolled past on
Post Road, and all talk at the inn turned to leaving. Plans
were made to rise at dawn and dig out.

Gilchrist Police Chief Roy Darrow came on the tube
after seven and read a statement outside the front doors
of the police station. He was asking the people of Gilchrist
not to panic: "No inmates have escaped, and this uprising
has been contained within the prison perimeter. No one
on the outside is at risk." But Rebecca knew that by giving
voice to people's fears, he was simply unleashing them.
She expected the number of cars out on Post Road to
double.

A scream came from across the room as Mia jumped
out of her seat, spilling a mug of warm cider on the floor.
"Scratching—at the window!"

It was Ruby. The cat had gotten herself locked outside

on the porch. Coe opened the French doors and she trotted back in, slinking guiltily along the fireplace to the dining room. Mia, however, was not relieved.

"I want to leave," she said, turning to Robert.

"Right now?" he stammered. "In this snow? In the dark?"

Coe interrupted then, asking that the television be turned down. Terry grumbled but muted the newscast. Coe went and stood at attention on the porch, just steps outside the open doors.

Rebecca listened too. Water moved through the house pipes from the dishwasher running in the kitchen. Blower heat breathed into the parlor. A wreath scraped mouselike against a window. But in the distance, the sound of fire-crackers echoed off the mountains.

"Shooting," Coe said, amazed at what was occurring in his hometown. "From the prison."

Mia gripped Robert's arm. "Right now," she said.

Robert said nothing. He looked to Fern for advice.

"You're my guests," she said, disappointed but firm. "You come and go as you please."

Mia searched for support, moving across the room to Rebecca. "What are you going to do, Miss Loden?"

Rebecca's visit to the prison made her the closest thing they had to an authority on the matter. The others looked to her as well.

The existential jury again. She had always thought that she would make a good leader, a moral being, the mantle she assumed every time she sat down at her writing desk to work. She knew she could set their fears at ease.

"From what little I know about prison riots," she said, "ninety-nine percent of the time, the inmates just give up. They can't go anywhere, and eventually they settle for concessions like better food or longer exercise privileges. I think the snow has everyone on edge. No one could break out of that prison. This will all blow over before too long."

Her answer greatly disappointed Mia, but the rest

seemed satisfied and the television volume was turned up again.

Rebecca, bolstered by the trust they had shown in her, decided to lead by example. She reminded Fern about the book reading, less than thirty minutes away. "Do you think anyone will show up?"

Fern was shocked that she had forgotten. "I think so. These are hardy people. Most of them will shrug it off and continue on their way, I'm sure of it."

Rebecca checked the time. "Shall we go?"

Darla spoke up. "Could I come? I've never been to one."

The others were politely uninterested, so the three of them bundled up and headed up the road on foot. The wind whipped snow as they followed a set of tire tracks, headlights from outbound cars passed them slowly. Only one vehicle came up behind them, the cavalry, a CNN satellite truck. It was primetime in Gilchrist, Vermont.

The common was still but for the line of cars. The police station was lit up at the end, a cruiser was parked out in front, blue spinners lit, and the streetlights illuminated a cone of falling snow. The library was small and new, tightly bricked with a granite block above the red front door reading, *Free To All*.

Inside, pastel-colored fliers heralded the reading on a bulletin board, with Rebecca's author photo pushpinned beneath the words *This Saturday Night!* But the lights were off inside the main room, the chairs unassembled. They waited a few more minutes, but it was obvious no one would appear. It was Rebecca who tried to console Fern, rather than the other way around. Rebecca had published two books before breaking out with *Last Words*; she had faced empty library rooms before.

The three of them went out onto the front steps of the library, watching the station wagons and four-wheel drives roll past. The slow-motion panic fascinated Rebecca, being such a purely human detail, the collective guilt of a community that had enriched itself on the rest of the country's crime-busting. This was the fear of a town founded on a fault line as the earth began to rumble.

Fern was devastated. For her, the exodus portended a more personal disappointment.

"Things will never be the same here," she said. "Gilchrist isn't a town anymore. We're just a prison now."

They pulled their scarves up over their faces and trudged back around the quarter-mile road bend to the inn. Mia and Robert were out in the driveway, trying to clear off their yellow Volkswagen. Fern, ever practical, pledged her help, but first went inside to put on some coffee. Rebecca needed only to change gloves, and passed Bert-and-Rita at the entryway, suiting up to help the younger couple get away.

Rebecca found Terry alone with the parlor television. He was a whiz with the remote control, as though staying on top of the media coverage somehow involved him in the crisis itself.

"They set part of the prison dispensary on fire," he told her. "That's smart. Burning your own house. And CNN finally got somebody on the scene."

"The truck passed us."

"Some bozo kid, it's awful." Terry chuckled. "His big break and he's blowing it."

"Did Kells come back? Hodgkins?"

Terry shook his head. "Nope."

The heavy snow came halfway to Rebecca's knees, thick stuff, coming down hard and sticking fast. It fell as quickly as Mia could clear it off the car windows. Fern was running her snowblower, shooting a plume of white onto the front lawn, but the machine kept choking and quitting. Robert sat behind the wheel, gunning the engine while Coe, wearing his fool's cap, helped Bert rock the car back and forth.

A snowmobile, sleek and black with yellow detail, cut slowly across the neighboring field, stopping in Fern's driveway. The engine idled and the driver removed his dark-visored helmet. It was a seventy-year-old man in a nylon racing suit. Fern left her snowblower to exchange a few words, then the old man replaced his helmet and turned back in the direction of Gilchrist Common.

Fern returned to them even more disappointed than before.

"Dickie Veal, he runs the public works. The outlying roads are all jammed up. Cars stuck in the smaller lanes near the edge of town. And there's some ice, people sliding off the shoulder. Everything would be clear, my driveway too, if Dickie's main plow hadn't gone missing two nights ago."

Robert looked at Mia, trying to make her understand that they were fighting a losing battle.

"Hey," said Coe. "Hey, listen." His many-tasseled hat was in his hands now, his head cocked toward the northern mountains. The absence of the snowblower brought out the snow-silence. "Check it out."

Rebecca heard a few car horns in the distance, faint and pitiable like quarreling children.

"No more gunshots," he said.

Back indoors, Terry sat in a club chair pulled into the center of the parlor, hands clasped before the TV as though watching a close basketball game. He muted the volume when the porch doors opened, and confirmed the absence of gunfire. "It's over," he said.

On screen, they were repeating footage of the distant prison fire. Fern said, "Did they say anything on the news?"

"Amateur night," Terry said, shaking his head disparagingly. "The CNN feed went to static almost as soon as they got it up. Nobody has anyone at the scene now."

Fern looked to her lamps. "Maybe we're going to lose power."

Rebecca said, "Wait a minute. Every remote feed was lost?"

"Power surge," dismissed Terry. "All those camera trucks out there in the middle of nowhere without enough juice. Or, maybe the FBI went in there with guns blazing, like Waco. Took out the cameras first in order to stage a surprise attack."

As the others began to relax, it was now Rebecca's turn to look concerned. Terry turned the sound back up as she shed her parka, keeping her reservations to herself while standing in the parlor with the rest, waiting for the television to tell them what to do.

REPRESSIVE SECURITY CONDITIONS INSIDE ADX GILCHRIST PRE-cluded the warning signs that traditionally anticipate prison disturbances, such as increases in disciplinary hearings, hints to well-liked guards that they should take vacation time or sick leave, or a high volume of outgoing personal items. There were no well-liked guards at ADX Gilchrist; there was no mail.

Despite the acute embarrassment of a full-blown riot raging in a so-called "unriotable" penitentiary—and the fact that correctional officers were rarely murdered during an uprising—Warden Barton James and his people relied on the usual reactive models. A prison riot has a reliable life cycle, from the inmates' violent euphoria of the first hours to the rejection of their initial, unreasonable demands—freedom, full pardons—to infighting among racial lines and the bloom of "preexisting intergroup tensions," and finally, to renegotiation and eventual collapse. The outcome of the riot was never in question; the only variable was its eventual cost, of human life, of damage to the physical plant, and of the loss of public faith in their federal prison system. Although in theory any prison riot can be ended at any moment by force, tactical assaults are prohibitively costly by all three criteria and ordered only as a strategy of last resort. The Bureau of Prisons's response was to allow the riot to run its course.

And that is exactly what the watchmen of ADX Gilchrist were doing: waiting, hoping to minimize cost. They never anticipated being evicted from their facility, and now they found themselves holed up on the access road well back from the front gate, inside two campers commandeered from a nearby construction site. ADX Gilchrist's onsite tactical unit, the Special Operations Response Team, was drinking cold coffee in the second camper. Off-duty guards manned the prison grounds outside the perimeter fence, and the government barricade—the twin campers, parked lengthwise across the road—was secured by local police and fire department officers. Communication with Bureau of Prisons headquarters at the Department of Justice was by cellular telephone only.

The only convenient sanitary facility was a single, wretched Porta-John from the same construction site. More popular was the snow-filled woods, which was fine for the men but not for FBI Special Agent Chloe Gimms now sharing on-scene command with a shaken Warden James. A thin woman with electric gray hair, she had survived forty-two years without peeing in the woods and was not about to break that streak now. She paced inside the small camper, ignoring the urge, tapping her thighs with red-mittened hands.

Warden James listened to the sporadic gunfire and the prison alarms. He sat in a small chair with his fists pressed to his eyebrows, wondering if he was supposed to be able to feel his pulse in his forehead. Chloe Gimms asked him about cutting power.

"No," he said. "The crash gates would all come down. We'd be trapping guards inside with the inmates, with no way to get them out."

"So even if we retook the Command Center, we couldn't wall off the units. Personnel would still be trapped inside."

Warden James looked up. "Correct."

"That's it, then. Nothing else we can do until more support arrives."

The warden stood and looked out one of the small camper windows. The outline of the facility was visible through the snow at the end of the long lane of trees lining Prison Road, black smoke from the dispensary fire rising behind. He tried reaching out to his charges, tried to un-

derstand them. "They'll have a lot of anxiety. After years
in isolation, of being spoon-fed—"

"It's a free-for-all," said Chloe Gimms. "Old scores are
being settled. A kill-off."

"No," said Warden James, shaking his head. "They'll
be looking for someone to take my place. A guiding force.
A leader."

"That's the nice thing about psychopaths. They're too
crazy to group up. Nobody could hold these cons together."

The warden turned. "Luther Trait could. For a while
anyway. The riot started in his unit."

"Trait? You think this is him?"

"It couldn't be anyone else." He stepped away from
the window, distressed. Correctional officers were rarely
murdered during an uprising. Something wasn't right.
"Where is your partner?"

"Police station in town. We needed a landline to talk
to Washington—regulations." She crossed her arms, tuck-
ing in her mittened hands and looking out the window the
warden vacated. Local police walked the barricade between the campers and the TV trucks. "Those cops better
keep the media away," she said.

Forty yards away, producer Justin Keane sat inside the
CNN satellite van on the phone with his boss back in
Atlanta, coordinating their live-report schedule and estab-
lishing a protocol in case of breaking news. They were
still the only cable channel on the scene, benefactors of
fortuitous timing, having detoured on their way back from
covering the birth of the Gallimard Sextuplets in
L'Assomption St. Jérôme, Canada, just as the snow was
really starting to hit. Their reporter had flown back sep-
arately, so Justin's cameraman, Buzzy—the suit jacket fit
him best—was doing what he could with the on-air re-
motes.

Justin hung up and scribbled his notes, then sat back
to stretch his arms in the confined quarters of the satellite
van. "May this all end so very, very soon."

"Amen," said Buzzy, wearing the jacket over sagging blue jeans. As he drained their last can of Mountain Dew, the overhead lights inside the truck flickered.

Justin checked the console. The image on his monitor snapped and went black.

"No, no," Justin said, rising. "No way. Not now."

He slid open the door, and two big guys in flannel and watch caps stood outside, looking up at him.

Locals. "Hiya," said Justin, surprised.

The first guy pulled a large silver handgun from his waistband. "Back inside."

Justin retreated obediently as, behind him, Buzzy's empty soda can *clink*ed and danced along the floor.

The armed man and his partner climbed inside.

GILCHRIST POLICE CHIEF ROY DARROW LIFTED OFF HIS HAT and ran his fingers through his hair. FBI agent Coté was talking on Chief Roy's phone and rooting around in Chief Roy's desk for a pen. But Chief Roy held his patience. The truth was that he was glad to have big law there, he was relieved to be in the presence of a higher power. This thing was more than his men could handle.

It was hysteria. What else to call it? The flight of the townspeople, which he first took for a lack of confidence in him personally, he saw now as something essentially helpful. Had they all stayed, every stray noise and they would be calling the new 911 system saying that an escaped serial killer was outside their door.

"Dad!"

It was Roy, Jr., waving him to the front. The floor of the station house was coarse with boot grit and Chief Roy winced at all the snow people were tracking in. This was like coming home early from a trip and finding your kids hosting a beer party.

Tom Duggan dogged Chief Roy to the glass doors, a shadow in undertaker's clothes, haunting him.

"Just go home, Tom. Or throw on a uniform and help

me out. One or the other. I'm up to my ears—"

"My mother, Roy."

"I know what I said. But I can't do anything for her right now."

"You said you'd send a car."

"I don't have a man or a car to spare. Hell, these aren't even my men anymore."

"She's all alone."

"She will be all right, and so will you. So will the rest of us. Just get her on the phone."

"You know she doesn't answer. She doesn't like the phone."

Roy, Jr., was holding the door, and the three of them moved out onto the stoop. The line of cars had diminished at that late hour, as word had gotten out that the roads were jammed. The town center was quiet and blue, five streetlights brightening the snowy common like an empty stage set for a pageant.

"Tom." Chief Roy put his hand on Tom Duggan's narrow shoulder, a strange gesture for him. "You're feeling guilty about this whole thing. My advice is: don't. Go on home. Don't try to drive out there yourself, we got enough problems on the road already and nobody to take care of them. Once things start to look better, maybe I can free up a man to check on her. And if, God forbid, things don't get better, I imagine the National Guard will be sweeping through here to check on her for you. All right?"

Tom Duggan nodded once in resignation, turning and moving in his somber way down the brick steps to the snow, toward Duggan's Funeral Home on the corner across the street.

Roy, Jr., came in front of the chief and adjusted his father's clip-on police necktie. "What the hell are you doing?" said Chief Roy.

"CNN, Dad. They want to interview you. Might want the both of us."

A crew of three men waited on the sidewalk below,

big guys, the bigger one holding a camera. "Can we do this inside?" said the chief.

"Want to get the snow and the brick in," one of them said.

The chief nodded as he fussed his way down four slippery steps. They had to think visually, he understood. Image is everything. "Good 'nough," he said. "But let's make it quick."

One of them regarded Roy, Jr. "This your son, Chief?"

"It's in the blood." Chief Roy nodded as he spoke his usual refrain. "My father and grandfather before me."

The reporter drew a revolver and cocked it at Roy, Jr.'s temple.

The click sounded dull in the snow. Chief Roy looked on wordlessly, feeling a hand at his waist. Someone relieved him of his side arm.

"Dad?" Roy, Jr., said, shying away from the short barrel of the gun.

Chief Roy could not grasp what was happening. He saw his son's face and staring eyes, but nothing made sense yet.

Beyond, he saw Tom Duggan walking away through the snow, his black-clad figure fading into the night.

They knocked Roy, Jr., to his knees, then laid him facedown in the snow. Another one of them stepped up to the chief and put a nine-millimeter handgun to his stomach.

"You walk right back inside and don't say nothing. Walk straight through to the side door and open it to us."

Nothing was real. "I've got a civil emergency here. . . ." said Chief Roy, but as soon as he heard his own words the spell was broken. He focused his attention on the snowy boot in his son's back. Roy, Jr., was lying still and limp in the snow as though he were already dead. A gun muzzle was pressed to the back of the head Chief Roy once cupped in his hand. "Jesus Christ," the chief said, his mind clearing. "I'll do anything."

"Do what I told you, and fast."

Roy Darrow turned and started up the four steps to the double glass doors, disoriented, gripping the handrail, unable to hear anything. He entered his station and passed through it slowly. He could not summon any speed. One of his men tried to hand him a telephone receiver but he passed him by, part of his mind remembering how irritated he had been when Ann insisted on driving down to her sister's in Cabot, "just to wait this thing out." Now he didn't care about his pride or the town or anything except his family and his son.

FBI Agent Coté was talking to him from the door of his office. "Got to clear some room here, Chief, this place is going to fill up with agents. Chief? Hey, Chief."

Roy Darrow turned left at the radio room, unlocking the doors to the side parking lot, admitting the three men and a fourth. They followed him inside and then rushed past him, moving quickly throughout the station.

Special Agent Lon Coté returned to the desk inside the police chief's office, rubbing his eyes and taking up the telephone again, still on hold. He was setting in motion the necessary mechanisms to use Title 18 violations—malicious destruction of federal property, hostage-taking—to upgrade the FBI's official response from "advisory" to "operational," thereby allowing them to take total command of the prison riot from the Bureau of Prisons.

A CNN cameraman walked past the office door and Coté shook his head at the lax security of the Gilchrist PD. All that would end . . . as soon as he could get somebody to pick up the damn phone. He looked out the room's only window, to the flakes dancing under the streetlamps around the town common. Then he became aware of voices rising in the outer rooms.

He set down the phone and was halfway to the door when the cameraman reappeared. In the man's free hand was a short-barreled Smith & Wesson.

Lon Coté felt the weight of the shoulder holster suddenly beneath his tan wool suit jacket. In his fourteen-year career he had never faced a loaded gun.

"Lay it on the floor," said the cameraman.

Coté saw another man behind him rounding up police. Except for the paramilitary Micro Uzi machine pistol in his hands, everything about these guys said *ex-cons*.

Coté set his piece down flat on the carpet and stood with his hands open and out at his sides. "My name is Lon Coté, special agent with the FBI," he said, plainly and without drama, surprised at the pride he felt in these words. "Now, what is this all about?"

WARDEN JAMES STOOD OUTSIDE THE TRAILER, WATCHING THE black smoke rising out of the compound as wet snow-flakes melted on his venous cheeks. "Fortresses," he said.

Chloe Gimms was behind him. "How's that, Bart?"

The warden looked straight up at the flakes falling to him and for a dizzying moment experienced the sensation of flight. "This was the end of the line. The worst of the worst. Now what? How do we punish this? Where does it go from here?"

Chloe frowned. "Just hang in there, Bart."

This was his last command. Thinking this bolstered Barton James. With the end in sight, anything is tolerable. Mrs. James had remained behind in Denver, too tired to follow him to one more prison town. Now he spent all his vacations traveling home. That was how upside-down things had been. She had wanted more time with him, now she was going to get it.

A roar behind him, machinery coming to life, almost like one of the campers starting up. But it was louder than that, Warden James felt the roar from the ground. Movement to his left. He turned, expecting police officers.

Three local men were walking toward them from the trees.

"The hell is this?" said Chloe Gimms, angered by the breach of security.

Headlights swirled behind the campers. Engine gears downshifted, and Chloe heard popping and felt thumps in

the ground near her feet, then noises like rocks striking
the camper hull and windows. With a crash and a wail of
steel, the camper next to her was rammed from behind.
She jumped out of the way as it was shoved over onto its
side in a crashing *whump* of snow.

Now she saw the attacking bulldozer rearing back and
raising its curved steel blade. The headlights swung
around and with a snort of exhaust the bulldozer rolled at
the second camper.

The Special Operations Response Team leader came
rushing out of the camper door. He saw the first camper
on its side and reached for his weapon—then jerked and
took a small step backward as though shoved. Chloe never
heard the gunshot. The SORT leader held his hands at his
chest as though cradling a baby bird. The bird was bleeding.

The bulldozer rammed the second camper, its raised
blade chewing and crumpling the roof, rocking the vehicle
but failing to overturn it on the first try. The bulldozer
rolled back, grinding snow, lowering its blade as a bull
does its horns, then rushing forward again.

Yelling and movement came from inside the jostled
second camper as members of the SORT team fled out
the only door, stunned.

With the second blow the camper tipped over like the
first, crushing the SORT team leader.

Gunshots cracked all around Chloe Gimms. SORT
team members were still climbing out of the windows of
the overturned second camper, only to be set upon by the
men dressed as locals. Those already outside drew their
weapons and looked for cover, but bullets smacked their
chests and legs and knocked them around. They tried to
return fire but they were shooting at ghosts. Snipers in the
trees. The ground snow was turning red.

Chloe was lying on her side, not knowing how she got
there. She turned to Warden James but he was being
dragged away by two armed men. She was rolled over

then by a man wearing a CNN ballcap, a gun jabbed into her face. He held a bloody SORT radio.

"Call in the guards from around the prison. Get them out here in two minutes."

"What is this—"

He fired two shots into the snow behind her head and she barely heard her own scream. "Do it!" he yelled, in a faraway voice.

She called them in. She didn't know if she was yelling or whispering into the radio. The man took her side arm from her and dragged her over to the rest.

Time blurred. Prison guards arriving from the perimeter were taken captive, made to sit in the snow like children, the local cops and reporters too. Guns, radios, and other equipment were all confiscated.

With the outside secured, some of the armed men headed for the prison entrance and the front gate, which opened magisterially. Gunfire was exchanged briefly, but then lights came on around the main entrance. Police cars, driven by more of these men, sped to the front gate with blue lights spinning.

Inmates exiting the penitentiary were picked up and chauffeured away. The rest of the guards were marched out of the prison, hands on their heads. A pickup truck pulled near the front entrance and a man standing in the bed raised a long, dark tube to his shoulder.

The missile obliterated the road sign heralding the entrance to ADX Gilchrist and federal property.

A cheer went up. Oddly, the prison structure itself, the gates and the watchtowers, were left intact.

Chloe Gimms saw it all then. The inmates were going to turn the tables on their captors and lock them up like prisoners of war. Chloe Gimms's mind flashed on every story of human degradation she had overheard in her six years working federal pens. She was one of the few women there and she was going to be passed around like their last cigarette.

But that was not what happened. A truck used for

transporting livestock was brought around and all the captives were loaded onto it like day laborers, including the
wounded and the dead. Armed prisoners in con scrubs
surrounded the truck and Chloe Gimms pushed toward the
center, trying to disappear with the rest. The back of
the truck was shut up and they began rolling away from
the prison, past the fallen campers and abandoned TV
trucks, turning the corner and following a bulldozer out
along the access road. Chloe's mind reeled. She looked
around for familiar faces, but they were packed so tightly
she could not move. Where were they being taken? The
phrase "mass grave" popped into her head, and Chloe
Gimms's bladder emptied, warming the insides of her
thighs. Hers was one of the last to go.

SPECIAL AGENT LON COTÉ RODE WITH THE REST OF THE GIL-
christ police force aboard a second truck, pulling in between the guard truck and the lead bulldozer. Ex-cons had
led a surprise attack on the prison from the outside, and
the liberated prisoners rode in pickups on either side of
the two trucks now, howling and hoisting rifles in their
hands.

The country road was dark but for the white snow. In
the distance Coté could see machines working, large vehicles: backhoes, tractors, a fork-bladed snowplow. The
organization mystified him. This was a coordinated effort,
not a riot of opportunity.

The trucks slowed near the machines, rolling past
cruisers and armed prisoners, AR-15s leaning casually on
shoulders. No one on Coté's truck uttered a sound. A huge
combine lit up, slowly threshing its way off the road to
allow them past. Suddenly Coté understood, and he was
amazed.

The voices of the cons below grew angry. An argument, back and forth, in Spanish and English. The Spanish
accent was Cuban. Gilchrist housed seven Mariel Cubans,
the worst of the six thousand or so degenerates, criminals,

and lunatics dispatched to the United States in Castro's "Freedom Flotilla" of 1980.

Coté chanced a look over the side of the truck. The arguing Marielito was wearing Chief Darrow's hat and brandishing his AR-15 in the direction of the cops on the trucks. One of the ex-cons was telling the Marielito to do as he was told, that he was not following the plan.

Then a yell from behind. Coté turned in time to see a young man in uniform slipping over the side of the truck, dropping wildly to the ground and taking off. It was the police chief's son, his arms pumping, boot treads kicking up bits of snow like sparks as he ran full-out for the trees.

Two shrill whistles from one of the ex-cons on the ground and a shot rang out.

The chief's son stumbled to his knees. A second shot stopped him from crawling.

People on both trucks screamed.

Armed cons and ex-cons jumped from their cars and rushed the trucks. A pickup with an M60 machine gun mounted on its bed pulled around from the shadows, high-beam headlights on, patrolling the road with a small man crouched behind the butt stock, hands at the ready. Coté began saying "The Lord's Prayer" in his head.

The Marielito was still going on, his debate with the white ex-con ratcheted up a few notches now. The hostages' fate was being decided. Cons and ex-cons waited on all sides with wild looks of freedom and desire in their eyes, their rifles trained on the trucks, waiting to be told what to do.

Blue police lights came on. There was a cruiser set just off the road. Four men in con scrubs stood outside it, mostly in shadow.

One man stood in front of the rest. That man slowly shook his head.

The Marielito in the police hat gave in. He shrugged grandly and lowered his rifle, swearing in Spanish.

Rifles went down all around the trucks. The man with

the mounted machine gun took his hand off the trigger and tipped the barrel toward the sky.

The trucks lurched and started forward again, past the rumbling combine and a sign marking Gilchrist's town limits. Coté's eyes remained fixed on the man who, with a simple command gesture to the renegade Marielito, had pardoned their lives. He was certain that blue-tinged silhouette was Luther Trait.

The combine rolled back into place behind them and the other machines crowded in, the snowplows starting to work, pushing snow from the fields onto the road. The prisoners were barricading the routes into Gilchrist. They were expelling every law-enforcement representative and closing off the town. It was a revolution.

THE CENTER OF TOWN WAS TAKEN WITHOUT RESISTANCE AND
Luther Trait entered the Gilchrist police station with little
fanfare, like a conquering general inspecting the abandoned enemy headquarters. The sensation was so like one
of his mental journeys that he had to remind himself that
he was in fact physically *in* the room. Coffee cups had
been left behind and coats were slung over chair backs
and the telephones still rang. Trait touched one of the
desks, feeling it under his fingers, still uncertain. He put
his hand on a ringing phone and the receiver was still
warm. He answered it.

The voice said, "This is Salvatore Richardsen of the
FBI. Get me Agent Coté."

Trait said, "He is not here right now to take your call."

"Who is this?" demanded the caller. "What the hell is
going on there?"

Trait hung up and turned to his crew. They were
stamping snow off their shoes and exploring the station,
except Spotty who stood by his side. Spotty had been
Trait's white shadow at Marion, the Brotherhood of Rebellion pledge a full head taller than anyone else in the
room, and loyal in the extreme. He would march at any
order. ADX Gilchrist had failed to break him mentally
because there was so little there to break. The rest were
ex-cons dressed as locals, Brotherhood of Rebellion click-
ups from the outside.

Dove Menckley entered the station shivering. Slender
and shifty, a compulsive arsonist with burned hands and
skin grafts obscuring the Hispanic features of his face,
Menckley took in the room with furtive glances out of

weepy, bloodshot eyes. Stacks of paperwork, partition drywall, roster notices: Menckley's world was full of kindling.

"Crazy out there," he said, rubbing his scarred fingers together thirstily. "No fires, anyway."

Trait said, "There better not be."

Menckley nodded, chastened. "They're rounding up the residents and bringing them to the prison."

"Good. How do the people look?"

"Bad," Menckley said, smiling until he realized he probably shouldn't. "Pretty bad."

"Cons staying inside town?"

"I think so. They're enjoying it too much to run off yet. A few will try their luck on the outside, but I think most are excited about assembling back at the pen tomorrow morning. They want to know what your plan is."

"We have the snow on our side, but not time. Get back to the pen. Some of them might be thinking about tearing it down. Discourage them. We need it for the next phase."

Menckley looked surprised. "How am I supposed to discourage them?"

"Just do it. See that they stay happy and occupied until tomorrow morning."

Trait left him and started down the hallway. He had been inside a few police stations in his time, he knew the general layout. He paused at the doorway to the radio room. Every line on the Enhanced 911 switchboard was flashing. An ex-con named DeYoung was working the console, and Trait motioned to him to put a call on speaker.

"Gilchrist Police," said DeYoung. "What's your emergency?"

"Oh, thank God, I've been calling." An elderly woman, whispering. "There're men snooping around my backyard."

Enhanced 911 displayed the name and street address of the caller. DeYoung said, "Is this forty-three Abenaki Way?"

"Yes." Relief, her voice growing louder. "Yes, that's me."

"Those are plainclothes police officers, ma'am. We're checking residents door to door. You can let them right in."

"Oh—thank heavens."

Trait moved on. He wore the police chief's key ring on his belt—having changed out of his hack clothes and back into regular prison issue—and found the lockup around the corner to the right. There were only two cells: Gilchrist was a safe community, once you factored out 312 reluctant residents. Trait found the key that fit the lock, and the steel-barred door swung open.

Warden Barton James sat turned toward the wall on one end of the thick plastic bench inside. He was hunched over, head hanging, hands tucked protectively between his legs. His bald skull was florid with yellow and purple bruises and blood from his face soaked the front of his white cotton shirt. He was beltless and shoeless and still.

Luther Trait entered and stood before him. Trait stooped for a good look at his face. The warden's right eye was a swollen, raspberry egg. Within the bruised orbit of his left, a pale green iris drifted toward Trait, a dilated pupil attempting to focus.

Trait sat down next to the warden. He relaxed and took in the clean, wide cell. Then, for a moment, he was sitting in his foster father's study, in an oversized, smoothly polished wooden college chair. Trait waited and the image cleared.

"There are things I want you to know," Trait said, "because no one else will truly appreciate what I have achieved here. I can tell you now, the break started with your guards. Brotherhood of Rebellion parolees got the home addresses of the E-Unit hacks and maintenance personnel. You all live in a neat little hack neighborhood, so it was easy to do surveillance on the hacks and their hack wives and little hack children enjoying their freedom. My men concentrated on dietary habits—specifically, break-fast foods. Getting into the houses was no big deal, and the sedatives were carefully measured with body size in mind, timed to release well into the hacks' work shifts. Yesterday was shakedown and sterilization in E-Unit. It was smooth, the hacks going down without any biological surges triggering their body alarms. We used the sight lines along the corridor to duck the cameras and swap clothes with the sleeping hacks. Then we played guard, signaling the cameras to open the rest of the pod doors. This same trick worked for the grate openings at the end of the hall, and the range upstairs, your hacks opening doors for us all the way to the Command Center. The battle there was bloody but quick, and then we owned the entire complex by remote control. Pod doors were opened in every security unit and the animals set free."

Warden James did not move, facing away from Trait, crumpled in pain. His only response was a tuneful wheeze.

"You're wondering how a man in solitary confinement in the highest security prison in the world could coordinate such an ambitious plan. I got a little help from my friends. The only times I was allowed out of the prison was to provide testimony for one of the members of my 'disruptive group.' A few minutes of face time, that was all I needed. You can thank my lawyers for that. I left most of the details to a trusted associate who has been lying low here in town a few days now, your average good citizen, preparing for my release. Other devoted Brotherhood parolees have been drifting steadily into town, getting the lay of the land and jacking tractors and heavy machinery to barricade the main roads and blitz you at the staging area. We took you from behind. You can see, I considered everything."

Trait was only now starting to appreciate the victory himself.

"You understand now why I had to see the writer? Her requesting a visit one day before the riot, after eighteen months of planning? I was worried the riot was off, but it wasn't. Tonight I have unleashed the wrath of ADX Gilchrist on its little host town. One night of rampage won't make up for years of torture, but it is a start. I'm putting their pent-up hostility to good use. The cons are rounding up every citizen in town and bringing them back to the prison. Tomorrow morning I will outline for them my great design."

The warden's voice was hushed and pained. "You'll never control them all."

Trait was pleased with the warden's impaired speech. "No more than you could. The difference between you and me is, I don't intend to try. Tonight I have their enthusiasm and that is enough."

The satisfaction of the past few hours drained as Trait looked ahead to the strength required to see this thing through to the end. He turned the warden toward him, eliciting a pitiful groan.

"I am not going to kill you, Warden. On the contrary, I am going to do everything within my power to keep you alive. You are my prisoner now. I am going to study you as you studied me."

Barton James's slanted jaw garbled his words. "The army will come in here and blow you all to hell."

Trait smiled. "I give your government two hours before it realizes what has happened here, and another six to eight to mass troops outside the town. By then I will have addressed the country, and that should put things into proper perspective. You think we got lucky breaking out of Gilchrist? I'm working on a fifty-year plan. This is only the beginning."

IT WAS MIDNIGHT AND CALLIE COLDWELL WAS SITTING IN THE dark with a loaded .38 in her lap. She never slept well when Ted was gone, but when Channel Seven's prison remote went to static, she really got scared. She couldn't see any lights on in the windows down Duggan Way, the

main road of the cookie-cutter village of correctional officers known as Gilchrist Falls. She wondered how many
other wives had already left.

Ted's last words to her on the phone that morning were
Just sit tight. And she had done that, making an afternoon
of it with Becky and C. C. after their early release from
school, building a family of snowmen in the front yard
and baking sugar cookies to welcome them to the neighborhood. Later, they went tramping over to Dinah's to go
sledding with her two girls. From the hill out back they
watched the minivans pulling away, she and Dinah dish-
ing cruelly on the younger wives. Callie was home in
plenty of time for Ted's next call, due six hours ago now.
Maybe mixing two highballs after the girls went to bed
wasn't such a good idea. She was getting really paranoid
now that something had gone wrong.

That was why Ted's old gun lay across her thighs. So
when the blue-lighted police cruiser turned onto her street,
she said aloud, "Thank you, God," going to the window,
leaving the gun behind. Just knowing that the Gilchrist
cops were out there—even though Ted called them *May-
berry RFD*—put her mind at ease. All it took was that
one little sign of authority.

Then the cruiser stopped outside her house. All grati-
tude melted away, and she felt her worst fears were about
to be confirmed: Something terrible had happened to Ted
at the prison. She stood behind the window sheers, hiding
from bad news, praying the cruiser would shine a light in
their yard and roll along.

It turned into her driveway, headlights brightening the
family room.

Callie rushed into the attached garage, hitting the button and hurrying to the rising door. It opened on bright,
flashing headlights and blowing snow.

Two officers were out of the car, closing their doors,
coming forward. Callie hugged herself inside her sweater,
one hand shading her eyes. "Yes?"

"Yes," they said, advancing through the flashing lights.

Callie was already backing away in confusion. Neither man wore a police uniform.

A HALF-MILE CLOSER TO THE CENTER OF TOWN, FRED BURN-glass awoke to the sound of voices in his yard. He crawled out of bed in threadbare long johns and felt around for his eyeglasses, only mildly aware of a rare, halfhearted erection. He pulled his specs behind his ears and squinted out his bedroom window. There were shadows prowling around the lumber mill. Those tractor thieves he had been hearing about.

He padded downstairs, barefoot in the dark. He froze near the bottom as a shadow passed his window. They were up on his front porch now. They were near the door.

Fred Burnglass was seventy-one years old. He lived alone, never having married for the simple reason that he had never gotten around to it. He owned six working radios, including the first one his grandfather ever brought home, but no television set—again, simply because he had never gotten around to buying one. He owned a telephone, hanging below his medicine shelf on the kitchen wall in the back of the house. Except for two years in the Army Signal Corps when he was stationed in New Jersey, Fred had never traveled any farther outside Gilchrist than Hardwick, fifteen minutes to the south, and then only for tractor parts. Everyone in the Northeast Kingdom knew to come to Fred Burnglass for good quality-milled wood at a fair price.

He heard more voices, whispering and near. He crept down the rest of the way to his hand axe on the straw mat next to his rubber boots. A flashlight shone through one of his side windows, splitting the darkness. As Fred's hand closed around the smoothly worn handle of the axe, he heard a single pane of glass pop out, busted.

The crack and tinkle in the rear of his house echoed in Fred's head. He was seeing shadows everywhere as he fought his way to the kitchen. He reached the cold linoleum of the dark room, fearful of broken glass. Voices outside, quiet and plain, but he was too rattled to make sense of them. He stopped beside the back door and felt the cold air spilling through the broken pane. The tractor thieves were right on the other side of the wall.

One hand came through the busted window, tattooed knuckles and fingernails pointed like saw teeth. It reached for the inside knob as Fred stood mutely, unable to raise his axe blade at a human hand, the trusted tool growing heavy in his grip. He spun it so that the flat edge was facing down, and with both hands steadying his aim he hammered at it once, crushing the tattooed knuckles against the door frame. Fred ran back to the front of the house, away from the howling and the angry voices.

Someone was trying his front doorknob. The door wasn't locked, but it tended to stick in winter. Fred watched the twisting knob and the entire door seemed to be moving. He stood before it, long johns sagging off his behind, axe halfheartedly raised.

"Get away," he said, not sounding like his voice at all, the words ran together as though choked.

There was a rattle outside and he could see his ten-foot ladder now up against the house, legs were running up past the window to the second floor. An engine started up outside—his Ford. Then something hard kicked at his back door, and kicked again. Fred spun to each noise like a man taking arrows from all directions. He backed to the railing at the bottom of the stairs. Footsteps crunched glass on the kitchen linoleum and a chair fell over. Fred backed along the side of the staircase to the angled closet door. He fumbled with the latch and backed inside.

Raincoats, his father's bagged suits, his old army jacket, all brushing against him like ghosts. He backed in deep and spun the axe again in his trembling hand, blade facing down now, Fred crazy with fear. He raised the axe over his head, and he lashed out at the first thing that appeared when he saw the door open a crack. There was a shriek of pain and an arm pulled back as the door was thrown wide open. Fred came out of the coats yelling and swinging at the shadows, but they immediately wrested the axe away from him. There were two men, each with their own hand tools. They were upon him.

TOM DUGGAN'S SHIP HAD RUN AGROUND. THE LONG, BLACK Fleetwood hit a frozen patch of road and the steering wheel turned uselessly in his hands as the funeral limousine slid off the shoulder and beached on a bed of densely packed snow. In frustration he threw it into reverse and gunned the engine and did everything he wasn't supposed to do, and the car sank and stuck there.

He threw open the door and hobbled through the deep snowfall to the road. From the downstairs window of his funeral parlor in the town common, he had watched the armed men load the Gilchrist police onto a truck. He left immediately after they did, his usual evening commute turned nightmarish by roaming prisoners and snow. But he was alone on this dark road, and less than a mile from his mother's house.

Tom Duggan ran through the trees. Branches tore at his undertaker's coat, grabbing after him like fingers. Snow and time obscured the landmarks he had known since a boy, but he pressed on, falling through the woods as much as running through them.

He emerged into a clearing and found himself right around the corner from her driveway. The house was dark when he reached it, the lamp timers switched off around ten. The side door was locked. Tom Duggan's mother never locked the door. His house key was hanging on the ring in the Fleetwood's ignition. He rang the doorbell impatiently, then without waiting he pulled his hand into his coat sleeve and punched through the windowpane nearest the knob.

He fumbled the door open without cutting himself and rushed through the kitchen and then upstairs to her bedroom. It was still made from the morning. The bathroom was also empty. He heard voices downstairs and ran to the dim parlor but her chair was empty. It was the radio playing, and he switched it off and called her name. He checked the floors in every room in case she had fallen. Then he saw that the front hallway door was open.

They never used the front door. The storm door was closed, but the threshold was sprinkled with snow.

He ran out onto the front walk. There were footsteps in the snow, one set, a short stride, already fading with the wind. He followed them around to the side of the house.

Tom Duggan found his mother lying in a drift a few steps behind the old woodpile. He rushed to her, stumbling, finding her curled up on her side, her hands pressed to her chest, her eyes closed. He rolled her over and let out a wail. Her mouth was shut in a grimace, her neck muscles clenched, her jaw set. He groped for a pulse even as he knew that she was gone.

He stepped back. The rest of the snow was undisturbed except for his own footsteps. What had possessed her to open the front door and wander outside with only a housecoat on? Was it the news on the radio? Was she disoriented and trying to walk for help? He knew only that his mother had died afraid and alone.

He knelt, weeping, and got her up into his arms. His impulse was to carry her back inside the house, but with the prisoners loose and the snowstorm, it could be days before he could get her to the funeral home. He would not allow her to decay inside the warm house. Tom Duggan cursed the prison then, cursed the uprising, standing with his dead mother in his arms. Slowly and regrettably he lowered her back into her cradle of snow. He would see to a proper and respectful end as he had always promised. With bare, shivering hands he heaped snow over her body, snow that would preserve her until his return.

Wind howled through the trees, breaking the spell of his anguish. Only after he stood again did he realize it was not the wind howling. It was the rowdy cries of escaped prisoners, borne on the wind.

The predators Tom Duggan had lured to Gilchrist were on the road. He started toward the house in search of a weapon. For the first time in his life, he considered objects in terms of killing potential, of which his mother's house held very few. Knives, yes, but nothing to fend off more than one convict at a time. They would not get him, he determined. He would survive this if only to see to his mother's final details.

Tom Duggan eyed the woods behind his mother's house. He entered them, slowly at first, still weighed down by despair. But by measures his pace increased. Murderous thoughts raged inside his head like the hungry voices of the prisoners as he headed north, tearing through the trees, not quite blindly, heading in the general direction of the old asbestos mine.

KELLS ENTERED THE PARLOR JUST BEFORE THE REPORT CAME through. He was holding his parka and gloves, his brown face flushed from the cold. All eyes turned to him.

"Where were you?" said Terry.

"Car ran off the road," he said, unwinding a snow-dusted scarf from around his neck. His thick, khaki pants were wet to his thighs. "Bad out there. Had to walk back."

"Where's Mr. Hodgkins?" asked Fern.

Kells said, "What do you mean?"

"He isn't with you?"

Terry upped the volume then, as the CNN anchor interrupted a taped piece. "We are going to the telephone now, where one of our news producers, Justin Keane, has breaking information on the Vermont prison break. Justin, where are you?"

There was no graphic available. The shot lingered on the anchorman's tanned face.

"Yes, Martin, there's been an extraordinary turn of events here . . . I am calling from a pay phone in Beckett,

Vermont, a few miles north of Gilchrist. Approximately three hours ago there was an attack upon the Gilchrist Penitentiary. A surprise attack, armed gunmen, believed to be parolees of a sympathetic national prison gang, opened fire on federal officials stationed outside the siege. The battle was brief, terribly one-sided, culminating in all law-enforcement and news-media personnel being loaded onto trucks and escorted out of town through a barricade of farm equipment. Martin, the prisoners of the Gilchrist penitentiary are free. And they have seized control of the town."

Everyone in the parlor was standing. Sentences unfinished, then shushing each other as the report resumed.

". . . equipment, radios, weapons. Also our satellite broadcast truck. My cameraman and I were taken at gunpoint."

The anchor's face reflected the nation's confused dismay. "You're saying you had a gun pointed—"

"I personally witnessed the shooting death of one Gilchrist police officer. None of us believed they were simply going to release us. . . . The only thing I can compare this to, Martin, is a military coup."

Fern was staring at the television, both hands covering her mouth. Terry looked dumbfounded.

The rest were like Rebecca: moving about, but not knowing which way to turn.

The anchorman said, "Justin—we know from earlier reports that many people have already left the town. What is being done for those who remain in Gilchrist tonight?"

"Martin . . . I can't imagine what they might be going through."

Kells switched off the television. It was as though all the oxygen had been sucked out of the room.

"We leave now," he said. "Everybody upstairs. Pack essentials only, the warmest clothes you have."

"Pack . . . ?" Terry said, incredulous.

"One bag. The police station is just up the road. They will be here any minute."

Terry said, "How can we drive—"

"We can't. They own the roads. We go on foot."

Mia cried, *"Where?"*

"Out of here. Right now, we just go."

Dr. Rosen said, "Shouldn't we wait here, for help?"

Terry was at the telephone next to the deacon's bench. He picked up the receiver, poised to dial. The numbers wouldn't come.

"You dial nine-one-one," Kells said, "you bring them right to us."

Terry dropped the receiver. "Cell phone," he said, and rushed out of the room.

Bert-and-Rita were the next to leave, starting past Kells and moving quickly up the stairs. Rebecca lingered near the doorway. Fleeing seemed so rash. Staying seemed so wrong.

The existential jury. Rebecca hurried out of the parlor and climbed the stairs behind Fern.

Inside her room, she got her cargo bag open on the bed and went around grabbing things, still not convinced. It was as though she were acting out a scene of people fleeing danger. Socks. Boots. Gloves and hat. Toothbrush, underwear. Moving automatically.

Kells's room was directly above Rebecca's, and she heard his heavy boots moving from bathroom to dresser to bed. It was beginning to sink in. She had no choice. All of a sudden they were running for their lives.

Her jewelry kit, a fleece pullover, her handbag, her cell phone. She nearly left without her laptop, and forgetting her manuscript heightened her panic more than anything. She slipped the laptop with battery charger into its carry-ing case and slung the leather bag over her shoulder, tak-ing up her cargo bag without zipping it, stopping at the door to look around the room. She was terrified to leave. She looked at the things she was leaving and wondered if she would ever return.

Kells's deep voice upstairs got her moving. She set her

bag down in the hall and ran up, ruffling the hanging quilts as she brushed past.

Fern was in the middle of her bedroom holding Ruby while Kells zipped up a bulging paisley carpetbag. "She'll be fine," he was saying. "They're not after cats."

"But she's never been alone, she doesn't—"

"She's fine," Kells said, reaching over and plucking the black cat from her arms.

Ruby squirted out of his hands, wriggling under the low bed. Kells clapped shut the wooden handles of Fern's carpetbag and moved to the door, leaving her looking at the empty bed. He went back and gripped Fern's arm and brought her along.

Rebecca followed them downstairs. The others stood in coats and hats at the reception desk. Each person carried one bag, except for Bert-and-Rita, who wore their matching backpacks, and Terry, who carried two. Bert-and-Rita's cross-country skis and poles stood against the reception desk. Robert held Mia, who was staring out from his dark coat. Terry was frantically punching buttons on his phone.

Fern went to Coe. "It's okay," he said, but a frightened boy had replaced the easygoing teenager in the fool's cap.

Kells pulled down an old hunting rifle from its mount over the front door. "This work?" he asked, checking the action. Flakes of rust twinkled to the floor.

"I . . . I think so," Fern said.

"Last time it was fired?"

"Ten years ago?"

Kells hung on to it anyway. "Cartridges?"

Fern looked spacey. "Maybe the side drawer."

He pawed around inside the reception desk, pocketing a few rounds.

"Where are we going?" asked Mia, her voice tremulous, tear-choked.

Kells came around to the front of the desk. "They don't know the town. They must be going by maps or street-to-street. We need someplace . . ." He found a brochure next to the burning candle—*Welcome to Vermont's Northeast Kingdom!*—and unfolded it. "Someplace not marked on a map. Someplace remote, where we can rest awhile, think."

He showed the map to Fern with Coe looking over their shoulders. "The golf course?" Coe said.

"Where? This empty area here?"

"There's a clubhouse there. Brand-new, they opened it this summer."

Fern said, "That's four or five miles away."

Kells folded the brochure and stuffed it into his coat pocket, ready to leave.

Terry, getting no satisfaction from his phone, collapsed it against the breast of his overcoat. "Five miles? In this weather?"

Kells nodded. "You're going to get your shoes wet."

Dr. Rosen said, "If we wait here, I'm sure help will come. If we leave, how will they find us?"

Darla's blond hair was tucked under a head wrap, ski-lift passes dangling from her parka. "They let the guards go free."

Kells looked at her. He seemed to be constantly in motion, even when standing still. "How many of those guards do you think were women?"

Darla blanched. Rebecca did too. Now all she wanted to do was run.

"Look!" said Coe.

He was pointing to the storm door. Blue lights spun through the snow and the trees. A cruiser was rolling along Post Road, but it was not the police.

Kells threw his bag strap over his shoulder and took up Fern's bulky carpetbag and the rusted rifle. "Out the back. We go now."

They rushed to the kitchen. Fern was the last to leave, blowing out the spiced candle on the reception desk and looking around one last time for Ruby. Rebecca called to her from the swinging doors.

They stole out into the backyard like criminals them-

selves, eleven fugitives blundering into the snow-muffled
night. Some drifts reached Rebecca's knees, pulling on
her legs like a soft floor in a dream, her bag cutting into
her shoulder. But with fear at her back she slogged ahead.
At the tree line she glanced back once at the inn, faded
into the snow except for a faint yellow light in an upstairs
window. Bert-and-Rita glided past her on their long skis,
arms pumping. Terry followed, struggling in his long coat,
eventually dumping one of his Louis Vuitton garment
bags. Kells was the last, breathing hard, toting his and
Fern's possessions. Their foot trail lay glaringly in the
white expanse, but the wind and snowfall followed them
late into the night. By morning all trace of their journey
was obscured.

THE THIRD DAY

MENCKLEY, THE ARSONIST, ENTERED THE CLEAN, CIRCULAR COM-
mand Center, the technological brain of ADX Gilchrist.
"The head count went better than expected," he reported.
"More than twenty confirmed dead. The Marielitos went
after a couple more—vengeance scores. Some others went
over the mountains."

Luther Trait eyed the penitentiary monitors as Spotty
stood next to him, impassive and broad. Cons roamed the
halls freely, still basking in their liberation, exhilarated
from running hard through the cold night. Trait switched
on the facility intercom.

"Brothers," he said, and watched their eyes go to the
ceilings. "This is Luther Trait. I have accomplished the
impossible. I have delivered you from your cages. This
morning you are free men." He saw their mouths twisted
by their war-whooping, but the thick walls of the Command Center were soundproof. "You have done well by
bringing the residents here. The breakout was a surprise
to all of you, and since then you have been operating
largely on faith. I accept your compliance as repayment
for your freedom. Consider us even. I know you have
concerns regarding government retaliation, but rest as-
sured that we have anticipated everything. My address to
the world will be broadcast over this same intercom in a
few short minutes, so please—stay tuned."

He switched off the microphone and watched the animals cheering throughout the facility.

Menckley worried his hands like a psoriatic. "Looting
was widespread outside the town center," he said. "Weap-

ons and booze mostly. They're drunk now, and happy, but it won't last."

"No, it won't," said Trait, turning to one of the men collecting rifles and tasers and mace from the room, an ex-con known as Burly. "How certain are you that all the residents have been rounded up?"

Burly, a murderer and strongman from Detroit, closely resembled the buzz-cut bank robber in police shooting galleries. "This town's a ghost town," he said confidently.

"All loaded onto trucks?"

"All loaded."

Trait turned to Menckley. "Start video recording. Set the system for exterior lockdown and then drop the package. Make sure you leave yourself enough time to get out."

Menckley was nervous but excited. "Don't worry," he said.

Trait glanced around at the Command Center. He was leaving ADX Gilchrist now, for the last time. But before he could, the police radio on his belt squawked.

It was DeYoung, his radioman back at the police station. "The FBI won't talk to you live on the air. They say they'll only speak to you privately."

Trait nodded. "Good. Then they can just listen like the rest of the country."

THE FIRST HOURS ALL RAN TOGETHER. THE MARCH TO THE GOLF course was an odyssey of whipping wind and gluelike snow, the coldest night Rebecca had ever known. Dawn brought neither sun nor heat, only milky light bleeding into the sky.

Kells kicked in a window in the pro shop to gain access to the country club. There was a stone hearth in the center of the main lounge, shaped like a wide, shallow well, and they gathered newspapers and dry wood for a fire. The flume smoke was a risk overshadowed by the need for heat. They sat around the growing fire, exhausted and smarting, feeling the heat on their cold-hardened faces and awaiting the sear of human thaw.

Rebecca's jaw defrosted, and she soon regained movement in her fingers and thumbs. She looked around. The lounge was all manufactured rusticity, dark wood and mounted moose heads and Indian hangings. Mia was staring deeply into the fire, her face florid. Darla was struggling to toe off her boots.

As Rebecca's head began to clear, the march began to fade into memory, supplanted by the outrageous reality of the present. Gilchrist had been overrun by criminals. There were three hundred sociopaths on the loose.

Kells shed his parka and went behind the front desk to the manager's office. Then he started away down the dark stone-and-timber hallway.

"Who is he?" said Terry, as soon as Kells disappeared around the corner at the long end. "Anybody know? Anybody talk to him?"

Blank stares, exhausted head shakes.

"What he does, where he's from?" Still no response from the rest. "He was out driving around town after the riot started. You realize—we're following this person, and we don't know who or what he is."

"He carries a gun," said Fern.

Everyone looked at her, Rebecca included. Fern spoke with regret, knowing she was betraying a trust. "I saw it in his bag when I was changing his towels."

Terry stood with effort, moving into the managers office. The voices startled them at first, but they were television voices, comforting, authoritative, and one by one they roused themselves to follow Terry. Rebecca was last, behind Coe and Fern, shuffling into the small office.

The screen showed ADX Gilchrist. The camera was set up outside the great fence, the view steady and peaceful, snow falling down.

Rebecca doped it out after a moment. "That must be CNN's equipment," she said. This was unprecedented, so far as she knew: The bad guys had broadcasting capability.

A man moved into view wearing prison blues. It was Luther Trait. Rebecca just stared.

He looked more commanding on television. He faced the camera and spoke into it without hesitation.

"Today is a great day," he began.

"A great day!" said Terry. Everybody shushed him.

"A day that has been a long time coming. A day you dreaded and yet never saw coming."

Kells returned, filling the only remaining space in the office, standing close over Rebecca's right shoulder. She tensed but did not turn.

"We have seized control of the Administrative Maximum Unit Penitentiary at Gilchrist. Overnight, we rounded up the citizens of this small town. I want you to know first that our invasion ends here. We have seized this town as fair trade for our mistreatment, and we have no plans to make any further acquisitions. We have no need. Our exile is self-imposed. We have no desire to rejoin your soft society. We ask nothing further from you, and provided that your government and law-enforcement representatives behave appropriately, we pose you no additional threat. As proof of this, we are releasing the captured residents to you at this hour."

"Releasing?" Dr. Rosen gripped his head, pointed at the television. "He's releasing the hostages!"

Rebecca could feel the force of Kells's attention over her shoulder, as though he were focused on Trait's every word.

"We hold no hostages, and we have no laundry list of demands. All we want is to be left alone. Gilchrist's geography is fairly self-isolating. Of course, should your government choose to attack us, we would be no match for them. However, we believe such an attack will not occur."

Terry said, "No?"

"Many of you are familiar with the concept of 'casualty insurance,' reimbursement in the event of a catastrophic loss. I have taken out a similar policy myself, in order to ensure our safety here. I call it '*multiple* casualty insurance.' "

She could feel Kells brace.

"Ricin is a natural protein poison extracted from the common castor bean. It is six thousand times more toxic than cyanide, and third overall behind plutonium and botulism. Inhalation of a single particle ignites a chain reaction beginning with flulike symptoms, progressing to exploding red blood cells, internal hemorrhaging, and finally death within a few days. The toxin is odorless and tasteless, and there is no antidote.

"My associates on the outside, fellow pledges of the Brotherhood of Rebellion, have devised a simple, effective mechanism to release the deadly ricin toxin in what is known as a 'controlled multiple casualty attack.' What we have done is install these devices in two randomly chosen communities within the United States of America."

She heard Kells say *"Oh, boy,"* under his breath.

"This claim may strike some as fantastic. It is difficult to accept the fact that you or your families may be at risk at this very moment, your survival contingent upon the actions of your elected government officials. You may simply think that we are bluffing. I cite an occurrence in Montana a few months ago, the traffic stop of a dedicated associate of mine. I understand that a small bag of white powder was seized, and later opened by an unfortunate police officer who unknowingly released the ricin into the police station, to lethal effect."

Rebecca's mind was racing. She remembered the news story as something she had printed offline for her clip file. Surface-to-air missiles, and ten or so policemen bleeding out from an unnamed contaminant.

"But words are cheap. You need to be taken by the hand. Things must be demonstrated for you in order to be believed and understood. What you will watch now is a live feed from the prison monitoring system inside ADX Gilchrist." The scene switched to surveillance images of prison corridors and offices occupied by cavorting ex-prisoners. "True warriors are rare in the modern world. Only the fittest are deserving of survival, and we will survive. But these weak men were weaned on the permissiveness of your society. They are criminals by occasion and opportunity, not will. They are learning their fate at the same time you are. The prison exits have been locked down. Less than thirty minutes ago we began introducing ricin into the facility's ventilation system. As you can see, these men feel nothing yet. They smell nothing, they taste nothing. Yet you will see that in a few short hours the first of them will begin to fall ill."

The inmates were stopping their partying. They were starting to look at one another and the vents in the walls.

Then back to Trait standing outside the penitentiary fence.

"Securing this broadcast facility was no accident. We will not be packaged and we will not be misrepresented.

We will not be spun. Any provocation by your government will place your lives, perhaps those of your family and friends, directly at risk. Two targets give us one to waste if we are needlessly tested or provoked. I urge you to contact your elected officials and make your voice heard. Any transgression toward the convict township of Gilchrist, from tampering with our utilities to a full-blown military assault, will result in the genocide of an innocent American town.

"There are plenty of us left here. You need not know who or how many. Only that we are dedicated and united. Along with this land we have claimed, we are also seeking reparations from your government in the amount equal to the total annual expenditure necessary to support the facility formerly known as ADX Gilchrist. Reports put the prison budget at $68 million. That sum, plus five percent for inflation, will be paid to us each year, in perpetuity. Consider it a tribute. And from this point forward, consider this town a separate nation from the rest of your United States.

"I hope I have impressed upon you the sincerity of our mission. We have secured the town, and we have proven our resolve to you. All you have to do from here on in is what you've always done: Forget us. Put us out of your mind and leave us alone, and we will do the same."

The image cut back to the prisoners roaming the Gilchrist halls, riled now, moving about in soundless confusion and anger.

Rebecca, like the others, stared dull-eyed at the screen, too shocked yet to speak. Having traveled so far that morning, they were due brighter news.

"They did it," said Kells.

The others turned toward Rebecca, looking at him. Terry was nearest to the television. "What do you mean, *'They did it'*?"

"A bluff," Bert said. "A fantasy. There's no such . . ."

Darla shivered. "He was so *calm*."

"They let the rest go," Dr. Rosen said. "They let everyone else go, so they would be alone here. We're the only ones left."

"Trapped," said Mia. She pressed against the others to get out of the small room, like a swimmer fighting toward surface air. Robert followed her out.

"What have we done?" Terry was becoming manic. "Why didn't we stay at the inn like I said?" His hat-rumpled hair made him appear bewildered. "He led us here. He took us deeper into town, instead of out."

They looked for Kells, but he had left the office. Darla pushed toward the doorway and the rest followed her.

Some returned to the fire, sinking deeply into chairs or just sitting on the floor, stunned. Kells remained apart from them, as always, standing on the top step of the lounge before the long hallway. A navy blue wool sweater with a seaman's collar covered his broad chest. If he was aware of Terry's insinuation, he did not show it. His mind was elsewhere, as though he were working through another problem entirely.

The others looked his way. Rebecca did too.

A muffled chirping noise broke the spell. Mia gasped in surprise. After a moment Rebecca looked for her cargo bag on the floor.

She unzipped the bag and dug through her clothes, finding her cell phone and feeling it vibrate in her hand. She hesitated before answering, but all eyes were on her now.

"Bec! Bec, do you believe this?" It was Jeb. He sounded far away. "Where are you now? Did you meet Trait?"

There was only one bar of reception showing on her display, and it was flashing. She nearly choked on her words, unwanted emotion rising. "I'm still here, Jeb. I'm still in Gilchrist."

"No, Bec. Everybody got out. They let everyone go."

Saying it was like confessing that she was in trouble, and she did not want to confess anything to him. "We didn't make it," she said.

"We? Who's we?"

She faced the rest to include them in the conversation. "My literary agent," she told them.

"The people I was staying with at the inn," she said into the phone. "We're at a golf course—a country club."

"A country club? Don't you know what's happened?"

"We know, Jeb. There's a TV here."

"Okay. And you're okay?"

"We walked all night."

"Okay. How do we get you out of there?"

"I don't know," she said, emotion rising again.

"Okay. This isn't good. Who have you talked to? Have you talked to anybody?"

"No one. No one knows we're here. It needs to stay that way, Jeb."

"Okay." The negotiating side of him had kicked in. "The Unabomer book I did with what's-his-name at the FBI, the special agent in charge of something. *Ginnie!*" He was calling his assistant. "What's that noise, Bec?"

Her phone was beeping. "Shit. My battery."

"Get me a land line number there. Is there a phone? I'll have somebody from the FBI call you back in ten minutes."

This was what Jeb did best: reassurance, hand-holding. Rebecca sent Coe to the reception desk for the phone number.

"Bec—I don't know what to say. You're okay there? These people you're with?"

"Yes," she said.

"And you did meet with Trait?"

"I met with him."

"This is very big. Hugely big, if we can get you out of there."

Coe had the number and Rebecca repeated it to Jeb. The line went dead before he could respond. She was left holding a dead telephone, yet something made her pretend he was still on the line for the sake of the others. "Okay. I'll be waiting. Right. Okay."

She collapsed the phone and dropped it into her bag. The others waited.

"Let's keep that main line open," she said. "The FBI will be calling in a couple of minutes."

Smiles, a surge of relief and hope—exactly what she had wanted.

Coe said, with awe, "The FBI?"

"Oh, thank *God*!" Darla exhaled.

Kells came down off the hall step, moving slowly to the hearth. He had everyone's attention. "They won't be able to do anything," he said.

Something popped in the fire. Fern's anxiety was beginning to show. "Why would you say a thing like that?"

Terry said, "Yeah, what do you know?"

Kells said, "We're on the wrong side of the fence here."

His manner put everyone off. He was squandering their hope. Rebecca stepped up for the others. "Look, I've met many of these agents. I've seen them in action. You'd be amazed by what they can do."

"They've already been outmaneuvered. Trait is a terrorist now, and even if the U.S. negotiated with terrorists—which it does not—there is no need for Trait to negotiate anything because he is in total control of this situation. He has taken the entire country hostage with one bold stroke."

"He's impressed!" said Terry.

The telephone rang on the reception desk. Rebecca answered it as the others—except for Kells, who remained at the fire—gathered near.

The voice said, "Is this Rebecca Loden?"

It was a male voice. Rebecca was cautious. "Who is this?"

"My name is Sam Raleigh, I'm with the FBI."

Rebecca turned and nodded to the others. "Yes," she said. "This is Rebecca Loden."

"The author?"

"Yes."

"Sorry—I was just handed this phone number. Can you tell me where are you, Ms. Loden?"

"At the country club. The golf course in town."

"In Gilchrist, Vermont."

"That's right. There are eleven of us, we walked here. We were all staying at the Gilchrist Country Inn. We were watching the riot on TV, and then they started to take over the town. We packed up and walked here." Strange pride in recounting this now.

"To a golf course?"

"It's new, it's not on the map. We're guessing the prisoners don't know about it yet."

"I see," he said, obviously surprised. "That's good."

"Are you in charge?"

"I am a crisis negotiator, I am assigned to this case."

She said, "So there are negotiations?"

"No. Not yet."

The others saw the answer in her face. Terry pushed through to the desk. "Tell him we want out," he said.

"What was that?" said Raleigh.

Rebecca turned away from Terry. "Can you help us?"

"Do you have a radio or television there?"

"Yes," she said. "We just watched Trait. We heard what he said."

"They've closed off all the roads. I don't know if you know. We learned from some of the released hostages this morning, they were collecting all the weapons they could find in town."

Rebecca repeated to the rest: "They've taken all the weapons."

Quiet alarm. Even Kells turned his head at that one.

Raleigh said, "Do you have any weapons?"

"Yes—one." She wasn't sure about Kells's gun yet.

"One. Okay. Any climbing gear perhaps?"

"Not really."

"I was just wondering if you were thinking about trying to escape. The snow right now would make for a treacherous ascent. Are you reasonably comfortable where you are?"

"For now."

"Because it sounds like you're in a pretty secure situation there. Probably the best position you could be in, considering the circumstances. I want to advise you strongly against attempting any escape at this time. The thing you most want to avoid is antagonizing the prisoners in any way. I'm sure you understand why. . . ."

"The ricin."

"Yes. We are taking this threat very, very seriously. There are thousands of lives at stake, apart from your own. You've got a good-sized group there. How many men?"

He was taking notes, which for some reason comforted her. "Five men, five women. A seventeen-year-old boy."

"Okay. Let me work out a few things here. My advice to you right now is to sit tight—"

"For how long?"

"Hard to say just now."

"What about a rescue attempt?"

"Impossible, given the current weather conditions and the fact that any incursion on our part would be perceived as a hostile action."

"You could do something. There's only a fraction of the prisoners left. You can sneak in some sort of Delta Team squad to take them out."

"It is much too early to decide anything, but even if we wanted to consider that, there is a constitutional problem here. Something called the Posse Comitatus Act forbids the use of armed force against U.S. citizens by federal troops, except by a special act of Congress."

"These aren't citizens," said Rebecca. "They're criminals. Terrorists."

"Yes, but unfortunately it seems the town incorporated the prisoners into the population a few years ago, for tax reasons. They are legal residents of Gilchrist."

She was exasperated. "So? What about the penitentiary? That's federal property."

"The president could issue a proclamation to disperse, but the only people occupying that facility now are basically dead men. Trait is right: There is no cure." Raleigh took a breath. "I have to do a difficult thing here, Ms. Loden. I have to ask you and your friends to wait. I understand how you must feel. But let me marshal resources here on my end. It might take a little time, but know that you have the full resources of the FBI and the U.S. government on your side. We will find a way to get you out, if you folks can just bear with us. I will call you back as soon as I can."

She realized with a chill that Kells was right. FBI negotiator Raleigh was playing her, talking the talk. He was stalling.

"Why don't you give me the names and addresses of everyone there," Raleigh continued.

The act of registering their identities with a higher power was supposed to comfort her, but it was just paperwork in place of real action. Rebecca turned to the hopeful faces watching her. Kells remained behind, arms folded, studying the fire.

"We can contact your families for you," Raleigh went on, through the silence. "Let them know you're all right."

"We have telephones here," said Rebecca. "We can call them ourselves."

"Right. Of course." He felt her cooling off. "But please impress upon the others the danger involved. The prisoners will be monitoring the media. You don't want to tip them off that you are still inside the town."

"No," she agreed, her spirit sinking.

"Let me give you a special direct phone number." Rebecca copied it down dutifully on a scorecard with a green-leaded golf pencil. "Just sit tight and stay low," FBI Special Agent Raleigh concluded, "and I'll get back to you shortly."

"Right," she said, numbly, hanging up the telephone.

Fern watched with a hand at her cheek. Rita was clutching Bert's arm, and Mia's eyes were wishing for the best while expecting the worst.

"They're not going to help us," Rebecca said.

Dr. Rosen's defeated gaze drifted to the floor. Mia just stared.

"They won't do anything to upset the prisoners," Rebecca went on. "They want us to sit here and wait."

"You weren't forceful enough," said Terry. "You've got to tell these people exactly what you want. You've got to be *explicitly* clear."

His reaction shamed the others. Rebecca was furious. "You call him back," she said. She threw the phone number at him and the scorecard hit his chest and fell to the floor. "Call him back yourself and be explicitly fucking clear."

"Okay," said Bert, stepping in. "Let's not fall apart here."

Rebecca went over to Kells, emboldened by her anger. "How did you know?" she asked.

Kells was infuriatingly even-tempered. "The FBI is out of it now," he answered. "This is a national security situation now. Department of Defense."

"Enough," said Terry, still near the reception desk, shaking. "I'm a bonds analyst. He's a doctor, she's an innkeeper, we have a social worker, a thriller writer, the rest. Who the hell are you, and how do you know so much about this, and why do you carry a gun?"

"I'm a government employee," said Kells. "I work for the Pentagon."

Terry kept pushing. "And what do you do for them?"

"Special investigations for the Defense Threat Reduction Agency."

"The 'Doomsday' Agency," said Rebecca.

Kells was mildly surprised. "That's right. We deal with weapons of mass destruction and unconventional warfare. Primarily the development of NBC weapons outside the dissolved Soviet Union. That's Nuclear, Biological, and Chemical."

"You're a physicist," she said. It was all she could remember about the agency.

"Not me. Just a street agent. That incident in Montana, the ricin exposure? The ex-con bled out in quarantine with the rest, but the FBI traced his movements back to a ranch outside Mesa, Arizona. There was a small factory in a work shed there on the property. Inside they found a partially constructed delivery device and nearly four pounds of ricin stored in coffee cans, baby food jars, thermoses. That's when I came onto the case. We don't get many domestic investigations, but the ex-con was carrying thousands in cash, semiautomatic rifles and ammunition, even a surface-to-air missile launcher. His intended target was never identified. Every lead dead-ended. I was delving deep into the con's background, which is how I wound up here. He had done some time in Marion with Trait and wore a Brotherhood of Rebellion tattoo on his arm." Again, he looked at Rebecca. "But even a government official on a special investigation couldn't get in to talk to Trait."

Much of the antagonism had evaporated and the others paid Kells careful attention now. "So—this ricin," said Bert.

"It's real and deadly, everything Trait says it is and more. But most importantly for us, the government will treat it as such. Gilchrist is this country's nightmare scenario. No one, certainly not the president, is going to put a couple of thousand of innocent lives on the line for us or for these cons. The prisoners are going to use the media to hold the entire country hostage in a high-tech, high-stakes blackmail, and it's going to work."

Rebecca said, "How can you be so certain?"

"Trait doesn't need to take out a million people. Probably couldn't. Variables such as wind, climate, transmission. But this is psychological warfare more than biological. There is no precedent for this. Doomsday always knew something like this might happen, we've discussed it, we've planned for it, but we've never had to deal with actual human lives. Trait's gambit here is solid. The best the FBI can possibly do is to maybe exploit the information chain. People other than Trait have to know the names of the targeted communities, including at least a few people on the outside. The FBI will be kicking in the doors of every Brotherhood of Rebellion ex-con out there."

"I don't understand," said Rebecca. "How can the prisoners be so organized? Trait's been in isolation all this time. And he's a killer, not a terrorist."

"Obviously he had help on the outside. Anyone remember the name Errol Inkman?"

Rebecca did, vaguely.

Kells said, "Resigned from the CIA in the early nineties, two years before Aldrich Ames. Inkman had been passing information to Libyans and other terrorist nations. He was arrested and held for months but never prosecuted. He's in his late-fifties now, thinner and worn, but still with a European mien. Graying hair. Bushy eyebrows."

"You don't mean," said Fern, with a start, "Mr. Hodgkins?"

"I didn't put it all together until last night," said Kells. "I thought I recognized him at dinner—I *did* recognize him—but could not place the face. Unlike Ames, Inkman's treachery hadn't resulted in the loss of any lives, so rather than risk airing the agency's dirty laundry in a public trial, the CIA quietly let him go."

Rebecca remembered the worn, particular man at dinner that first night. "Why would he bother springing a killer like Trait?"

"Just because they didn't prosecute doesn't mean they let Inkman off scot-free. He betrayed the United States. I'm certain they pulled his life apart brick by brick. Bankrupted him with lawsuits, scared away potential employers, harassed his friends, searched his home. I know his

wife left him, and he started drinking. I imagine now he's
a very bitter man with an intense anti-American grudge.
As the former second-in-command of the CIA's counter-
terrorism station, he's got a lot of specialized information
lying fallow. Now he's putting that expertise to work. He
is one of those people who thinks he's smarter than everyone else, whose latent genius went underappreciated and
unacknowledged. A large ego in a marginalized man. I
don't know how he could have gotten involved with Trait
and the Brotherhood of Revolution. I do know that, in
order to pull off something of this magnitude, he needed
absolute secrecy and unwavering dedication of the men
involved—something perhaps only Luther Trait could de-
liver."

"But if he was ruined—bankrupt—then how did they
finance this thing?"

"Inkman could have bankrolled this with bottle returns.
Biowarfare hasn't changed much since the Romans used
dead dogs to foul their enemy's water supply. Only the
methods of delivery have matured. The cost of a controlled multiple-casualty attack on a one square kilometer
area using conventional weapons is about two thousand
dollars. With nukes, you drop to around eight hundred
dollars. Chemical weapons, about six hundred dollars. But
biological weapons? About one hundred, one fifty."

Dr. Rosen said, "Look—they seem reasonable. What
if we throw ourselves on their mercy? They don't want
us here, and we don't want to be here. They let the others
go."

Terry said, "These are psychos. We should wait,
shouldn't we? The FBI knows we're here now. They'll
find a way to get us out. They have to."

In the corner, Darla sank down the dark wall paneling
to sit the floor, gripping her stomach.

"We could hide here," said Rita, looking around.

Fern nodded. "There's a kitchen. We have a fire."

"Fire makes smoke," said Rebecca. "We might as well
dial nine one one. We can't just hide here and wait this

thing out. The prisoners could hold the FBI off for months like this—*months*. Do you realize?"

"She's right," said Kells. "We need to keep moving. Tonight."

Rebecca nodded at having found an unlikely ally. "We have to escape. There is no other way."

"Not escape," contradicted Kells. "The snow is three feet deep in places and still falling. With the short days, there's no way we could cross the mountains or walk through the trees in the dark. Even with skis for everyone. The cons have sealed off the town and sealed us in. We can't go backward or forward."

Rebecca was staring at him. "Then, what?"

"We make a stand here in town. We fight."

Dr. Rosen said, "Fight?"

Terry dropped his arms and walked away.

Mia was crying silently, Robert was holding her hand.

Rebecca was shaking her head. "We can't provoke them like that," said Rebecca. "The FBI said—"

"The FBI said, *Wait to be captured.* They said, *Better eleven dead than eleven thousand.*"

The others were shocked. Hearing it put so bluntly chilled Rebecca.

Terry said, "That's not true."

"You're in finance, Terry," said Kells. "You crunch the numbers." He looked to the rest. Rebecca could feel Kells's pull on the group's orbit, like a finger nudging a gyroscope off course. "Right now Trait and his men think the town is evacuated. So, long as we keep moving, we've got the snow to shield and the long winter nights. Sitting here and waiting will only get us killed."

"Killed?" said Dr. Rosen. "And going out and fighting them won't?"

"Not if we do it right. Not if they don't know we're here."

"You were wrong," Dr. Rosen said. "You were wrong about running. If they had caught us at the inn, we would all be home now."

Kells said, "I wasn't wrong. You think the hostages were well-treated? These men escaped from cages. What about your girlfriend?"

Kells nodded at Darla sitting against the wall. She just stared at the floor, but public acknowledgment of the affair chastened Dr. Rosen.

Rebecca was tired and scared. "Just say the word. *Rape*. Just say it."

"That would be just the beginning."

"You think only women? Don't pretend it couldn't be any one of you."

Terry said, "Jesus Christ!"

Kells said, "All the more reason to keep moving. Fighting these escaped convicts is the only way."

Rebecca said, "Won't they assume the attacks, or whatever you're proposing, are coming from outside? They'll drop the ricin on those towns."

Kells was growing impatient. "Those towns are already lost. The mechanism has already been set in motion. No matter how it happens, Trait's going to be forced to do those towns someday. Otherwise, if he's allowed to profit from this threat, you're going to see these situations popping up all over. No one can get in his way right now except us."

"Are you kidding?" said Terry, laughing fearfully. "Do we look like fighters to you?"

"You look like people with a simple choice: Fight or die."

Bert said, "How many killers are left out there? What do we think? Twenty-five? Thirty?"

"Assume more. But even forty, even forty-five, that's still a four-to-one ratio. Favorable odds when surprise is on your side."

"But these aren't just men," Rebecca reminded him. "These aren't just convicts. These are the worst of the worst."

"They are just men. But they are also the establishment now. They are the law in this town, and we are the criminals. It's a lot easier to create chaos than it is to prevent it."

"That sounds good in theory," said Bert, looking interestedly at Kells. "But they have all the weapons. We have yours and Fern's turn-of-the-century rifle. We're outgunned. How do you propose to get more?"

Kells looked to Fern. "They couldn't have collected all the guns. Not here in Vermont. You've got hunters, farmers, sportsmen. Let's use their unfamiliarity with the town to our advantage. Give me someplace the cons wouldn't have looked, or couldn't have found."

Fern tried to think but could not concentrate.

Coe looked up then, his face bright. "What about Marshall Polk?"

Fern looked to him, more shocked than chagrined. "Marshall Polk?" she said.

Kells said, "Who is Marshall Polk?"

"A crazy man," said Coe. "Lives in the mountains."

"A recluse," said Fern, "an old kook. A former selectman and town postmaster until he started fighting the prison plans. He was always kind of wacky with his theories, but something went wrong in his mind. Maybe just age. It ended up with him seceding from town. He lives in a shack somewhere in the northeast mountains."

"He declared war on Gilchrist," Coe said. "He's a one-man militia."

"Barbershop talk," scoffed Fern. "Marshall never actually *did* anything."

Kells directed his question at Coe. "You know where he lives?"

"Cold Hollow, on the ridge somewhere over the old asbestos mine. I know it pretty good."

"Think he's still there?"

"Don't know. But maybe he left behind some guns."

Fern said, "That's a day's walk."

Kells was still looking at the kid. Coe was thinking. "We could take the sleds," he said.

"What sleds?"

"The snowmobiles. The greens crew here has some. A couple of them came out to chase us off the fairways a few weeks ago."

"You know how to ride?"

Coe's confidence was growing under Kells's examination. "Me and my buds, we carve up the old asbestos mine all the time."

"This is what we need," said Kells, pointing Coe out to the others. "Someone resourceful, someone who knows the town, who notices things. How long?"

"To get there? Two hours, maybe? Depends on the sleds. And two hours back."

Fern said to Kells, "Wait. He's only seventeen."

Kells asked if anyone else could operate a snowmobile. No one else volunteered.

"It's settled," said Kells, looking at Fern. "I wouldn't take him if it didn't mean our survival." He turned to Coe. "You and I will go together?"

"Sure," agreed Coe.

Terry said, "But what about the rest of us?"

"Keep a lookout, and be ready to leave after sundown. We'll scout for a new hideout along the way."

"Wait." Darla got to her feet, still distressed. "What if something happens? What if you don't come back?"

Kells had his bag open and his revolver in his hand for everyone to see. He said, "We're coming back."

TRAIT STOOD LISTENING TO THE INN. AN ASTRONAUT RETURNING to Earth after years in an orbiting capsule would also move about clumsily, grabbing walls. Trait was doing this mentally. He was a man coping with his freedom. The sensations overwhelmed: the cold air, bright rooms, doorknobs that opened under his hand. For five years he had done so much wandering with only his mind that now he doubted his physical presence in each new space.

The joy of freedom would come. Little gifts of will. Music. Sunlight. Women.

The pain in his head was like the flames that buffet a spacecraft's return to Earth. It was a neurological reaction to an abrupt change in atmosphere, and it was to be expected. These were the birth pangs of a mind expanding to its new environment.

He continued past the hanging quilts in the upstairs hallway, turning into the next bedroom and feeling a pulse of familiar energy. A burgundy sweater was folded next on the dresser. He picked it up by its shoulders, letting it fall open before him. The fabric was smooth against his fingers, cooled of body heat but still redolent of her scent. Clean and fragrant, like soap right out of the package. He looked into the mirror.

For a moment he was standing inside his foster sister's room, waiting for her, hearing her blue jeans swishing down the hall. He had gotten into trouble with that girl, and had been killing her ever since.

A man appeared in the doorway, and Trait was back inside the inn. Errol Inkman wore the same collared shirt and loose corduroy pants he had worn at their very first meeting, that morning. His belt buckle was small and bright gold. Trait found Inkman a strange little man, nothing at all as he had imagined him. "A quarter mile outside the center of town," Inkman said, "just a few minutes down the road from the police station. We can store weapons in each place and work out of both. Plenty of space here, and a good-sized kitchen—the perfect location."

Trait folded the sweater and laid it back on the counter. "Perfect."

"I checked all the rooms. Most of the luggage is gone. Looks like everyone left in a hurry."

Trait wondered if she had been among those he released that morning. "One thing I learned in Gilchrist was that there is no such thing as coincidence."

"The writer?" surmised Inkman. "That she requested a meeting with you the day before the breakout?" He ventured a step over the threshold. "I wonder about things like that sometimes. Connections. Like my sitting next to Deacon on that bus trip to Baltimore. Him hearing my ramblings and, once I sobered up, drawing me out about bio-terror and revenge. Was it fate? Or just a random occurrence that, in light of our success here, in retrospect seems like destiny?"

For a moment Trait was inside his Marion cell with Deacon, a wizened man of seventy years, shuffling out on parole, promising to keep the faith. Trait owed his freedom to that old hard-timer, as well as his sanity: Deacon was a legitimate criminal psychiatrist in 1960s Baltimore before coercing patients into pulling jobs for him. In their cell at Marion, he had taught Trait how to survive in the life of the mind.

Trait said, "There are omens, good and bad."

"She was no more notable than the rest," said Inkman. "An unremarkable bunch. But gone now."

Trait nodded, coming out of it. "Gone."

"Except the warden." Inkman had stopped near the brass bed and its lilac comforter. "I just came from the

police station. Jailing him is a foolish indulgence. I was
very specific about there being no hostages. Putting a human face on this siege will force an assault. If the Cold
War had involved a handful of Americans in a gulag in
the Ural Mountains, it would not have lasted six months.
Better to hold an entire nation hostage than one of its pale
citizens."

Inkman's knowledge of the world impressed Trait, but
not enough to change his mind. "No one knows," Trait
said. "To the outside world, he is dead."

"This is a battle for public opinion. Killing or impris-
oning innocent people makes us madmen. But releasing
civilians and downsizing the country's unwanted prison
population—that makes us revolutionaries."

"The warden is an indulgence," conceded Trait. "But
he is *my* indulgence. And he will remain."

"It's bad form. To hold a man without ransom, without
any potential benefit—it is dangerous."

Trait started past Inkman, leaving the room for the
stairs. "If you had been with us inside Gilchrist, you
would understand."

"My point is," said Inkman, following, continuing, "if
you are going to *bend* any other rules of our agreement,
I'd like to know first."

Trait reached the bottom of the stairs where Spotty was
eating a bowl of cereal as he stood guard at the inn doors.
His hand and opposing wrist were wrapped with gauze,
blood-dotted bite marks apparent on his forearm.

Trait said to him, "I warned you about those guard
dogs."

Spotty had insisted on saving the German shepherds
from ADX Gilchrist before the ricin dropped.

"I can break them," Spotty said.

"They were bred to attack cons."

Spotty nodded awhile, swallowing. "I'm going to
change my clothes."

"It's not the scrubs. It's the smell or something. Something the hacks put in our food. I don't know how they know, but they know. They know cons from guards and civilians. You get torn up bad, Spotty, there's no doctor here. No one here to treat you. You realize that?" Now Trait could hear their barking, deep-throated in the distance. "Where are you keeping them?"

"The church. Good fence around the cemetery, room to run."

"If they get out and hurt somebody, you'll have to put them all down. All of them, understood?"

Spotty answered with quiet confidence. "I can break them."

Menckley came in from outside then, hunched over and shivering, tears from his watery eyes were frozen high on his cheeks like bits of broken glass.

"What's going on?" asked Trait.

"They've given up trying the pen doors," Menckley reported. "Also the Command Center. Too stupid to know they can't beat the lockdown that way. Panic seems to take them in waves. A few symptoms are starting. That stuff will start to wear them out."

"How's it playing on TV?"

"The government tried to censor our feed but the networks keep cutting to it now and then."

"Good. Keep the live feed running."

"How many cons do you have riding around town?"

"None. Everyone is either here in town or walking the barricades."

Menckley's facial expressions were limited to his thin, ointment-slick lips. Now they curled in suspicion. "I heard engines when I was out there."

"What kind of engines?"

"Snowmobiles, had to be. On the wind from the east."

Trait looked to Inkman. "A few stragglers, perhaps," said Inkman. He appeared unconcerned. "Inmates who failed to return for the count, still riding around. They probably don't even know what happened at the prison yet."

Trait said, "Send somebody out there to sweep the area. Give it to the Marielitos. They seem anxious for something to do."

AT A HARD-PACKED ROAD LINED WITH BARE, BLACK TREES, COE opened up his sled and Kells throttled to keep pace, doing thirty miles per hour over the snow. Flickering through the trunks to his left was the asbestos mine, a skeleton of a tower with connecting feeder bridges atop a bald hill. Beyond it rose an outlying ring of mountains.

They turned off the road and kept to the safety of the trees, cutting wide around the outermost mine buildings before reaching the hills and starting to climb. They topped out on the first hill and Coe led the way onto a curling footpath up the next rise that only a kid would know about, just wide enough to admit their sleds.

The shack they came to was windowless and leaning, built tree-to-tree on a guarded plateau under the grizzled chin of a sloping stone cliff. The roof was off-kilter, like a bad hat worn roguishly, and the buckled front porch gave the shack a goofy grin. A thick clump of trees sheltered the plateau from the mine and the rest of the town.

They cut their engines and stood off the sleds, shedding their helmets in the sudden, ringing silence. Kells stayed near his sled, as did Coe.

"Chimney," Kells said.

Smoke dawdled out of the roof pipe. Footpaths were shoveled from the warped porch, and recent footprints led from the door to the trees.

Kells was unzipping his parka when a tubby old man in a lumberjack coat stepped out of the trees with a gun in his hand. He wore boots with dirty fur halfway up the calves and moved as slowly as he spoke, seemingly made up of equal parts granite, grit, and wood.

"I thought someone'd come," he said, pushing his plaid hunting cap off his forehead and pointing the gun in their direction.

Kells's hands were empty and open. "Easy with that," he said.

"Easy yourself." The old man paid careful attention to where he planted each boot as he sized up Kells. "Got the ground wired for booby traps but the whole shebang's buried under this snow. Funny way of sneaking up on a man. I heard your engines running a mile off."

Kells glanced at Coe and the kid gave him a nervous nod.

"Marshall Polk?" asked Kells.

"Seventy-three years now."

"We came from the inn. Do you know what's happened in town?"

"I know a gunshot when I hear one. Know a gunfight when I hear more. I warned them. I did my part. But all they saw was tax breaks and more streetlights. Now I got a black man standing in my front yard."

Kells had dealt with the Polks of the world before. "If you thought I was a prisoner you'd have fired that thing by now."

"Don't try and out-think me," he said, cocking his head.

"My name is Kells. Do you recognize the boy?"

Polk came a few steps closer, scrutinized Coe. "Looks like the Provost fella, Matthew Provost."

Coe seemed surprised. "That's my dad."

"Except for the hair. Your dad's was longer, girly. Always got hippie magazines in the mail. How you mixed up in this?"

"We came here to . . . I brought Mr. Kells to see you."

"The rest of the residents are gone," said Kells. "Do you know what has happened?"

"I got two radios but no batteries. Same could be said for my ears. But I know enough."

Kells noticed a second set of footprints, leading

out of the trees. "Someone come to you an hour or two before we did?"

The old man called, "Come on out, Tom."

A man in a long black overcoat opened the front door of the shack. His face was long and the shins and the tails of his coat were soaked through. He held a revolver in his hand as though he hadn't held many.

"Mr. Duggan?" said Coe.

"Look here, Tom," said Polk. "The Provost kid brought a friend around."

It was anger, not nerves, making his weapon shake. Kells faced him. "There's a group of us holed up at the golf course. Fern Iredale, the innkeeper, and some of her guests."

"Fern?" said Tom Duggan.

Polk said, "Tom stumbled in like that two hours ago— frozen solid. No boots or gloves or hat. Could barely see the black of his coat under the snow. He told me what he could."

Tom Duggan's gun hand had fallen, and he was leaning against the skewed door frame, looking away.

Kells briefed them on the takeover and the ricin threat. At the end, Polk was squinting up into the falling snow.

"It's funny," Polk said, with satisfaction. "You can wait for a thing to happen, anticipate it, plan and prepare, but when it comes it still packs a punch."

"We came up here looking for help," Kells said.

"Seven years and no visitors. Now three in one day. They remember you when they need you. Let's take this inside. My manners are rusty."

The porch was a row of wooden pallets nailed together. Inside, the shack was warm, dim, airless. Like the old man, it was arranged around a potbelly, a sizzling black stove. The sagging army cot must have been hell on Polk's back, and there were a desk table and two chairs lifted from the abandoned mine. Half of the table was a workshop, cluttered with rags and twine and radio parts. The other half was cleared for eating. Jars of preserved fruit and boxes of Quaker Oats and other dry foods were stacked on slanting shelves, no toilet or bathtub in sight.

Tom Duggan had taken a seat in a wooden folding chair near the stove, a puddle of melted water beneath him. The revolver rested in his hands in his lap.

Kells ducked to keep from butting one of the rafters and bringing down the roof. Coe's face was screwed up at the smell.

Polk pulled the door shut and came around near the cot. "Never thought I'd see the ditchdigger visit me in my own house, at least not with me on two feet to greet him. Tom's the town's favorite son. That'd make me its poorest relation. He brought in the prison and the money. Now his mother's dead."

"Mrs. Duggan?" said Coe.

Tom Duggan's head turned a bit at the mention of her name.

"It's the riot that killed her," Polk said. He had given up on his .38, no longer aiming it at Kells. "Terrible thing. It's the government behind it all. They've wanted this town from the start."

"I work for the government," said Kells.

Polk's gun came back up. "That's two strikes against you."

"The other being that I am black?"

"The other being that you're a flatlander. Not from the Kingdom. Don't be so race-sensitive. I hate everybody."

Kells said, "We were hoping you might have some guns."

"Guns. What do you want them for?"

"To fight."

"Fight the prisoners?" Polk was constantly reevaluating Kells. "Say I did have some guns. If I gave them to you, how would I get by?"

"You could join us."

"I've been fighting this fight for seven years. Way I see it, you'd be joining me. You got a plan?"

"Our plan is to find some weapons and fight."

Polk nodded. "I must say I like your plan."

The old man went to his cot and got down on one knee and pulled out an old army blanket. He carried the bundle to the cleared end of the table and unrolled it ceremoniously, like an ancient scroll.

Inside was one long rifle, a shotgun, a revolver, a pistol, and a greasy paper bag.

"All cleaned and oiled," Polk pronounced.

Kells studied the bounty. "Where's the rest?"

"Well, there's my thirty-eight. But I keep that on my person. And Tom has the other revolver."

Kells nodded. "And?"

"That's about it."

Kells looked again at the mouse-chewed blanket and the four measly weapons. "And you call yourself a militia?"

"Guns cost money. I gave that up when they started putting them metal stripes in the bills. Microchips. Your government trying to control our purchases."

"We're big on that. What about hunting for food? A crossbow?"

"Broke a few months ago. That's a jug of gasoline over there."

Kells found it under a scrap of tarpaulin. It was a milk gallon carton and its contents sloshed around inside. It was not even half-full.

"Like little eyeballs in your pocket," continued Polk. "Tracking our movements."

Kells looked sternly at Coe. The kid looked embarrassed. He was blocking his nose by pretending to wipe it.

Kells picked up the long rifle. A sling was attached. He was incredulous. "This is a biathlon rifle."

"I got most of them from friends. Some die, will 'em to me."

Kells tried the bolt action. "A *biathlon* rifle?"

"Straight pull. Damn accurate. Pretty good stopping power, and light."

Kells picked up the pistol, a Beretta 9mm. "You have friends who deal drugs?"

"That's a police-only model, loads fifteen plus one. Good old Eddie Bakerfield, God rest. But it's foreign-made—I never trusted it."

"What's in the paper bag?"

"Some extra rounds. Most of them fit."

Kells nodded, reconciling himself to the situation. "Fine. How soon can you pack?"

Polk plucked an old Pan Am flight bag from behind his bed. He said, "I've been packed for seven years."

"You ride with Coe." Kells wrapped up the blanket of oily weapons and looked to Tom Duggan. "The undertaker and I will take the guns."

Tom Duggan looked up, then rose to face Kells. He looked slightly crazed, but mainly just lost. Demons were running roughshod over his thoughts much like the marauders raiding the town. Despair over his mother's death and fantasies of vengeance crowded his mind.

"I thought you were one of them," he said.

Kells shook his head dismissively. "Don't worry about it."

Tom Duggan wore the look of the dispossessed. It was a look Kells knew well.

REBECCA STOOD ALONE IN THE SHADOWY FUNCTION ROOM AT THE
end of the wide hallway, chairs up on the round tables,
the bar empty of glass. For two high-school summers, she
had waitressed every weekend at a country club outside
Hartford, called Pleasant Valley. All she could remember
of it now was the downtime after cleanup when the lights
were dim, and the kids were all flirting with each other
as they waited for their rides: The valets raced golf carts
out on the fairways, the busboys stole swigs from behind
the bar, and she and the other waitresses chatted with their
legs swinging off the bar stools. There had been something very grown-up and reassuringly innocent about it at
the same time, a free zone between adolescence and ma-
turity—a safe place of limbo, as opposed to where she
was now.

You have something for me, Luther Trait had said.

She pulled the gold cord on the glowing red curtain
and opened the wall of windows on the last green. A flag
had been left planted in the snow, a red number eighteen
fluttering before a vista of sculpted white fairways and
high, tamed trees. She could feel the cold pushing through
the glass as she scanned the grounds for sociopaths. Hearing gunshots in the distance had been one thing. Running
for her life was quite another.

She returned to the service kitchen as the coil beneath
the glass kettle began to glow orange. Rebecca was boiling water for tea, though all she really wanted was something to keep her hands warm. You can't fight criminals
with cold hands. She was trying hard to stave off despair.

One of the swinging doors pushed open and Darla

stepped inside, looking childlike in her matching lilac ski parka and pants. "Hi," she said, hesitantly. Her bright blond hair stood out in stark relief to her dark eyebrows, forced and desperate like the rest of her.

Rebecca had heard Dr. Rosen on the telephone in the manager's office earlier. *I'm all right, dear. No, just some others who are also stranded.*

"Plenty of water," offered Rebecca.

Darla moved to the long prep table in the middle of the kitchen. "I just wanted to move around," she said. "It's like . . . it's not really real, you know?"

Rebecca nodded. She did know.

"Ever been to one of those murder mystery dinners, where they kill someone between courses, and it's kind of shocking but you just play along? I feel like I'm just playing along."

"Yes, I know."

"I never had a brother. I've never been in a fight before in my life. I don't know why I'm not crying right now."

Darla's expression tightened and Rebecca had to look away. She was angry that Darla needed consoling. They all needed consoling.

"I don't think I can fight," Darla said. "I know you can, from reading your book. But I'd be afraid to hold a gun."

Rebecca was about to set Darla straight on her weapons experience when she heard the motor in the distance. The engine ran faint, then loud, then faint again, like a motorcycle riding toward them up and down hills.

"Do you hear that?" said Rebecca, stepping past Darla and through the swinging doors to the function room, looking out over the course. The sound was louder there.

"The snowmobiles," said Darla, following. "Thank God."

Rebecca saw the sleds now, skimming over the creamy golf course, riders weaving in and out of formation.

She counted three sleds and pointed this out to Darla.

Darla said, "Maybe they found a third and brought it back."

Rebecca studied the distant riders, their jackets and helmets. She was backing away from the window.

Darla was still rationalizing. "They might have changed their clothes. . . ."

Rebecca turned and started through the function room to the hallway, running to the end, her boots clumping into the lounge. The others were rising and moving to the windows.

"Get back!" she yelled fearfully. "It's not them. It's prisoners."

They all stared. Rebecca moved to the edge of the front-facing window as the noise of the engines grew to its loudest, revving like angry dirt bikes. Then they quieted to an idle.

The others shrank away, dropping to the floor. Rebecca knelt and peered over the sill.

One of the prisoners already had his helmet off. He was a compactly built, dark-skinned man standing astride his sled, smoky breath curling out of his mouth. He looked to be in his forties. All of them wore heavy jackets and boots. Their idling snowmobiles looked like sleek black insects.

The standing prisoner stepped off his sled and sized up the building, disappearing to the right.

Terry's scared voice asked, "What is it? What's happening?"

Rebecca slid down and turned her back flat to the wall, pressing her hands against the solid planking of the wood floor. "They're looking around on foot," she whispered.

Rebecca saw Fern lying on her side against the bottom of the sofa. Her rifle, their only weapon, was hugged to her chest.

Rebecca heard boot steps crunching in the snow. A vague shadow darkened the gloomy window light above her and she closed her eyes, waiting for it to pass. She opened her eyes and the room seemed to float before her.

The shadow was gone. It took all she had to turn and peer outside again.

The other two prisoners remained on their sleds. The one on foot was missing.

Rebecca ducked back, slanted against the wall. It was as though the lounge were hurtling through space. "They're going to see the smoke," she said.

"We've got to run," said Bert, huddled low against the far wall with Rita.

Rebecca heard sniffling. Mia was with Robert somewhere behind the hearth.

"Maybe they'll just go," said Darla, a small voice. She sat near the hall steps, hands clenched to her chest.

"No," said Rebecca, her own words making her feel sick. "They're going to come inside."

"We're getting the hell out," said Bert. It sounded like he was moving.

"Where?" Rebecca whispered.

Another noise now. Faint, distant as the engines had been. A high-pitched squeal getting louder. It was a whistle, growing. . . .

"Ohmigod."

Rebecca scrambled to her feet. She took off running down the weaving hall to the function room, rounding the tables and breaking through the swinging doors to the kitchen where the kettle was screaming with steam. She slid the glass pot off the burner and burned her hand holding the spout open to silence the noise. The kitchen doors swung behind her, slowing until only the whistle echoed in her head.

She put the kettle down on a cold burner. It hissed at her and she turned without breathing. She was separated from the others now. She had backed herself into a blind corner.

Footsteps, hard and quick through the function room. Fern entered with her rifle, barrel-first.

"Maybe they didn't hear it," said Rebecca, fooling herself now.

Fern said, "They heard it."

Rebecca held on to the stove as more footsteps approached and the rest of them pushed through the black doors behind Fern. Everyone except Bert and Rita.

"Weapons," Rebecca said. It was all she could think of. "We need weapons."

She pulled open counter drawers, looking for knives. A noise outside made her pause: a single snowmobile engine running past the delivery door.

Rebecca could feel the hysteria rising in herself and in the room. She found a drawer full of cutlery and was pulling out knives when the panic started behind her.

"I need a gun," said Terry, grabbing at Fern. "I need a gun!"

Terry began to wrestle with her for the rifle. Fern twisted away in amazement. "Who do you—?"

"Give me the gun!" Others tried to intervene, and Terry began to fight them too. "Get away from me!"

Dr. Rosen and Robert tried to lock Terry's arms behind him, but he shook them off with flailing elbows and then ran to the delivery door. He was working the handle, trying to get outside. He got it unlocked before Rebecca and the rest seized him, pulling him back and forcing him up against the walk-in freezer door. His face was red and grunting. A full-blown panic. They handled him roughly, fighting Terry instead of the prisoners.

Only the sled engine stopped them. It passed the door again, this time followed by footsteps.

And Terry had unlocked the delivery door.

The steps stopped outside as the sled engine thrummed in the distance.

Then glass broke at the far end of the building.

They could not lock the outside door. They would be heard. They all stood frozen in the kitchen as though darkness hid them. Dr. Rosen was holding Terry by his collar and Mia's raw nose was buried in her tight, mittened fists.

Fern stepped away from the rest with her rifle. She

trained it on the swinging doors leading to the function room.

More glass shattering. The prisoners were inside the country club.

Terry moved again, and this time no one stopped him. He left Dr. Rosen holding a torn scrap of collar as he raced away through the swinging doors into the function room.

All reason fled with him. Darla inexplicably ran out too. Dr. Rosen stood immobile for a few seconds, watching the doors swing, then went after her. The black doors swung and swung.

The first gunshot sounded far away. A man yelling, perhaps Terry. Rebecca shrank into the corner. Hiding helplessly was the worst feeling she had ever known.

Two quick screams in the hallway, and gunshots to match. In her mind's eye Rebecca saw Darla twist and fall.

Another yell and then footsteps charging through the function room. Fern steadied her rifle and the swinging doors burst open and a man ran inside. Fern shot him in the face. It was Terry.

Terry's hand went to the hole in his cheek. He fell forward against the center prep table.

Mia was screaming, Rebecca was screaming. Fern was stunned and shrouded in smoke.

Terry continued on his knees to the outside door, a man possessed. He fumbled at the handle, finally pulling it open.

A prisoner with a deeply grooved face was waiting for him. Terry fell back with two gunshots in his chest.

Everyone was moving in the room except Rebecca. Fern doggedly worked the bolt on her rifle for another shot as the prisoner rushed inside, yelling in Spanish, firing at the first person he saw. Robert crumpled to the floor. Mia screamed through her hands.

Fern raised and fired again. The shot jolted the prisoner. A bit of insulating fluff flew out his right sleeve.

Then he kept coming. She was working the bolt again when he shot her in the stomach. Fern sagged a bit and raised the rifle but the mechanism had jammed. The prisoner walked up to her with her barrel trained on his crotch and shot Fern in the chest. She fell back and the rifle clattered to the floor as the prisoner stood over her.

Rebecca reached blindly into the open drawer. She was standing there holding a two-pronged serving fork. The prisoner laughed and came at her as the swinging doors opened behind him.

It was Kells. The gun in his hand went off and the prisoner's shoulders flew back. Kells advanced with the gun held in front of him and fired twice more before the prisoner could turn. Kells kept coming and firing until the prisoner was lying dead.

The revolver did not explode in Kells's hand. It made only a dull loud cracking noise. There was no explosion of flesh, only coin-sized holes that gurgled blood. And he did not grin. He appeared deadly purposeful and short of breath.

Silence then, the strangest, loudest silence, a smoky moment in the room. Kells heard words spoken in the hallway and walked back out through the swinging doors. The doors rocked back and forth.

For some reason Rebecca followed him. Kells strode around the tables with his gun ahead of him like a flashlight. The second prisoner, dark like the first, turned the corner into the function room and Kells fired first and fast, hitting him in the stomach, the face, and a leg. The prisoner stumbled to the empty bar, slipping to the brass foot rail and falling still. He was alive and concentrating hard on his breathing. Kells kicked the man's gun away.

"How many more?"

Kells was talking to her.

"One," she answered, shocked that she was even visible.

Kells proceeded into the hall. Rebecca went only as far as the edge of the carpet.

Halfway to the main doors, lying twisted and still in a lilac ski suit, was Darla.

An older man inside the front doors wore a long black overcoat and wielded a long rifle. Kells stopped near him and called down the hall in Spanish. He yelled again, then started along the opposite wall toward the reception desk.

A prisoner rushed out of the manager's office firing a rifle. Kells cut him down. The prisoner collapsed in the hallway, and Kells advanced, sticking his revolver back into his shoulder holster. The prisoner was dragging himself toward his dropped rifle.

The man in the overcoat stepped next to Kells. He raised his long rifle over the prisoner but could not shoot.

Kells reached down for the prisoner's rifle and finished him with a single shot to the back of the neck.

There were no flourishes. He killed without style and without hesitance. Dutifully, he killed.

The man in the overcoat just stood there. Kells started back past Darla to the function room, right around Rebecca to the prisoner lying at the bar. He searched the inside of the man's unzipped North Face jacket as the prisoner watched, for some reason unable to move. He flexed his hands but his legs were still and loose. He was saying something over and over in Spanish, with what sounded like a Cuban accent. Kells responded in Spanish, finding a small, thin canister inside the prisoner's jacket.

It was a can of mace. Kells stood and sprayed the prisoner in the face, and the prisoner coughed and seethed.

Kells moved on to the kitchen doors as the man in the hangman's coat approached. Rebecca recognized him now. Tom Duggan, the undertaker from the town ceremony the day before.

Rebecca heard weeping behind the bar. She circled it, wide around the agonized prisoner.

Dr. Rosen was sitting there with his head in his hands.

Tom Duggan had followed Kells into the kitchen and Rebecca went too. Kells was kneeling next to Fern. She was dead and Terry was dead and Robert was dead. Shy, goofy Robert looked bewildered as Mia screamed over him.

The doors opened behind her and Coe appeared with a short, round-bellied old man wearing furry boots. The mountain man, Polk. He limped forward a step or two, then stopped.

Kells was on his feet again. "Get the kid out of here," he told her. "Take the girl."

Rebecca reached for Coe's shoulder, but he shrugged her off. "Fern," he said. It was Kells who stepped up and pushed Coe out the swinging doors. Rebecca needed help with Mia too, tearing her away from Robert's body. The undertaker just stood in the middle of it all and watched.

Rebecca led them down the long hallway to the lounge, past Darla and the dead prisoner. Rebecca left them there to go back for Dr. Rosen, helping him to his feet. The maced prisoner sputtered something in Spanish as they left.

She had to walk Dr. Rosen past Darla. His gaze stayed on her fallen body as they passed.

There was glass on the floor of the lounge and wind and snow blowing through the broken window. Rebecca sat with Mia on the couch, Coe across from them crying into his fists. Rebecca laid one hand on Mia's shivering shoulder, the other on her thigh. The old man wandered in and took a chair in the corner without saying anything.

Rebecca's despair was too general for tears. For a while her mind went black, a deep, lightless place. She tried to will herself back by focusing on the physical, staring at the hearth fire that had cooled. She noticed a bloodstain on one wall, perhaps where Darla had been shot, the spatter like an augury portending a terrible future.

Luggage lay about the lounge like bodies. Terry's designer suitcase. Darla's thick American Tourister. Robert's hockey duffel. Fern's carpetbag.

Bert-and-Rita's backpacks were there but their skis and poles were gone.

At one point the undertaker appeared in the hallway to drag the third prisoner back to the function room, then to carry Darla.

The old man had fallen asleep. Mia's heaving slowed, her eyes settled into a deep stare. Coe emerged from the stones of his fists every now and then to look around the four corners of the room, searching for something, like a way out.

Finally Rebecca had to leave Mia and walk about. She was leaping with nervous energy and it took all her concentration to move slowly and not alarm the others. She went to the cracked window, feeling the cold. The light was fading. The short, terrible day was ending, the snow turning luminescent, and the flakes draping them in silence.

Staring into the snowfall made her light-headed. Before turning away, she thought she saw a form disengage from one of a cluster of tree trunks to stand on two legs. Bert-and-Rita again came to mind and Rebecca blinked and squinted into the darkness but saw nothing.

She waited awhile longer for it to return, until she doubted her own vision. A thread in the bullet-cracked glass had tampered with the fading light, she decided, deceiving her. She turned from the window and her nerves compelled her to the hallway.

She could hear whimpering coming from the function room. It was doglike, a kind of dry crying. Maybe she was hearing things too. What was taking them so long? Still light-headed, she reached out for the glazed stones of the wall, making her way past the bloodstains toward the end.

She turned the corner and onto the royal blue rug of the function room. The prisoner was still alive. He was seated in a chair set against the great wall of windows overlooking the dark eighteenth hole. He was a broken man, shirtless and bloody, with tears and all manner of mucus and saliva running down his pulpy face, the small hole in his stomach clogged with blood. He would have collapsed to the floor were he not bound to the chair with the gold cord from the curtain. He had been tortured, and he had talked. She could tell this just by looking at him.

The corpses of the two dead prisoners were arranged against the window, sitting, heads to the side, empty hands in their laps. Their faces and palms had been mutilated. Arched over their heads were two words painted onto the glass, the drippy green letters reading like a comic book scream:

TICK TOCK

The scene was arranged for maximum impact, like a macabre piece of performance art.

Kells walked out of the kitchen then. He was wearing a police radio copped from one of the prisoners. His hands glistened clean though there were specks of blood on the lap of his pants.

He walked past the chair and picked up the prisoner's black North Face jacket, lighter and warmer than his own. He examined it for bullet holes before putting it on.

Tom Duggan pushed through the kitchen doors in his slender, stiff way; and Rebecca could see behind him that the others' bodies were gone.

The prisoner groaned and the room reeked of chemical mace and Rebecca's head continued to swim.

Kells gathered the prisoners' rifles and revolvers and mace and started past her without a word. She did not attempt to question him. She had seen too much that day. The prisoner groaned as she followed Tom Duggan back down the hall to the lounge.

Kells scavenged the others' bags, emptying Robert's hockey duffel of his clothes and toiletries and filling it with the prisoners' weapons, including a guard's taser. Mia watched him with a hard, blank stare.

"Where's the older couple?" asked Kells.

"Bert and Rita?" said Rebecca. "They're gone. Their skis are gone."

"Then we have enough sleds to transport everyone in one trip. Coe and I passed a farmhouse a few miles out, backed up into trees off the road, good approach views."

They were leaving. That was something everyone wanted. "What about the others?" asked Rebecca.

Tom Duggan spoke. "The freezer. It will preserve them."

Rebecca picked up her cargo bag and laptop case and found her gloves among the others lining the hearth. As she pulled them on, she noticed Kells saying something to a downcast Coe, standing near Fern's old paisley carpetbag. Coe nodded reluctantly and went to find his knapsack.

Kells turned to the reception desk telephone. He pushed only three buttons.

Rebecca turned to Dr. Rosen. He had stopped in the middle of putting on his long coat, one arm halfway in the sleeve, watching Kells.

"I have a message for Errol Inkman," Kells said into the phone. "Tell him his friends from the inn were looking for him. You have the address."

Kells replaced the receiver and picked up his own bag and the weapon-filled duffel.

"What did you just do?" said Dr. Rosen, pointing. "You called nine one one?"

"It'll take them hours to get here in the dark." Kells was moving to the hallway. "The snow will have swallowed our sled tracks by then."

"What happened to the element of surprise?" Dr. Rosen cried.

"Things are moving more quickly than I expected."

"Than you *expected*?"

"The next wave will be prepared. Better to take the upper hand now. Intimidation can be just as effective as surprise."

"Intimidation? You're baiting them? A challenge?"

But he was talking to the hall. Kells had gone out the front doors. They could see him through the front window now, carrying his bags to the prisoners' sleds.

Dr. Rosen looked at Rebecca and the others. "He's crazy. We're following a killer."

Rebecca nodded in agreement. Then she and the rest of them took their bags and made their way to the door.

LUTHER TRAIT STOOD BEFORE THE MARIELITO SAGGING IN THE chair. The bullet hole in the Cuban's gut cried out like a little mouth of pain. "A miracle you are still breathing, Octavio."

Octavio blinked up at Trait, slumping off the chair like a forgotten attic doll. "Cut me down," he whispered, huskily.

"You were left alive to scare us."

"I told you everything."

"You told *them* everything."

Inkman entered just in time to watch Trait pull a revolver out of his waistband and execute Octavio with a bullet to the forehead. The Marielito's neck flopped back and Trait knocked over his chair with a kick to the dead man's chest.

Inkman took in the carnage as the smoky report rang in the room. It was the bleeding green words, dark against the night glass, that grabbed his attention.

TICK TOCK

Inkman's face washed white. He felt for the back of a chair and lowered himself into it.

Trait stepped away from the smell of the cordite and seared flesh, returning the gun to his belt. He saw Inkman sitting there. "Your friends from the inn," Trait said. "You called them, 'an unremarkable bunch.'"

Inkman's eyes were unbelieving. He was holding on to the seat of his chair as though the room were in danger of being overturned.

"At least two were killed," Trait went on. "Between five and ten of them got away on snowmobiles."

"They asked for me by name?" said Inkman.

"By your real name. Explain '*Tick Tock.*' "

"It is 'Clock,' " said Inkman. He was deeply affected by the scene, and Trait was patient. "A code name."

"Whose code name? Yours?"

"Not mine. I never met him. Not that I know of. Might have dealt with him indirectly. I did a year in Belize in the mid-eighties—"

"Are we still talking about the guests from the inn?"

"He was a legend. I didn't know anybody in the CIA who knew who he was. Only rumors."

"CIA, code names, Guatemala. I'm asking you how this person could have been at the inn."

Inkman looked stricken. "I-I can't explain it."

Jazzed by the violence, Trait's mind worked quickly and reasonably. "Someone is playing you. Somebody got into the town somehow—"

"Nobody got into town."

"Then your inn friends are getting help by phone. Someone at the CIA came up with this."

Inkman shook his head stridently. "It's bad juju even to invoke his name. The Company itself was afraid of him. Look what he did to their faces. You think some retired florist from Hartford did that?"

"So this man was staying at the inn somehow, and you did not know it."

"It was said he could turn it on and off. That you could stand next to him in a hotel elevator and never look twice—that was his greatest talent. He was faceless. The coldest of the Cold Warriors."

"To the central question: How did he get here? And what does he want with you?"

But Inkman was still making sense of the past. "He was a devil to the Guatemalans—a demon, a spirit. His was the highest bounty ever offered by the leftists. He vanished in the early nineties just as the human-rights crimes were coming to light. It was said that he had been captured and tortured, then thrown into an active volcano or chopped up and fed to jackals. They never found his body."

"Octavio said a black man did the killing and the cutting."

Inkman remembered the inn guests. "It could be," he said, chilled. "I don't know. It could be he's been following me the whole time, but . . . no. They dropped my surveillance when I went to Mexico. I'm sure of it." But his gaze had fallen. "Why won't they ever leave me alone?"

"The writer was here also. She remained in town."

Inkman was suddenly disgusted, aroused. "Who cares about the writer? Listen to me. Clock's brief was counterinsurgency warfare. He ran proxy wars. Toppling unfriendly governments in Central America and propping them back up with the CIA's own. Drafting, organizing, and training indigenous fighters, that was the game. It was said he could melt plowshares into swords with just one glance. Subverting the economic and social fabric of a small country is textbook stuff—but every culture has character, a national psychology, and Clock knew how to exploit its weaknesses. He knew how to give an entire society a nervous breakdown in the name of America."

"Octavio saw an old man, a teenaged boy, the writer. You are too easily impressed. This is a scare tactic. He is trying to rattle you, and he is succeeding."

"He left this for us. He wanted us here." Inkman jumped to his feet. "He could be outside right now."

Trait pushed him back into the chair. "He's not. We were too careful."

"If he's here in town, then he's not just coming after me. Do you understand that? He's coming after all of it—the town, you, everything." Inkman looked again at the bodies and the writing. "He wants you to go after him. I'm telling you: Don't."

"I won't. Not tonight, not in the dark. But tomorrow. We will put an end to this tomorrow."

Trait signaled to Spotty to admit the remaining Marielitos. The burn hole in Octavio's forehead had stopped smoking, and the snowmobiles idling outside had masked the revolver's report.

Trait met the four at the edge of the carpet. Four middle-aged Cubans coming off twenty years of U.S. incarceration, their eyes were bright as they tried to see around him into the room, skin tanned, builds tight and compact. Trait nodded solemnly and allowed them inside.

The Marielitos shouted words of anguish and one man gripped the shoulder of another as they viewed their fallen comrades. Their eyes glared with rage.

"Your brothers-in-arms were ambushed," Trait told them. "We have a handful of citizens who foolishly decided to hide in town. Your brothers killed at least two."

The one who spoke English turned to Trait, his top lip curled in fury. *"Faces,"* he said.

Trait glanced at Inkman. "There might be one among them who knows torture and revolt."

The man translated this to others, furiously, before turning back to Trait. "Where they go?"

"The snow will keep them slow tonight. They can't go anywhere except deeper into town. You will have your day. I promise you an opportunity for vengeance."

"No," said the spokesman, the smallest and angriest of the four Marielitos. "We promise you."

THE FOURTH DAY

IT WAS HOURS BEFORE DAWN AT THE FARMHOUSE THEY HAD BRO-ken into. The lingering stink of cigarette smoke and the childproof catches on the lower kitchen cabinets were the only signs of an adult ever having been in residence. At some point children and pets had taken over. Food was ground into the shag carpeting, toys lay overturned on the stairs, and a handprint smudged the bottom third of every wall and door. So lived-in was the house that the absence of little voices and the tapping of paws brought out for Rebecca the deathlike stillness of the town.

Rebecca had been paired with Coe for the hour's journey from the country club, sitting against his back as they ran without headlights along property lines and iced fences, slipping across the countryside like field mice. He had worked the sled hard through the unspoiled snow like a dirt bike in soft sand, while she had been vigilant for prisoners.

Once they reached the house, Kells made each of them take a turn tooling around the yard behind the barn before letting them rest. Rebecca found the sled easy to operate, less like a motorcycle than a moped. Kells explored the barn, silo, and dairy stables while Rebecca took the first watch at the upstairs windows, too distracted to sleep. She understood why he liked the location of the farmhouse—the view from the front looked west over a mile of fields, as far as they could see through the falling snow—but Rebecca found it too inviting and open. She thought of all the questions she wanted to ask Kells, but when he came to relieve her she had been crying, and she hid her face and said nothing as she returned downstairs.

The scent of dog urine puffed out of the rocking chair cushion as Rebecca sat in the playroom, bundled in her coat and a pair of ski pants she discovered in the downstairs closet. She tried to stay warm as she listened to Kells's boots on the creaky floor above. Mia sat unmoving on the small sofa, wrapped in a heavy sage-green quilt, her sad, vague gaze boring a hole of memory in the jelly-stained wall. Dr. Rosen sat in a corner scribbling on country club stationery, presumably a letter to his wife. Young Coe fought sleep like a little boy, embarrassed as he roused himself from dozing, only to blink and nod off again.

Rebecca found herself neither tired nor hungry. As she had learned in the days following the breakup of her marriage, the human body needs little to sustain itself when overstimulated emotionally. Fear piled up like the snowdrifts outside.

Later the footfalls changed overhead, as Tom Duggan relieved Kells. Boots came down the stairs, a refrigerator opened, glass clinked, light glowed in the kitchen. The refrigerator door light went out and a chair scraped linoleum. Coe jerked awake as Rebecca stood, but she waved him back to sleep.

The kitchen was dark-paneled and dim around a deeply scored central island. The red vinyl backs of the kitchen table chairs were cat-clawed and oozing cushion foam. Blood throbbed in her head as she watched the manslayer, Kells, drinking water and plucking sardines from an open tin, eating them one by one.

He saw her there and slid his meal toward her. "Protein," he said.

She declined. He switched on a small, sticky television and they watched footage from the ADX Gilchrist video feed. The prisoners lay in the corridors and on cell beds, coughing without sound, their hands pulling at their throats.

The Cuban's police radio was coiled in front of Kells like a snake, hissing occasionally. Kells popped another sardine in his mouth, swallowing it back like medicine, and she did not fear him. She sat down.

"Why haven't you contacted anyone at Doomsday?" she asked him.

"Because it's better if they don't know I'm here. That way they can't ask me to stop."

"That agency is only about two years old, I think. What did you do before that?"

"I was with the Department of State."

His precise wording was telltale. "The CIA," she said.

Kells ate a sardine.

"In Cuba?" she said.

"For a brief time. Mainly in Central America."

"How many years total?"

"Twenty-one."

"That's how you know about Inkman. You're retired?"

"Doomsday is a second career."

"What did you do for them in Central America?"

"Embassy work. Diplomatic cover. Cold recruiting, handling."

"Embassy work?" she said, unbelieving. "You learned how to do what you did to those men's faces in an diplomacy school?"

Kells took a long drink of water from a plastic Rugrats cup. "These Marielitos are a bad bunch. That's why Trait kept seven alive for himself. He has four left, and he'll have to work to keep them happy. The convict said the others' deaths would be avenged. Disrespecting the corpse, that's a cultural thing. We need to make these convicts crazy."

"You have a plan," she said. "I think you've had a plan the entire time."

"Running straight at Trait will get us nowhere. You've researched him, you know that. Inkman—Hodgkins, as you knew him—he is the weak link."

"The Cuban told you this?"

"No one told me this, I know it myself. Inkman is no hardened criminal like these others. He's a bitter bastard who thought he had pulled off the crime of the century and now knows he's in this thing way over his head. These aren't his people. He's used to liaising with corrupt generals over lemonade, running countries by remote control. Inkman is vulnerable here, and Trait is vulnerable through him. They've made the inn their headquarters."

Rebecca was shocked. The inn.

"There and the police station," Kells went on, "where most of the weapons are stockpiled. We're up against about fifty men—thirty prisoners and roughly twenty ex-cons. They have the center of town all sealed up and the access roads barricaded."

He pulled a brochure out of his back pocket, unfolding the town map from the inn. The town was almost a perfect diamond, rotated slightly clockwise. The prison was situated due north, the common and the inn just south of the diamond's center. Kells tapped the east-northeast corner. "We're out here," he said. "We've got to degrade their defenses bit by bit, all the while moving closer to the center of town. Hit them hard and fast and keep moving."

"And that doesn't seem the least bit unrealistic to you? With the few people you have left?"

"Do we have a choice?" He folded the map and shoved it back into his pocket.

"What is 'Tick Tock?'"

He selected another sardine. "The trademark of an infamous Central American CIA agent, code-named Clock. Clock was 'old' CIA. The invisible hand and all that, legends and ghosts. The breeze you only feel at night, the birdcall from an empty tree. Clock was sangfroid personified. Except for one thing."

She waited. "What?"

"He never existed. He was a psywar chimera, a Killroy invented to intimidate the natives, but the legend took on a life of its own. The perfect agent: brutal yet principled, unwaveringly loyal, perfectly invisible and therefore blameless. Not plausibly deniable but *absolutely* deniable. Every unexplained disappearance or massacre, every unsolved atrocity on either side, was eventually attributed to him. The CIA reaped the upside with no downside whatsoever. Very few people at Langley knew the truth."

"How did you?"

"I was attached to the American embassy in Guatemala, I had to know these things. Inkman spent a year in Central America, so he was definitely familiar with Clock. I'm working on Inkman's fear. The CIA ruined him completely. Now he thinks he has the upper hand, and Clock being here is like the id of the CIA coming after him again. Much better than a handful of weekenders and an ex-spook doing cop work for nuclear physicists."

"You're so certain about Inkman."

"As the vulnerable point? He's the one with the terrorist know-how. He's the one who put this thing together. He's invaluable to Trait, and the albatross around his neck."

"And the ricin? If they kill a town full of people in retaliation?"

"Why bother? We'll still be here. They'll have to deal with us sooner or later."

His tone chilled her. *Deal with us.*

He finished off the water, setting down the cup with finality. "I'm going out to the north barricade before daylight. I want to exert some pressure on them from the inside."

She didn't like the thought of him leaving. "Alone?"

"With the kid. He should know a shortcut to get us back here after sunup."

"Coe?" Rebecca thought of Fern, and felt someone should stand in her place. "He's only seventeen."

"All he has to do is lead me out there."

"The undertaker knows the town."

"I considered that. But that would leave you alone."

"Alone? Dr. Rosen, Marshall Polk—"

"The old man is a fighter all right, but not too agile. The good doctor is still in denial. And the girl—Mia? That would leave you and Coe."

"Then how can you expect to beat these prisoners?"

"We have a lot on our side. I don't need more than two or three warm bodies who can fight."

"You're saying that Tom Duggan is a fighter?"

He reminded her about the undertaker's dead mother. "That's how it was in Guatemala. Indigenous people robbed of their land, their lives stripped away, having no choice but to fight. Not brave men, but desperate men. Men forced to become something they did not think they could be."

"But Coe," she said. "He's just a small-town kid."

Kells pulled out the pager he had scavenged off Terry and copied the phone number onto a piece of napkin. "If you need to move, page me and we'll rendezvous. But I wouldn't travel too far on those sleds. The engine noise is like chum in a shark tank."

THEY TOOK TWO SLEDS, COE IN THE LEAD AND KELLS BEHIND him with one of the prisoner's rifles. Rebecca watched from the family room as they faded into the dark cloud of night snow. Barely visible mountains loomed like an electrified prison fence. On the other side was freedom, normality, home.

There was too much time to think, too much time to contemplate the danger awaiting them. She wandered the rooms of the ground floor. The farmhouse rambled, the contents of one room spilling over into the next, playroom to kitchen to family room to den, a swirl of country domesticity, of children and animals turned loose. She felt like a detective investigating a family disappearance, and took care not to disturb or even right the overturned toys. She looked down at an action figure stripped naked, devoid of gender, and thought about being thirty-seven years old and alone.

The telephone cord stretched across the hall floor from the kitchen into the dining room. She turned away, not wanting to hear Dr. Rosen lying to his wife.

She stopped inside the playroom. Mia sat on the threadbare sofa next to an untouched glass of water. "Drink," said Rebecca, hoping to rouse the girl. Mia looked at her blankly, her short hair flat and defeated. Rebecca touched her quilt-covered shoulder and sat there for a while. A long road of grief lay ahead of Mia with nothing to forestall it.

Dawn came gloomily to the windows. Shoes descended the staircase. Tom Duggan paused in the playroom doorway, tall and dour, looking like a country lawyer in his rumpled undertaker's suit, then withdrew to the kitchen.

Rebecca patted Mia's shoulder. She found Tom Duggan standing with his arms crossed, turning as she entered.

"Sorry," he said. "Didn't mean to intrude."

"Not at all. I wasn't very good company for her."

"May I ask . . . ?"

She noted the inconsistency of his face, pale cheeks chipped with acne scars beneath a pink and smooth forehead.

"The young man you loaded into the freezer. He was her husband."

"Terrible," he said, though his regret was professional and passed quickly. He sized her up as only a box maker can. "I was looking forward to your reading at the library."

"Oh." She was surprised he knew who she was. "I was at your dedication two days ago."

He nodded. It was obviously an unpleasant memory.

A silence passed without any awkwardness. Rebecca asked, "What happened back there, at the country club?"

His face became even more serious as he recalled it. "I'm still not sure. I was taking care of the others in the freezer when he was talking to the prisoner. In Spanish—I don't speak the language. He arranged the others by the time I was done. Why he cut them, I can't imagine."

She told him everything she knew about Kells.

"Do you trust him?" asked Tom Duggan.

"I don't have a choice right now. None of us do. You

saw him. He killed two prisoners and tortured information out of a third." A small, brittle laugh escaped. "Who's going to top that?"

"His hands shook a little after you took the rest away." Tom Duggan seemed reassured by that. "But he seems serious about fighting to take back Gilchrist." Tom Duggan's expression darkened.

Marshall Polk entered just then from the opposite doorway, suspenders supporting his waistband below his considerable gut. He had just awoken and he shuffled from side-to-side like an old man doing an impression of a toddler. "Take back?" he said. "It's all gone. Who's the crazy one now?"

Tom Duggan said dryly, "I didn't spend the last six years living over an asbestos mine without a toilet."

The old man smiled, his wispy hair ridiculous with static as he turned to Rebecca. "This is an old argument, Miss . . ."

"Loden. Rebecca."

Polk leaned on the table, fists down, smelling of old man. Each word came slowly, as though he had forgotten the next.

"A town is not a business, Becky, like Tommy here thinks. It's people and people sometimes die. And Tommy's an undertaker who won't let go. Hope someone shows me better consideration when I'm at the end. Don't plug me in to a machine and pretend I'm dandy." He looked around the kitchen, rubbing his belly. "Where's the black?"

Rebecca said, " 'The black'?"

"Don't look so offended. He's a good shepherd. This town needs a fighter."

"Now you want to fight?" said Tom Duggan. "What happened to blowing up the town?"

"I want to go out with every tree ablaze. At least I'll do more than just clean up the bodies."

Tom Duggan's slender hand squeezed the torn foam back of a chair. "You think I won't? This is my fight more than it is yours, Marshall." He glanced at Rebecca, his manner growing milder. He looked down at his long-fingered hands. "I just hope I can distinguish myself."

Polk said, "I don't suffer any self-doubts."

Tom Duggan said, "The insane rarely do." Then he turned to Rebecca. "How do you feel about it?"

"If given the choice—fight or escape—I would choose escape."

"Do you have a choice?"

Rebecca admitted she didn't.

"None of us do," said Polk. There was a shimmer of glee in his eye.

Hurried footsteps above, then a hushed voice calling down the stairs. "Hey. Hey."

Tom Duggan went to the bottom step, Rebecca after him.

Dr. Rosen gripped the banister at the top. "I think I see something."

Tom Duggan rushed up the stairs, Rebecca followed less enthusiastically. If Dr. Rosen had actually seen anything, he would have come running.

His beige cardigan flapped under his arms and his soft corduroy pant legs *shush*ed as Dr. Rosen led them into a child's room of bunk beds, board games, and broken toys. Through a window spotted with Pokémon stickers, there was a side view of the barn, old and bowed and lurching, one bent nail away from collapse. Snow was piled thick and heavy on its soft roof.

"Behind the barn. Leading to the trees."

Rebecca could see the little holes in the knee-high snow. The footprints were recent, winding from the side of the barn to the woods in back.

Tom Duggan straightened. "You haven't seen anybody?"

Dr. Rosen shook his head nervously. Their growing anxiety confirmed his own distress. "I don't know how they got there."

Tom Duggan went to each second-floor window, leav-

ing Dr. Rosen and Rebecca studying the barn together. It
was a single pair of footprints. The rest of the snow was
clean and unbroken. No footprints approached the house.

"I hoped you were going to tell me I was seeing
things," said Dr. Rosen.

Polk hauled himself over the top step as Tom Duggan
returned, shaking his head. Polk came to the window,
squinting into the brightness of the morning snow.

"Could be someone hunkered down inside," he said,
"waiting for reinforcements. Or there's more than one already. They all could have walked in the first man's footprints."

"We would have seen them," said Rebecca. "They
couldn't have followed us through that snow last night."

Dr. Rosen nodded anxiously. "Kells said that."

Polk was shaking his head. "Never count out luck."

The thought of a prisoner stumbling upon them so soon
after dawn was unlikely at best. "No one here heard a
sled," said Rebecca, optimistically.

They all agreed on that. It was good to agree. They
would have heard something.

Tom Duggan backed away from the window, and in
doing so stepped on a squeaky toy. "Sorry," he said,
having startled them with his clumsiness. Then, seizing
on their attention, he said, "We have to go out there to
take a look."

"I'll do it," said Polk.

Tom Duggan ignored him. "It should probably be two
of us."

"I don't know," said Rebecca, nervous now. "Why
would a prisoner hide in the barn? Could be Bert or Rita
out there, I suppose—but why wouldn't they have come
right up to the house? Unless they're hurt." She shook her
head quickly, as though she could clear it that way, like
the cracked Etch A Sketch lying on the floor. "I don't like
us splitting up."

Dr. Rosen agreed. "We should wait for Kells."

Tom Duggan said, "Those are footprints out there. You're suggesting we do nothing?"

Rebecca said, "Splitting up is a bad idea. If we go, we should all go together."

"And walk into an ambush?" said Polk.

Rebecca said, "They were *hours* behind us last night. Kells made *certain* of that. The snow covered our tracks—there's no way." She was trying to convince herself as she tried to convince them.

Then Dr. Rosen's eyes grew wide. "What if they got to Kells on his way to the barricade?"

She followed that train of thought. "He wouldn't have told them where we are."

"How do you know?" said Dr. Rosen. "They could have made him talk."

"He wouldn't have to say a word," said Polk. "His tracks lead right back here."

"This isn't helping," said Tom Duggan. "We heard no engines. And why would they stage this, hiding in a barn? If they knew where we were right now, they would come in here and get us."

"Then who is it out there?" said Dr. Rosen, exasperated.

Polk started toward the hall. "You three keep talking," he said. "I'll be right back."

"Marshall." Tom Duggan's voice was sharp. It turned the old man around. "You're not going anywhere." He looked at the others. "In theory, I think Rebecca is right about not splitting up. But he can't go anywhere with those legs."

Polk said, "Poor circulation or no circulation, I can hold my own."

"And the young lady downstairs. We all can't go together, it's that simple." He turned to Dr. Rosen. "Doctor? I'll go alone if I have to. But we can't ignore this."

Dr. Rosen looked stricken.

"I'll go," said Rebecca. The others turned in surprise, increasing her anxiety. But she was desperate not to be trapped inside the house in case something went wrong. Outside, at least she could run.

Tom Duggan said, "We'll get you a chair, Marshall. I'll bring you a rifle to cover us. You can see the barn all right?"

Polk waved his hand at the window. "I see fine."

Tom looked to Dr. Rosen one last time.

Dr. Rosen said, "I think they came across Kells's tracks. I think they followed them back here."

Tom Duggan said, "Then there's no sense waiting for him, is there?"

Dr. Rosen's eyes fell, but when they went downstairs he pulled on his coat. He dressed himself with great care, winding a brown-patterned scarf around his neck and slowly fastening his coat toggles as though preparing his own body for a funeral.

Rebecca found a brown knit cap in the closet, and Tom Duggan put on an ear-flapped hunting cap that looked warm. Mia watched them pull weapons from her dead husband's hockey duffel. Tom Duggan chose a revolver and took the biathlon rifle up to Polk. Rebecca picked the 9mm Beretta. It looked the newest. She shoved the weapon deep into her coat pocket.

Outside the kitchen door, the air was arctic cold. They waded through snowdrifts past the sleds hidden against the rear of the house. They paused at the corner of the house, like swimmers treading water at the last safety buoy, then started across the open yard toward the barn.

The snow was thick and sandlike. The wind whipped up sheets of curling white, and Rebecca was torn between the impulse to rush ahead to the barn and the dread of actually approaching it. Drooping, snow-burdened trees stood behind the barn like ancients with their heads bowed. She glanced over her shoulder to Polk's window but could not make him out through the swarm of white.

They reached the sagging corner of the barn. Tom Duggan pointed to Dr. Rosen to stay there, theoretically within sight of Polk, then went ahead with Rebecca, plodding through the snow to the tall double doors.

There were the boot prints, blunted and deep. The barn doors were unlocked and hanging ajar. Snowfall beneath the outside threshold was skimmed back from the door indicating it had been recently pulled open.

Rebecca removed one glove and pulled the heavy pistol out of her coat pocket. Rebecca Loden, author, standing in a near-blizzard with a loaded gun in her hand. She looked up at the sky and the snow spilling out of it.

Tom Duggan hurried past the doors to the far corner of the barn. He pulled off his hunting cap and ducked his head around the corner, two quick glances, pulling back fast. Then he pushed his cap back on his head and crept around the corner.

Rebecca shivered, anticipating a hail of bullets. She twisted to look back at Dr. Rosen, who was hunched under the sagging corner stud, his gun gripped in two gloved hands.

Tom Duggan reappeared, shaking his head. Nothing there.

He retraced his steps next to the stranger's tracks to the doors. He pulled on the handle and the big door swept open before he could catch it, stopping with a clatter. The entire barn quivered and snow slipped angrily off the roof. Something fluttered inside. Tom Duggan peered into the opening, and so did Rebecca.

There was a half-dismantled tractor, bales of hay stacked high, a rusted jungle gym lying on its side, horse blankets and rusted tools. In the rear sagged a ladder-less loft of rotting wood. Below that, a sun-faded billboard advertisement for Barclay cigarettes against the far wall.

Tom Duggan glanced both ways as he stepped inside. Rebecca followed, at once relieved to have dirt under her feet instead of the sucking snow, but wary of the weakened roof overhead. It looked like a dark cloud about to burst.

Tom Duggan pointed out the clumps of snow on the floor, spaced like footsteps, diminishing ahead. Other than the rear of the loft above, the only area hidden from their view was the space behind the stacked bales of hay. That was where the snow droppings led.

Rebecca backed just outside the door so that Dr. Rosen would see her and not panic. He looked miserable, stealing a glance back at the snow-shrouded house. Then she returned to Tom Duggan and started toward the hay.

He moved deliberately. She wondered where he found his courage, or maybe it was simple determination. Maybe "bravery" was a task-specific term. Digging a grave in the frozen earth wasn't brave, but walking alone to those hay bales was, and yet she supposed the same impulse lay behind each act. Maybe she could be brave too.

A crow lifted from behind the stinking bales of hay, fluttering to the rafters. Tom Duggan grabbed her arm and she grabbed his. Neither of their guns went off. She was ready to turn back, but he kept going forward, now pulling her along with him toward the corner of hay.

There were two bodies. They were seated shoulder to shoulder against the warped wall, inordinately still, one head tipped forward at a ludicrous angle and the other set back crooked, bloodied mouth open. Rebecca recognized Bert and Rita's cross-country snowsuits and a scream caught in her throat, cutting off all breath.

She was weak with revulsion. Her mind was sluggish and the particulars came to her in waves.

The half-open eyes.

The splayed legs.

The slashed necks.

There was something inside Bert's mouth. It looked like a piece of paper, pastel blue and wrinkled. Tom Duggan went to him. He had attended to hundreds of dead bodies, but none of them murder victims. He was haggard and red-cheeked. He reached for Bert's downturned head and pulled the paper from his mouth, then backed away to Rebecca and opened it.

It was a flier. *Gilchrist Public Library. Rebecca Loden tonight, reading from her bestselling novel* Last Words.

Rebecca stared at the piece of paper, still slow to think. She turned back fearfully to the twin corpses. Their boots were off and she could see their ankles, their severed Achilles tendons.

Rebecca turned and looked wildly about the barn. She remembered the loft overhead, previously dismissed as uninhabitable. He could be anywhere. Panic began to suffocate her.

She ran for the door of the barn as though it were being closed. Outside, she forgot her stride in the high snow and flopped forward on all fours. She expected him there, waiting for her, but it was only Dr. Rosen, a drip hanging off his nose, wondering what was taking them so long.

She ran back through the snow. She ran as though she were being chased, the cold and the flakes disorienting her, fear stinging her eyes. She reached the corner of the house and stumbled past the sleds to the back door, fumbling with the handle. She fell inside, scuttling across the kitchen linoleum as though he were at her heels, knocking over a chair as she hit the corner cabinets and turned holding her gun.

She trained it on the open kitchen door, waiting for him. Noises in the house, shoes on the stairs, like gunshots in her mind. A form filled the doorway, and Dr. Rosen saw her on the floor with the gun and reeled backward into Tom Duggan.

"Shut it!" Rebecca screamed. "Shut the door!"

Tom Duggan shut the door behind them.

"Lock it!" she said.

Tom Duggan turned back to the knob. "There isn't one."

"That chair!"

He picked up the chair she had knocked over and jammed it securely under the knob.

Still, Rebecca aimed, training the gun on the part in the window curtain.

"What?" yelled Dr. Rosen, crazed. He hadn't seen anything. "What is it?"

A form appeared around the center island. Rebecca swung her gun madly, but it was just Polk with the biathlon rifle. She stopped then and set the handgun down on the floor between her legs and stripped off her knit cap and unzipped her coat collar, choking for air.

Tom Duggan told the others about the bodies in the barn, then showed them the flier.

She tried to speak but the words forming in her mind made her sick and she waited through a tangy wave of nausea. "Jasper Grue," she said. "My killer in *Last Words*."

DR. ROSEN HURRIED AWAY FROM THE DOOR. "JASPER GRUE—HE was out in that barn?"

"It was Bert and Rita," said Rebecca, starting to cry. "Bert and Rita."

"Okay," said Tom Duggan, approaching her slowly. He helped her up off the floor with a hand to her arm and got her into a chair. "How are you so certain it's Grue?"

"Because I know him!"

Polk said, "Who is Grue?"

Tom Duggan explained, "Some sort of serial killer, if I recall. Ms. Loden writes thriller books. Her villain was Jasper Grue."

"Inspired by," she said. "Inspired by Jasper Grue. And he's not a serial." She tried to collect herself. "The Achilles tendon. Grue cuts them with bolt cutters to cripple his captives so they can't run. Kills them by cutting their throats."

"He was here?" said Dr. Rosen.

"He *is* here." She pointed, aware that she was yelling. "He's out there."

"Then why haven't they come after us?"

"He won't be with the other prisoners," said Rebecca, shaking her head. "He's on his own."

"On his own?"

The questions were good, they kept her from hysteria. "Trait's black. Grue would never trust him."

Tom Duggan said, "But how did he find us?"

It came to Rebecca right then. "He followed us from the country club. He followed us last night."

Polk pointed upstairs. "You said Kells said no one could follow."

"Right—no one except Grue. He's a survivalist, an expert tracker. A hunter. He was raised on nature. Never uses a gun, doesn't trust them. He likes the knife because it's personal. Also crossbows, but he prefers hunting knives with serrated edges. He likes to do it face-to-face, talking you through. He collects last words. That's what it's all about. Used to keep them in a notebook, that was the main piece of evidence at his trial. And, if he has time, he pulls teeth for trophies. Makes jewelry out of them. Bragged to the press that he'd make a tiara out of me if he ever got the chance—"

"Easy," said Tom Duggan. "Easy."

"Last night before we left the country club—I thought I saw someone outside. He saw me there. He had picked up one of the fliers around town, checked the date, and stayed for me. The sound of the snowmobiles must have drawn him, same as the Cubans. Bert and Rita came across him and he killed them and carried them all that way. He brought them one by one into the barn. He set them up in there and put that flier in Bert's mouth so that I would know he's here for me. What Kells did for Inkman at the country club: My God, it's the same thing. Grue is coming after me."

"After you?" said Dr. Rosen. "*Only* you?"

"Weather doesn't matter to him, snow, cold, nothing. He'll wait me out. He'll be as patient as the snow."

Turning, she saw Mia standing behind her, looking like a child who happened upon something she was not meant to see. Her gaze quieted Rebecca.

In the ensuing silence, Rebecca heard a far-off sled engine.

"Kells," said Tom Duggan.

Great relief from the others, and Rebecca jumped to her feet.

Then Dr. Rosen said, "But what if Grue is waiting for him?"

They rushed upstairs to try to signal Kells. Rebecca followed Tom Duggan to the master bedroom—strewn with clothes and chewed-up pet toys—with the others behind.

She could just make out the sled riding toward them over the white landscape—just the one sled, carrying two men. Moments later she was certain those were Coe's jacket sleeves at the handlebars.

Polk joined them, out of breath from climbing the stairs. By then Rebecca was positive: It was Kells behind Coe, same body type, same jacket. "How do we signal them?"

Tom Duggan looked for a way to open the window as Dr. Rosen began to recoil. "Oh, no," Dr. Rosen said, pointing. "Oh, no."

Rebecca saw nothing at first. Kells and Coe were five hundred yards from the house, moving straight.

Then she noticed the dark shapes appearing off to the left. Two more sleds, running side-by-side.

"Found us," said Polk.

A low rise separated the sleds from Kells and Coe, shielding them from view. But both parties were running like arrows converging on a point.

The prisoners' sleds moved steadily through the snow, without great speed, each carrying a pair of cons. "They haven't seen each other yet," said Tom Duggan. "Kells doesn't see them."

The glass was fogging. Rebecca pressed her fists against the cold pane.

The prisoners' sleds disappeared behind the last rise, then reemerged, first one and then the other, cresting the top and slowing at the head of the downslope.

They had spotted Kells and Coe moving below them.

"No," said Dr. Rosen, behind them.

Coe saw them now. He was slowing. His sled came to a stop halfway across the rolling fields, still a few hundred yards away.

The two animals spied one another across the frozen

plain. For a moment everything was still except the falling snow.

She knew that Kells was judging their chances of making it to the house. She watched with blazing attention. He never looked at the house. He was deciding whether or not he needed to involve the rest of them.

Black spots appeared on the snow at his sides, his shed gloves. He raised his rifle as Coe dug into the snow, wheeling the sled around and shooting off in the opposite direction.

Kells fired to his left. Four or five muffled reports. Coe cut sharply at an angle, running back toward the trees.

The cons' sleds plowed down the bluff, gaining speed at the bottom, leaving two sets of grooves in the clean white frosting.

"He's leaving us," said Dr. Rosen.

Tom Duggan said tensely, "He's leading them away."

One sled took the lead, its passenger rising and leaning on the driver, firing.

Kells returned fire behind him, then tossed away the empty rifle and pulled a smaller gun as Coe made for the woods. They were fading from view now, disappearing into the trees.

Rebecca pushed away from the window. "What do we do?" she said. "Do we wait? Do we help?"

"Look!" cried Mia.

One of the prisoners' sleds turned back. It had left the chase, following Coe's tracks back toward the house.

"They figured it out," said Tom Duggan.

The sled stopped at Coe's turnaround. One of the helmeted prisoners pointed up at the house like he was pointing right at their window. Then they left Coe's tracks and headed for the front yard.

Polk was already limping toward the stairs.

"Everybody take a window," said Tom Duggan nervously, rushing after Polk. "We can't let them in."

Mia was still staring out the window. Rebecca took her arm and brought her across the hall to the other front-facing bedroom, the pink-painted nursery. "You need a gun," said Rebecca.

Instead, Mia found a narrow recess between the changing table and a closet that fit her perfectly.

Rebecca stripped the gauzy cloud curtains from their rods. She peered around the edge of the window, watching the sled ease into the yard below. The land was broad and uneven, spaced by bare, snow-crusted oaks and clusters of gnarly birches. The prisoners drove slowly, cautiously.

Rebecca backed up. Across the hall, she could see Dr. Rosen on his knees before the picture window in the bedroom. He was talking to himself, gun in hand.

Mia gripped the changing table near a short stack of onesies. "Rebecca?" she said.

Rebecca returned to the side of the window. "What?"

"I'm pregnant."

It was a long moment before Rebecca turned to look at her. Mia stood sad-eyed, trembling. The rumble of the snowmobile turned Rebecca back to the window.

"Just stay by the wall," Rebecca said.

Below, the sled stopped and the prisoners climbed off holding their helmets. One carrying a compact, Uzi-like weapon, the other a handgun. The one with the Uzi spoke into a police radio. It was only a matter of time now. The snow in the front yard was unblemished, but once they went around back it was all over.

Then a gunshot below, a crack of breaking glass. It must have been Polk below her. The cons dropped their helmets, scattering, each to a separate cluster of trees. The trunks shielded them well and only a shoulder or a tuft of hair showed against the snow.

Rebecca was trying to raise her storm window when the *rat-a-tat* sound started, matched by a *thump*ing noise. The prisoner to the right sprayed the house with automatic fire. The stream lashed at her window, lingering there, ten or twelve holes smacking through the double glass as Rebecca ducked away and the rounds lodged in the ceiling, chipping plaster and spinning a Winnie-the-Pooh mobile.

The bedtime tune jingled along with Mia's screaming.

Rebecca blindly fired back twice through the cracked window. It felt scary, random, and futile. Not daring like it looked on TV.

The bullets had not pierced the walls of the house. Mia sank to the floor.

More answering gunfire from below—a slight response to the cons' barrage—then just the plinking lullaby.

Convict reinforcements would be on their way by now. Rebecca scanned the horizon for Kells, but it was hopeless. His sled tracks were already fading in the swirling snow.

Mia was sitting on the floor with her hands blocking her ears. "Get out of here," said Rebecca. "Find someplace to hide."

Mia heard her through her hands. "I want to stay with you."

Rebecca was shaking. "You hide. They're going to kill the rest of us."

Another spray of gunfire and glass cracked and fell to the braided rug. Mia got on all fours and crawled out of the room.

Rebecca aimed through a wide break in the double glass, firing one quick shot at each cluster of trees. She was turning away in anticipation of another barrage when something caught her eye.

Something was moving in the snow. It looked as though the snow itself were moving, something rippling beneath its surface like a worm beneath the skin—to the left of the nest of trees hiding the semiautomatic gun. Rebecca risked another long look and saw a patch of snow creeping along the front yard. A stray shot spat through the glass and Rebecca flinched but could not turn away. She was transfixed. The shape moved behind the trees.

The prisoner reared up with the small Uzi-like weapon in his hands and then something else reared up behind him. Two white arms wrapped the con's chest and yanked him backward, the gun wasting rounds into the highest branches. The snow form rolled on top of the convict and a bright metal blade flashed.

At first she thought it was Kells. The figure turned on all fours and glanced up momentarily at the house, and Rebecca saw small, dark eyes, a bleached-white coat, and a bloody knife blade. The thrill of victory dropped away.

It was Jasper Grue. He released the dead convict and returned to the blankness of the snow.

The moment possessed the awful inevitability of a dream. She understood now that she was his to hunt and no one else's.

The other con rose hesitantly, eyeing the other cluster of trees. He had heard the automatic fire. He saw the ripped branches and snow clumps falling down. He was calling his partner's name.

Footsteps on the hall stairs. A voice, Tom Duggan's. "Let's go! Let's go!"

She ran to the top step, and for a moment the staircase was all white, her eyes stinging with the brightness of the early morning snow. Tom Duggan materialized at the bottom and she hurried down.

"You saw him?" she said.

He nodded. "We have to get away while they fight it out. Now or never."

Mia was there and they grabbed their things in a frenzy, Rebecca throwing her computer case over her shoulder as another gunshot cracked outside. She hurried to the kitchen and Polk was sitting on a chair near the door. He appeared oddly relaxed. Rebecca yelled at him, "Come on!"

Dr. Rosen entered from the bathroom with a roll of gauze and a handful of Muppet bandages. He knelt next to Polk and Rebecca stopped and took a closer look at the old man.

She saw the bloodstain on his shirt, spreading over the lower left side of his gut.

"Damned lucky shot," he said, wincing with disappointment.

Dr. Rosen was frantic. "This won't work. I need real medical supplies."

Tom Duggan rushed in. "Where?"

"A hospital, a clinic. A doctor's office."

Tom Duggan shook his head. "Nearest hospital's in Beckett."

Rebecca said, "What about an animal hospital?"

"There's the vet. Dr. Chalbee."

Dr. Rosen nodded quickly. "We should go there."

Tom Duggan said, "I know the way."

He buttoned Polk's jacket over the wound and helped him to his feet. Outside, he loaded the old man onto a sled and sat in front.

Rebecca mounted the other two-man sled as Mia stood by. "Get on!" yelled Rebecca, and Mia did, clasping her hands around Rebecca's waist. Dr. Rosen took the one-man sled and they pulled out after Tom Duggan.

They rounded the house the long way, riding in tandem along the tree line. Mia's hug tightened as they crossed into the front yard.

Grue was working over the prisoner in the second clutch of trees. The sled noise turned his head. Rebecca opened up her throttle. She wanted as much distance between her and Jasper Grue as possible. She crouched closer to the handlebars and Mia gripped her tight, the laptop pressed between them as they raced across the yard to the field beyond, gathering speed.

She looked back once. Grue was distinct against the dark trees, watching them go, the second convict lying dead at his feet. She saw something in Grue's hands: a hunting bow. He was in no rush. The town was a trap and Rebecca's sled tracks left a long thin shadow she would not outrun.

COE DANCED THE TWO-MAN SLED ALONG A HUNTER'S PATH THROUGH the crowded wood.

The kid obeyed every instruction Kells yelled into his helmet. He held on to Coe's midsection with one hand, reaching back to fire with the other. But Kells could not get off a clear shot, even as bursts of gunfire chipped the tree trunks around them.

They jumped free of the tree cover, hopping a curb of snow onto a meadow road, the rear track fishtailing until the treads bit and the sled straightened out. The road was clear and rising and Coe surfed it hard. The cons' sled broke out of the trees and Kells aimed for the headlight. He noted that the second sled did not follow.

Coe topped the incline and the land up ahead opened around them, too widely. They would be an easy target there. The kid was driving for the lower hills where the road rejoined the trees, but they weren't going to make it. Kells heard cracks over the growl of the sled engine, then a sound like a rock striking his helmet. He saw the cons' sled in the shaky side-view mirror, two road dips behind them and closing.

Then the view in the mirror went white. Coe had peeled off the road in a wild, skidding turn, nearly tossing an unprepared Kells, hurtling them down the steep face of a bluff. Kells's stomach floated as they dipped, coming up short and hard at the bottom. The other sled followed them off the road, gaining over the slower track, firing. Snow chunks popped around them like white corks. They rejoined the winding road on the far side and hit another straightaway and Coe got them back up to speed. But the sled behind them was still gaining. Kells turned and fired three more shots, to no real effect.

The cons were closing the gap on their left wing. They were within shooting range but the kid kept his head down and pushed the sled. Kells turned to fire. He saw the rear passenger on the con sled fooling with his Micro Uzi, trying to reload and hold on at that speed.

Kells barked an order into Coe's ear and the kid braked obediently, immediately, fishtailing a bit as the cons' sled burst ahead, coming even with them suddenly, not more than an arm's length away. Kells looked over at the surprised criminals, the con in back working frantically to reload.

Kells's revolver was in his left hand now. He fired at the sled, picking holes in its side and biting the driver's leg, who twisted away. The sled began to wobble. The con driver was losing the skid and the sled ran nose-first into the far shoulder of the road, momentum carrying the machine and its passengers cartwheeling away.

Coe pulled to a stop and Kells jumped off and ran fifty yards back to the cons. The passenger was dead. His neck was wrenched at an impossible angle, his body crumpled at the base of a tree. The driver lay on his stomach, half-buried in the snow, moaning.

Kells dug the man out and rolled him over. He pulled off the con's helmet and tossed it into the snow. It was a white guy in his early thirties, still reaching for his bloody thigh. The gun in his face did nothing to ease his grimace. The con cursed in pain and rage.

Kells unzipped the man's coat and found a police radio on his belt.

Kells told him, "Say what I tell you to say."

The man cursed and gripped his leg, trying to look at his wounds.

Kells kneeled on the man's chest, pressing the muzzle of his Astra .357 against the con's Adam's apple. "Say what I tell you to say or I'll kill you."

The man was settling down, breathing through bared teeth.

"Give them your handle," Kells said. He turned on the transmitter with his free hand and held it to the man's mouth.

"Dog Two," said the con, his eyes fierce on Kells.

"Dog Two, come in, over."

Kells told him what to say and the con's voice was strained as he repeated it into the radio. *"Clock is running,"* he said.

"Again, Dog Two?"

Kells nodded and the man repeated himself. *"Clock is running."*

Kells shot the man twice, two rounds into the meat of his opposite thigh.

Kells stood and turned off the radio, tossing it into the snow, leaving the con screaming.

At the sled, Coe pulled off his helmet with some difficulty and held it in his trembling hands as though it were his head. There was a chip in the black enamel. A bullet had glanced his right ear. Kells's gunshots shook him and he dropped the helmet to the snow. He saw Kells standing over one of the prisoner's bodies with his gun in his hand, and all at once the chase, the killers, the bullets, the take-over—everything caught up with him and Coe vomited, forcefully voiding the bile from his stomach, sinking weakly to his knees on the side of the road.

"'CLOCK IS RUNNING,'" SAID INKMAN, PACING THE DINING ROOM.
His hands squirmed behind his back. He wore a guard's
flak jacket now, obvious beneath his soft wool sweater,
barreling his thin torso.

Trait found Inkman's veneration of Clock offensive.

"I told you not to go after him," said Inkman.

Gunfire popped again, muffled and distant. The four
surviving Marielitos were performing a Santeria ritual
over their countrymen's remains in the funeral home.
Menckley had seen them smearing ashes on the foreheads
of the dead and placing empty bottles of rum into their
stiff hands, waving guns and occasionally firing into the
walls.

Trait let them grieve. The ammunition they wasted was
a modest investment in vengeance. He was glad he had
not sent any of them to be lost with the morning patrol.

"What if he starts to get to the others, shaking them
up?" continued Inkman. "You can't have them question-
ing your judgment."

Trait said contemptuously, "So far you are the only
one doing that."

At the northern barricade before dawn, a riderless
snowmobile had crashed into the tractors and combines
blocking the road, bursting into flames. It did no signifi-
cant damage, but sniper fire dropped three of the four
watchmen who tried to put out the blaze.

An hour later, the two-sled search patrol reported engine noise in the northeast. They sighted the sled, one
taking pursuit, the other continuing ahead taking fire from
a nearby farmhouse. Trait sent Menckley to alert the Mar-

ielitos, but then received the "Clock" transmission from
Dog Two and called him back. There had been no more
radio reports.

Trait pulled his concerns inward while Inkman paced
and talked.

"We use the ricin leverage here," Inkman suggested.
"Demand the insurgents' surrender. Tell Clock and the
rest to back off or else we take out a town."

Incoherence. "You keep going on about how cold-
blooded he is. Wouldn't holding a town over his head
only increase his resolve?"

"We threaten the government, then. Have them call
him off."

"And show weakness? This is an internal problem."

"No—it would show strength. The threat would rein-
force our superiority."

"This is cowardice," insisted Trait. "Are we a nation
of warriors, or a gang of cheap extortionists?" Inkman's
increasing desperation had eroded Trait's patience. "Clock
is a distraction, nothing more. The only thing we can
threaten him with is failure."

"Don't turn this into a contest," said Inkman. "If you
get into a tug-of-war with him—"

"What? I'll lose?"

Inkman closed his mouth and looked away.

Trait simmered under Inkman's impudence. He had to
remind himself that Inkman had delivered him from
Gilchrist and that the future of the town depended in part
on his expertise. That was the only thing stopping Trait
from beating Inkman to death right there in the dining
room.

The black cat peeked out again from beneath the saloon doors of the kitchen. It eyed Trait and shrank back,
fur rising as it turned and trotted archly away.

Menckley came when Trait called him, massaging oint-
ment into his scarred hands. It had been Menckley's job
to dispose of the cat.

"She's too quick," said Menckley. "I don't know what to do."

"You trap her the same way we're going to trap these rebels—by setting out a nice big bowl of milk."

A THIRTEEN-INCH TELEVISION ATOP A FILE CABINET IN FRONT of the holding cell showed the dying, blood-vomiting cons. Trait sat on the cushioned swivel chair from the police chief's office, watching Warden Barton James through the door. The warden's back sagged and his hands gripped the edge of the plastic bed, his arms lax. Trait had issued him a clean T-shirt and the warden had used his button-up Arrow to clean the dried blood off his face. His right eye was misshapen and dark but his jaw was less twisted.

The warden's unlaced shoes were twinned on the floor beneath the hard bed. They had also confiscated his belt. Around his waist instead was the thick black nylon stun belt that Trait once wore. Trait sat with the remote electronic trigger in his hand.

Trait had given the warden a copy of his own obituary, downloaded from a Denver newspaper that morning. Barton James, thirty-seven-year employee of the Federal Bureau of Prisons, left a wife in Colorado and two married daughters.

"Four inches of newsprint," said Trait. "And only because you were murdered by someone famous like me."

The warden shifted uncomfortably on the bench, rolling his head away from the television. If he was thinking about his wife and children now, he was too smart to let it show.

"There are other riots now," Trait went on. "Terre Haute, Fort Dix. Otisville, Millington, Terminal Island. The BOP came down hard with a nationwide lockdown, but a little too late. It's spreading. We've shown them it can be done, and done with style. The news opinion polls are asking, 'What do you think the government should do about the prisoners occupying Gilchrist?' And guess what the American public is saying?"

"They are saying, 'Leave them alone.' "

"Same as always. 'Bury them. Forget. Do whatever you have to, we don't want to know.' And you were their *man*. And now they are abandoning you."

"They believe I am dead."

"And you are dead. As I was. Welcome to your afterlife. Here you will answer for your prison. I spent five years talking to walls that would not talk back. Now I will have some satisfaction." He pointed to the television. "Why didn't you just kill us? Why didn't you end it as I have? You call it humane, you say, *We are not evil because we do not kill evil men.* So you torture us instead. We were your whipping boys."

"You were being punished for your crimes—"

"We were being punished for the country's crimes. We were someone they could point to. We were there for them. My name strikes fear and awe into peoples' hearts, like that of a god. All you did was imprison that god for a while. My crimes gave you whatever power you had. Gilchrist was my prison, not yours."

"And that is why I am being punished?"

"For failing to recognize that. But unlike you, I have no interest in torture. All I want to do is talk."

"That's what most cons want. To be heard."

Trait nodded. "To cry on the shoulder of a society that never loved them. But not me. I don't *need* your society. Man is the most resourceful creature on this earth—the greatest hunter, the greatest survivor—and I am the very best of that breed. Too great even for my own time, for this thin veil of civilization the world has drawn over its face. Man's primal impulses—to take for himself, to fight, to own—I have answered here. Your society hasn't cast me out. I have cast out your society."

"Then why me?"

"Because you are the prison. I have taken my prison,

the external walls and bars, and imprisoned it, internalized it. I have mastered it."

"Mentally, you're still there. Is that what you're saying?"

"Don't try to crawl inside my head. There's no room for you there."

"This can't last, Luther. You can't win, not here."

"Your naivete is showing—your belief in freedom, in safety, in peace. In this place called *America*. The only thing that keeps America going is exactly your *illusion* of America, this myth of sanctity, this adolescent dream. A pyramid scheme of better tomorrows. The myth that they can leave the dark side of their culture in the care of others, that it has been segregated and controlled. 'Bury them. Forget.' Like their garbage and their ghettos. We have already won. We will be left alone here."

"But there is a resistance effort in town."

Trait held his poise, pleased he had kept the warden alive. "You have overheard things," he said. "Good. We'll have no secrets from each other."

Trait told him everything then, from Inkman to Clock. He saved mention of the writer for last.

"You are as surprised as I was," said Trait.

The warden looked shocked. "What do you want with her?" he said.

Trait had lost all sense of Rebecca Loden as an actual person. In his mind she was the daughter of his foster family, the one who had caused all the trouble.

Trait said, "I think the question is: What does she want with me?"

THE SNOW-TOPPED, HAND-PAINTED SHINGLE HUNG FROM A BLACK yard lamp, *Pet's Best Friend, Mending and Grooming, Dr. Roke Chalbee.* The house behind it was an untidy ranch tucked away from the road with a novelty street sign posted over the carport: *Ford Cars Only.* Snowfall humped the shrubs in front so that from a distance the house looked like it was sinking in a bowl of meringue. A sore-thumb addition off one side of the house was the veterinarian's office.

They paged Kells as soon as they arrived. He and Coe were all right. They told him what had happened at the farmhouse, about Polk and Grue, and Kells was on his way back with Coe.

Rebecca wandered from room to room with the Beretta still in her coat pocket. It would take Grue perhaps a full day to track them on foot. He had never even operated a motor vehicle and would not follow by sled. He mistrusted most machines, although there was evidence he had used a chain saw once, and wiretap records once captured his voice on the telephone. It had once seemed fitting that he would serve out his sentence trapped inside the technological fortress of ADX Gilchrist.

In the office, Polk sat next to a small steel examining table with his shirt unbuttoned. Dr. Rosen snipped away his stained T-shirt to expose his pale, protuberant gut and downturned nipples. The bandage, as it came away, was soaked with blood. Dr. Rosen cleaned the wound until it looked benign, a neat little tear in the soft handle of the old man's lower right side, bleeding feebly.

Dogs howled behind the door leading to the kennel.

Dr. Rosen asked Polk over the din, "How's it feel?"

The old man was ashen-faced, breathing deeply. "Oh," he said, "not bad."

"Numbness anywhere? Tingling? Legs moving all right?"

"Legs fine."

"No pain, walking?"

"Put some music on, I'll dance."

Dr. Rosen patted his shoulder and moved to a medicine cabinet over the sink. Tom Duggan had broken the lock.

"Look at poor Tommy," said Polk. Tom Duggan was standing in the doorway with his arms crossed. "He's all bothered about his commission."

Tom Duggan said, "You shouldn't have shot at them so early."

"Don't measure me just yet, box maker. This is a scratch."

Rebecca joined Dr. Rosen while the others bickered. "He's lying about the pain," said Dr. Rosen, selecting a glass bottle. "I'm going to give him an animal sedative. It'll have to do."

"What about the dogs?" she said. Their barking was like an alarm.

Dr. Rosen nodded unhappily. "The same, I guess."

"I want you to take a look at Mia when you're through here."

"Why?" he said. "What's wrong?"

"Nothing. Just look her over, make sure she's okay."

Polk saw Dr. Rosen with the glass bottle in hand. "No putting me out," said Polk. "You people need me awake."

Dr. Rosen filled a syringe. "Some rest will do you good."

Polk tried to stand as Dr. Rosen approached. "Don't come at me with that," he said.

"Your heart rate is way up. You're wasting recuperative energy on yelling at everybody. You need to sleep."

"Come at me with that thing," Polk said, "and you'll get a fight."

Dr. Rosen stopped, needle in hand, unsure how to proceed. Tom Duggan came forward from the door. "Tell me where," he said.

"The muscle," said Dr. Rosen. "Anywhere."

Tom Duggan took the syringe and faced Polk. The old man's breathing was rapid now, blood pushing more quickly out of the tear in his side. "You need rest," said Tom Duggan.

Polk grinned, half out of his chair. "Cadavers ever fight back, Tommy?"

Tom Duggan advanced and the old man's arm came up. Tom Duggan grasped Polk's wrist and twisted his arm, jabbing the needle into the man's sagging biceps. He held him there as he emptied the barrel, then released Polk, and handed the syringe needle back to Dr. Rosen.

Polk snickered, rubbing his wrist. He looked angrily dazed. "Bet that felt good, eh, Tommy? Why don't you take it out on me, your mother's death. It's your prison." He slumped back in the chair. "She came into the post office. A cape coat she wore. Package for Tommy. From the Lionel Train company, for Tommy's birthday." He stared off as Tom Duggan left the room. "For Tommy's birthday."

Rebecca helped Dr. Rosen walk the tired, mumbling old man down the hall to the bedroom. They lay him on top of the comforter with a pillow under his legs, untucking the edges of the blanket and sheets and folding them over him. They left him wrapped tight and mumbling about Lionel Trains and overdue postage.

Rebecca returned with Dr. Rosen to the kennel. The vet had left behind three small, yipping dogs, a clumsy Newfoundland woofing in the biggest cage, and a handful of cats lounging in a carpet-lined habitat, scratching and mewling. They dosed the noisy animals' food, and in fifteen minutes there was quiet in the house, except the Newfoundland's snoring and the twenty-four-hour news.

The TV room blended with the decor of the rest of the

house, that of the aging bachelor pad. There was a thin-cushioned den couch squared off in front of the dusty set, a stack of blank videocassettes and *Sports Illustrated* magazines on the crumb-covered coffee table, beer label coasters, a food-stained remote control.

The news ran footage of American servicemen camping in the Vermont snow. Eleven thousand United States Army and National Guard personnel surrounded Gilchrist. A report on "small-town paranoia," recounted the flight to larger population centers across the country and reports of vigilante gangs roaming rural towns, looking for outsiders.

There was much more, such as the stock market, down nineteen percent since the takeover—but the usually news-hungry Rebecca did not care. Reason played no role in her vigilance as she returned to pacing the long central hallway, watching the windows for Grue. She made a detour later into the back room of slumbering animals, coming upon Mia. She had her short-nailed finger inside the wire wall of the cat cage, rubbing a kitten's velvety snout.

Rebecca went to her, watching her baby the sleeping kitten. "Fern had a cat," said Rebecca, remembering.

She saw suddenly how empty her life had been over the past year. How she had been hiding in Vermont, nursing her wounds—pretending to get stronger, but in truth just hiding. Polk's secession from Gilchrist seemed reasonable to her now. He had abandoned his hometown before it could abandon him. She hadn't walked away from Manhattan so much as she had declared war on it, the Manhattan that had once been her and Jeb's. The Gilchrist that had once been Polk's.

Mia withdrew her finger from the cage. "Do you think you'll ever write about this?" she said.

The notebook computer Rebecca was lugging around everywhere with her. The novel gestating inside. The writing life seemed so far away now.

Rebecca shrugged. "Do you think I'll ever get the chance?"

*   *   *

SHE LATER CHECKED ON POLK AT THE OTHER END OF THE house. Swathed in sheets and blankets, unshaven, his hair mussed and his aged skin grubby, he could have been wrapped in mover's quilts in a doorway off Lexington Avenue. They were all homeless now.

There was a portable telephone next to a packet of Jokers on the dresser. A cartoon dog eraser capped the antenna. Rebecca could have called Jeb again, but what was the point? In theory, she could imagine the relief of hearing a familiar voice. Just not his.

Rebecca got her case and set up her laptop on the table desk inside the vet's office. She risked tying up the phone line for a few minutes and fed her modem wire into the wall socket. Her America Online account came up and she signed on.

The front page headline hyperlink read:

CRISIS IN VERMONT, NATION ON ALERT: TALK ABOUT IT LIVE.

She went to Google and typed in *"Errol Inkman."* The returned list of newspaper headlines told the story:

SUSPECTED SPY FREED

"INTELLIGENCE SENSITIVITY" THWARTS INKMAN SPY CASE

ALLEGED SPY ENTERS PLEA IN SECOND DRUNK DRIVING CHARGE

And so on. She pursued it no further. Instead, she searched *Kells,* realizing she did not know his first name.

She scrolled through such random sites as the home-page for a Boston bar and a gamer's favorite death-match foes. Tenth on the list of ten returns was a year-old article from the *New York Post*, but the link only gave her the first few paragraphs:

"DOOMSDAY" AGENT DEFENDS NY SUBWAY GAS PANIC

An agent of the Pentagon's "Doomsday" Agency remained unrepentant yesterday, defending his unauthorized simulated gas attack as a necessary wake-up call to the city.

In a scene eerily reminiscent of the 1995 Tokyo sarin attack, midday shoppers emptied onto 14th Street yesterday in a panic after a parcel inside a Barneys shopping bag began to sizzle and smoke inside Union Square station, filling the station with a sweet-smelling gas.

No injuries were reported.

Defense Department authorities were embarrassed by the unauthorized simulation, although the agent responsible for the midday drill, Alex Kells, offered no apologies.

"There is no defense against this type of attack except increased public awareness," he wrote in a prepared fax distributed to media outlets. "The materials involved in assembling this device cost me less than the price of a hardcover book. It could have been substantially more than the scent of jasmine filling your lungs."

The Defense Threat Reduction Agency was created to counter the emerging threat of unconventional warfare attacks by terrorist cells and rogue nations.

Emergency personnel cleared the scene just before rush hour, and many evening commuters, unaware that any emergency had existed, praised the improved smell inside the station.

That was why he had not contacted his superiors. Alex Kells was the last person the government wanted running loose inside Gilchrist.

She signed off her account and unplugged her modem. Just then the task of packing up her computer seemed too daunting. Instead, she pointed her cursor at her novel-in-progress and the document scrolled onto her screen. She scanned the first few sentences. They thudded like notes banged out on an old piano. She switched off the computer before upsetting herself any further. Too exhausted to sleep, she lay her head down on her crossed arms anyway.

THE SUBWAY STATION WAS CROWDED WITH PRISONERS dressed as prison guards. Rebecca stood among them, still and tense. A train pulled up and all the doors opened and Kells stepped off wearing a three-piece suit. The cons all watched him in a complicit manner but no one said a word.

Kells approached her. Rebecca waited to catch his eye but he passed without a glance.

A parcel he left on the subway car started to sizzle. Smoke began to flow out of the sliding doors, becoming snow that fell inside the subway station, piling up on the platform. The snow was deadly poisonous and the disguised prisoners ran for the turnstiles while Rebecca stood there cradling her laptop, open and swaddled in a blanket of soft pink chenille. The infant's face on the screen blinked and smiled at her, then began to cry. Its wailing turned heads. Jeb rushed over, dressed as the prison warden, trying to wrest the laptop from her arms. Rebecca fought him off until he became Jasper Grue. The laptop screamed and wriggled in her arms as she ran through the poisoned snow to the turnstiles, where Luther Trait was waiting to take her ticket. *You have something for me*, he said.

She awoke from the dream—back in her bed at the inn. The quilt comforter was warm and heavy on her chest and legs. It was night still, and the relief Rebecca felt was immeasurable. It all fell quickly into place: the prison interview, the evening snow, meeting the inn guests, sleuth-

ing around after the mysterious Mr. Kells. She was
fascinated by the way her unconscious mind had sorted
these things into the fantasia of a prison riot and the takeover of the town, and meant to think on it some more.
She reached for a glass of water on the night table, and
that was when she saw the man watching her from the
foot of her bed. He came at her out of the shadows with
incredible speed.

SHE AWOKE IN THE VET'S OFFICE WITH A GRUNT AND THE
squeak of the chair. She looked about, confused that she
had dozed, then greatly disappointed not to be in her bed
at the inn.

She felt a cold draft, as though somewhere in the house
a door had been opened. She heard voices and stood at
once, following them down the hall to the pantry.

Everyone was at the open back door. Two men were
walking out of the trees. The larger one, Kells, wore a
black ski mask and carried a large camouflage bag slung
over his back. Coe trudged a step or two behind.

Inside, Kells pulled off his mask with a crackle of
static. Coe's cheeks and chin were windblown red, his
eyes bleary. They stood in the kitchen, emanating cold,
stamping their feet.

Tom Duggan said, "Where are the sleds?"

Kells's mask had left his jaw muscles warm enough
for speech. "Ditched them. Too noisy. More trouble than
they're worth. We have something better."

He slid the camouflage bag off his back to the linoleum
floor, its contents clattering, bulging strangely. He left it
there, too stiff from cold to kneel, so Dr. Rosen got down
on the floor and unzipped the bag.

"Snowshoes," said Kells.

Not the old wood-and-rawhide kind, but modern
aluminum frames with waterproof decking and step-in
bindings and toe crampons. There were three pairs. Underneath was other gear for winter trekking: ankle gaiters,

full-boot crampons, thermoses, an ice axe. And one of the strapped Micro Uzis favored by the prisoners.

"A hunter's lodge," he said. "Where we called you from. They had taken the guns." He frowned at the last part. "Where's Polk?"

Dr. Rosen led him into the bedroom. Rebecca remained in the kitchen, a little shocked. She thought her situation with Grue merited immediate concern.

They helped Coe into the TV room and onto the couch, pulling off his jacket and his boots. Mia draped a red-and-black throw over him, and Coe swallowed and worked at loosening up his facial muscles as they questioned him.

In broken sentences, he recounted Kells's sniper work at the northern barricade, then the snowmobile chase from the farmhouse. "He shot them," Coe said, and Rebecca was unable to tell if this excited or disgusted him. Perhaps both.

He let his head fall back against the top of the threadbare cushion. He described the hunter's lodge on the shore of the frozen lake, then was relating Kells's 911 call when his voice began to trail away. His eyes were closing and none of them tried to rouse him. His head slipped to the side and he looked so young asleep. Rebecca tucked the throw around him.

Kells returned, having shed his coat. "Good," he said, seeing Coe sleeping. He dropped into an easy chair himself, the armrests worn to strings at the elbows.

"You called nine one one?" asked Tom Duggan.

"To draw them out there. Keep them off balance, expend more of their energy. We torched the place before we left." Dr. Rosen entered, returning from the bedroom. "Can you go after the bullet?"

"Without a transfusion, that would only do more damage. I don't think it hit any organs."

"Who thought to bring him here to a vet?"

Dr. Rosen said, "Ms. Loden."

Kells looked at her, nodding, impressed. "So tell me about Grue."

Where to start? She told him about Bert and, Rita, then about having seen someone in the trees at the country club. At the end she handed Kells the library flier.

He nodded, yawning. "This definitely complicates things."

Rebecca stared. "Complicates things?"

"How accurate was your portrayal of him in the book?"

"I didn't portray him. The character was *based on* Jasper Grue."

"So you made him a little worse than he really was. But other than that, it was him. The thing about collecting last words?"

"That was him."

"And his tracking abilities?"

"He bleached his coat and pants to blend in with the snow. The cons never saw him coming."

"Bleach." Kells nodded again. "That's good, we should have thought of that. Never fired a gun?"

"Right."

"Won't use a sled."

"Yes."

"Stalking, rape."

"Yes."

"Okay. So he's on foot, and by all accounts still hours away."

"But he'll get here. And if we move before that he'll follow us again. He's used to living off the land. That's what made it so difficult for the FBI. Before his capture, he hadn't slept with a roof over his head since age six. He could survive out there indefinitely."

Kells yawned again. He pulled at some of the armrest strings, thinking. "Do you want my advice?"

"Yes—of course."

"I would kill him."

"Oh. I see, thanks. Knew you'd come up with something."

"There are no restraining orders in Gilchrist, no police to call. He knows we're armed so he'll hang back awhile, because this is playtime for him. But you can't just wait him out. You can't hide and you can't run away."

"I was hoping you might help me."

"Me? I'm waging a guerilla war here. Kind of have my plate full."

She stared at him, unbelieving. "So what am I supposed to do?"

"What you need to do. Survival has a way of uniquely focusing the mind."

That last sentence stuck Rebecca and she rolled it over and over in her head. "Survival . . ."

" 'Survival has a way of uniquely focusing the mind.' I read your book. That line was one of the few truthful things in there. You have a mind for crime, but there's distance in your fiction, a shallowness, a dishonesty. You're better than that. Some of the things you wrote, the throwaways, the minor insights into the criminal mind. You're intrigued by criminals and bad men, but you dress up this interest as entertainment. You're hiding behind your prose."

Here, finally, was the foreman of her existential jury. "Are you a killer or a book critic?" she said.

"I know you think it's a mistake you're here. Wrong place, wrong time. But there are no mistakes, only choices. Choices you've dreamed about in order to avoid actually making."

Rebecca was too stunned to be offended. Did he have to do this in front of the others? "You think you know me because you read my book?"

"You took a criminal and dressed him up as a bogeyman for your fictional counterpart to slay. Now you're stuck fighting your own ghost. He's not interested in the rest of us except as impediments. You built him up, you're going to have to tear him down again."

Kells yawned again and settled deeper into the chair. "I have to check out for a few hours now," he said. He turned to Tom Duggan. "The gas station, the one with the old-fashioned tanks. Is that the only one in town?"

Tom Duggan nodded. "Just the one," he said.

"It's outside the center of town. That makes it easy." Kells crossed his arms snugly and put his head back. "Wake me at sundown. The three of us, the undertaker, the thriller writer, and the killer," one last sideways glance at Rebecca before closing his eyes, "are going for a walk."

WHAT SHE REMEMBERED MOST ABOUT THEIR JOURNEY THAT NIGHT,
three hours trekking on snowshoes through frozen backyards and deserted country roads, was the sound of the
bird's wings. In the windless snow-silence, Rebecca heard
an eager *flip flip flip* as a woodpecker took flight, leaving
one pine tree for another. The din of civilization had
tricked her into believing that birds flew in silence.

It is a staple of science fiction that characters undergo
"hyper-sleep" during space travel, their bodies working at
a metabolic crawl in order to survive a voyage of
thousands of light-years. That was how her mind was
working now. Every hour spent in Gilchrist seemed to
speed her farther away from her former existence, as
though if she did not turn back soon, her home world
would be forever lost.

The snow did not glow that night. The landscape
stretched before them like deep space. She was soaked in
blackness, as though imbued with invisibility. Kells was
somewhere behind her, Tom Duggan a few steps in front.
In the gloom it was like walking between two ghosts.

Only the eerie calm spared her total sensory deprivation. She concentrated on the sound of their snowshoe
crampons chewing the snow crust.

Tom Duggan's navigational skills impressed her. He
went forward with determination, leading them out of the
trees on the far side of a hill along a hump of snow that
might have been a buried stone wall, joining what seemed
to her an old logging road.

Snowshoeing had not come easily. Rebecca was just
getting the hang of it when Tom Duggan stopped. She

sensed him next to her, and they waited for Kells in the dark.

Kells's bearpaws were undersized for his weight. He was huffing a bit, the outline of the shotgun barrel poking out of his backpack just visible. It occurred to her that he had not taken the smaller Uzi.

"Through these trees at the bottom," whispered Tom Duggan.

Kells's voice was disembodied, haunting. "Let's go."

A light shone faintly through the tree trunks. Kells led the way down the sloping wood until Rebecca made out the slowly rotating sign. *IRVING*, it read, between the top red half and bottom white half of a diamond. Below that: *Quality Gasoline*.

She saw a pair of old-fashioned pumps in front of a clapboard building, across a road scarred with sled tracks. It was almost a mystical scene, the snow falling around the lazy twirl of the illuminated sign. If ever a gas station could be described as being beautiful, this was it. Rebecca shrugged off her small pack and sat down behind a tree trunk to unstrap her snowshoes.

The only thing more miserable than shoeing through the snow was sitting in it. Light from the *IRVING* sign was spare, but it was the only torch in the night. The lonely gas station occupied one corner of a densely wooded intersection. A small house was just visible to the far right, shadowed and quiet. She made out more tread marks in the snow around the pumps, and a large, hand-lettered sign over the garage: *No Car Foreign To Us*. The building itself appeared abandoned, just like the rest of the town.

Perhaps "Enemy Fuel Supply and Storage Facilities" was at the top of the strategic objectives list in the standard CIA primer on civil insurrection. Rebecca had expected to be Kells's lookout. Hanging back and observing was the perfect job for a writer. But when Kells donned his ski mask back on and started to move, both she and Tom Duggan followed. She did not want to be left behind.

Shotgun now in hand, Kells led them down through the rest of the trees, hunched low, continuing along the shoulder of the road until the station garage blocked their view of the pump island and the twirling light. They crossed the road there, some feeling returning to Rebecca's legs as they reached the neighboring house. A shingle under the mailbox told her it was the home of the town taxidermist. From there they turned and doubled back through trees to the rear of the gas station.

They stopped at the tree edge. Fifteen or so feet of open space separated them from the building. Kells pointed out dim tracks in the snow along the rear wall, leading to a barely visible back door. They were boot prints and they were recent.

"Wait here," Kells said, and started along the tree line, moving the long way around the station, treading lightly on the snow, disappearing around the right side of the station. ·

Rebecca looked at Tom Duggan. He wore his flannel hunting cap with the ear flaps down. He was scanning the trees behind them, nervous.

"What do you think?" she asked.

Smoke blew out of his mouth. "I think there's someone here."

Kells returned, moving tree to tree.

"Four of them inside," he whispered.

Rebecca stared. She wanted so much more information, and none at all.

"They're huddled around a space heater," continued Kells. "Too cold to wait outside."

"Wait for what?" she said.

"This trap."

She was actually relieved. She looked back through the trees to the taxidermist's house. Now they would retreat.

Kells pulled off his ski mask, eyeing the rear of the station. His head turned as though he were listening to something. He was not leaving.

"Listen," he said.

There were too many thoughts going through her head to focus on any one thing. Her own breath came like a roar in the windless night.

She heard a click, crisp in the cold air. A door somewhere. Maybe low voices. Now the soft crunching of footsteps over hardened snow, advancing.

"Oh, my God," she whispered.

Kells's eyes worked quickly over the station as he handed her his shotgun. Rebecca took it and backed behind a wide tree trunk across from him. Tom Duggan also hid.

Kells stood still. She watched his eyes track the source of the footsteps as it rounded the corner of the garage. His eyes narrowed and brightened.

She heard a key being inserted, a knob being turned. A soft bumping noise and a door opening and closing.

Kells stepped from the side of the tree trunk. Steam came thickly out of his nose.

"Now do we go?" she said, panicked.

He held up his palm to silence her, then emerged from the tree cover to stand in full view of the closed door.

Rebecca hugged the long gun to her chest. "Don't," she said.

But he was already crossing the snow boundary to the light-rimmed bathroom door. The crunching of his boots was soft and quick, then silence ruled again. Rebecca could barely see him in the shadows against the station wall.

A soft flushing noise.

Rebecca could not take her eyes off Kells's form. She could see him breathing deeply in some strange, meditative way.

The knob clicked. The door opened and the figure of a man emerged from the dark room. Rebecca saw him only briefly. There was something round and flat in his hands, keys hanging from it. A weapon was slung over his shoulder.

The man noticed the extra footprints, stark and violent

over the crust of snow. He followed them back with his eyes to where Rebecca stood, reaching for his weapon as an arm appeared behind him.

Kells's right hand cuffed the man's throat. He pulled him down backward without a cry.

Rebecca turned quickly to the taxidermist's house. She listened to the thumping struggle of one desperate man trying to overpower another. She wanted to run and keep running.

Tom Duggan watched the gas station with narrowed eyes, as though staring into a raging wind. Rebecca heard the snow being thrashed. She could not run and she could not stand still.

She looked back. She had to.

Kells's knee was on the man's chest. He had the strap of the man's weapon wound around his neck, strangling him. The man's legs were kicking slowly in the over-turned snow.

It would not end. She turned and watched Tom Duggan instead, and eventually his expression relaxed. Then Kells rejoined them, carrying the man's weapon.

"Now can we go?" she said. It was what she had been saying over and over in her mind.

Kells's eyes were shining and there was sweat on his neck. "They're going to come looking for him," he said. "We'll finish this here."

He was pulling off his gloves. He unzipped Rebecca's coat and she let him. She was wearing Polk's old gun belt, notched tight, the excess strap tucked into her waist-band. Kells pulled the Beretta out of her holster and stuffed it into the back of his pants. Then he took the shotgun from her. He emptied the rounds, dropping them into his pocket.

"Pull off your gloves," he said.

"Why?"

"Pull off your gloves."

She stepped back, one pace closer to the taxidermist's house. "What are you doing?"

"I can't take all three by myself. Not without firing."

"Without . . . firing?"

"We're too close to the center of town. The noise would carry. We'd be overrun in minutes."

"But you said, 'take all three'?"

"You're coming with me to the garage. I can't do this alone."

"Why take a gun?"

"You can hold it on them. They won't know you can't shoot. Now pull off your gloves."

"I'll go," offered Tom Duggan.

"No," said Kells. "You wait here. Neither one of us will make it back without you."

She was sick but the symptoms would not manifest themselves. "Don't make me do this," she said.

He was holding the shotgun out to her. He had that purposeful look in his face again, the killer standing in front of her.

"Think about Fern," he said. "Remember what they did to her."

Rebecca stopped protesting and Kells pulled off her gloves. He put the shotgun into her cold hands.

Kells started across to the corner of the back wall. With a glance back at Tom Duggan, Rebecca followed.

She was on the threshold of nausea, tipsy with violence and fear. The oppressive cold settled in her head, making her mind heavy. Something washed through Rebecca, a chill separate from the outside air, a bracing mania she had never before known. Her grip tightened on the slide handle of the unloaded weapon.

Attached to the corner of the wall was a small box bearing the old Ma Bell symbol. Kells opened it and plucked out the wires.

They carefully retraced the dead man's footsteps to the front. Kells peered around the corner, then started ahead. For a brief moment the *IRVING* light bathed them from above, and a shiver like a silent scream ripped through her body.

The bay door was slanted, half raised, as though jammed. They ducked inside and moved low, aware of a closed office door to their left. There was an old Volkswagen Rabbit, its dark green hood open, a greasy rag hanging off the engine. They squatted behind the driver's door and peered through the car's windows to the office.

Rebecca saw vague shadows moving against the glass. They were heads lit mildly by an orange glow.

Kells dropped back down, eyeing their surroundings. He was breathing deeply again, trancelike. A knife was in his right hand.

She was numb from the cold and could barely move. She felt dazed.

A noise from the office and Kells looked through the car windows again, then ducked back quick.

The door opened. Two pairs of boots hit the oil-stained floor and the door clicked shut and the boots sounded like they were coming right toward them. Rebecca gripped the shotgun to keep it from rattling in her hands and giving them away.

The boots passed the VW's rusted front bumper. She turned her head slowly, as though her neck would make noise. The men ducked underneath the open garage door into the *IRVING* light, looked around, then turned left, back toward the rear.

Kells was ready to move. He pointed forcefully toward the office door, then rose to pursue the pursuers. Rebecca grabbed after him but he was already away, creeping agilely along the wall of the garage, ducking under the door, turning after them.

Then she was alone in the awful silence of the service station garage. She was still a moment, then shuffled around to the rear of the VW. It was as though Kells had put her in a trance too. She was amazed she was moving at all.

She crossed the garage to the office door. She waited

a long time there, far too long, clutching the empty shotgun. She was waiting for Kells to return.

She would look just once. Then she would pull back and keep waiting.

She turned toward the door glass. One man sat in a wooden folding chair, his face and hands inches from the space heater of glowing orange coils. He was a white man, his heated, brassy face bore the broad insolence of a lifelong bully.

She turned back after only a second, secretly thrilled with her invisibility, waiting, waiting. The shotgun was weightless in her hands. Her breathing was still problematic, but she rode it out like a swimmer tumbling beneath a breaking wave, waiting to float to the surface.

The squeak of the office chair turned her head. A familiar *click-click-click* noise inside, buttons being punched. She held her breath, turning for another quick glance.

The con was on his feet now. A big man, broad and sloppy. He was trying to dial out on the dead telephone.

Rebecca's hands tightened on the shotgun. There was a police radio coiled on the service counter. The con was moving to it.

She did not know what was happening until she was standing inside the office and facing him, the shotgun leveled at his chest.

"Right there," she said. By that she meant, "Don't move." She jabbed the shotgun barrel toward the radio in his hand. "Down. Put it." The power of speech was failing her.

With the shock of her entrance came a dose of fear. At first the con obeyed, setting the radio back down on the counter.

Then the initial scare began to wear off. He saw that she was a woman. He recognized fright in her face.

"The writer," he said, his expression becoming a crooked smile.

A swallow caught in her throat. They knew her. Again she tightened her grip on the shotgun.

He looked her over slowly. Seconds passed and she could sense him growing bolder and bolder.

Now he was looking at the shotgun. He said, "What are you waiting for?"

Kells, she thought, but Rebecca could not reply. Her mouth was tight, lips fixed, her mind cracking like an ice cube in a hot water.

The con's pistol lay on one of the wooden chairs, oranged by the glowing heater. She saw his eyes cheat there and she was on the verge of panic. She wished she had bullets to shoot him.

The con was relaxing, his arms growing loose. His fingers twitched.

"You can't shoot me," he said. "Can you."

She could not find the words. She could not say or move or do anything.

Slowly and defiantly, eyes trained on her, he moved a half-step closer to the chair. "You're too afraid," he said.

The word *Don't* would not fall from her lips.

His smile spread, fierce and jagged, like a crack threading through thick glass. All at once he lunged for his weapon.

Rebecca rushed forward. She hit him with the shotgun. In movies they usually swing the butt end around, but all Rebecca could do was run the muzzle at him like a sword. She had aimed for his chest but as he ducked for his gun she caught him on the side of the forehead over his right eye. There was a snap of broken bone and the con staggered backward, off balance.

He stopped there, holding his head. His hand came away and blood filled the indentation over his eye socket and spilled in a thin line down the side of his face.

"Fuck!" he said. "Oh, you *fucking*—"

Correcting her previous bad form, Rebecca pivoted and brought the butt end around before he could move again, cracking the man sharply across his left ear. The blow whipped his head around and rocked him sideways. He fell throat-first against the edge of the counter, then sagged to one side, spilling to the floor.

The counter edge had crushed his windpipe. Rich, red blood from his head wound pooled beneath him as he lay choking to death. Rebecca stood over him, poised to strike again as the man went into convulsions. His hands opened and closed on nothing, forming tight, trembling fists, then opening slowly and for the last time.

Awful silence again. She stumbled backward against the heater, never taking her eyes off him.

Kells entered behind her with Tom Duggan. Kells took one look at the dead man and pulled the shotgun out of her hands. The butt end was cracked and he tossed the broken weapon away. He grabbed her arms, shaking her until her eyes rose to meet his.

There was a strange bit of fluff in his tight black hair. She reached up for it, fascinated. It was a tiny feather, a shred of down from one of the prisoners' jackets.

Suddenly everything seemed hundreds of yards away. Adrenaline swirled in her mouth like sugar and her legs would not support her anymore.

Kells seemed to understand. He left her sitting in a wooden folding chair inside the front glass door of the station office while he worked. The Volkswagen Rabbit's diesel engine turned over, and he ran it out of the service garage, plowing through the snow to knock over both pumps. Gasoline came spurting and there was no overhang, no safety devices, foam sprinklers, or alarms. He located, dug up, and pried off the underground storage tank caps on either side of the small island, while Tom Duggan dutifully tied together oily rags from the garage, feeding them into the holes. Kells moved seemingly on instinct, arranging his sabotage like a muralist working in a creative frenzy, while Rebecca watched and felt no sense of exigency at all.

He tasked her only once, handing over two red jugs of gasoline with instructions to stash them on the other side of the taxidermist's house. She did this, passing the tangled bodies of the other two cons in the bloodied snow. Behind the taxidermist's she was finally sick, watching her vomit splash into the virgin snow, hearing herself gurgle, but feeling nothing. She returned to Kells and the smell of gasoline was thick now, the cold air turned sticky, the station undulating like a mirage, rising fumes meeting the falling snow. There was a large, white propane refilling tank in one corner of the lot and Kells left it hissing, striding through the haze back inside the station. He reemerged with a Zippo lighter and a smaller red jug, pouring out a trail of diesel fuel as the three of them retreated across Post Road. He lit the fuse there. He did not wait to watch it burn.

Rebecca was stepping into a snowshoe binding as the first underground tank blew. A moment of hissing wind and a tremor, as though the earth had sucked in a full breath, then a tremendous eruption that dropped all three of them to the snow. The ground buckled and roared and the heat was immediate, oranging the snow and bowing the trees. Tree trunks snapped back and ice and snow plummeted down from above, pelting and nearly burying them.

A second, smaller blast followed, lacking the oxygen resources of the first. Rebecca felt a hand grip her coat collar and she got to her feet, shaking off the snow and branch debris, some of it flaming. The *IRVING* sign had fallen and Tom Duggan watched with the fire in his eyes, light and shadow flaring on his face. The wind swirled and smaller explosions ripped behind them as they turned and fled back up the slope, Kells paced them through the raining fire and ice.

TOM DUGGAN TOOK THEM ALONG ICE STREAMS TO OBSCURE THEIR snowshoe tracks, and the rising winds ensured that they could not be followed back to the vet's. By the time they returned, the wind was such that the snow was blowing sideways past the windows, as though the house were in a spin. It was a kind of madness, this town she had lost herself in.

Polk lay on the bed with his arms at his sides, his feet propped up on the pillows. His shirt was tugged up to his chest, exposing flesh as pale as turkey meat. He was very weak, but his only complaint was thirst. He kept glancing up at the ceiling as though he saw someone there.

Tom Duggan took a chair next to him, and in a quiet voice he told him about the gas station.

"Blow it all up." The old man chuckled. "Burn it all down."

Rebecca leaned against the cologne-stained dresser. She felt wasted, observing the room rather than existing in it. She had killed a man and stood over him as he died. Like suicide, murder took precious little effort in relation to the decision to act. The will to murder was all.

Kells was redolent of the gasoline and smoke, having carried all the fury of the explosion back with him. To leave the bedroom, he had to walk past Rebecca.

"You knew they would be there," she said. "Why did you do that to me?"

He stopped in the doorway. "What did I do?"

"You made me kill him."

"No. He made you kill him."

She remembered the way she had looked at Kells after

the killings at the country club. She wondered how people would look at her if she ever made it out of Gilchrist. Then she thought how strange it seemed to contemplate any existence outside the town. This was how murder occurred, she realized: The killer believed she was acting inside a closed system.

Tom Duggan was standing now, looking down at Polk.

"No hospitals, Tommy," Polk said. "No transfusions. Diseases in the blood."

Even his paranoid rantings were losing fervor. "We'll see, Marshall."

"In the end, Tom. In the end . . ."

"Don't talk about the end," Tom Duggan said. "Don't worry about anything."

As they were leaving, Coe met them in the hallway. He was rested now and excitable again. The patchy stubble on his face made him look slightly goofy. "He asked me for the phone number to the inn," he said.

They followed Coe back to the vet's office. Rebecca moved clumsily, as though inhabiting a new body, uncertain how well it worked.

The speakerphone was ringing. Inside, Kells stood behind the vet's desk. Mia and Dr. Rosen were there, and Dr. Rosen asked Kells what he was doing. Then the telephone was answered.

Kells said, "This is Clock. I want to speak to Luther Trait."

The rest of them held fast. Rebecca remained inside the doorway, near Tom Duggan.

Muffled words, then Trait's unmistakable voice through the exaggerated speakerphone. "This is Trait."

"We took out your fuel supply and four more men. That brings your total population down to about forty, by my count."

Trait paused, then answered with confidence. "Gasoline means nothing to us right now. Once the snow clears we will take delivery of whatever supplies we need."

Kells said, "You will not last here that long."

"You underestimate me. As I have underestimated you—until now. There are some Marielitos here who would like to meet with you to discuss the killing and mutilation of their countrymen."

"They have to catch me first. How long until their frustration turns on you?"

"We all share a bond here, the persecution we suffered at ADX Gilchrist. We all wear the same battle scar."

"All except one."

"Yes. Except one. I wonder why you didn't ask to speak to him?"

"Inkman will betray you. You must know this by now. The takeover of this town was a classic CIA coup, only Inkman is bankrolling it with your lives instead of cash. We put up governments and tore them down again, and walked away unscathed every time. Does the term 'puppet dictator' mean anything to you? How long will it be before he kills you and takes over?"

Trait emitted a practiced laugh. "You are trying to play me," he said. "Inkman views your presence here as a threat. I do not. To me you are an opportunity, a challenge. The takeover here was too easy, too efficient, too programmed. We are warriors. What is a warrior without a war?"

"A criminal."

"Your death will be the rock upon which this community of warriors is forged. I think you being here might turn out to be the best thing that could have happened to us."

"You will find I am not a problem to be solved. I am more of a problem-solver."

"Is the writer there with you?"

The rest of them turned. Rebecca thought she was going to fall to the floor.

Kells was silent, waiting. Rebecca wanted to rush away.

She heard herself speak. She heard herself say: "Yes."

A long pause on the other side.

"You stayed," said Trait.

Bewilderment and terror. Simply to have made an impression on a monster such as Luther Trait was appalling.

He continued, "I said we would meet again on my terms."

She searched for a response. Kells's eyes were dark, his killer's face sharp.

Trait went on, "I won't be responsible for what happens if my men find you first. But tell me where you are right now, and I will come get you. I will treat you well. You know you can't win here. What chance do you have against a crew of motivated killers? You know Clock must fail. You have one chance to survive—and I say this to anyone else listening as well. Kill Clock in his sleep. Kill him before he gets you killed. You will be spared and rewarded."

Her anger surprised her. "I won't be your prize," she said quickly.

"All in time," he said. "I said if there were no jails or laws, you would align yourself with a warrior like me. Only, for now, you picked the wrong warrior. But this town is getting smaller by the hour. Look outside your window tonight and you will see."

The click told her Trait had hung up.

Kells turned off the vet's phone with a beep. He was contemplative for a moment. "He's thinking about Inkman now."

Tom Duggan said, "What did he mean about looking out our window?"

Kells was listening now. Rebecca heard it too.

Noises outside. A soft thumping, rhythmic, like feet running hard through the thick snow.

Kells dashed from the windowless office past Rebecca into the hallway, and she followed him into the TV room. She was certain it was Jasper Grue.

Kells sidled up to the front window. He showed her an open hand to quiet her footsteps on the uncarpeted floor as the noise of the tramping grew closer. Kells drew the Beretta from the back of his pants and held it at his side, turning to the glass. The room was dark enough for her to see the snow blowing outside. She gripped the wall as Tom Duggan appeared behind her.

Kells relaxed, standing full in front of the window, the gun hanging loose.

A riderless horse pranced into view. He was black and kicking in the delirious snow, snorting lungfuls of steam, an orange and brown blanket leaping off his back. He spun around and around before the window, triggering the outside motion light which illuminated his dark coat and ebony eyes, spooking him into wheeling and galloping away.

Rebecca moved to the cold window as the snow-kicks faded from view.

"Look out there," said Kells, next to her.

She shook her head. The horse was magnificent and strange. "He's gone."

"Way out there. Keep looking."

They had a good view of the southern section of town. The snow was whipping but thin, and through it, well in the distance, she picked out a slight glow.

"Sunrise?" she said.

"Keep looking."

Like an optical illusion coming into focus, a distant pattern emerged. Rebecca's eyes adjusted to the sight of small fires burning along the outer hills.

Tom Duggan moved behind them. "Cabins and hunting shacks in the woods. They're burning them down."

"To cut us off," said Kells, "draw us closer. This is good."

Rebecca turned. "How is that good?"

"Because it shows respect. Trait was cool on the phone, but we're getting to him. We need to keep applying pressure. We need to keep moving."

He backed away as the others emerged into the room. He was looking at Tom Duggan.

"We need to be close to the town common," Kells said. "Someplace well-hidden, but within striking distance."

Tom Duggan nodded somberly. "I know of a place."

THE FIFTH DAY

SPOTTY ENTERED THE INN DINING ROOM THAT MORNING LOOKING
like the rising of the sun had caught him off guard. He
left his long coat in a heap on the floor before the corner
hutch and lowered himself carefully into a chair. They
had a strange way of collapsing beneath his bulk.

He still wore his prison scrub shirt, untucked over the
drab farmer's pants and huge, unlaced work boots. There
were many more aspirin-sized holes of dried blood on his
hands and forearms, as though carpenter nails had been
plucked out of them.

Trait sat across from him. "Can you tell me what is it
you see in those dogs?"

Spotty looked surly and distant, the way he always
looked. "They'll come around," he said. "I need more
time."

Trait saw that Spotty would never admit defeat. He was
a loyal man who wanted someone to be loyal to him. He
trusted that loyalty would be returned in kind.

Inkman fidgeted to Trait's right. The inn dining room
was their center of strategic operations, buffet tables
pushed side-to-side, covered with town maps and notes
composed in Inkman's inscrutable scrawl. Only one serving table remained against the wall, the padded cloth
empty except for crumbs and coffee stains and prints from
dirty cat paws.

Map ink blued Inkman's fingertips. His hands were
always moving now, and sweat dampened anything
he touched. He wore a hooded coat back and forth from
the inn to the center of town, to confound imagined snipers. More and more he looked like a frightened little man.

He had asked Trait that Spotty be assigned to him full
time, and Trait had refused.

Trait looked at Spotty. "The fireball at the gas station
got Menckley all horny. That gave me the idea to dispatch
the hairless firebug with Burly to every house, shack, and
cabin, working from the border in. We're going to suffocate the rebels by torching their hiding places, drawing
them here."

"Let him come," said Spotty.

Trait enjoyed Spotty's confidence. "That's what this is
about. Fortifying the town."

They schemed. Sentries were reassigned to guard against
surprise attacks. Inkman said that the inn was vulnerable,
and Trait agreed. They decided to abandon it and circle
their wagons around the town common. Trait was determined not to suffer any further embarrassment at Clock's
hands.

Trait paid careful attention to Inkman's counsel. Inkman exhibited a desperate enthusiasm for the security arrangements, while Spotty needed only to be told what to
do. They were like two planets in divergent orbits around
Trait's sun.

Heavy footsteps interrupted. The four Marielitos rode
a wave of cold air inside, moving into the dining room
with their sled helmets in hand. They had searched for
the rebels all night after the gas station blast. Trait had
known it would be pure futility, but he left them to it.
The solidarity of the convict township was waning under
Clock's pressure. They required the purifying ritual of the
hunt. Victory over the insurgents would unite them again.

The Marielitos stood jackal-eyed and edgy. Trait saw
Spotty stiffen and knew there might be trouble. Spotty
had been Trait's golem ever since Marion, and his fealty
was perhaps the only fixed value in the ever-changing
Gilchrist equation. Spotty's back remained toward the
men.

"Good news," announced Trait. "Your search is over.
We are luring Clock to us."

The leader translated for the others. "We want the warden," he said.

Trait's eyes grew cool. "You're just frustrated. You can't get Clock and you're angry."

The Marielito spokesman frowned sulkily. "We know you have him in the jail. We want the *hijo de puta*."

Inkman shifted in his chair. The Marielitos wore guns on their belts and their coats were swept open to display them.

Trait remained impeccably still. "You can't have him," he said.

"Why don't you let them take the warden?" Inkman offered. "For their troubles."

"We no ask," the Marielito said. "We tell."

Trait's eyes never left his. "You don't get the warden," Trait said. "Now go back to the funeral home and wait for further instructions."

The Marielitos remained. Fear was a challenge to these men, a taunt, something to be answered with action.

Spotty planted his feet firmly on the floor and rose out of his chair. He did not turn to face them. He did not even look their way. He just stood ready.

First one Marielito backed away. Then another. Finally the spokesman yielded and, dismissed like children, they went sullenly to the door.

Inkman sprang from his chair as soon as they were gone. Trait anticipated some comment but Inkman just donned his hood and went out into the snow alone.

Spotty followed Trait out to the front steps of the inn. As they watched Inkman trudging back into town, angry barking came out of the snow in the distance.

Trait turned to Spotty with a sudden rush of affinity. "Leave the dogs alone," he said. "We need to concentrate on security now."

Spotty's shoulders tested the seams of his coat sleeves as he acquiesced with a shrug. They split up inside the police station, Trait continuing to the cells in back.

Warden James sat on his plastic slab, his shoulders

sagging against the wall as he listened to what Trait had to say. "Now you come to me for advice?"

Trait stood outside the jail cell, his feet firmly planted. "I'm just telling you what has happened."

"You are the warden now, Luther. They are the prisoners. They have the motivation. You refused to be broken, and now so do they. How quickly the satisfied forget their hunger."

In a flash Trait was back inside his E-Unit pod in ADX Gilchrist, sitting alone in his old cell. He was happy there. "I relied too much on Inkman, who is not one of us."

"All kingdoms are illusory, Luther. Even yours. There is no satisfaction in holding power, only taking it. I am your example. You exist now only to incite rebellion, to be overthrown or killed."

His insubordination surprised Trait. "Today you are much more opinionated."

"A man with nothing to lose will get that way. If you don't like what you're hearing, confide in someone else. Go to Inkman if you still think you can trust him. I've been thinking about what you said, about criminals being the purest of men, the best of their breed, feared and reviled for their strength. You believe in survival of the fittest. You think you will prevail here because you are a warrior. But *fittest* does not mean *strongest*. It means *most adaptive*. It means *most suitable for survival*. Strength has played less of a hand in human evolution than luck. Dinosaurs were strong until a meteorite kicked up a cloud of dust that blanked the earth, and they could not adapt to the changed conditions. These rebels are your meteorite, the snow outside is your cloud of dust. You are a killer and a sadist, Luther, motivated by forces you do not understand. You are *mad*adaptive. Clock and the others, they are motivated purely by self-preservation now, they have nothing to lose."

Trait hated to concede anything, but the question was an important one. "Clock said Inkman would betray me."

"Inkman betrayed his country for his ego. Now Gil-

christ is his country." The warden lowered his head, and
the look he showed Trait was one of fatherly disappointment. "Why do you think it would be any different this
time around?"

THE PHYSICAL CHALLENGE OF THEIR EXPEDITIONS NO LONGER MADE
any impression upon Rebecca. Only the daylight made
this one different. They paired off and took turns pulling
Polk's toboggan. Her mind kept returning to the gas station in a perverse attempt to reconstruct the series of
events leading to the convict's death, forming only the
fractured narrative of an interrupted dream.

The house Tom Duggan led them to was modest and
crowded by trees. From the front door, just a sliver of
street showed beyond a twist in the driveway, and only
from the upstairs bedroom window could you see the
nearest neighbor, a farmhouse and stable set well across
the road. To Kells, the house was neatly hidden. To Rebecca, it was a remote, wooded cul-de-sac tempting to
Grue.

Inside, snow fell in the living room. Ghostly flakes
haunted her retina and no amount of blinking would clear
them. Through a hall window she saw Tom Duggan's
dark figure standing alone in the side yard. The real snow
falling outside was soothing to her vision, so she pulled
her coat back on and went out.

Down the front steps and around a stack of snow-
covered firewood, into a side yard bound by dark, leafless
trees. Tom Duggan stood hat in hand over a smooth,
broad, gravelike hump of snow. His eyes were downturned and he stood rigid as though expecting a sudden
gust of wind. Dull white stubble aged his angular face.
She stood near and waited for him to speak.

He said, "This was my mother's house."

She had sensed this from his familiar manner as he

entered the house and moved through the rooms.

"She wandered out here," he said. "I found her curled up."

Rebecca remembered her first impression of Tom Duggan, at the ceremony on the town common: a proud, reasonable man who had humbly saved his hometown from extinction.

"There was nothing you could have done," she said, aiming for empathy but hitting only emptiness.

He replaced his hunting cap. He said, "It's just not right."

"I'm really sorry."

He sunk his hands deep into his overcoat pockets. "Kells wants me to take him into town."

"Just you?"

He nodded. "I want to go. I want to see it."

She found Kells inside, boiling water in a black pan. The kitchen had been updated recently, with clean buttercup-yellow countertops, natural wood cabinets, and new appliances except for the thin, whirring avocado-colored refrigerator.

He emptied a packet of Lipton's Cup-a-Soup into an "Irish Blessing" mug. His whiskers were coming in dark with gray hints, giving his chin more of a spadelike jut.

Rebecca said, "You're going into town?"

"With the undertaker. To get a look at the setup."

"How long?"

"Don't worry about Grue. The guns will keep him away. You can handle yourself here. You've proved that."

"I proved nothing. The gas station counter killed that man, not me. All it proved was that you can force me into situations I don't want to be in."

Kells looked at her probingly. "Why did you come here?" he asked.

"What do you mean? To this house?"

"To Gilchrist. To the prison. You came for something."

"You know why. To interview Luther Trait."

"And he represents what to you? Besides publicity and book sales."

"I was doing research on a character."

"No." He shook his head. "What about fear?"

"You mean, was I afraid? Of course."

"Trait was especially cruel to women. Maybe that's why you came. You told him on the phone that you wouldn't be his 'prize'."

She still resented him for that phone call. "Well, he was right about one thing. That I would align myself with a killer."

"He meant that you would let a man do the killing for you. You know that the only way you can avoid being the prize is to participate, to do your own fighting."

She didn't like that. "I don't know what he meant," she protested.

"Look here, at Gilchrist. The government was oppressing the prisoners who finally reached their breaking point and revolted. Now they are in charge of the town—but here we come, fighting back. That's the price of power. The history of the human race was built on insurrection. Now look at you. In a world run by men, you've won real independence—money, a position of some influence. You've beat the system. The problem now is that as you move into power, getting a taste of it, you find it's a lot easier to tear down the establishment than to build one up. Trait is learning that now. So there's trepidation. There's a stall, a pullback. Before you cut the emperor's throat, you think: Do I really want to do this? Do I want the responsibility this will bring? That moment of hesitation is when most people fail. You've got to move past that fear. You've got to kill that fear, however it manifests itself."

She shook her head as though to clear it. "Are you talking about Gilchrist now, or a gender war?"

"You came here to meet Trait so that you could go back and tell the world, *I looked the beast in the eye. I faced the Minotaur and here is what I learned.* Trait is a butcher and a sadist, with a special brutality toward women, and you came here to take away his power to scare you. You want to capture him in your book and trap him there for good. For you, killing a man and writing about him are the same thing. You came here to kill Luther Trait."

She must have been even wearier than she realized. His words almost made sense. Her thoughts were like doll furniture and he was reaching inside her head and rearranging it to his liking. His persuasion was both seductive and alarming. "Why are you doing this to me?" she said.

Dr. Rosen entered carrying Polk's sopping red bandage to the trash. If he noticed them talking, he didn't care. "Forget the soup," he said, washing his hands in the sink. "He's asleep now."

"Later?" said Kells.

"Maybe."

Kells turned off the boiling water. "How long?"

Dr. Rosen was washing his hands forcefully under the steaming water. "He's losing too much blood," he said, then stopped and turned off the faucet and shook his head. He returned to the sitting room.

Kells added water and stirred, pulling a small plastic bag from his pocket and crumbling some brown herbs into the broth.

Rebecca looked again. Kells was stirring small buds of marijuana into the soup.

"From Coe's pack," he said. "If he wakes up again, give this to him."

The scent of the pot rose with the steam as Rebecca watched the buds spin in the middle of the mug. Instead of flakes falling before her eyes, it snowed behind them now, the drifts piling up inside her head.

Kells and Tom Duggan left and Rebecca stood at the front door, looking past the driveway to the sliver of street. The snow fell in silence and nothing moved. She shut the door on the white yard and locked it behind her.

TOM DUGGAN LED KELLS ALONG THE ABANDONED TRAIN ROUTE IN-to town. The railway was canopied with trees, narrow and straight. With their three-day beards and sullied clothes they looked like tramps who didn't know the trains had stopped running.

There was no high ground from which to spy or mount an ambush on Gilchrist Common. The only way to view it was to go there. Post Road ran straight through it, start-ing with the general store and library, and ending at Dug-gan's Funeral Home and the police station. The loop around the common itself was optional. The land sagged behind the buildings along the bend, the school, town hall, and church. That was where Tom Duggan figured to make their approach.

It was mid-morning by the time they reached the inn, a quarter mile outside the center. From behind a snow-frosted evergreen, they watched men in parkas unloading storage from Fern's garage onto waiting sleds. One con carried an armful of rifles.

"They're pulling back," said Kells. "Moving every-thing into the center of town."

A man with a rifle on his hip stood under the oak near Fern's country swing. He turned his back to the road and Kells and Tom Duggan withdrew deeper into the trees.

They skirted the western perimeter where the land dipped to the farms below. Stout Scotch pines provided cover near the top of the rise, Kells staying close to the backs of the buildings, watching for convicts.

The barking frightened Tom Duggan. He was worried about being scented and betrayed. It grew more spirited as they approached. "What do we do?" he asked.

"Where are they?"

The dogs sounded like they were on the other side of the church, to the left. "There were never dogs here before."

"They'd be on us now. Must be tied up." Kells looked at the backs of the buildings. Tom Duggan had never viewed Gilchrist Common from this perspective. "We need to get inside one of these buildings."

Tom Duggan looked down the lane and settled on the building he knew best.

"There's a dirt room in back of the church. They buried the dead there before the town was incorporated, stored munitions there during the Revolutionary War. It's where I keep my digging tools now. The old door doesn't lock. Stairs lead right up into the sacristy."

Kells nodded and followed him along the crest of the rise, past the back of the town hall, moving toward the dogs. The barking turned to howling, though its intensity began to wane. Tom Duggan could finally see them, dark German shepherds racing around the cemetery left of the church. About ten of them were penned there, strong, black beasts snapping at the air behind the spiked iron fence, baring their teeth and trampling the graveyard snow.

The narrow lane behind the buildings was clear on both sides. The square wooden door was now twenty steps away.

Tom Duggan ran for it. The old knob turned and the hinge squeaked as usual and the familiar scent of machine oil and earthy musk wafted out of the dark cellar.

Kells was at his side. The dogs were whimpering now, crying and no longer howling. They stood on the fence, dancing on their hind legs and pawing at the spikes. No more ferocity, just dogs whining to be let out.

They entered the cellar. Tom Duggan tugged the noisy door shut and they stood in earthen darkness. "Guard dogs," said Kells.

"What are they doing here?"

"I don't know. But they seemed to like us."

No movement above. Light outlined the ceiling trap-door and Tom Duggan led Kells past his workbench to the stairs. Their boots croaked guiltily on the wood planks.

Tom Duggan lingered in the downcast light as Kells eased open the trapdoor and moved to the front of the church. When no other noise followed Kells's boot treads, he surfaced.

There was a long vestment closet in the sacristy and an old bowl sink and stacks of printed announcements. Tom Duggan ventured out past the backdrop wall and onto the modest altar overlooking the empty pews. Kells was halfway down the center aisle. Muddy paw prints stained the red carpet and the church reeked of wet dog. It was like the yellow snow on the graves outside. The desecration gnawed at Tom Duggan.

Special collections from the prison-enriched congregation paid for the new stained-glass windows, four to each side wall and two tall lancets on either side of the double front doors. The colored glass impeded the view of the town center—Tom Duggan hadn't considered this—but the hinge windows opened at the bottom for ventilation, and even better, the front windows featured clear pieces of glass mixed in with the stained ones. He joined Kells near the doors.

The flakes were coming down wetter and smaller outside, a slow, white rain over Gilchrist Common. For just an instant Tom Duggan saw the town center as it had always been—the row of storefronts from the police station to the general store, the high flagpole, the snow-washed gazebo—everything normal and fixed. Then two slow-moving men in heavy coats approached with rifles in their hands, shuffling along the sidewalk.

Kells ducked and moved to the left of the church and Tom Duggan followed. They looked out from the honey-tinted glass of Jesus' feet.

The cons had paused at the front of the cemetery fence. The dogs turned ferocious again, racing around the small stone markers, jaws snapping hungrily. The men barked back at them and continued on in the direction of the Masonic Hall.

Kells pried open the bottom of the window. The barking had tailed off again as the dogs returned their attention to the church, whining and jumping over one another at the rear fence.

Kells made a grunt of interest and they walked back to the front windows. A sled from the inn skied along Post Road, moving right to left, past the library and the bank and stopping to unload at the police station. The brick station was the center of activity. Three figures lurked on its cleared front steps, guarding the entrance, too far away for Tom Duggan to make out faces or weapons. At the curb in front was a beaten pickup with a large machine gun mounted on its bed.

Duggan's Funeral Home was across the corner from the station. A bulldozer was working on his front lawn, plugging up the street with mounds of snow, frozen sod and all.

The loop road was recently plowed, and a large van was parked directly across the street from the church. Bold red letters on its sliding door spelled *CNN*.

"They must have cut the prison broadcast," said Kells. "They're hunkering down here in the center. They brought the TV van back for safekeeping." Kells stood back from the window. "I'm going to take it out."

"You're not going out there," said Tom Duggan.

But Kells had a way of announcing things that precluded debate. "I can eliminate their broadcast capability."

"What if someone's inside?"

Kells was unsnapping his parka. He had the taser on his belt. He moved it to his coat pocket.

"What about me?" asked Tom Duggan.

Kells pulled his ski mask on, then rolled it up to look

like a wool cap. "Just wait here and tell me when I'm
clear to go."

Tom Duggan looked outside again. There was plenty
of activity in the center but none near the church. The van
would block him from sight. The only worry was another
two-man patrol.

"Clear," said Tom Duggan.

A gust of snow and the door closed and Tom Duggan
was alone.

He watched Kells cross the road to the van, head down,
shoulders hunched, walking slow. From behind, he easily
passed for a prisoner.

He knocked on the van door, two sharp raps. Tom
Duggan heard a garbled exchange of words. Kells stood
waiting for what seemed like a long time, then the door
slid open. Kells nodded up to the form inside—a black
man, wearing earmuffs and a long, loose coat—then
jabbed him with the taser and jumped inside.

Tom Duggan saw the con's legs twitching. Kells
turned and glanced back once at the church before shut-
ting the door.

He watched until he was confident Kells had raised no
alarms, then Tom Duggan turned back to the empty
church, moving from the vestibule to the rear pews. He
had held out hope that some sense of decency or even
superstition would have kept the marauders away from
his shop, but as the dogs in the cemetery proved, nothing
in Gilchrist was sacred anymore, not faith or death or
personal property. They were tearing up his land, they
were running through his house.

He needed to see this. He needed to know that there
was no going back.

Raucous barking intruded upon his thoughts. He realized he should have been watching the windows. The
front door opened behind him, too soon for it to be Kells.
Even before Tom Duggan turned, he knew he was in trouble.

The prisoner, hulking and broad-faced, pale with

brown hair matted flat on his hatless head, stood holding an automatic weapon on Tom Duggan. He stepped forward smiling like a retarded boy at the entrance to a zoo.

REBECCA HAD HER LAPTOP OPEN ON A TRAY TABLE IN THE parlor. On the screen was a page from her long-gestating sequel to *Last Words*. She read the prose again. It was flat and meaningless. Writing had become a safe haven for her, a place she escaped to in order to avoid life's conflicts, rather than confront them. She had been hiding inside her work just as she had spent the past year hiding in Vermont.

She selected the entire text of her manuscript, beginning to end, blackening the display. The delete button was smooth under her fingertip. She scooped a tiny thread of dust off it, coming within a few pressure-pounds of executing the self-destruct command. She wanted to know what it would feel like. She tested the tension of the key spring, the machine gently whirring beneath her finger. But caution prevailed in the end. She closed her notebook before doing any permanent damage.

She went to the kitchen. The pantry jars held only cookie crumbs and cracker salt, the refrigerator an open liter of ginger ale. She was hungry finally, her stomach so empty it hurt. She took in the kitchen and tried to picture Tom Duggan's mother puttering around there. There were safety rails in the shower stall upstairs and handlebars around the raised toilet, triggering memories of Rebecca's own grandmother near the end, and the house in Manchester with the sun porch and the dishwasher that connected to the sink by a hose. She remembered her grandmother's sweet tooth, and Rebecca pursued this instinct into the dining room, to the buffet table there, but found only table linens and tarnished silverware. She climbed the stairs to the master bedroom, undaunted, zeroing in on the night table at the sunken side of the mattress. The drawer handle was still slick with cream.

Jackpot. An open bag of Brach's candies and a package of Nestlé Crunch bars.

Rebecca hurried downstairs to share this bounty with the others. They were in the living room, Dr. Rosen watching the TV and Mia sitting with Polk. The old man lay on a brocaded sofa, his potbelly barely rising beneath an unfinished brown-and-orange afghan with crocheting needles still hooked in the corner. His skin was papery and his lips were downturned at the corners, parted as though in whisper. He looked like a thing ravaged by the elements. She thought of a downed tree in the woods, the bark husk rotting away, the wood core brittled and infested.

His eyes opened. He brows knit when he saw her.

Rebecca dropped the candy in the kitchen. She heated up the soup in a microwave oven and took Mia's place, sitting in the cushioned rocking chair at Polk's head.

She blew on the first spoonful and touched it to his cracked bottom lip. He swallowed and she fed him a second spoonful and a third. His throat worked sluggishly.

"This is service," he said hoarsely.

She smiled and shook her head to keep him quiet. A drop escaped to his bristly chin. His eyes lingered on Rebecca's face, exploring it like a feeding infant.

After a few minutes of patient swallowing his eyes began to drift. She kept feeding him. The soup had cooled enough for her to lift the mug to his lips, and he gazed at the ceiling as he sipped. His interest lagged and she pulled the afghan back up to his neck, then lay her hand over his forehead where fresh beads of sweat glistened. It was like touching a warm ball of cracked leather. She felt the transfer of heat from his fevered head to her palm.

"Oh, boy," he whispered.

She took the mug and the spoon back into the kitchen. Coe was there. He was supposed to be watching the windows. He could smell the soup's secret ingredient. Re-

becca offered him the rest, but he declined with a
sorrowful shake of his head. He wanted a clear mind for
whatever was coming. So did she. That surprised her.

She brought out the candy and they sat and ate. The
television reported that the prison feed had been terminated at the source. They kept replaying the moment of
interruption: cons sprawled out dead or dying in the
corridors, languid with dementia, choking on their own
blood—suddenly effaced by static.

Polk had a fit of sleepy mumbling behind them, clutching at his afghan. Coe looked particularly distressed. Rebecca tried to get him talking. She asked him what his
plans were after high school.

"Going to Austin, Texas," he said. "A friend of mine
moved down there with his dad two years ago. I went last
summer for a visit. He lives on a ranch. Do you ride?"

"Horses?" she said. "Not since I was a girl."

"I've been practicing. His dad's company does web
pages, and he said he could get me work to pay for college. Only, my parents have problems with it being so far
away. These are two people who met in South America
in the Peace Corps."

"You should go," interjected Dr. Rosen.

Coe was surprised by this unlikely source of support.
"I'm working on them," he said.

"My son, when he was about your age, went out to
school in California, and it was the best thing for him.
You need to do these things young. You never know what
time will bring."

Rebecca was interested. "How do you mean?"

Dr. Rosen had the rocking chair, but he was still. "My
son was lost six years ago. An avalanche on his honeymoon. One last run before dark."

Mia said, "How awful."

"They say that, if the force of the falling snow doesn't
kill you, it's a gradual suffocation. The snow freezes and
you re-breathe your own carbon dioxide. I just wonder
what he thought of at the end. He was completely im-

mobilized, and it was dark. I wonder if he thought of me at all. How did he see me? Waving to him on the first day of school? Cheering him on at some game? Sitting around the kitchen table? But probably it was all just panic, senseless, formless." He smiled wistfully. "Rhonda and I, we just drifted apart. The tide separated us and we could have fought it, but neither one did. Because who has the strength? We stayed together for Jacob, for his memory. Darla—she was young. She was open to things. Full of life, yet with her own troubles. She needed encouragement and guidance. I know these are just excuses."

The telephone interrupted him. They others jumped a little at the ring. Polk gasped.

Rebecca stood and went to the kitchen. It scared her at first, but Kells was the only one who knew they were there. He must have brought a cell phone with him.

She picked up the cordless receiver. It smelled faintly of old lady. "Hello?"

"You made me use the phone. I don't like to use the phone."

The drawl was slight but distinct. A chill came over Rebecca, a creeping dread, the room becoming smaller.

"I saw you writing," said Jasper Grue. "In your computer."

Rebecca shrank into a crouch. She tried not to make any noise. She could hear him breathing in her ear. She looked at the kitchen windows. He was on a phone somewhere, he was—

Crouching, Rebecca made her way down the front hallway to the dining room. Opaque yellow curtains draped the windows like desert veils. She turned and saw the parlor tray table from there.

Rebecca crept to the windows. The curtains were parted in the middle, and outside she saw boot prints in the snow. They came out of the woods and right up to the snow-mounded shrubs. There, a small patch of snow was yellowed.

The address on the mailbox. He looked her up in the phonebook. But where was he calling from?

Was he in the house?

She pulled back from the window, striking the table and rattling the crystal punch bowl centerpiece.

"Where'd your men go?" he said.

He had been near when they left. Had he killed them?

She went ducking back into the kitchen to the weapons bag. She was pawing through it.

Mia and Dr. Rosen stood in the doorway, frightened, and Rebecca motioned for them to duck down.

"Did they go to town?" he said.

Rebecca pulled a gun from the duffel bag and forced the words. "I've got a gun. We all do."

"All of you? The girl and the boy too? And the sick old man in the toboggan? You think guns'll keep me away?"

Rebecca sat against the wall near the door, out of sight from all the windows. She gripped the phone hard and did not know what to do.

His slow drawl was just as she had imagined it. "Here's Bert's final testament. *'Don't do this, dear God, I have money, please.'* He was crying. I wrote that just after I cut him. The wife was trying to scream through her gag, but when I pulled it off her she went quiet, like she weren't there anymore. *'Gloria,'* she said. Just once, just like that. *'Gloria.'* Must be a daughter. 'Course, you're a great artist. Your last words count. I expect much more from you."

Rebecca pushed the on/off button and the receiver clattered across the kitchen floor.

SPOTTY STOOD FOR AWHILE NEAR THE BULLDOZER WORKING outside the funeral home. He was watching the snow fall in front of his face.

Something had been bothering him, and now he knew what it was. The church looked a lot like the town hall except that there was no cross on top of the white spire. The TV van was parked outside of it now. Next to the church was the graveyard where Spotty kept his dogs.

They were quiet. No stray barks or howls.

Spotty walked across the common. He went in a straight line, stepping over the low white post fence with almost no change in his stride, snow swirling in his wake. Passing the bandstand, he saw the dogs congregating at the rear of the graveyard. He heard a little whimpering.

One of the dogs heard him as he passed the TV van. She barked once, jumping to her feet leading the charge at him across the cemetery. They planted their front paws in the beaten snow there and raged at him, full-throatedly, though Spotty noticed a couple of them backing off. Two or three of them whined and trotted back to the church wall with a grace Spotty himself lacked.

He bore their hatred without understanding it. Something in the church had their attention. Something there pleased them. Spotty felt more jealousy than either confusion or anger. With one stride he mounted the steps to the double doors.

The man standing inside wore a long, black coat and a hunting cap with ear flaps. Spotty got the drop on him and the man turned but did not otherwise move. Spotty saw the fear right away. He knew there was no one else inside the church.

"Hands," Spotty said.

The man's hands went up very slowly. They were gloved. This was one of the rebels who blew up the gas station.

"Coat off," Spotty said.

Carefully, like a man removing wet clothes, the rebel pulled off his coat and laid it over one of the pews. He wore a gun belt.

"Gun out," Spotty said.

The gaunt man took his gun out and set it on the bench next to him.

"Turn around," Spotty said.

The rebel was obedient. He stood with his arms above his head as though the church were flooded and water was rising.

The front doors opened and Spotty wheeled. He saw the earmuffs and black skin and long coat of the TV van ex-con. Spotty nodded to him, easing up on his gun, a quick glance back at the rebel.

"Got one," Spotty said. Disappointment became pride. "My dogs led me to him."

Spotty was pleased with himself. He knew that saving the guard dogs was a good idea. He wished he had a radio to call Luther.

The ex-con closed the doors on the snow. "Get his gun," Spotty said, turning back to cover the rebel.

He never felt the crack on the side of his head. He never heard it, he never saw it coming. He knew only he was on the floor now and the church was roaring. It tilted like a dream room and he clutched at the floor, rolling, sliding off.

When he opened his eyes again, the church righted itself. He was sitting up, clawing at the armrests of a high-backed wooden chair. He was tied to it by ropes around his neck, waist, arms, and legs. The ropes were tasseled at the ends, though it took several moments of confused staring to discern this.

He was coughing and spitting and his vision was blurred. Spotty had tasted mace before.

They had him at the foot of the church altar. The black ex-con from the TV van was there, standing before the big table like a priest.

But he was not the black ex-con from the TV van. This revelation sank in slowly. There was a hunting knife in the man's hand.

"Whathis . . . ?"

Spotty hissed a spray of blood, finding several of his teeth broken. He tested the ropes, but his neck was lashed to his wrists in such a way that the throat cord tightened with each squirm. Mace tears rolled down his face. The big chair was made of heavy wood. It would not crack under his great weight.

Kells said, "You know what this is."

Spotty understood only that there was more hurting to come.

Kells showed him a missile launcher. "We found this in the cloakroom."

Spotty said nothing. Spotty was confident he could stall them a long time.

Kells said, "Do you have one of these stored in every building?"

Spotty said nothing. The man finally just nodded and set the launcher back down on the table. Spotty wondered for a moment if he had somehow let on something. He was disoriented.

Kells said, "I want to know about the security arrangements here."

Spotty shook his head as best he could.

Another voice then, the rebel in the hunting cap, lurking on the periphery of Spotty's vision. "And the names of the two ricin towns."

Spotty blinked. He played like he was unaware what they were talking about.

Kells stepped off the altar to stand in front of him. He was playing with the knife in a casual, threatening way.

"You don't have to die. You should know that. This isn't the end unless you want it to be."

Pride surged in his veins and Spotty showed him his best face. The sweat squeezing out of his forehead was pure anticipation. He was eager to prove himself. He welcomed this test of will.

"We have little time," Kells said, checking the door, "so here is how we will proceed. I am going to ask you a question. If you fail to answer it quickly and truthfully, then you will choose where I cut you. You have five senses and therefore five choices: eyes, ears, nose, tongue, or hands. You select the sense you can best do without and then we start it all over. I ask the same question again, and you get another chance to avoid becoming a vegetable."

Spotty's throat swallowed beneath the rigid rope.

Kells said, "Most people choose the nose first. Smell is the most undervalued sense. Rarely has anyone progressed beyond sight."

Spotty tried to shake his head and was choked for the effort. He was tearing up again, not from fear but from the mace and the rope tension and his clumsiness in getting caught. He thrust his chin upward as best he could, straining against the cord, as though to say, *Ready.*

Kells studied him, waggling the knife in his hand. After a long moment, he backed off.

"Good soldier," Kells said. "I believe you will maintain your loyalty to Trait right to the end. Pride is all you have. I won't break your loyalty with pain."

He moved back onto the altar. Spotty watched him disappear behind the backdrop. They had to kill him. Stalling was Spotty's only chance, until a patrol noticed the dogs' silence and investigated.

He heard steps, numerous and confused, growing louder in the rear of the church. He smelled the German shepherd before he saw it. Kells came around from the sacristy holding one of the guard dogs by the collar.

She was nosing his leg and trying to jump up on him. Spotty's eyes burned at her playfulness.

The dog scented Spotty and stiffened. It lurched toward him, testing Kells's grip on her collar, a snarl strangled in her throat. She crouched on the crimson-red rug, growling menacingly at Spotty.

"You said these were your dogs," Kells said.

He patted her dark, silky coat, touching her in a way Spotty never could. The dog's eyes never left Spotty's, even as she dipped her head toward Kells, begging his hand.

Kells smiled. "Good *girl*," he said. "Trusting sort. They know cons from civilians."

Spotty swallowed his distress. The dog was so eager for affection, so immediately loyal.

As Kells held the collar with his left hand, the hunting knife reappeared in his right.

"I want you to tell me about the security arrangements here in town."

Spotty foolishly tested the rope again and paid the price. It scored the broad base of his neck, choking him as the dog's collar choked her.

Tom Duggan spoke. "Not on the altar," he said.

But Kells ignored him, stroking the dog's belly with the knife hand now. The dog lay contentedly and vulnerably on her side, still glaring at Spotty. Kells's stroke worked its way up to her throat.

Kells said, "Start with the police station."

Spotty tried to lift his feet. He tried to will himself out of the strangling chair.

The dog wriggled under Kells's hand, nuzzling the rug. Spotty saw the rebel's eyes darken as sometimes Luther's would.

Kells's hands moved quickly. The knife went *swish-swish* and up he stood.

The dog let out a half-yelp and rolled onto its legs, standing and stepping forward before slumping, blood gushing from her throat. She pushed forward on hind paws, crawling, then gave up, rolling off the altar step and bleeding out at Spotty's feet.

Spotty was choking. He could not breathe. The throbbing in his head reminded him of beatings from parents whose love he was refused.

Blood ran down the altar steps. Kells's voice came to him as though on a crazy breeze. "Nine more. Only you can spare them."

The stink of the opened dog. Spotty choked out two words, a gasp. "You Clock?"

Kells looked down at him from the altar. He nodded once.

Spotty felt a flicker of relief. If he was going to be broken, at least he was going to be broken by the best.

TOM DUGGAN MOVED TOWARD THE ALTAR, CRAWLING WITH anxiety and repulsion. Kells had gone too far, and they had been there too long. Three dog carcasses lay around the altar. The hulking prisoner was slumped in the pastor's chair, head down, wheezing.

"We need to go," Tom Duggan said. "Someone's going to come."

There was blood on Kells's hands and a few flecks on his coat sleeves but none on his boots. He said, "We can't leave him here."

In his distress, Tom Duggan thought Kells was proposing that they take the con back with them. "What do you mean?"

"We can't let him tell the cons what we know."

He understood then. "But if they find him dead, won't they know we did it? Won't they assume we know everything anyway?"

Kells's expression blanked as though he were looking at something terrible but inevitable. "You wait here," he said.

He pulled out his taser and hit the con with a paralyzing charge. He sliced the ropes with his knife and the prisoner fell hard, flopping to the floor near one of the dogs. He twitched there, immobilized.

Kells replaced the pastor's chair on the altar and dropped his knife on the rug. He returned the rope and the launcher to the sacristy cloakroom, then started down the old planks underneath the trapdoor.

Tom Duggan regarded the prisoner, oafish and shivering like some great beast stranded outside its natural habitat. "You should never have escaped," Tom Duggan said.

The man's eyes were more sad than fierce. He heard

the paws running up behind the altar and his vision rolled to the backdrop.

The rest of the guard dogs came trotting into the sacristy before scenting Tom Duggan, bounding out to him, their cold bodies dancing around his legs.

He remained very still.

First one let out a low, feral growl and then the rest turned. Their coats grew prickly, teeth flashing white. The prisoner's eyes were tragic as the dogs broke for him: a many-mouthed beast, roaring.

THE MANIA-FRIGHT OF IMPENDING RAPE AND MURDER WAS NOT A wild, electric feeling. It was more like bugs and fungus of immense weight, creeping over Rebecca's skin to her mouth and nose, slowly suffocating her.

Kells and Tom Duggan returned an hour too late for Polk. Tom Duggan lifted his mother's unfinished afghan off Polk's face. His manner was studied and formal, and he replaced the shroud with great care.

Polk's body was bundled in flowery bedsheets and carried out to the side yard and laid next to Tom Duggan's mother. With shovels and gloved hands they buried him in the preserving snow. Tom Duggan said a few words at the end. *He was a true revolutionary. He was willing to tear down his world rather than see it compromised.*

The rest stood with head bowed, except for Rebecca, who never took her eyes off the woods.

Inside, they shed coats and gloves in the hallway and regrouped in the parlor.

"We know the other two towns," announced Tom Duggan, Kells standing behind him. "We got the information from one of the prisoners."

Rebecca reached for the easy chair and sat in it. She was reluctant at first to give in to elation. Any dashed hope would crush her now.

Dr. Rosen stammered. "How do you know it's true?"

"The zip codes of the two towns correspond to Luther Trait's ten-digit inmate number. That's how he selected them. The first five digits are the zip code of the first town, the second five are the second."

This was typical of Trait, a backward stab at the tech-nocracy that had imprisoned him.

Rebecca said, "Then it's over?"

"That part of it," said Tom Duggan.

Dr. Rosen blinked as though waking from sleep. Coe's graveside tears were gone. Mia's hand gripped her sweater over her belly.

It was over. Just like that. Grue and Trait and every-thing.

"What other part is there?" asked Rebecca, looking at Kells. "We just wait to be rescued now. You'll call your agency, and they'll end this."

Tom Duggan deferred to Kells, backlit by the window overlooking the snow graves. "They'll have to evacuate both towns before moving into Gilchrist. That will take time. We have a window of maybe ten hours."

Tom Duggan said, "We also learned their security setup. We were inside the center of town. We know where their manpower and firepower are concentrated."

"Of the forty or so cons left," said Kells, "at least half of them are out manning the barricades. A few others are out riding around burning down houses. That leaves less than twenty inside the center of town itself."

Rebecca was dizzy with relief. "Then it'll be easy for the army to come in and take them out."

Tom Duggan's face was serious and still. His were eyes of purposefulness, not victory. "They're vulnerable," he said.

Kells said, "We're going back in. We're going to hit the center of town at nightfall."

Bewilderment, then anger clouding out joy. Kells, she could understand. But not Tom Duggan.

Kells said, "This has never been about the other towns."

"Yes, it has," said Rebecca. "Yes, it has."

"This has been about this town, about us, and about them."

"That's crazy," said Rebecca. "You ended it. *You just ended it.*"

Kells shook his head sternly. "Polk," he said. "Fern. Mrs. Duggan."

Rebecca was growing frantic. "No!" she said. "Shooting your way into town isn't going to do anything for Polk or your mother. It is *over*!"

Tom Duggan was nodding, standing near his mother's crystal lamp. "It might not mean anything to you," he said, "but I was there. I saw them crawling all over the common like it was their own. If they were in your house, and you were tied up and forced to watch them tear down everything you worked to build, all the time thinking, 'If only I could get free . . .' We just got free. I don't want the government to finish this. They were going to give us up. I want to end this myself. Maybe I've got more at stake than the rest of you."

"You don't," said Kells.

"Those prisoners need to know what it's like. To lose everything. To be humbled."

Dr. Rosen was standing before the mantel. There was a mirror there, and he was looking at himself in it. He turned toward Tom Duggan and Kells. Rebecca almost reached after him.

"I want to go with you," Dr. Rosen said.

Rebecca got to her feet. "This is crazy!" She felt betrayed. "It's over! Don't you understand? You don't have to fight! No one has to fight!"

Dr. Rosen went to stand with the others. He looked pained, like a tired drunk lacking the sense to sleep it off. "They can't go alone," he said, then turned to Kells. "I'll go so long as the boy doesn't have to."

Coe looked shocked. His youthful fascination with the takeover had long since faded. He looked older now, and younger at the same time. He looked relieved.

"The kid stays here," said Kells. "Mia, too."

No one looked at Rebecca. Her face was flushed. She was all alone. She was desperate, searching for excuses.

"What if they can't clear out the towns in time?" she said. "What if Trait calls in the ricin too early?"

Kells said, "I can have them kill the telephone service from the outside."

"But there are cell phones. Pagers."

"They can move satellites if they need to."

"The television," she said weakly, knowing the feed had been cut.

"That's been taken care of."

It was Kells's censure that she felt most piercingly. "It's over," she said, pleading with him. "Why can't you just let it be over?"

No one moved until Kells started away. "I have a phone call to make."

Tom Duggan and Dr. Rosen went out after him, and Mia came to her side. "Why didn't you tell them?" she said. "Why didn't you say Grue called?"

Rebecca just shook her head. She couldn't even speak anymore. There were two Rebeccas, one who was angry, one who was scared. Right now the one who was scared was in full control. All she had to do was hide for a few more hours and she would be safe.

She was all alone in the parlor when Kells approached her, as she feared he would. He wore a flak jacket over his sweater now, a Micro Uzi hanging from his shoulder.

"Dr. Rosen said Grue called."

"It doesn't matter," she said. "It won't matter in a few more hours."

"What makes you think you'd be any safer here?"

She was beyond reason and she knew it. "A few more hours," she repeated.

"We need you."

She shook her head. She was trying not to cry.

"Instead of taking control, you're giving up all control. If we end this thing, then it's ours. We claim it. We give it meaning."

"There is no meaning. There's no meaning to any of this."

"You're still the writer here, aren't you? Still hanging back and observing, believing you can never be touched. Trying to outrun this vague fear that's chasing you. Spinning your fragile little fictions, these morality tales parroting empty truths. People standing up and fighting simply because that's the right thing to do. Only, as we see here, that's not exactly how it works. You lack the conviction of your characters."

She would not be shamed into action. "That sort of thing may work with Tom Duggan and Dr. Rosen—"

"You think I'm running some sort of game? Have you spent so much time making up cardboard heroes that you don't recognize plainspoken valor? I show people the path, either they walk it or they don't. You want to tag along and just make notes. You're like a thief, stealing lives for your books, then casting yourself as the hero. How did I become your villain here and not Trait?"

She was indignant, burning. "I am never going to write about this."

"Sure you will. You're a thief, that's what you do. But when you betray the rest of us in print, don't make this into anything more or less than it was. Others will want to forget, they'll want to deny what really happened here. People like yourself. They want to go on believing their freedom is actually free."

She sensed as much disappointment as anger from him, which wounded her more. *"I'm sorry,"* she whispered. "Is that what you want me to say?"

"I was just a guy doing a job," he said, starting away. "Write that."

THE FIFTH NIGHT

LUTHER TRAIT WAS IN THE POLICE STATION WHEN THE FIRST SHOTS were fired. He took an AR-15 rifle from the front table and was out on the front steps before the tarp was off the M60.

Gunfire burst about the common. The first thing he noticed was that the guard dogs were loose. Their black bodies were sharp against the whitened scene, legs working hard in the deep snow. Two remained near the cemetery, tearing at a screaming con.

The Marielitos rushed down the walkway from the funeral home, ready for a fight.

Trait advanced along the curved road, scanning the common for rebels. Two snarling German shepherds were cut down, but no rounds landed anywhere near him. The random pistol cracks and rifle bursts lacked the cadence of an exchange.

Then loud reports blasted behind him. Quintano, the head of the Mexican Mafia, fired the pickup-mounted M60. The *bam-bam-bam-bam* flipped a dog near the gazebo. But lacking human targets, the M60 fire stopped. The yelling and the barking died away.

Silence fell with the snow. Trait paused before the Masonic Hall, awaiting a second wave of attack, or perhaps even the first.

One of the ex-cons was running toward him, pointing back at the church with his gun. "The dogs!" he yelled.

Trait said, "The rebels! Where are they?"

"I don't know. The dogs came at us out of the church."

Trait saw the open church doors past the CNN van.

Trait looked for a familiar hulking figure as the cons began emerging from their hiding places.

"Where's Spotty?" he said.

The ex-con was holding his wrist, his hand bloodied from a dog bite.

Trait started for the church. His fury increased with his speed. Spotty and his fucking dogs. Trait passed the con at the cemetery fence, his coat in rags, two gutted dogs whimpering at his feet.

Trait rushed inside the church. Two more dogs stood on the altar, turning and running at him. Trait dropped both of them in the center aisle as he advanced to the front pews.

He saw Spotty twisted on the altar steps. Trait slowed and reached for the back of the first pew before going to him. He rolled the big man over.

Spotty was dead. The dogs had been eating him.

Trait sat down on the first step. He looked out at the empty church, the rifle resting across his lap. Trait felt something leave him then.

Trait turned back to the altar in a daze. He saw the dog carcasses. He saw the bloody knife on the rug. Spotty had fought them off.

Immediately something wasn't right. Trait resisted his hunch. He didn't like where it was taking him.

He had never seen Spotty use a knife. Spotty's trusted Micro Uzi was nowhere to be seen.

Then he noticed the blood on the armrests of the celebrant's chair.

Others were coming in the doors now. It was instinct that kept Trait from telegraphing his concerns to the approaching cons.

He went behind the altar to the wide closet there. The rocket launcher lay under the choir robes, just as they had left it. If the rebels had gotten to Spotty, wouldn't they have found the launcher?

He returned to the altar. The cons were coming to the front rows near Spotty's body, sitting down. The Marielitos entered but remained at the far end of the center aisle. Their clannish impudence angered Trait now. Like Spotty, he had saved them from slaughter when he didn't have to. He had delivered them from ADX Gilchrist, asking only loyalty in return.

The thing that had driven them apart, the threat of Clock and the rebels, was now the only thing holding them together.

Inkman slipped inside the front door in his hooded coat, the ruckus having drawn him out of wherever he was hiding. He came down the left side of the church, steering clear of the Marielitos.

Some were looking at Trait now. Maybe they wanted words from him. Maybe they wanted an explanation. Maybe they wanted him to rally them to battle.

Of all of them, Spotty should have been the last man standing. His sudden death took something out of the rest.

Trait's voice was dead. "Get back to your posts."

Hard, tired stares. Trait moved into the center aisle. The Marielitos stood between the last rows, and Trait came up against them. He met the leader's smug, shiny eyes.

One of the others moved slightly to let him through. There were no words, nothing.

He stopped on the bottom step outside even as the cons pushed past him. Daylight was dying in the sky.

Something else wasn't right in the common. He faced the news van they had brought back from the prison. It was parked across the street from the church doors, yet no one had come out of it during the shooting.

Trait went inside alone. He showed no reaction when he saw the coatless ex-con slumped dead on the floor. The tangle of cut wires concerned him more, but again his instinct was to do nothing—not out of respect for Spotty this time, but out of disdain for Inkman, for the Marielitos, and all the rest.

He set the inside lock before stepping back outside and closing the van door.

Inkman was waiting for him in the snow. There was
concern on his face, and fear, and still a bit of the condescension in his manner that Trait had come to despise.

"Did Spotty know?" said Inkman.

Trait stared hard. Doing the weak man then and there
would have been like admitting he was right. The Marielitos lurked inside the church, almost within listening
range.

"Did Spotty know about the zip codes?" Inkman said.

Trait grabbed the soft fabric over Inkman's shoulder.
Inkman tried to pull away in surprise. Trait could feel him
shivering through his coat.

"You stay with me now," said Trait. Inkman tried to
twist away as Trait muscled him across the common toward the police station. "I don't want you out of my sight
again."

REBECCA ONCE DREAMED THERE WAS A KILLER LOOSE ON WEST 95th Street.

She was home writing when detectives from the 24th Precinct buzzed. She answered all their questions while drawing them out as to the particulars of the crimes. As they rose to leave, one of the detectives noticed a copy of *Sexual Homicides: Pattern and Motives* on her bookshelf. He asked her about it. His partner scanned a few manuscript pages, then proceeded to her office. Rebecca followed, explaining to them who she was, but they would not allow her past the door. Inside her file cabinet they found newspaper clippings following their case. They pulled down books from her shelves: *Bite Mark Protocol, Bloodstain Pattern Interpretation, Suspect Interview and Interrogation.* There were police texts on evidence gathering, forensics, suspect profiling, sexual deviance. Detailed notes on knife wounds, ligature marks, tire impressions, and the amount of time the human body takes to decompose.

These were reference tools, she told them. She was Rebecca Loden, the author. She went through her apartment searching for a copy of *Last Words* but failed to find one. Even her framed dust jacket, with her photograph on the back cover—hands folded behind an elegant writing desk, radiating confidence, auburn hair shining—was missing from the wall. One detective recited her Miranda rights as the other clasped his handcuffs around her wrists.

*   *   *

SHE REMEMBERED THE DREAM NOW AS SHE STOOD AT MRS. Duggan's kitchen window, watching the daylight bleed out of the Vermont sky. Her books were her alibis. Who else but a psychopath has such interests?

The snow was falling gently now, finally tapering off. Everything was ending, it seemed. Just not soon enough.

They heard the sled engine again. It varied, ranging from a growl to a distant purr. When the wind changed, she smelled smoke.

The house-burning cons were circling closer. She was anxious for dusk. The glow of the flames would give her some idea of how close they were. From the upstairs windows, she had seen black smoke in the distance through the fading snow.

Be patient, she told herself. She wanted so badly for this all to be over. *All you have to do now is wait.*

She turned from the window to Coe and Mia. Mia sat on a chair near the oven with her hands folded between her thighs to keep them from trembling. Coe was rocking back and forth as though trying to stay warm.

"We'll be out of here by morning," Rebecca said, hoping to reassure them all.

The telephone rang and Mia jumped to her feet. Rebecca tried to ignore it. Coe looked at Rebecca as though she had done something terrible.

There was no answering machine, and each ring pealed through the house like a scream.

"Don't answer it," said Mia, both an admonition and a plea.

But the phone kept ringing. He knew she was there.

"He'll come if I don't," Rebecca decided. "I can stall him," she said, and went to the wall phone.

She gave it one more chance to stop ringing before she lifted the receiver.

"Saw 'em go," said Grue. "All three men. Leaving you alone."

"Not alone." She nearly screamed it, trying to calm down.

"They looked geared up for a fight. They were going to town, weren't they."

It's over, she wanted to tell him. But that would only force him to act.

"Funny thing," he said, his voice unreal in her ear. "I just called nine one one. Me, calling the police number. Only, it weren't the police that answered."

Before she could stop herself, Rebecca said, *"No."*

"I told them your men were on the way. An ambush will leave you all alone here, for good."

Rebecca slammed the phone back into its wall cradle and the others looked at her in alarm. When she realized she was covering her mouth, she removed her hands.

"He called the cons," she said. "He told them Kells and Tom Duggan and Dr. Rosen were coming."

"But . . ." said Mia.

"They're walking into a trap," said Coe.

Rebecca moved down the hallway to the front door, gaining speed. "I have to warn them."

"But how?" said Coe, following. "They have a . . . a thirty-minute head start on you."

She pulled on her coat as she moved into the parlor. "They were stopping to rest at the inn. Maybe I can catch them there."

"But how?" said Mia. "With Grue waiting outside for you."

Rebecca shouldered the laptop case containing her abortive novel.

"I'll go with you," said Coe.

Rebecca shot him an angry look as she moved. "No, you will not."

He followed her back into the kitchen to the weapons bag. "But what if it's a trap? What if he just wants you out there alone?"

Rebecca pulled a rifle out of the duffel bag and handed it to Coe. "You're staying here with Mia. Anyone tries to get into the house before you hear helicopters, shoot them through the door."

Mia was crying. "But you can't catch them. How will you make up the time without a sled?"

Rebecca stopped a moment. She looked around the kitchen but she was actually visualizing the area outside the house, the woods, the street, the neighbors. "Horses," she said. "That farmhouse across the street. There's a stable." She went back into the bag for guns.

"What if he's there?" said Coe.

The only gun left was Polk's old snub-nosed .38 revolver. She took it and stuffed it into her waistband against her back, grabbing a can of mace and an ice axe also. She stood and zipped her coat and fixed the Velcro loop of the axe to her laptop strap.

"You can't go out there alone," said Coe, gripping the rifle.

"How do you know that farmhouse isn't where Grue is calling from?" said Mia. "What if the horses are dead? What if—"

"Stop!" Rebecca grasped their shoulders to get them to shut up. Speed was everything now, and if she didn't get moving and keep moving, the others were done for. "Grue is out there. And now he knows I'm going out there." She shook these off as mere facts. "I have to do this. Grue is only here because of me. He's my responsibility." She released them and moved to the door. If she paused to think anymore about it—her odds of success, the dangers she faced—she would not be able to leave. "Just hide. Please."

She hurried out of the door into the freezing air. The snow formed a thick, luminous crust in the twilight. The woods were dark, and she stayed as far away from them as she could, moving along the driveway to the road.

He would be there soon. He would immediately pick up her trail. All her agonizing about Grue had been for nothing, all her running like standing still. And so near the end. Even in her lowest moments, Rebecca had always secretly believed she would walk away from Gilchrist. That was the arrogance of a born storyteller, a fantasist, a fabricator. Instead, she should have foreseen this happening and conserved her energy.

At least now she had a clear cause and direction. Necessity, not bravery, compelled her toward the road. It was smooth, white, silent. The axe handle flopped against her back. As she crossed to the other side, she shed a glove and took the revolver into her hand. Grue would anticipate the gun, but childishly she clung to this imagined advantage. She remained a number of paces away from the trees, tense and alert.

The faint sound of neighing horses thrilled her. She hurried along the roadside until she realized she was too far away for her presence to be disturbing them. Something else was making them cry.

She started to smell the smoke. Looking up, she noticed the glow beyond the trees, and Rebecca began to run again, leaping through the deep, crusty snow. A downed tree marked the end of the woods and the beginning of the wide clearing.

The farmhouse was on fire. Flames were taking the walls, and second-floor windows were popping, black smoke rushing out. A stable to the right of the house was not burning, though embers floating on the excited air drifted toward the haystacks like fireflies.

The blaze entranced her and for a few moments everything near—the forbidding trees, the distressed horses, the flames, and the flaring orange embers mixing with the dancing snow—took on an enchanted air. The conflagration of the farmhouse took on a poignancy she could not explain, and watching it rage, she felt at once a queer inner peace.

The horses whinnying returned her to the urgency of her task. The arsonist cons were near, as was Grue. She labored across the snow, hurrying in a straight line toward the stable to rescue the horses and take one for herself.

She did not see the ski tracks until she was nearly upon them. The bold light of the flames shadowed the grooves before the house and made them quiver. Rebecca slowed, following the tracks with her eyes to a two-passenger sled parked a safe distance away from the house.

A gruff voice called out to her over the crackling roar. Rebecca froze as the backlit form of a man emerged from behind the house, between it and the stable.

He was impossibly broad, a block form of a man, all shoulders and waist. He ran a few more steps toward her, aiming a silvery handgun.

It was not Grue. A second form then appeared behind the first, shorter and slightly hunched, wearing a dark pea coat and carrying a clublike torch.

They were the house-burning cons. Rebecca's revolver was weightless in her hand, pointed down at the ground snow.

Burly, the ex-con, yelled something at her that was lost to the blaze. Menckley came next to him, moving more tentatively, the house flames enlivening his scarred face and making it seem even more grotesque. Burly shook his handgun and she heard his voice now, demanding to know who she was and if she was alone.

Rebecca was so dumbfounded by this sudden turn of events that she gave no consideration to answering. She was focused on only two things: The cons' yells would bring Grue more quickly; and they would keep her from catching up with Kells and the others at the inn.

Burly came a few steps closer and ordered her to drop her gun.

Caught, she found herself wondering what Kells would do, and suddenly her choice was clear. Burly was agitated and would lose nothing by cutting her down right there.

She tossed Polk's revolver out to the side. It made a perfect impression in the top layer of snow and promptly disappeared below.

Burly yelled at her to take off her pack. She would have done anything to quiet him. She slipped the strap off her shoulder and set it down at her feet.

Menckley was telling him to shoot her. Instead Burly

ordered her away from the pack and she complied, moving back just a step or two.

Burly directed Menckley to retrieve the pack. They were close enough to Rebecca now that she could understand them.

Menckley wanted no part of it. "Just shoot!" he cried.

But Burly was ranting, "Get over there and see what she has in her goddamn pack!"

Menckley eyed the trees bordering the land, alive with flame shadow. "What about Clock?"

His fear resonated with Rebecca. It was the cons' belief in the fictional Clock that gave him real power. In the same way his imagined omnipotence excused the cons' failure to contain him, Grue was—to Rebecca—a mystical ghoul tracking her through the snow of her literary guilt, rather than just a man: a vicious killer, but still a living, breathing, fallible man. Her demonization of Grue in part relieved her of the responsibility of facing a mere mortal, endowing him with the force of all her fears.

The fearful side of her began to retreat. The angry side—the smarter side—was emerging.

She looked at the stable. Pockets of flame had burst to life in the dried hay bales, borne on cinders drifting in through the open front wall. The horses reared and kicked the wooden stalls.

Burly was pointing his gun at Menckley now. The two cons were yelling at each other, loud enough to be heard deep into the woods. The farmhouse was now fully engulfed, time slipping away like the smoke sailing into the night sky. Finally, with a howl of protest, Menckley doused his torch and shuffled toward her.

Burly's gun was trained on her again as Menckley reached the pack, just a few feet away. Menckley eyed her with apprehension and distaste. His face was a waxy swirl of scar tissue glistening with sweat.

Snowflakes became water on Rebecca's cheeks. She knew she had to make something happen here.

"It's over," she told him.

Menckley squinted at her, looking up from the pack. "What's over?"

"The army is on their way. Clock found out the ricin towns. This place will be swarming with FBI agents in another hour. Don't you two have a radio?"

Menckley straightened, looking at her with distrust. "We have a radio."

"Check it then. Why else would I be running around freezing my ass off out here?"

Menckley eyed her a second longer, then turned back to call to Burly. "She says that we should——"

Burly yelled and twisted, dropping to the snow as the rifle report echoed off the mountains.

Menckley screamed. Burly lay still before the consumed farmhouse. Menckley whipped around and looked frantically into the trees.

The noise shocked Rebecca but she was primed for action. She lunged forward and tore the ice axe from her laptop case with one pull. From her knees she brought it around low, burying the pick blade deep in the meat of Menckley's upper left thigh.

He howled and fell to one side. He gripped his leg just above the exposed blade and started to crawl, looking feverishly for Clock.

Rebecca, too, searched the farmland now, the horses neighing crazily behind her. She found a figure advancing from the street, nearing the light of the blaze. There was a rifle outlined in his hands. It was not Clock, and it was not Grue.

It was Coe. The flames oranged him, his eyes darting from the man he had killed to the flaming house to the scarred man trying to pull himself away. Then finally to Rebecca.

"I saw the glow from the window . . ." he began.

"Don't," Rebecca said, meaning *Don't waste time*. She moved quickly to the impression her revolver had left in the snow. "Where's Mia?"

"Back at the house." Coe was dazed but wired. "She wanted me to go."

Rebecca gave up her search, realizing she could have Burly's gun instead.

"You're going right back to her."

"No," Coe said. "I'm coming with you. You don't even know the way back to town."

She realized he was right.

Menckley had given up escape, and instead now lay cowering from Coe, pleading for his life. Coe watched him, perplexed.

The arrow silenced Menckley. A whittled wooden shaft with crow feathers and a sharp stone point entered his neck just above his clavicle, lodging there as his eyes went wide and blood spurted into the snow.

Coe spun, firing into the trees. Rebecca gave a quick, crazed glance that way—then started toward the stable at a run.

The horses were going wild as fire took the inside walls. The smoke was thick and gray as Rebecca fought her way along the stalls, throwing open doors and getting out of the way.

The farmhouse started collapsing just as she got clear, showering her with cinders. The crazed horses scattered, all except two, bucking and dancing in confusion. Two horses without saddle or bridle.

The ash cloud provided their cover. Coe helped throw her onto the jibing black colt, and after two attempts mounted the snorting palomino, the rifle slung over his shoulder.

Rebecca crouched for balance, gripping the colt's neck and mane. The flames moved things in the trees behind them and she did not trust the shadows. She was as spooked as her horse. Only at the last second did she realize her laptop case was still lying in the snow.

When the rest of the farmhouse slumped forward, the burning timber crushed the thin box into which she had emptied the past year of her life.

And the horses broke. Rebecca held on, hands, thighs, and heels, seeing nothing but white and black. At least one arrow whizzed past her head. The horses kicked hard through the deep snow, fleeing to the street.

KELLS, TOM DUGGAN, AND DR. ROSEN STOOD BEFORE ONE OF THE old telegraph poles across the street from the abandoned inn. They were trying to figure out how to blackout the center of town—how to bring down the live power and phone lines safely without electrocuting themselves. The wooden pole was too deep in the frozen earth to uproot. Kells was about to head to the inn garage for a ladder when he heard the horse hooves. He drew his gun, Tom Duggan and Dr. Rosen doing the same.

Rebecca's colt reared at the sight of the men. She swung off him, her legs weak from gripping. Coe dismounted onto the packed snow behind her. The horses were as glad to have them off their backs as Rebecca and Coe were to be off them.

The men lowered their weapons. Kells was the first to meet her.

"They're waiting for you in town," she said, breathless but relieved. "They know you're coming."

"How?"

"Grue saw you leave. He called nine one one."

"Grue?" Kells said, looking past her down the road.

"He might have taken another horse." She turned and looked back now, as did Coe. "We ran into the arsonists." She hurriedly told them the rest. At the end of it, Kells looked proud. "What will you do?" she asked.

The others waited for his response. Kells moved a step or two back away from them, his face unreadable. Then he spun and opened up his Micro Uzi on the crossbar of the telegraph pole.

The rounds chewed the brittle wood and the wires

snapped and gave way, sparking and falling to the snow.

A quarter mile ahead of them, beyond the trees at the turn in the road, the dim aura of artificial light winked out like a snuffed candle.

Rebecca turned at the sound of the hooves. The horses were galloping back the way they came. They disappeared around the darkness of the bend, and as the gun burst echoed off the mountains, silence returned, more gravid than before.

Kells lowered his weapon. "We're going in," he said. "The circumstances haven't really changed. Only they're expecting three now—not five."

He looked to Rebecca and Coe. "Right," Rebecca confirmed. "Five."

Kells nodded confidently. "We'll let them steep in darkness a minute before starting in."

The others remained quiet. Rebecca was quietest of all, listening for Grue's galloping hooves. The inn loomed on the roadside like a dark sarcophagus sealed in ice. The country swing was coated with snow like the white dust of a thousand years. Rebecca spotted something small moving at the foot of the sprawling oak that formed one leg of the swing. It was Ruby, Fern's cat, working diligently atop the frozen crust. Excited, Rebecca looked closer—only to find Ruby picking meat off a dead woodpecker's carcass, watching Rebecca with bright, hungry eyes.

Rebecca's bare hand went to her throat. There was violence in the air, like pollen or plague, descending on them with the snow. She retreated to Kells who held the two plastic fuel jugs from the Irving station. He handed one to Tom Duggan.

"You two take the kid," he said. "Move to the church steeple as quickly as you can, and make a lot of noise on the way. I'll take the writer."

Kells's matter-of-fact bravado excited Rebecca. She was glad to be paired with him. For some reason she wanted to be near when he struck.

"They don't have any flak vests," said Tom Duggan.

"We're two short," said Kells. "Whoever wears the vest takes the lead."

Dr. Rosen turned to Coe. "You stay behind me, no matter what. I mean it."

Coe nodded, his rifle hanging low. "Yes, sir."

Kells handed Rebecca the second gasoline jug, and she was surprised to find herself anxious to get into town. "See you at the police station," Kells told the others, with neither ceremony nor good-bye, and Rebecca walked beside him toward the dark thickness of the trees.

A RICH, RURAL BLACKNESS SOAKED THE COMMON, WITH ONLY THE ground snow retaining some light. From the police station window, Trait could barely see the outlines of the other buildings.

Inkman was starting to flip out in the darkness behind him. "I told you that call was no hoax," he said.

The thought of a renegade convict tracking the rebels across the countryside exasperated Trait. With five such soldiers he could have put down this insurgence before it began.

He saw shadows emerge from the school, two of his cons stepping outside like children ignored too long in a game of hide-and-seek. He wanted to shoot them himself.

The silence and the blackout were too much for Inkman. "Why did we let them cut the power?"

"Because we knew we could not prevent it," said Trait. He turned and found Inkman in the gloom. "Three men, the caller said. Do you think we can handle three men?"

"One of them is Clock."

Inkman's weakness chafed Trait's warrior ethic. Trait started toward him. "We were all just hired hands," Trait said. "Isn't that how you saw it? Employees. Instruments of your revenge."

Inkman took one step backward. "What are you talking—"

"Once the money started rolling in, you were going to force another coup. Only this time you were going to see to it that *I* was killed and *you* were put into power. Tear down one government, set up another in its place. That's what you said you and Clock used to do. As soon as we got clear, you were going to run this town like it was your own little country. That was going to be your ultimate revenge on the CIA."

"And you thought *I* was cracking under pressure," said Inkman. "You thought Clock was getting to *me*."

Inkman was unconvincing. "I think he will get to you," said Trait. "Any minute now."

Gunshots erupted at the far end of the street. Pistol fire, answered by rapid automatic bursts. Inkman's eyes jumped and he backed away toward the radio room.

DeYoung came out past him, rushing from the radio room with his headset wire dangling. "Luther, they—"

"I know. They cut everything."

It was a brief exchange, just long enough for Inkman to go into his boot for a gun.

He aimed it at Trait and DeYoung. Trait said nothing, staring at Inkman.

Fear raised Inkman's voice. "Stand together, you two."

Trait would not move. DeYoung drifted slowly to him. Trait's eyes never left Inkman.

Inkman reached for a desk phone, listened a moment, then dropped the receiver and moved to another desk. He punched buttons to be sure. The phone lines were dead.

Trait said, "Who are you calling, Errol?"

Inkman remembered the cell phones in the battery chargers near the door. He flipped one open, working the buttons with manic confidence. "They took everything away from me," he said. "My wife, my life, everything." The phone was dead. He put another to his ear. "They thought they ruined me. They thought I was broken, done." He dialed quickly with his thumb. "Now I'm taking away one of their towns."

"What for?"

"Spite. And it will force the government to cooperate with us here. I'll make them call off the rebels."

Inkman had lost all sense. A beeping noise signaled a disruption in service, and he tried to dial out again, hammering the desk with the cell phone when it failed.

"They took out the wireless," he said, troubled. "They would never have risked killing the service, unless . . ."

"Unless they were coming over the mountains," said Trait.

"Spotty," realized Inkman, looking at Trait. "What have you done? What have you done?"

"What have I done?" Trait knew then what it was like for Spotty to have lain there while his dogs tore at him. Trait had had enough. "Get out of here," he told Inkman, barely controlling his fury.

Inkman blinked, confused. He had the gun.

Trait took a step toward him. "Clock is coming for you now, and you will meet him."

The window glass rattled as Quintano opened up the M60 outside the doors. The racket was tremendous.

Inkman backed to the twin doors, stopping there, still covering Trait.

Trait took another step toward him.

Inkman threw open the door and was gone.

Trait turned quickly, directing DeYoung to grab a rifle from the front table. "I'll get him," DeYoung said.

"No," said Trait. "Stay here and man the windows. This is the fallback point. We have to hold this place."

The volume of the gun report rose again as the door opened. Trait spun angrily, expecting Inkman.

It was the leader of the Marielitos. He was alone, coatless, twin holsters strapped across his flak vest bandito-style. Two more guns were in his hands, aimed at Trait and DeYoung.

DeYoung was at the weapons table. Trait held his open hand toward DeYoung to keep him still.

The Marielito's eyes were merry with savagery. He had come there to kill.

Trait yelled over the M60 noise. "Inkman just left," he said. "Clock's mark."

The Marielito glanced back at the door. He wanted killing, but he wanted vengeance more.

Trait yelled, "He's the one to shadow—if you still think you can beat Clock."

Challenged, the Marielito straightened and backed to the doors. He smiled with gritted teeth, to let Trait know he was next, and then swung out of the door.

Trait left DeYoung to cover the windows and hurried down the dark hallway to the twinned cells at the end.

A backup bulb over the fire-alarm box cast the room dim red. Warden James was standing at the bars, listening to the gunfire outside.

"It's happening," the warden said.

Trait unlocked the cell door and tossed away the keys, grabbing the warden by the shoulder. He walked him roughly back along the hallway to the door by the radio room.

Outside, Trait could see Inkman's footprints cutting diagonally across the smooth parking lot snow. He could just make out the backstop of a baseball field in the distance.

The Marielito had skirted the lot to the trees. Trait saw his shadow disappearing there.

Inkman's run, leading Clock away from the center of town, gave Trait a fighting chance. And if the Marielito got lucky and ambushed Clock, all the better.

Trait saw someone coming toward them from the bulldozer, a dark shadow holding two guns. Trait pushed the limping warden ahead of him with one hand, drawing his gun with the other.

It was another of the Marielitos. Something had split them up. He was pointing his guns and yelling but Trait could not hear him over the roar of the M60. Trait raised his gun hand behind the warden.

When the Marielito got close enough, Trait shot him three times. The second round pierced the con's forehead above his eye and dropped him. He never returned fire. The warden was pulling on Trait, but Trait had him firmly by the back of the neck and forced him around toward the rear of the station. They turned the corner and Trait hustled him down the narrow lane between the buildings and the trees, skirting the gun battle inside the town common.

REBECCA STOPPED WITH KELLS INSIDE THE TREES AT THE EDGE of the blacked-out Gilchrist Common. The general store was outlined before them. She had bought a sandwich there a long time ago.

"Do you hear drums?" she whispered.

He indicated that he did. He was kneeling in the snow, looking out over the darkened center of town.

"Where are they coming from?" she asked.

Kells said, "Your head."

The first gunshot split the night. It was answered by two more, then yells and scattered bursts. She made out three figures running toward the old schoolhouse, and recognized Tom Duggan by his long coat. She heard Coe's rifle. They were taking fire from inside.

Louder reports close by. A convict shooting from the other side of the general store, between it and the library. Kells pressed his revolver into Rebecca's free hand and pointed her to the rear of the store. "He's going to run," he said, rising and starting for the store's front porch.

Rebecca hurried out of the trees and along the side of the store to the back. Wooden pallets were stacked by the rear door, and there was a picnic table submerged in snow.

The gunplay nearby went *tat-tat-tat,* crisp and particular. She could tell that Kells was firing, swapping shots with the shooter. She dropped the gasoline jug near the door.

She heard boots thumping in the snow. Someone was running toward her along the side of the store. She pressed tightly against the wooden door, arms stiff, keeping a two-handed grip on Kells's gun.

More shots and rounds spit into the pine branches behind the store.

A dark figure turned the corner. He was holding a long weapon and he was not Kells. Rebecca saw small, bright eyes at the same time the con spotted her hiding in the shadows not six feet away.

She fired twice. The noise and recoil of Kells's revolver shook her.

The con staggered backward with a startled grunt. But he stayed on his feet. He looked down at his chest and the rips in his parka exposing his flak vest.

He yelled and brought his long gun up again, but a spray of bullets stopped him, ripping him knee-to-head.

Rebecca's bullets had pushed the con back into Kells's sight line.

The con twisted hard and fell facedown in the snow. As he lay there his semiautomatic gun kept firing into the ground, a muffled *pum-pum-pum-pum*.

Kells moved into her view, silencing the con's gun with a kick to the man's arm. He grabbed the con by his boot and dragged him behind the store, leaving a streak of blood-darkened snow.

Rebecca's arms remained straight, the gun still aimed and ready. Kells moved into her sight and eased her muzzle away from his chest before reaching down to seize the con's weapon. He kicked the man over. The con was dead.

"Get his vest," Kells told her, taking the gas jug and opening the back door.

The sound of more gunfire got her moving. She knelt carefully next to the dead man, touching only his green parka, drawing the zipper down and pulling it open. She saw the dimples she had left in his black vest. She pulled at his coat sleeve and used her boot to roll him over, twisting the jacket off him. Then she unstrapped the vest and tugged it over his head.

She shed her own coat and strapped the vest over her sweater as Kells reemerged carrying the fuel jug and a flare. Rebecca smelled smoke on him, and light flickered orange inside the store.

Kells checked the load of the con's weapon and then handed it to Rebecca, trading it for his revolver.

The alarm tower behind the library—a narrow granite obelisk, dark against the darker sky—was the last remnant of Gilchrist's volunteer fire department. "Cover the common from the top," Kells told her. "The others are working toward the church for a good angle on the police station. That's where I'm headed. You've got about thirty rounds left. Use them sparingly. Don't draw any attention to yourself and don't get found. Just snipe. Keep them off balance."

She felt proud of Kells's respect, even if she had had to shoot a man to earn it. She grabbed his arm before he could leave. "What was it?" she asked him. "What was it that you saw in me that I never knew was there?"

"It was all right there in your book."

She released him but for a moment he did not run. Light from the flames starting inside the general store showed the steam rising out of his sweater collar. She wanted him to stay. She was only just starting to understand him. She realized she wanted to know more.

"You'll be all right," he said, starting away.

He took off running for the brick library. Rebecca ducked inside the stone archway, rusted iron rungs leading to the top of the narrow tower. There was a short ledge below the old horn, iced but flat, a perch for her to stand on and look out over the common.

She was only a few feet higher than the one-story library. She could see spurts of gun flame here and there, and made out some movement between the old buildings across the common.

Kells was at the side corner of the library. He stepped out and fired three quick volleys, one across the common and two more straight up the street. Then he curled back, weapon up, as chunks of brick cracked off the library facing.

The loudest answering fire came from a gun in front of the police station. Despite her poor sight angle, Rebecca issued two rounds in that direction, and the con's weapon jerked and felt good kicking at her chest. She looked back along the tree line, scanning it for a form in white moving slow against the terrain, but, of course, she saw nothing. When she looked back at the library, Kells was gone.

GUNFIRE RATTLED IN THE NIGHT. ANY ONE OF THEM MIGHT HAVE fired the shot that killed the convict guarding the door to the town hall. But Dr. Rosen was certain that it was his rifle and not Coe's that felled the man firing at them from inside the school.

He stole through the foyer with Coe, under the watchful, granite eyes of Gilchrist's town fathers. But the missile launcher supposedly stashed inside the town hall was gone.

They gave up the search and found Tom Duggan in the back hall. An old-fashioned hip door swung behind him. Behind that, the room marked *Archives* was alive with an angry orange glow. The gasoline jug was gone.

Tom Duggan's brow was soaked with sweat. Dr. Rosen recalled seeing his granite bust sitting on the foyer floor, waiting to be installed with the rest. Now his flames fed thirstily on the ancient paper, the Gilchrist archives beginning to whip and roar.

"For Polk," Tom Duggan explained.

He was the first out the side door, Coe second, and Dr. Rosen taking up the rear with ammunition clacking in his coat pockets, hopping the rail of the handicap ramp into the snow. Gunfire cracked, but it was a short, clear run to the rear of the church. Kells's strategy appeared to be succeeding. The convicts were shooting wildly, and only the occasional bullet thudded a wall or cracked a pane of glass.

Tom Duggan led them to the gravelike dirt room and Dr. Rosen took the lead, running up the stairs to the trapdoor and firing quickly at a robe hanging in the cloakroom. But he was alone in the sacristy, and as the others surfaced he advanced to the front. The church was empty except for the corpse at the foot of the altar and the eviscerated dogs.

Back inside the sacristy, Tom Duggan and Coe lifted a bazooka-shaped weapon out of the cloakroom with the care afforded a religious relic.

"Can we do with one?" asked Dr. Rosen.

Tom Duggan said, "We'll have to. You get up to the steeple. I'm heading out."

Dr. Rosen grabbed Coe and pulled him over the altar into the body of the dark church. Dr. Rosen scanned the pews as they passed them. The smell was terrible but Coe gripped his rifle and soldiered on.

They ran up the stairs to the choir balcony over the entrance. Behind the organ, wooden rungs climbed to another trapdoor some twenty feet above. There were a few bullet holes in the wall.

"Stay here and stay down," said Dr. Rosen.

Coe crouched on the floor as Dr. Rosen climbed the rungs to the ceiling, popping the clasp latch on the trapdoor and finding himself looking straight up into the church bell. Cold air washed his face as he slid the rifle into the belfry and hoisted himself up.

Kells had been right. The belfry offered an excellent vantage point, overlooking the entire common. Dr. Rosen knelt next to the copper bell and looked down over the roofs and snow. He saw the general store burning to the east. To the west, the machine gun barked from the pickup truck in front of the police station, tonguing flame. That was his target.

There was little room there next to the bell, but Dr. Rosen knelt and sighted the rifle the way Kells had told him to, steadying the weapon against his shoulder, exhaling slowly. He squeezed the trigger and the rifle jumped. He squeezed and squeezed again, the rifle cracking, Dr. Rosen going on faith that his shots were landing somewhere near the gunner.

*   *   *

TOM DUGGAN HOPPED THE IRON FENCE INTO THE CHURCH cemetery, creeping through it with the missile launcher in his hands. The M60 was across the common, he could see its fiery bursts.

Three times he stopped and set himself, only to decide that he must move closer. He had no idea what the launcher in his hands could do. Kells had instructed him only to aim straight at the gun.

Just one row from the front of the fence, he knelt behind one of the larger headstones. He lifted the launcher onto his right shoulder, double-checking that he had the shooting end pointed forward.

The machine gun barked. A *pang-pang-pang* reverberated, the church bell was being struck.

Tom Duggan got to his feet. With the long barrel balanced on his shaking shoulder, hands shaking, he aimed and thumbed the trigger.

There was a second or so delay, and then the *whooshing* noise of the missile starting out of the tube. It was during that unexpected delay that he may have come up a bit on his aim.

The missile voided the barrel, filling the air with acrid smoke. It drove across the common in a perfectly straight line, as though being led along a fixed string.

But it missed the gun. It overshot the pickup truck by a few inches and instead struck the left corner of the police station.

There was a furious shudder and the cracking of mortar—and then a brief silence. Dust from the punched corner of the police station rose and blew over the pickup like a cloud. Stillness in the common, no gunfire, no yelling. The spent launcher slipped off Tom Duggan's shoulder and fell to the ground.

The respite was short-lived. In a moment the machine gun started up again, firing out of the smoke, smacking and shattering the gravestones around Tom Duggan. He

dove to the ground and covered his head as a tremendous
barrage filled the cemetery with lead and splintering stone.

KELLS WORKED HIS WAY PAST THE BANK TO THE CRAFT STORE.
He had taken one round in the lower back of his vest, a
lucky shot fired from somewhere in the woods near the
school. Sniping from the church steeple kept the M60
gunner distracted as Kells approached the police station.
A single, high-caliber round from the M60 would have
bored through Kells's vest and dropped him cold.

Two figures hustled across the street from the funeral
home, behind the pickup. Kells ducked between the pot-
tery store and the police station, expecting a gunfire, when
the missile launched from the church cemetery. It drove
across the common just six feet off the ground, but missed
the pickup truck, slamming the stationhouse and blowing
out windows and shaking the ground. Glass landed at
Kells's feet and snow plummeted from the branches of a
nearby pine.

Kells ran to the corner. The gunner had been knocked
off the truck bed by the missile impact, but he was coughing now and climbing back aboard through the dust.

Kells pulled his knife. He poked holes in the half-full
fuel jug as the convict spun the M60 and opened up on
the cemetery. Kells stepped out into the expanding dust
and hurled the jug into the bed of the pickup with a *thump*.

The shooting slowed. The gunner smelled the gasoline.

Kells lit the flare and tossed it end-over-end into the
pickup. There was a *whup* of oxygen-sucking flame, then
a ripping hush as the jug ignited and burst.

The gunner was splashed with flame. He screamed and
spun away, tumbling out of the truck bed and thrashing
around in the snow.

Kells wasted no time. He ran up the front steps and in
through the shattered doors of the police station, his boots
crunching broken glass. Inside the dusty darkness he
found only one man, moaning, dazed, and sitting against

a buckled wall, blood running out of his ears.

The weapons had fallen to the floor. Kells picked through the AR-15s, finding a MAC 10 machine pistol just as he heard movement behind him. He turned firing.

Two rounds punched him in the gut of his vest, rocking him backward as he shot up the convict from groin to face, dropping him.

Kells grunted in pain and moved to cover the con, standing over him. But the man, dying now, was not Inkman. Kells left him there, discarding his Micro Uzi for the heavier MAC 10.

He found no one in the rest of the building. Next to the radio room was a side door leading out to a parking lot, and at the foot of the stairs there lay another convict. Kells checked the body and guessed that it was one of the Marielitos. The man had been tapped in the forehead at close range.

Footprints surrounding him were fresh and clear and Kells read them quickly. Two men, the shooters, had exited the station through the same door as Kells, their footsteps closely paired as though one were holding on to the other. Then behind the dead Marielito came two more pairs, long, running strides, very likely the two men Kells had seen running from the funeral home before the missile struck. They had stopped to attend to the con, then moved on in pursuit of the first pair of tracks, following the shooters around the back of the station.

Kells was moving in that direction when he noticed a lone set of footsteps farther out in the parking lot. The holes were widely spaced, plain and straight as little black arrows, leading toward a baseball backstop in the distance.

A lone man had raced away from the center of town. With deadly certainty Kells started after Errol Inkman.

THE TOWN HALL WAS FULLY ENGULFED NOW, WHICH REBECCA AT-
tributed to self-immolation: the symbolic heart of a ravaged town, flaming out.

She choked off volleys at the police station, the Masonic Hall, the woods behind the school. It was call-and-
answer: a burst of gunfire from anywhere in the common
except the church and she responded with a short, controlled discharge. Yet she felt disassociated from the battle, hidden behind the row of buildings, high above it all.
She was still one step removed, still a writer. The gun in
her hands was a pen and she was shooting ink, highlight-
ing the action throughout the common. It was as though
the entire assault were being authored by her, spilling out
of her mind.

Grue was near. She could feel him somehow, and being holed up atop the tower with only one escape route
made her jittery. She searched the tree line for him, in
vain.

Two men appeared in the narrow lane below her. They
emerged from the trees behind the bank at the rear of the
library, and Rebecca rose up, unseen, aiming her machine
pistol down at a sharp angle.

One man was holding a gun to the other's head. The
hostage was an older white male, wearing neither a coat
nor a flak vest, limping weakly. His face was obscured,
but his bald head and stooped shoulders brought a strange
association to her mind. It was the Virgil to her Dante:
Barton James, the butlerlike warden of ADX Gilchrist.
But he was surely dead, a casualty of the initial riot. The

quality of his memory made her hesitate, turning aside the barrel of her gun.

They stopped in the glow of the burning general store. The bald man's captor was Luther Trait. Rebecca's mind reeled as Trait threw the warden—it *was* the warden—against the rear of the library. He opened a back door and pushed the warden inside.

Rebecca stood staring after they were gone. The old fear returned in a rush of smothering panic, as though no time had passed since her interview with Trait. She was back again inside that disciplinary hearing room inside ADX Gilchrist, worried about the body alarm wired beneath her sweater.

She was safe in the alarm tower. He had not seen her. He did not know she was there. He was inside the building right below her, but she could continue on as she had before.

She looked out over the battlefield of the town common. She took aim at the police station again and squeezed. The machine pistol fired one shot, then clicked dry. She squeezed the trigger again and again until she realized the gun was empty.

How had the warden stayed alive? Why was he with Trait?

A great *thud* shook the stone tower. A cloud of dust rose from the police station and for a few moments the shooting stopped and everything was quiet. She looked way across the common and saw, dimly, the figure of a black-cloaked man standing in the cemetery, a missile launcher falling from his shoulder.

It was Tom Duggan. She knew then that he had also started the fire inside the town hall. Gilchrist was his life and he was tearing it all down. He had finally accepted its death. Now he was liberating himself in the only way he could, and Rebecca found real meaning in that.

Killing a man and writing about him are the same thing.

But Trait had not bowed to such easy treatment. She

had come for him here in the hope that an encounter with
the demon would somehow free him up for sacrificing in
print. Then he had invited her to stay in Gilchrist and she
had accepted.

Next time we meet, it will be on my terms.

Now two more men appeared below. Convicts in wool
caps, holsters crisscrossing their vests, following Trait's
and the warden's tracks out of the woods to the library
door. They advanced with guns drawn—tracking Luther
Trait. These two convicts were hunting him down.

Rebecca watched from above as they eased open the
back door, crouched, and entered.

Their manner enraged her. Two unknown assassins
were stalking *her* criminal. As though in expression of
her sudden fury, the gun in front of the police station
exploded into flames.

You came here to kill Luther Trait.

The words were Kells's, but the voice in her head was
her own.

BUILDINGS BURNED BELOW AS DR. ROSEN FIRED AT ANYTHING THAT moved. He understood now the allure that clock towers held for the powerless, the afraid. He was a fifty-four-year-old podiatrist from Boston crouching in a church belfry, holding off a town full of killers.

A snowmobile came revving out of the woods near the school, shooting into the common through an opening in the post fence. Dr. Rosen turned and paced the dim shadow cutting across the snow, firing but missing as the rider ditched the sled and took cover behind the gazebo. He became an immediate nuisance, pecking away at the church steeple as Dr. Rosen chipped holes in the bandstand roof.

Sparking music on the bell, *pang, poong, ping,* and Dr. Rosen ducked and covered his head. The pickup bed was still burning and the M60 dripped flame, but another con had climbed in behind the big gun. Ricochets splintered the wood inside the cramped belfry and Dr. Rosen tried to get a shot off.

Then the bulldozer roared to life. Headlights swung brightly across the common from the funeral parlor, chewing snow past the upturned barrel of the M60, crushing the low post fence. The wide steel scoop blade reared high to shield the cab from Dr. Rosen's aim, though he wasted two rounds on it anyway. The great machine was headed straight for the church.

The action was heavy now, the fixed gun barking, the gazebo con sniping, Dr. Rosen taking noise and splinters. His right arm jerked forward after two particularly harsh tones off the big bell. The pain was searing and he fell back, rolling until the floor disappeared beneath him.

He did not know where he was until he looked up and saw the belfry trapdoor above him. He had fallen through and landed on the choir balcony near Coe. He gripped his bloody arm. "I'm shot!" he said.

Rounds from the fixed gun ripped into the balcony wall, low over the floor. Coe flattened out near him and they covered their heads and waited.

Dr. Rosen could move his arm but the tingling pain made his right hand useless. He looked for the rifle and saw that it had fallen near, still in one piece. He reached for it with his left hand, but Coe grabbed it first.

Dr. Rosen said, "Give me that—"

The kid was already alligator crawling across the floor to the ladder rungs. Dr. Rosen rolled toward him but his injured arm held him back.

The kid scuttled up the ladder with both rifles in one hand, pausing once as rounds bit through the wall. He hoisted himself safely into the belfry.

"Coe!" yelled Dr. Rosen.

The teenager's face appeared through the trapdoor.

"Behind the gazebo," Dr. Rosen said.

Coe nodded once and disappeared.

The bulldozer noise grew louder. Dr. Rosen rolled over again and fished in his coat pocket for his handgun. As he was getting to his feet, the engine surged and the bulldozer rammed the front of the church.

The foundation shuddered and brought him to his knees. Wood and glass ripped out of the church entrance, headlights illuminating the altar.

A churning noise as the machine tried to turn beneath him. It wanted to bring the entire structure down.

The engine sputtered and stalled. There was swearing below, the clicking of a dead engine. A door opened and heavy footsteps crunched over fallen debris.

The convict was out of the bulldozer, moving on foot. Dr. Rosen knelt on the floor above him with the gun in his hand.

*   *   *

TOM DUGGAN SNAGGED HIS BLACK OVERCOAT AS HE FELL OVER
the cemetery fence. The hem caught and the lining ripped
and he had to twist free, leaving the coat hanging from
an iron spike.

He crept through the snow to the left, along the road
past the Masonic Hall toward his black-shuttered funeral
home. The bulldozer had started up there. The headlights
came on bright and it rolled past the pickup, crushing the
fence post, roaring across the common toward the church.

The barrel of the big gun still dripped fire. The prisoner
who had stumbled out of the ruined police station burned
his hands as he opened it up on the church belfry. Yet the
M60 continued to rock furiously as Tom Duggan stole
along the snowy hedge fronting his home. The con was
yelling between each burst of fire, ripping into the steeple,
and Tom Duggan could see bright sparks flying off the
bell.

The bulldozer rammed the church, opening up the
mouth of the entrance. Its headlights illuminated the
stained-glass windows like a jack-o'-lantern.

Rounds resumed from the belfry, picking at the snow
around the pickup and punching holes in the bumper. But
the con would not stop. He kept yelling and firing the hot
M60.

Tom Duggan pulled the revolver from his belt. He
crossed his front walk, going the wide way around the
pickup, approaching the gun from behind.

DIESEL SMOKE AND DRYWALL DUST, THE SOUND OF DEBRIS
breaking off the wall.

Dr. Rosen was listening to the convict below as a sudden volley of automatic fire ripped through the floor
planks.

Spit holes pitted the wood all around him, dropping
him to his side. He was not hit, but he landed hard on his

bad arm and the groan upon impact was automatic and forceful.

He was given away. He froze where he was there on the choir floor, but the damage was done.

Near his head was the bloodstain from his first fall. One of the rounds had splintered the stain, dead center. That was what gave him the desperate idea.

He rolled forward so that his injured arm lay across the hole. The splinters were jagged and biting and Dr. Rosen's groan authentic. Fresh blood ran down through the floor.

COE SAT WITH HIS EYES CLOSED AND HIS BACK TO THE WOOD stanchion as rounds rang off the big bell. He held the rifle ready and rushed a count of five before opening his eyes and turning and firing twice in the direction of the police station.

Answering fire was loud and quick, rounds sparking off the copper bell, but Coe had already spun back into a tight crouch.

He was no match for the M60 gunner making frenzied music off the bell. He had a much better chance at getting the gazebo sniper below. That angle was safer and more favorable. Coe poked the rifle sight over the edge and fired down at the dark rotunda roof.

A distant rumbling began to make itself felt under his feet. First he thought it was the bulldozer rolling through the church. Then he saw lights moving over the jagged horizon of the Green Mountains.

Helicopters were crossing into town. The army was moving in.

Another discordant volley off the bell, Coe curled up tight. The gazebo had gone quiet and he wondered if he had hit someone. He peered over the edge of the belfry platform.

He could just make out the convict beyond the cover of the roof. The man was crouched and there was something balanced on his shoulder, long-barreled, pointed at Coe.

Coe saw the smoke as the Stinger left its launcher. There was no time for any other reaction. He jerked backward and the rifle slipped from his hands.

DR. ROSEN'S HEART RACED AS THE INTRUDER CLIMBED THE stairs to the choir balcony. He lay still but his hands and feet were trembling and he was certain that with one look the convict would know that he was not dead. What he concentrated on was patience and the young life of the boy upstairs.

A rumbling in the distance, growing, obscuring the creaking of the con's boots on the old stairs. Dr. Rosen had to rely on his instincts. The gun was heavy in his off-hand.

His muscles were tense with the urge to spring, but he waited, waited, until he could wait no more.

He opened his eyes and brought the gun up and saw the convict on the top step, standing in a drab green parka and wet denim jeans, looking up at the open trapdoor. As Coe came diving headfirst out of the belfry, Dr. Rosen emptied his gun into the convict's legs and chest and the convict fell back. Coe crashed to the floor next to Dr. Rosen as a windy, whistling noise filled the air, splitting slate and wood, ripping apart the church steeple overhead.

TOM DUGGAN YELLED AT THE CON TO STOP, BUT THE MAN'S ears were bleeding and the noise of the gun obliterated all human voice. So Tom Duggan shot him once from behind. The bullet struck the convict in the shoulder, and DeYoung stiffened and turned fast. He brought the steaming gun around with him.

He never stopped firing. Rounds ripped into the ground, stitching the snow toward Tom Duggan. He lunged forward to the grill of the pickup and the hot rounds thumped behind him, the M60 barrel unable to get below the front cab. Tom Duggan was readying his revolver as fire from the belfry plunked the body of the pickup, driving him back. He ducked to the other headlight and came up shooting.

His gunshots struck DeYoung in both arms and square in the throat, driving him back from the machine gun, knocking him out of the pickup.

The gun tipped skyward of its own accord—silent now, though Tom Duggan's ears screamed as though it were still firing. He saw lights moving across the dark night sky and knew they were helicopters in the distance.

He climbed up into the scorched bed of the pickup. He got behind the M60, but was too late in turning to the gazebo. The Stinger lit out and pierced the belfry, smashing the steeple and lopping off the high white cross before going off corkscrewing into the night.

Tom Duggan opened up the gun. He shuddered as round after round discharged, first felling the missile-firing con, then all but obliterating the old gazebo. He turned the spray on the blazing town hall, wasting bullets into the hungry fire, then wheeled hard and ripped into each building along Post Road, from the library all the way to the wounded police station behind him. He stopped then, looking over his shoulder at his beloved funeral parlor, his home. The lawn was all torn up, bullet holes in the clapboard siding, the front door hanging open. Tom Duggan turned the gun, gripping it hard as he tore into the white walls, popping the lead-glass windows and shredding the generations-old sign.

THE M60 NOISE GREW DISTANT, AND INKMAN'S PACE SLOWED AS his breathing suffered, the freezing air choking his lungs. He tumbled over the short right-field fence and picked himself up and slogged through the knee-high snow toward the farm. The openness of the land pulled at him. The nearest hiding place was a silo at the top of the rise, but from there it looked terribly far away.

Over his shoulder, Inkman's own footprints pursued him like a shadowy version of himself. This phantom trail failed to symbolize guilt for Inkman, standing instead as just another example of his ongoing bad luck. Misfortune had dogged him for years, always conspiring to keep him from achieving his goals.

Way beyond the tall, bare trees, the sky over the center of town glowed ruddy, and Inkman was glad.

A dark figure crossed the pitcher's mound of the baseball field. The form was moving across the snow with quick deliberateness—and Inkman turned and ran as fast as his desperation would take him.

He expected a bullet in the back at every step. There was a tree farm before the silo, neat rows of fat spruces shaking wildly in his vision. They were neither many nor tall, but they were his only potential cover.

The flak vest weighed heavy on his shoulders as the snow sucked at his feet. Every time he looked back, Clock was gaining.

He would not make it to the trees. Clock was closing too fast. Inkman could see the breath swirling around his pursuer's shadowed face.

So Inkman took to favoring his right leg, giving up

before the trees. It was a Christmas tree farm, bushy spruces in rows of ascending height—and Inkman stopped just yards away, doubled over as Clock came up fast behind him.

"Wait," Inkman said. "Please wait."

He kept his right leg stiff, gripping his knee, sliding his hand down to his shin.

The muzzle of the MAC 10 poked into his cheek, stopping him. Inkman froze as Clock reached down and pulled Inkman's pant leg over his right ankle, finding the holster inside his boot.

Relieved of his gun, Inkman dropped to one knee, hands over his head, suppliant. He looked up at the face of the black man from the inn, changed only by a few days' growth of beard and angrily glowing eyes.

Clock hurled Inkman's handgun into the trees. "Get up," he said.

Inkman stood, snow sticking to his pant knees. Even in the grip of fear, Inkman was confident he could scheme his way out of anything. Just keep Clock talking.

He spoke slowly as his shortness of breath required. "Fitting," he said. "That I staged a revolution here . . . and you overthrew it."

Clock said nothing, but neither did he shoot him.

"Too fitting," concluded Inkman. "How did you know I was here? Or have you been following me ever since . . ."

Rotors beat in the distance, helicopters approaching in the night sky.

Inkman went on, "Why wouldn't you have stopped me before? You wouldn't have allowed this to happen . . . unless you wanted the country to go through this? A public-policy lesson? A vaccination shot against future biowarfare?"

"Your problem is, you're not as smart as you think you are," said Clock. "You should have taken your lumps and crawled away."

Confusion fueled Inkman's pitiful defiance. "I want back what you took from me."

"You'll take what's coming to you," said Clock. "What's been coming to you for a long time."

Three gunshots cracked at close range. Inkman yelled and jerked backward, but it was Clock who had been struck: two shots off his vest, one in his left arm.

As Clock twisted, Inkman wasted not a moment turning and running into the trees. He drew no fire. After scooting across a few rows, he stopped to get his bearings, kneeling low and trembling. He was trying to figure out in which direction his handgun had been thrown.

KELLS RUSHED INTO A ROW OF SIX-FOOTERS FOR COVER. INKman had scrambled off to the left and the third gunman was somewhere along the right. Inkman had seemed as surprised by the gunshots as Kells was. There was pain in his left arm but he was more concerned that spilled blood would mark his tracks in the snow.

He crouched still a few more moments, listening for footsteps, branch snaps, breathing.

The snow in the narrow lanes was soft and unbroken. He realized he had to get moving and cross the shooter's tracks before the shooter crossed his.

Kells hurried along, gun out, eyes and ears alert. He ducked through gaps between tree rows, moving fast but sure.

Crunching snow in the direction of the smaller trees. Boot steps, moving fast. Through the branches he saw a body fleeing the farm, plodding up the short rise toward a barn.

It was Inkman, running away. The sight invigorated Kells. No longer on the defensive, he moved confidently from lane to lane.

He found the opposing tracks in a low row. He knew Inkman's tread and this pattern was different. He set off after them at top speed, weaving in and out of rows. He

knew that the gunman must have crossed his telltale tracks
by now.

A form moved to Kells's right, two rows over. He
slowed and waited, pushing into the next lane, crouching
at the end of the row.

Boots rushed along the adjacent lane, coming toward
Kells, then right past him. Kells rose fast and burst into
the shooter's lane in a flurry of snow.

The convict spun and fired high. Kells was on his
knees and let the gunfire sweep the lane above his head
once before firing up at the man's legs and arms. The
convict flailed and twin guns jumped out of his hands and
he fell backward, settling deep into the snow.

Kells got to his feet. It was another of the Marielitos,
the man's mouth curled in pain as his wet eyes stared up.
"El Reloj," he said.

The Marielito watched the snow falling out of the sky
and whispered to himself in Spanish. Kells dropped the
MAC 10 and pulled the revolvers from the holsters crisscrossing the man's vest.

The barn was a short walk up a low rise. Cows lowed
plaintively as the helicopters beat overhead, searchlights
focused on the center of town.

Kells crossed the white tableau with a gun in each
hand.

It was a cow barn, long and dirt-floored, doors open at
both ends. Inkman had released the jerseys in an attempt
to slow Kells, but the cows just moaned past him, looking
for food.

Inkman was staggering toward the opposite end of the
barn. The air was thick with bovine sweat and dung as
Kells advanced over the dirt. He raised both arms, the
good one higher than the bad one, aiming at Inkman's
back and calling his name.

Inkman stopped, swaying in the doorway. Below him
stretched acres of wide-open, snow-coated meadows. He

turned and faced Kells, exhausted, showing him an open hand.

"Wait," Inkman said.

The revolvers fired, and then there was only one man standing in the barn.

A CAROUSEL OF ROMANCES CREAKED AS TRAIT BRUSHED PAST IT to the library window, looking at the town hall in flames across the common. The M60 rattled proudly against the cracking of the smaller arms, but it should never have come to this. Defending their own turf was failure in itself.

The new library reeked of old paper. It was dark but for the flames from the general store casting flickering light through the side windows, shadows shifting and creeping in the stacks. The warden leaned heavily against the front counter. Near him, a library calendar sleeved in a clear plastic standee highlighted a Saturday evening reading by bestselling author Rebecca Loden.

"What are we doing here?" asked the warden. "You're trapped."

Bullets cracked the front window, fluttering a white shade as Trait paced, gun in hand, head screaming. "Shut up," he said. He was trying to think.

If Clock had taken the Inkman bait, then all they had to contend with here were a few civilians. The launchers would scare off the first wave of army helicopters. Maybe he could retreat to the prison with a few remaining men. Maybe there was some ricin left over—

The floor shuddered and books dropped off the shelves. Trait realized a missile had struck one of the buildings. He sensed it was not a blow for his side.

"You are no longer the leader of this revolution," said Warden James. "You are its victim."

Trait turned on him, eyes flashing. He crossed the library to the front desk and brought the butt of his gun across the warden's face.

The warden dropped to the floor. He lay still a moment before rolling onto his back.

"One more word," said Trait, brandishing the gun above him.

The warden's face, shaded by old and new contusions, remained defiant. "You just keep trading one locked closet for another."

Trait thought of his E-Unit cell. All the dreams he had dreamed there. All the journeys he had taken.

The front door opened onto Post Road and the common, and Trait was a few moments too slow in turning.

The man who entered wore all white: a bleached coat, pants, boots, gloves, and hood. He was crouched low, a small bow and arrow poised in his hands, the bowstring pulled taut to his nose. The nocked arrow was aimed at Trait's face. Trait's gun was aimed at the stranger's heart.

"Drop it!" yelled Trait.

But the intruder froze and held his crouch as the door opened wide on the fire-brightened snow and the gunplay behind him. The flames of the general store painted a white man with blunt features under a sloppy beard. He slowly rose to full height, lowering the bow to his chest, revealing his face while keeping the arrow point aimed dead at Trait's eyes.

"I said drop it," said Trait.

"Naw," said the archer. "Go ahead and shoot. You'll be wearing an arrow shaft in your neck."

The archer smiled a pale grin. Trait kept his aim and his distance.

"Jasper Grue," said the warden, amazement filling his voice from where he lay on the floor.

Trait said, from behind his gun, "You the cowboy who's been tracking the rebels?"

"Not all them," said Grue. "Just one. You the Negro who set everyone free?"

Grue, Trait remembered. A race-hater. Militia leader. Backwoods survivalist. He had to be handled carefully.

Trait said, "What brings you here now?"

"I ain't come to say thank you."

Trait showed Grue his free hand as he circled away from the counter, keeping a respectful distance. Grue turned with him. "The FBI is coming with the U.S. Army. We've got to run. Maybe you know something about the terrain here. Maybe together you and I could . . ."

Grue shook his head slowly. The sound of the gunfire through the open door did not impel him at all.

"Why not?" said Trait.

"Because the second you drop your aim, I'm going to put you down."

Trait breathed deeply through his fury. "I turned you loose. You owe me."

"You made a distraction. I got out on my own."

"Then what did you come here for?"

"The writer. I want to know where she's at."

Trait smirked cruelly. "She tried to write about you too?"

"I got a little book of my own," Grue said. "She's getting her own chapter."

Shadows produced by the fire next door had been shifting the entire time.

Now all at once, whole silhouettes emerged from the dark stacks. Two men, wielding handguns.

Grue was the first to react, getting off an arrow at the most visible shooter. He dropped fast and rolled behind a table of current periodicals.

Trait swung and fired three times, and simultaneously there were flashes of light from the gunmen. Trait ducked back behind a row and looked for Grue, seeing only the warden lying on the floor, playing dead. He heard yelling in Spanish and understood that the other two Marielitos had come to collect for their murdered comrade.

The searing in his ribs was acute and he had trouble keeping his gun arm up. The bullet had gone in below his heart but had not come out. He slumped against the book-shelf, switching gun hands and then came out blasting.

One Marielito was down already. The second was half-turned by an arrow in his shoulder and Trait finished him off with two shots to the head. The third trigger pull clicked empty as the Marielito fell dead.

Trait dropped his empty gun and stood hunched, his hand pressed hard against his side. Grue emerged from behind the front desk, eyeing Trait, his empty hands, and the bloody wound. In one fluid motion Grue plucked an arrow from his pouch and strung it taut.

Trait turned toward him. Smoke hung in the air. The room smelled of cordite and sweat and the musk of decaying paper.

Grue moved in front of the desk, holding his aim. "Where is she?" asked Grue.

Trait frowned, grunting. "I don't know."

The warden was looking up from the floor now. "He doesn't," he insisted.

Grue's eyes lingered on the warden in dim recognition. He looked back to Trait and let the arrow fly.

The point pierced Trait beneath his right breast, knocking him backward into the end of a row of shelves. Trait stood there looking down at the black-feathered arrow sticking out of his chest. He looked at Grue.

Grue set his bow down calmly on the table of current periodicals and advanced.

With a defiant growl, Trait summoned the strength to remain on his feet. There was a blur of disgust and impassivity on the race-hater's face. This was the will of the fatherless cons, turning on him now.

He managed an impudent smile as the first blow came. Grue roundhoused him flush in the face, shattering his nose and cheek and driving him back against the metal row end, jerking the arrow for extra despair. Grue's knee came up next, then his fists again, Trait accepting his judgment boldly, tasting in his mouth not blood but the bitterness of defeat.

He was going unconscious. Just as he was slipping into the black undertow of the room, Grue released him and backed away.

The voice calling to him was high and crazed. "Stop it! Get away from him!"

Trait twisted on the floor at the bottom of the row. He felt little pain now, drifting on a nimbus of brain-released opiates.

Someone was standing in the firelight near the Mariel- itos, aiming a gun. The room listed as Trait tried to focus on the face.

He saw auburn hair blazing in the flame light, and the revelation came in waves.

Rebecca stood near the front of the stacks—motion- less, almost floating, the Marielito's revolver still warm in her hand. Grue moved with incredible agility, releasing Trait upon her order, but then darting behind the warden who had been almost at his feet. Now Grue's white- gloved hand gripped the warden by the throat. His other hand clutched the handle of a large hunting knife, held vertically, the gleaming silver point touching the crown of Warden James's bald head. Grue's arm was ready-bent to drive the wide blade down into the warden's skull.

The two Marielitos lay dead at her feet. Trait was bloodied and crumpled, barely moving.

"Put that thing down," drawled Grue. Beating up on Trait had exhilarated him, his dark, beady eyes bore a bright sheen.

The warden looked forlorn, his eyes downcast—scared but too weak to express it.

"No," Rebecca told him. "You put down the knife."

"I will," said Grue. "Right down through his skull."

She shook her head, still yelling. "You won't kill him. You've got nothing if you kill him."

Grue's glove tightened around the warden's throat. The knife blade twisted as with a grin Grue slowly rotated his wrist back and forth. A single drip of blood appeared on Warden James's head, rolling down over his temple and streaming to his chin.

"We'll stand here like this then," said Grue. "See who moves first."

Grue continued to twirl the knife point, holding the warden close.

As the revolver shook in her two-handed grip, she said, "I'm not afraid of you anymore."

She was overheating inside her sweater and flak vest. She smelled him now, the sickening funk of his unwashed body. Outside, gunfire raged as the big gun continued to fire.

Grue just grinned and kept twisting the knife. Her senses plagued her as she stood by helplessly, watching him bore into the warden's head.

Trait's groaning, until then ignored, stopped as a hand came free from beneath his chest. Rebecca saw something in his fingers, perhaps a weapon, but did not have time to react.

Trait thumbed the switch on the stun-belt trigger. The warden rocked violently, thrashing with an immediacy and force that shook him free of Grue's grip, dropping him hard to the floor.

Grue was left wide open and Rebecca did not hesitate. She squeezed once and Grue shuddered and stepped back.

He looked down at his chest as blood oozed out of the small hole, seeping into the white fabric. He looked again at Rebecca, arms hanging at his sides, a child's expression of hurt on his face.

She fired four more times, emptying the revolver into his chest and neck and driving him back onto the table of periodicals. He lay still a moment, bent backward over the tabletop, then sagged and fell to one side, pulling some of the magazines with him to the floor.

Trait released the switch that freed the warden, leaving him quaking involuntarily before the front counter.

Rebecca carried the empty gun to Grue. He lay on his side, throat gurgling as his lifeblood coughed out of his neck and mouth. He was sagging like a balloon losing air, looking bewildered and small.

She knelt beside him and set the gun down near his wide, staring eyes.

"I don't want your last words," she said.

But he could no longer see her or the flame-lit book stacks of the Gilchrist Public Library. Death panic had tricked his mind out to a place in his past. His mother had run a slaughterhouse, and it occurred to Rebecca that he might have returned there to die.

Rebecca used the table to get to her feet, momentarily leaning on it for support.

When she turned around, Luther Trait was standing before the row of bookshelves behind her.

Rebecca reeled back wildly, stumbling into a smaller table set near the far stacks.

Trait was a broken man. His face was ripped apart and swelling and his jaw hung open. He could not summon a full breath. The black feathers of the arrow in his right breast were wet with blood. His head drooped to the side such that he watched her out of his one good eye, the yellow-brown pupil piercing.

He spit out blood in order to speak. "You look different," he slurred.

"I am different."

She stood her ground, gripping the table as books tumbled off display stands. One struck her boot and its familiar jacket design distracted her. The prim, satisfied woman behind the writing desk in the author photograph was someone she barely knew. Rebecca was standing against a table of *Last Words* display copies, arranged for her ill-fated reading.

Trait took one short step toward her, then another, holding his balance. This brought a determined, if lopsided, grin.

"Don't come any closer," she warned him.

"You saved me," he said.

"They're coming now. Stay where you are."

But he came forward two more steps. She felt oddly relaxed—out of control and in control at the same time. Suddenly she was glad she had stayed in Gilchrist, if only to defy him.

"Here I am," she said. "Here's your prize."

The rumbling grew tremendous overhead, the rotor hum of the helicopters sweeping near the center of town. Warden James crawled to a sitting position against the front desk, looking up now, hearing them, as did Trait.

Trait pushed ahead. He was dying and yet somehow he kept moving toward her.

"Don't do this," Rebecca said.

He was close now, only a few steps away.

Something in his broken face told her he was stronger than he seemed.

"I'm not afraid," Rebecca said. Her hand went into her pants pocket, closing around the mace. "I won't be any-one's victim."

The warden called to Trait in a worn, tremulous voice, "Luther! Don't!"

Trait paused, a spark of aggression in his one good eye—then he lunged for Rebecca, one arm raised, groping for her neck.

Rebecca pulled her hand out of her pocket. She maced him as he came.

Trait hit her sputtering, grabbing at her face as they went down, overturning the display table.

He was on top of her, blindly, pulling at her hair, trying to work his other fist free. The mace mist irritated her eyes, and as they rolled Rebecca felt around the floor until her hand gripped something with a familiar heft. As Trait was raising his hand to strike her, Rebecca let out a yell from a long-forgotten self-defense class and brought the *Last Words* hardcover across his temple.

Trait sagged, dazed. Rebecca shoved him off her and rolled over, gagged by mace, but he would not give her up. He gripped her vest, pawing at her face and hair, and she could not get free of him. Above him now, with both hands she brought the book spine down forcefully against the back of his head. She struck him with it again and again, hammering his head into the floor until the binding cracked and the creased cover boards and bloody endpapers collapsed in her hands, the freed pages fluttering around the room like snow.

WARDEN JAMES WAS RECEIVED BY THE ARRIVING GOVERNMENT AND
law-enforcement agencies as a hero on par with the res-
urrected Christ. A hush came over the heavily armed men
as Rebecca walked him out of the library, and they took
him from her shoulder like a child pulled from a well.

Stunned FBI agents eagerly questioned him while they
waited for the medical helicopter. Foremost on their
minds was the whereabouts of Luther Trait. When the
battered warden pointed at the brick library, a handful of
agents started toward it with guns drawn.

"He's dead," Warden James said, stopping them.

"Dead?" said one. "Who did it?" The supervisory agent
scanned the destroyed town common. "Who did all this?"

The warden looked at Rebecca, standing outside the
ring of men.

"They did," he said. "Trait's men. A power struggle.
They brought down the town."

He kept looking at Rebecca as they peppered him with
questions, until finally he glanced away.

"Perhaps one of you could do me a favor," Warden
James said. "My wife thinks she is a widow. The sooner
I get to a working telephone, the sooner I can correct
that."

The helicopter touched down near the gazebo and he
was strapped inside, and Rebecca felt better once he had
risen out of Gilchrist and puttered away.

They were all detained as suspected prisoners until
positively identified. Rebecca, as the only woman, was the
first to be cleared. They told her she was in shock and

Rebecca allowed them that assumption because it precluded her answering questions about the blood on her sweater sleeves. Her opinion, and that of the rest, was that they owed the FBI nothing.

She felt wired and out of sorts, sick one minute, sleepy the next. Her throat was still raw from the mace, her muscles tired and tight. The snow had stopped but for a few straggling flakes, the sky brightening with morning as she took in the war-torn town. The smoldering husk of the town hall, the smashed front of the church, the rocket-punched police station. Nothing was fixed anymore. Molecules were being continually rearranged and transformed. It seemed to her now that the snow had not been falling that week so much as she had been rising through it.

The sounds of gunfire in the distance. The barricade cons still putting up a fight.

Mia was returned to the center of town by sled, wrapped in a thick blanket. "You're okay," she said, starting to cry when she saw them. "You're all okay."

Rebecca thought of Mia as an orphan entrusted into their care, a child they had to protect and carry home. In turn, Mia had carried a part of each of them, something innocent and untouched, from the beginning.

Dr. Rosen, still giddy from the gunshot and the battle, insisted on dressing his own arm wound. When the FBI informed him his wife was waiting at the hospital in Beckett, Dr. Rosen thanked them with tears in his eyes.

Coe's parents would also be at the hospital, and he joined Mia and Dr. Rosen on the second medical helicopter. Rebecca was relieved not to have to meet Coe's parents. For some reason she felt responsible for Coe, and that she had failed him. She wished she had been able to shelter him more.

The FBI wanted Rebecca to go with them, but Rebecca was waiting for Kells. "Make sure Mr. Kells comes to see me," Coe called to her, on his way to the waiting helicopter.

She did not know where Kells was. She assumed he was somewhere being debriefed.

Tom Duggan remained behind, standing with her outside his funeral home. His black overcoat was gone, residual adrenaline keeping him warm in his wrinkled funeral suit. He said he wasn't sure where Kells was either.

"What did you tell them?" Rebecca asked Tom Duggan, now that they were alone.

"Nothing, same as the rest," he said. "What can they do?" He shrugged. Then he resumed looking her over. "I am worried about you."

She didn't know how much he knew. "Me?" she said, turning and looking at the sign, *Duggan's Funeral Home*, riddled with bullet holes.

Tom Duggan nodded, contrite but not quite ashamed.

"So what now?" she asked.

"For me or for the town?"

Rebecca shrugged.

"First order of business is burying the dead," he said. "I'll take some of these men to the country club to get the others. I'll go to my mother's house alone."

"And the town?"

He looked out at all the activity in the common. "Like a forest after a great fire. Either it comes back or it doesn't. If it does come back, usually it comes back stronger. But if it doesn't, then you have to move on, you don't have a choice. Animals know it, I don't know why people don't. It pains me to say it, but the old fool was right. We've had a good fire here, long overdue. I'll miss my mother terribly, but I'm free now, and there are other forests." He nodded, still partly convincing himself. "What about you? Are you going to write about this?"

"I don't know," she said. "I truly don't."

"Well," he decided, "I'd buy a copy."

She hugged him then, and in feeling some of his stiffness dissolving in her arms, she began to feel better herself. When they separated he was smiling, and with a modest wave he started away.

A voice called to her, loud, startling, familiar. "Bec!"

Jeb climbed out of an arriving army jeep and hurried toward her through the snow. He was wearing a soft orange ski parka, tan corduroys, and new snow boots, trailing a cashmere scarf.

He gripped her in a tight hug. Now it was Rebecca's stiffness that needed dissolving.

"A miracle," he exulted. "I don't want to say I gave up hope, but—"

"Where did you come from?"

"Stowe—I've been waiting day and night for some word from you. Soon as the news broke, I had an agent friend of a friend get me in here. Look . . . at you." His enthusiasm suffered as he took her in: She was scraped up, bruised, and exhausted. Perhaps he could tell that she had not merely survived the assault on Gilchrist, she had participated in it. And perhaps just as intuitively he put it straight out of his mind. "Let's get you away from here. We'll check you out, get you cleaned up. There is so much heat right now, so much buzz on this revolution thing, you would not—"

"Jeb."

"Okay, I know, I know. But we've got to strike while the iron is hot." He gripped her shoulders. "I know this is a monster cliché, so forgive me in advance . . . but you truly don't realize how much you miss someone until you think they're gone. I mean, really, really gone."

She reached for his hands, gently pulling them from her shoulders, holding them.

Jeb smiled. He nodded and calmed down.

She leaned forward and planted a kiss on his smooth, scented cheek, then withdrew before he could reciprocate.

"You're fired," Rebecca said.

Jeb's smile lingered as the words took a few moments to register.

"I'm moving on," she said. "The *Last Words* sequel isn't working out. My heart isn't in it."

"Fired?" he said. "We have a legal agreement."

"Sue me. Nothing's guaranteed in life, nothing's fixed. You're the one who taught me that."

Four men passed behind Jeb, two of them wearing black windbreakers with the acronym *DTRA* in bold white letters on the back. The Defense Threat Reduction Agency.

"I have to go now, Jeb," she told him. And she left him standing there.

"Excuse me!" she called, hurrying after the men, following them around an army jeep.

While the pair in windbreakers were fairly young, the older two could have passed for nuclear physicists. All looked haggard, like men who had just dodged a bullet. The ricin had indeed fallen on the target towns—Trait's Brotherhood had dropped the poison when news of the town invasion broke—but too late, just after the evacuations. Rebecca was glad the country had gotten a little taste of doomsday.

"Excuse me," she said again, getting their attention that time. "Can you tell me where Alex Kells is?"

One of the younger ones glanced at the older pair. "We wouldn't know."

"I've been looking for him."

The agent turned to continue on with the rest. "We have no idea where he is," he said.

Rebecca was standing there, perplexed, until after a few steps one of the older men stopped and turned back. "You're a friend of his?" he asked.

Strange to hear it put that way. "Yes."

"We don't know where Alex Kells is," he explained, in apology for his associate's short manner. "After the stunt he pulled in the New York City Transit System, he was placed on administrative leave. We've neither heard from nor seen him since."

Rebecca smiled at first, as though she were being put on. Then a thick fog began to settle in her head.

"But how did you know about the ricin towns?" Rebecca asked him. "The zip codes?"

"We were contacted by the CIA." He looked at her strangely. "You'd have to ask them."

They continued on busily, leaving Rebecca alone on the edge of the common.

If Kells hadn't been working for Doomsday, then who had he been working for? And if he was not being debriefed . . .

A female FBI agent hurried past in a heavy blue parka, reacting to a report on her radio. *"Body in a tree farm, just outside the center of town."*

The agent turned at the police station and headed out across a baseball field scored with boot tracks. Rebecca followed her into the open pasture beyond and over a hump of snow marking a property line. There was a Christmas tree farm in the distance, and a group of men in windbreakers standing near the end of a tall row.

Rebecca was accustomed to moving through the snow now, and even in her exhaustion she overtook the agent before the farm. A male agent there tried to get in her way, but Rebecca sidestepped him. In their eyes, she was a victim. Victims needed to emote.

It was another of the Marielitos, lying on his back in the snow, empty holsters crisscrossed over his flak vest, eyes frozen open.

"Inkman," she said. "Where is he?"

The agents looked at her strangely. But their unquestioning silence told her they knew something. She repeated the question, and one of the earphone-wearing agents glanced to the top of the nearby rise.

Rebecca walked to the barn. Her weariness was complete, her fatigued mind swimming as she trudged up the last snowy hill.

The doors were open at both ends. The cow stalls were

empty and only a handful of men stood about. She smelled manure and cordite.

The body lay in the dirt at the far end of the barn, just inside the snow line. "Mr. Hodgkins" bore a slurred expression in death, his head tipped to one side, eyes glancing away as though forever in search of a better angle. She pitied Inkman then. She realized he never had a chance.

A single pair of footprints, deep and widely spaced, led out from the barn over meadows toward the tree line and the mountains in the distance.

Three men stood together outside the door. They were in their fifties, dressed conservatively in parkas and suit pants, engaged in close conversation. Rebecca absorbed their scrutiny without reflecting anything back at them.

"Clock," she said.

Two of them looked over, as though uncertain she was speaking to them. One said, "Excuse me?"

But it was in their eyes. A shimmer of recognition, like a pupil contracting from a flash of unexpected light.

Looking out at the footprints leading away from town, Rebecca felt the first stirrings of a novel taking form in her mind.